## PRAISE FOR *FALLING*

"…I can't say enough good things about this well-crafted jewel of a book. It's not often that a story causes me to get a little teary…this one did…on more than one occasion…I heartily recommend it…"
—Mystical Nymph, a 5 nymph review
at *Literary Nymphs Reviews Only*

"…Well written with an excellent plot…Falling is a book that grips you and doesn't let you go…I fell in love with Cain and Luke…I highly recommend this book…"
—Hayley, a 5 Angel *Recommended Read*
from *Fallen Angels Reviews*

"...I'm not sure where to begin…other than to say I loved it…unable to put it down. I can't recall ever reading a more passionate, and at times, painful book…highly recommend it…an emotional thrill ride…"
—Sandra, for *The Romance Studio*

# FALLING

Cain Hawkins is a master at suppressing his desires. After all, he's been doing it for more than a century. What Cain wants more than anything is a man to love, but he knows that no matter how much he craves it, it can never be. Cain is a Naverto demon, and to desire another man is more than forbidden, it is an act that will bring about his death. Cain keeps to himself, working with abused horses on a small patch of land, all on his own.

Then Cain's brother makes a request he can't refuse.

Luke Forrester just wants a job and a place where he can recover from a brutal beating. He dreams of a place where he can work with the horses he loves so much. He can't let the fact that he's had a crush on Cain for more than two years matter. Luke is determined not to screw things up. He will prove to Cain it wasn't a mistake to hire him, and he won't allow the secret that he dreams about Cain every night interfere with his work.

But working and living in such close proximity can test the best of intentions, and when one kiss leads to something much, much more, everything changes. Cain must trust Luke completely. And together, he and Luke must find a way to fight for Cain's humanity and save him from his demon clan before he is found out and they are ripped apart forever.

# FALLING

CAMERON DANE

ISBN-13: 978-1475159769
ISBN-10: 1475159765

FALLING

Copyright © 2012 by Cameron Dane
Originally released in e-book format in January 2008
Cover Art, Print Design, and Formatting by April Martinez
*Falling* edited by CB Calsing

Manufactured in the USA

# DEDICATION

For my brother S... It all started back in the fourth grade with a story about an invisible boy. Thanks for making me do your homework that one time; it really paid off. Love you, CD.

# CHAPTER ONE

Cain Hawkins had been summoned to a meeting at his brother Connor's home. He was to attend immediately. Connor's voice had sounded strained and clipped through the telephone, and Cain had grinned devilishly as he imagined the tight lips and clenching jaw on the other end of the line. Only one thing ruffled his brother's feathers these days -- Cassie Hawkins, Connor's spitfire of a wife. With a smile, Cain pulled his truck to a stop in front of the sprawling home on their Montana property. He couldn't wait to hear what Cassie had done this time.

Taking the stairs up to the porch two at a time, Cain let himself in through the front door. "Hello? Con! I'm here. Where are you?" Cain hadn't lived in this house for over a year but he still had his own key and knew he was always welcome to visit. And in this instance, since Connor had been the one to drag him away from where he lived on the other side of the property, Cain had no intention of feeling guilty for shouting through the house to make his presence known.

"I'm in the office!" came the familiar growl of his older brother. "Get the hell in here, right now!"

Cain moved down the hall in an easy, long-legged lope until he reached Connor's office. When he got there, he crossed his arms against his chest and leaned a shoulder against the door frame, waiting for his brother to look up from his desk to acknowledge him.

It didn't take long.

"Thank God, you're finally here," Connor said. He looked up from his paperwork, his black eyes blazing in a way that let Cain know he hadn't been focused on his work anyway.

"Hello to you too." Cain nodded and then went ahead and took one of the visitor seats on the other side of the desk. "What has Cassie done that I have to talk you out of locking her in your room forever this time?" At the sight of his brother sneering, Cain just raised an answering eyebrow right back. "Come on, Con," he said, his voice teasing, "you wouldn't have pulled me away from my work in the middle of the day for nothing. You know how important it is to me, and you know damn well I'd go demon on your newly human ass and beat the shit out of you if you ordered me over here just to talk about the weather. So, let's have it. What has your wife done now?"

Connor's jaw started clenching in earnest, and he threw his pen down on the desk. "Damn it, Cain. She brought home a stray, and if he stays here one more day, I think I might kill him."

Cain looked upon Connor's unforgiving face and hard jaw, on dark brown wavy hair, then to the big, muscular body hidden beneath his work clothes. Except for the fact that Connor's eyes were almost black while Cain's were blue, it sometimes shocked Cain to remember they were not true brothers-in-blood, but rather by choice. Which was why Connor's harsh tone had Cain sitting forward in his chair and looking at his brother in a whole new way. For all of Connor's gruffness, he would never hurt an animal. More than that, the man could never deny his wife anything. An-y-thing.

"Excuse me?" Cain finally managed to utter, once he'd digested the serious nature of Connor's vow. "What kind of stray did Cassie bring home? A horse?" Now that made sense. "Do you have an injured horse you want me to nurse and house in my stable?"

"No." Connor shook his head. "I have a man I want you to nurse and house in your stable."

That one rocked Cain back against the chair. "What?" His voice went decidedly hoarse. "You did not just say what I think you just said."

Connor's gaze never wavered. "Yes, I did." When Cain opened his mouth, Connor held up a hand. "Hear me out. Please."

Cain could only nod. At this point, there were no words to express his horror. Worse, his fear.

"He's a friend of Cassandra's from high school," Connor began. "About a month ago, she gets a call that sends her out of here like a bat outta hell, straight to Billings. Turns out this friend of hers called her from the hospital. He'd apparently had the shit beaten out of him in a bar fight and was in pretty bad shape."

Cain knew all of Connor's inflections as well as he knew his own. The fine hairs on the back of his neck suddenly stood on end. "Why do you use the word 'apparently'?"

"Because something in the way my wife relayed the incident set my radar out of control. I know she's either outright lying to me or she's not giving me the whole truth. Trust me when I say that I can tell when Cassandra is holding something back from me."

"I guess that comes from being in love." Cain could only speculate. He'd never been in love, and he never could be. To do so was to risk his very life. "What do you think happened?"

"I don't know. At this point, I don't much care. I just want the man out of my house so I can have my wife back."

"Wait a minute." The puzzle pieces weren't coming together for Cain. He felt as if Connor had left out about fifty parts of this story, which just went to show his agitation. "He's here? In your house? Right now?"

"Yes, and you would know that if you checked in with us a little more often. You're holing yourself up with your horses, Cain, and none of us feel like we get more than five minutes to talk to you lately."

"Sorry." Cain's jaw ticked. "I've been busy."

"Be less busy." Connor's stare softened and the lecture slid away from his tone. "For your family, at least. Okay?"

Cain nodded. "Got it."

"Thank you. So anyway, this guy was released from the hospital two weeks ago. He still needed some tending to, though, and Cassandra wouldn't hear of him going anywhere else."

"Oh, I get it." Laughter erupted, and Cain didn't bother trying to hide it. "You're jealous of the face time this man is getting with your wife. He's taking up her precious time that should be spent with you."

"So?" Connor practically growled the word. "She is *my* wife. For God's sake, we've only been married for two years."

Wearing a wicked grin, Cain said, "And you think you should be able to grab her up whenever you want her, and take her on any surface in this house, at any time you want to make love to her. You can't do that with a guest in your home. Does that sound about right?"

"Yes." Connor's lips narrowed down to a tight line, and Cain knew what the admission had cost him. "Christ, we haven't been married that long. Is it so wrong to want her to myself as much as possible?"

"No," Cain replied. What the hell else could he say? With Cain also living in the main house for most of the first year of Connor and Cassie's marriage, he had been part of the problem. Caleb, their other brother, still lived in the main house too, but he rarely spent a night in his own bed, so he hadn't cramped the newlyweds' style in the way Cain had done. *In the way this friend of Cassie's apparently now does.* "I can see why you're frustrated."

"I am," Connor admitted. "The guy might still be a little bit bruised up but he's basically healed. I know Cassandra, though, and she's not going to let him out of this house until he has somewhere to go."

Cain slipped back to being confused again. "Wait. Doesn't he have an apartment? Or a house?"

"Used to work another ranch," Connor explained. "He says they fired him when he got into that bar fight and couldn't go to work, something about that being his last chance to stay out of trouble. He says he'll work to repay the time I've let him recover here, and I believe he's sincere. There's only one problem with that…"

Cain finished, "He'll still be too close by, and Cassie will dog his heels making sure he's okay. Ergo, you still don't get your wife back. How am I doin'?"

"You're batting a thousand."

The weight of familial responsibility settled on Cain's shoulders, heavy enough to bow him under. "So how am I supposed to help you?"

"He's great with horses," Connor shared. "In fact, I've seen him working with them when I've had occasion to visit MacLesten's ranch."

"Whoa. Whoa." Cain sat up ramrod straight. "MacLesten's a bastard, and you know it. I despise the way he does business, and I've seen fear in his animals' eyes that I don't like one damn bit."

"I know," Connor cut in. "You know I feel the same way about MacLesten. But this kid, man" -- Connor gestured with his hands -- "he has an ease with horses I've only ever seen in you, Cain. You know Cassandra would never befriend someone who abuses animals. They've known each other since just after Cassandra moved here, all the way back to when she was a senior in high school."

Panic suddenly filled Cain, making his heart race terribly. "Wait a minute." Memories of listening to Cassie talk about her few close friends all those years ago flooded Cain's brain, filling in the gaps of what hadn't yet been said. "Are you talking about Luke Forrester? Is he the guy who was beaten up?"

"Yeah," Connor confirmed, and Cain's stomach twisted with sickness. "Why? Do you know him?"

Cain nodded. "He gave me and Cassie a ride home from the Halloween party a few years ago. Remember?"

"Oh, right." Connor's gaze turned wistful and a secret smile briefly touched his lips. "Other events that evening ended up being much more important to me than who brought you home." Connor had declared his love for Cassie that night, and through a demon ritual, Cassie's love for Connor had allowed him to become human. Their other chosen brother, Caleb, was of the same demon species Connor had been, a Dastetier, of the first beasts, while Cain was a Naverto, a flying creature. Connor added, "I'd forgotten Luke gave you guys a ride home."

"It was him." Cain's stomach fluttered as he remembered, but he determinedly shook it off. "You're right; he does have a good reputation among the local hands for being a hard worker, with a gentle hand for the most skittish of mustangs."

Connor's face lit up like a Christmas tree, and Cain knew his own peace of mind was over.

"Then you'll take him on?" Hope laced each of Connor's words.

"Where will I put him?" Cain scrambled, reaching for one last escape from this mess. "My cabin only has the one room. I don't have a bunkhouse."

"You have that room in the barn. Put him there. He's willing to work. I think he's eager to, even. What do you say? Will you give him a chance? For me?"

The room in the barn was small, and it likely wouldn't be comfortable, but Cain didn't feel as though he had a lot of options. How in the hell did one refuse the man who'd saved him from squalor and maddening loneliness some one hundred and fifty years ago? How did one deny anything to the man who had given him a family in himself and Caleb, when he'd had nothing for twenty-five years before that?

Simple answer: *I don't.*

"Send him over tomorrow." A chill swept through Cain as he gave his agreement. He had a terrifying feeling he'd just signed his own death warrant. "I'll give him a shot. That's all I can promise."

Connor reached across the desk with his hand outstretched. "That's all I ask."

After shaking on it, Cain backed away. "I have to get back to work. Say hi to Cassie for me. I'll talk to you soon."

As Cain let himself out and made the drive to his cabin, memories of the few times he'd crossed paths with Luke Forrester assaulted him with a vengeance. The night of the Halloween party -- the night they'd officially met -- still held the strongest pull for Cain. The ride home from the party had happened in virtual silence, but it had been ripe with tension. Cassie sat between him and Luke, upset and trying not to cry after a fight between her and Connor. Above Cassie's head, Cain's gaze had met Luke's in the darkened cab of the truck. The small glance had ended before it had even started, but Luke's kind and empathetic gray eyes had stayed in Cain's memory for many a lonely night afterward. On the few instances they'd crossed paths since, knowledge of how aroused Cain became every time he thought of Luke made him fumbling and uncomfortable. Whether it was at the diner or the feed store, Cain would mumble a rough "Hi," barely make eye contact, and then get the hell away as quickly as possible. But even those brief encounters... Christ, they'd left Cain sweating...and hard.

There was no denying Luke was stunning. A lean, hard body that knew how to mold a pair of jeans and a cowboy shirt to his frame; dark hair that had a tendency to curl at the edges when he perspired; and the palest gray eyes Cain had ever seen. Top that with a face that wasn't the least bit pretty but all man and it was a recipe guaranteed to keep Cain up at night jerking off. Add to the picture that the man loved horses as much as Cain did and this little arrangement had disaster written all over it.

Luke Forrester was the very image of what Cain found attractive and sexy in a man.

And that was the one thing Cain Hawkins could not afford to feel.

"Shit."

# Chapter Two

A high-pitched beeping assaulted Cain's ears. He yanked a pillow over his head with one hand as he reached out and banged the alarm clock with the other. Exhaustion ruled every muscle and bone in his body. Even if he hadn't used half of his sleep time letting the demon within him out to fly, Cain still hated mornings like the very devil anyway.

He knew once he dragged himself out of bed and put his body under a shower for five minutes he would be raring to start work. But fuckin' A, the ten minutes it took every morning to talk himself out of bed were always the very worst of his day.

That all changed the second Cain heard his dog, Whisky, barking up a storm on the porch. The dog rarely barked, and when she did Cain was always grateful to be alerted to whatever had grabbed the mutt's attention. He rolled out of bed and into a discarded pair of jeans in one smooth move, and pulled his front door open with a shotgun raised to his shoulder in the next.

That was how Cain officially greeted his first employee, Luke

Forrester.

"Whoa, don't shoot." Luke's hands went from stretched out to ward off Whisky to up in the air in surrender. "Connor sent me over for work; one of his guys dropped me off. I'm Luke Forrester. We met a few years ago on Halloween. I gave you and Cassie a ride home."

Cain lowered his gun and leaned it against the split-log wall of his cabin. "I remember." His tone came across terser than he would have liked, but Christ, it wasn't even six a.m. yet. How was he supposed to function in front of a guy he'd had wet dreams about before he'd even had a cup of coffee to help him wake up? After clearing his throat, Cain tried again. "That Halloween was one hell of a night."

"Yeah." Luke chuckled and smiled. Even through the yellowing bruises still marring his face, the torrent of raw masculinity radiating off the man struck Cain hard in the gut. "I think it's safe to say Cassie has forgiven Connor for whatever had her so pissed off that night."

Cain found himself smiling back. "You could say that. I'm surprised she's not here with you right now reading me a list of jobs I'm not to let you do until you're fully healed."

Luke looked away then, and Cain could have kicked himself for making a joke at the younger man's expense. If Luke and Cassie had been together in school, then he couldn't be more than twenty-five years old. At that age, young men often still felt the need to prove their toughness.

After a few beats, Luke turned back, his gray gaze unwavering as it landed on Cain. "I won't cause you any trouble." Such rawness laced Luke's voice it twisted Cain's stomach. "Not from my injuries and how I got them, and not from anyone wanting to coddle me and prevent me from working. I aim to earn every penny you and Hawkins Ranch pays me, and I don't intend to ever let you regret being coerced into giving me this job."

Cain's respect for Luke went up a notch. "You show me that your reputation with horses isn't all talk, and I won't have any problems with you. But just in case it needs to be said, I don't agree with MacLesten's methods for taming his animals. I will give you a beating worse than the one you've already taken if I see you mistreating any of the horses on this property. Got me?"

"Crystal clear. I didn't approve of my old boss's decisions on much of anything. I'm happy to be out of there, if you want the truth." Storm clouds churned in Luke's gaze; Cain couldn't mistake them for anything but troubled. "Sometimes you don't have any choice but to go where the work is, and that was the only reason I stayed on with Justin MacLesten's outfit for as long as I did."

Unspoken layers of deeper sentiment lived in Luke's comment, ones that left Cain aching and curious to ask for more. Danger lay in that direction, though, so he held his tongue. Belatedly, he realized he stood on his porch half clothed, and that was not a position he ever needed to be in with Luke Forrester.

"Let me get a shirt, and then I'll walk with you to the barn to show you where you're going to bunk down. I'll introduce you to the horses so you can get started."

Luke dipped his head. "Sounds good. Oh, and Mr. Hawkins?"

Cain almost growled at that. "I'm not some pompous ass who stands on ceremony, *Luke*. Call me Cain, or don't call me anything at all."

"Right." The man blushed, and Cain had to turn away before his new employee noticed his cock suddenly twitching in his jeans. "Anyway, I just wanted to say thank you for this opportunity. You won't regret it."

*I seriously doubt that.* Instead Cain said, "I hope not. I'll be back in a minute."

"I'll be waiting right here."

"I'm sure you will." Cain got through the door and closed it, quickly. Once inside the sanctuary of his cabin, he muttered, "And I have a feeling that's going to be a huge problem."


Once Luke Forrester felt certain Cain Hawkins had moved away from the front door, he took a deep, calming breath. His heart had started racing the minute the man had walked out onto his porch dressed in only a faded pair of jeans. The man was beautiful in the simplest, most basic ways, and Luke had been fighting a massive crush on him since the night Cassie had introduced them some two years ago. Ever since the Halloween party and the ride home, on the dozen or so times they'd had reason to cross paths, Luke had taken to not saying much of anything other than, "Hey, how's it going?" and then quickly moving on. Luke had been so tongue-tied that first time Cassie had introduced her "big brother" that he'd hidden for fear of looking like an idiot.

When Connor had approached Luke with this position within the Hawkins organization, Luke had come to accept his infatuation with Cain Hawkins had to come to an end. Luke needed the work. He couldn't go back to MacLesten's property, but by the same token, his mother and sister needed his financial assistance in order to pay their bills every month. He'd had to dip into the little bit of money he'd managed to save in order to provide for them this past month, but his savings wouldn't last long. If he didn't have a steady paycheck coming in soon they would figure out he'd left the job with MacLesten. The questions would start then. Luke could never let his mother and sister learn the truth about where he'd been for the last month, and why he'd had to be there. Their safety absolutely depended on them never knowing.

It was time for Luke to just man up and get over his silly crush on a guy he could never have anyway, and just do the job so damn well that Cain Hawkins never had any reason to let him go.

That was what Luke would do, because he had no other choice.

---

"So," CAIN SAID, "THIS IS where you'll be staying." He kicked open the door to the little room at the back of the barn. Luke followed Cain in and set his duffel bag down on the floor. "You have a bed," Cain continued, "and a nightstand with an alarm clock. There's a fridge and a microwave in the office; you are welcome to use both. I'm sorry it's not more, but I only ever intended for it to be used when I need to keep hourly watch on one of the horses. I guess when you get the rest of your gear in here it'll start to feel a little bit more like home."

Sickness flooded Luke's belly but he forced himself past the mortification and turned to face Cain head on. He had to start facing his new truth or he'd be too embarrassed to look the man in the eye for anything. "This is my gear." He picked up the duffel bag he'd just set down and forced his way past Cain to place it on the single bed. "When I didn't immediately claim my stuff from the bunkhouse, MacLesten distributed it to the other men." Luke kept his head high, determined not to be ashamed. "The clothing I have now Cassie bought for me at some secondhand stores. Your brother said he would give me a saddle and a few other things on credit, so I'll have all my own gear by the end of the day."

"Justin MacLesten is one of the foulest human beings I've ever had the displeasure to come across." Cain's voice was clipped and hard. "And let me tell you something, Luke, in the course of my life, that's saying something."

Cain's anger had come so fast that Luke had blanched, fearing it was aimed at him. When he realized it wasn't, blood rushed through his body and left him swaying where he stood. The man had looked ferocious, and Luke made a mental note never to piss him off.

"What's done is done." Luke did his best to appear as though the theft wasn't a big deal to him. "I hate to lose my saddle but it's worth it in trade to be working here for you instead of over there for MacLesten even one more day." The subject of how and why he'd left his old job still made Luke's stomach sick, and he preferred not to think or talk about it if he could avoid it. "So, *Cain*" -- Luke made a point to follow that first rule he'd been given -- "why don't you introduce me to the horses, and we'll get started."

"Ahh, now you're talking about my one true love." Cain practically purred as he beckoned Luke to follow him.

The man smiled, and Luke tripped over his own feet. Cain reached out and grabbed Luke's arm to steady him. The small contact, even through the fabric of his shirt, sent frissons of complete sexual awareness through Luke and burned his skin to heated life.

"Sorry." Luke pulled away immediately. Heat rushed to his face and he knew he was blushing like mad. "I'm not normally clumsy. I promise."

"Don't worry about it." Cain winked as he backtracked to the door. "It's not like you set off a series of bombs. You tripped. Now" -- once again, he gestured to Luke -- "follow me, and I'll introduce you to my children."

The unnecessary, unexpected kindness from Cain tripped even more wires in Luke. He couldn't make the buzz of awareness go away. He followed Cain Hawkins out into the body of the barn anyway, all the while reminding himself not to stare at his new boss's fine ass.

---

THREE NIGHTS LATER, CAIN CAUGHT up to Luke as the younger man led Fancy Face, one of Cain's most tentative new horses, back into the barn. He hadn't wanted to disturb Luke while he worked with the horse, so Cain had split his time doing paperwork by his front window and watching the path from the main paddock for the rangy man.

"So…" Cain stepped in line alongside Luke rather than the temperamental horse. "How'd you do with her? What are your thoughts?"

"Geez." Chuckling, Luke glanced at Cain sideways. "You don't waste any time, do you? Can I at least rub her down and feed her before we talk?"

Cain smiled sheepishly. "I'll help you with that, and we can talk while we do it."

Luke laughed again. "You are what the experts refer to as a dog with a bone, Hawk."

*Hawk?* Visions of the sleek, brown bird in flight assaulted Cain's senses. The apparent discovery of one of his secrets sent Cain's heart to pounding in triple time. How in the hell had this guy figured out Cain could fly in his demon form? Or that he was a demon, period? Cain snagged Luke's arm and spun him around until they faced each other. "Why did you call me a hawk?"

"Oh God, I am so sorry. I know you told me to call you Cain or nothing at all." Luke reached out as he apologized, but his hand quickly dropped back to his side. "I didn't mean to offend you. I just do that sometimes when I'm around a person a lot. I don't know why. I shorten people's names, and before I know it I'm calling them by a nickname. I apologize. I won't do it again."

*Fuck.* Cain hadn't meant to terrify Luke. And by the darkening of his silver gaze, Cain could tell he had. "No, Luke," Cain murmured, "I'm the one who is sorry. You can call me whatever you want. It's fine." *Stupid. Stupid. Stupid.*

With another curse under his breath, Cain turned and started walking toward the barn. He didn't dare let Luke see the relief flooding every inch of his body, leaving him lightheaded. He couldn't risk giving himself away. For just a split second, paranoia had grabbed at Cain and had him thinking that somehow Luke had found out about the flying demon that lived within him. Only, nobody except his brothers and Cassie knew about that cursed being, and Cassie had never seen him in full demon form. There was no way Luke could know about the flying.

Snapping out of his silent lecture to himself, Cain suddenly realized he was staring at Luke while the man removed Fancy Face's equipment and started to rub her down. Cain quickly moved in to help, but the horse shied from too much attention, so Cain put the tack away instead.

Cain spoke from farther down in the barn, compelled to explain himself to Luke for reasons he could not afford to feel. "It's just that nobody has ever given me a nickname before, so it kind of startled me for a moment. I don't dislike it. If Hawk is how you think of me, then you can call me that. This isn't MacLesten's outfit; I don't push everyone under my thumb and always have to have everything done my way." Forcing out a chuckle, Cain made a feeble attempt to lighten the mood. "But don't tell my brothers that. As far as they need to know, on this piece of the property it is my way or the highway."

"And what is your way, Cain?" Luke finished Fancy Face's

rubdown. Cain caught Luke glance across the barn, but before the man could catch him staring, Cain quickly turned back to his work. Luke added, "That is, if you don't mind my asking?"

"That's the million-dollar question." Cain found himself sharing the truth, revealing more than he probably should. Something about this man made Cain want to tell him all of his secrets. The pull to connect with Luke was vicious. So very quickly, Cain found Luke damn hard to ignore. "When I approached Con and Caleb about this project, I told them I would rescue these abused and mistreated horses, rehabilitate them, and then resell them for a tidy profit."

"Sounds like a good plan," Luke commented. "Noble idea and profitable at the same time. Can't argue with that."

Cain didn't want to acknowledge how much such a simple compliment from this man filled him up with pride. "Yeah, in theory it was great."

Luke locked the latch on the stall door and leaned his shoulder against the wood. "So, if it's such a good idea, then what's the problem?"

Cain was very afraid of the confession he was about to make. It could, in more ways than one, break him. He leaned on the stall opposite Luke, stared at his handsome face, the man so clearly curious and interested -- things Cain couldn't afford in a friend -- and did it anyway. "I've fallen in love with each and every one of these animals, Luke. And when I love something, I don't ever let it go."

# CHAPTER THREE

Later that night, Cain cursed up a blue streak as he paced the length of his cabin, fighting the conflicting need and panic roiling within his body, each challenging for dominance. Fear of his immediate attraction to Luke did battle with an excitement of sexual discovery Cain couldn't deny. Once again, he chided himself for saying what he'd said to Luke in the barn earlier that night.

"I keep what I love." Cain rolled his eyes. "What a pansified idiot you are, Hawkins." An unforgiving edge laced his lecturing tone. "Why didn't you just come right out and say you're attracted to him and want to fuck him, you jackass."

When Cain had made his declaration, Luke had just said, "Oh." The guy had to think Cain was a total freak now. Which, Cain reminded himself brutally, he was. The demon pushed to get out when Cain wasn't in harmony, and right now, he wasn't even close to feeling at peace inside his soul.

"Fuck it." Cain moved through the small cabin to his bedroom and started to remove his clothes. "You want out?" He talked to his reflection in the big mirror above his ash wood bureau. "Show yourself, Naverto, and we'll go fly."

Standing nude before the mirror, Cain stared, determined to remind himself of the most important reason why he could never act on his attraction to Luke Forrester. As the change began, Cain's breathing shifted to low in his belly. He was so accustomed to the feeling that it no longer registered as painful. Everything happened simultaneously, but Cain bookmarked each element as it occurred, his focus darting from one image to the next, forcing the transformation down his throat to a place of acceptance. The hard, sharp angles of his face shifted to mountainous, squared off, and compressed. His ears flattened against his head, stretching up and back until the tips were elongated points. The muscles in his chest, shoulders, arms and thighs thickened with bulk, while at the same time, the color of his flesh changed from naturally tan to the richest copper tone in the color wheel. His fingernails and toenails thickened and curved to clawlike appendages, and his back split open, unfurling a set of wings that would span eighteen feet from tip to tip when fully extended. Cain growled with pleasure as his cock hardened and lengthened to over ten inches, the sensation of growth very similar to what it felt like when he stroked himself to release. Sexual arousal was the final phase in the change, and in the aftermath, the face and body of Cain Hawkins was no more.

This was what Cain was, a demon. And as he did not have sexual desires for human women, it was something he had no hope of ever changing.

———

AN HOUR LATER, CAIN SOARED THROUGH the moonless, black sky, keeping high above the tree line and out of sight of human eyes. His blood coursed hot and fast through his body, reminding him he would need to make an animal kill soon. All demons required fresh meat for survival. He hated taking the life of any breathing thing, but accepted the necessity of the task if he desired to continue breathing.

Cain imagined that were he fully human, he would be a vegetarian. Over time, he had managed to train his demon's need to accept blood-rare cooked meats on a regular basis in place of the weekly fresh kills he'd have to otherwise make. He was now only forced to take down a deer, elk, or ram once a month instead of four times. And while he hated taking any animal's life, it was something he lived with as a consequence of what he was.

Exhaustion ruled Cain's body, and he knew he had to get home soon or else he would not be able to work tomorrow. He pumped higher and higher with his wings, up into air so thin it made him dizzy. When he reached the height he wanted, euphoria took over and pumped his blood full of endorphins. He angled down quickly, spreading his wings all the way out as he started to glide back to earth on a cushion of brisk air. Wind sluiced over his flesh and speared through his hair, the sensation coating him in pleasure that he imagined sex could bring to a body. The floating motion caused every inch of his skin to tingle with life, from the separation of his toes all the way up to the smattering of hair on his chest.

Cain loved flying. He gave himself free reign to love it to the full extent of his body's need to feel pleasure. He did it in place of the sex with another man his body so craved.

———

BACK DOWN TO EARTH, CAIN let himself into his darkened home through the back door. As he walked to his bathroom to put on pair of sweats, the demon's features slid from his face and body as easily as they'd appeared. That was as it should be, Cain snorted derisively, as this was the second night in less than a week he'd let the demon out to fly. Not a usual situation for him. He normally had complete control over the demon, more so than many others did.

The mental separation of human and demon was a product of not embracing the full demon life, Cain knew this. It was rare that an individual didn't relish being a demon, especially if he or she was born to the creation as Cain had been. But he'd known from a very young age that he didn't enjoy playing tricks on humans. Cain had never liked showing himself to lonely people in the dead of night, terrifying them, and then laughing from the shadows when they were called unbalanced and occasionally even locked away by their fellow humans if they refused to retract their claims. Knowing that, and understanding he did not have a desire to mate with Naverto females when in demon form, Cain had run from the place of his birth, separating himself almost completely from his demon clan. He'd --

"No! No! Stooopppp! Pleeeease!" A low, almost inhuman cry rent the dead silence of the night. The sound had Cain tearing out his front door, wearing only his sweats, and breaking into a dead run for the barn. Some of his horses had been abused terribly, and while they were learning how to trust people again, they sometimes attacked out of a primal fear. If Luke had tried to force interaction for some reason, he could be seriously injured or killed for his mistake.

Fear lodged deep in Cain's throat, for his horses and for Luke. If something happened to Luke because Cain hadn't properly explained the behavior of the abused animals, Cain would never forgive himself. He ripped open the sliding barn door and stormed inside. Moving down the line of occupied stalls, eight in all, Cain soothed the neighing panic in each horse before moving on to the next to repeat the process. Pain still weighing on his chest, Cain looked for a body inside each stall, perhaps stretched out and trampled on the ground. There wasn't one.

*Thank God.*

A guttural moan and then a sob filled the air, and Cain's relief gave way to panic once again. Without thinking, he took a dozen long-legged strides to Luke's door. He found himself inside the room standing next to the bed in two additional quick steps. A nightlight beside the bed illuminated Luke as he thrashed, his face buried in his pillow, moaning, clearly in the throes of a nightmare. Perspiration glistened on his bared back -- highlighting a number of scars -- but Luke cried out for help again right then, and Cain's anger at seeing the marks quickly gave way to gut-wrenching need.

Unable to stand there and do nothing, Cain sat down on the edge of the bed and reached out to touch Luke's shoulder. "Luke? Luke?" He spoke softly, much as he would with one of his skittish horses. He didn't want to spook the man into lashing out at him. "Luke?" Cain nudged the finely sculpted shoulder once again. "It's Hawk, Luke. You're having a dream. You need to wake up."

One second the man moaned terrible noises into his pillow, the next he keened and buried his face against Cain's stomach. He wrapped his arms firmly around Cain's waist, and his entire body quaked. Luke clearly still lived in the aftermath of his dream, and Cain had never experienced such an all-encompassing pull to protect another being in his one hundred and seventy-five years of life.

"Shhh, shhh. It's okay now," Cain crooned softly. He smoothed his palm over Luke's sweat-drenched hair again and again, petting him with a gentle touch. "You're not in that bad place anymore. You're right here with me." He rubbed up and down Luke's back, ignoring the need to ask for an explanation about the ridges of marred flesh under his fingers. Instead, he just tried to settle the heaving radiating through the tension-filled body he held. "You're perfectly safe here, Luke. I'm not going to hurt you, not for anything."

The arms squeezing Cain's middle with a powerful hold loosened just a little bit. The breathing slowed from choppy to merely labored. Finally, after what felt like an eternity, Luke pulled away and leaned back against the wall. Wildness still eclipsed his eyes, and he wouldn't fully meet Cain's gaze.

"Were you dreaming about the beating?" Cain asked, keeping his voice to a whisper. Vulnerability radiated off of Luke, and Cain fought the urge to haul the younger man back into his arms and hold him close until all the fear went away. Instead, he clasped his hands together in his lap. "Is that what the nightmare was about?"

Luke swiped his hand across his cheek, clearly trying to push away proof that the power of his dream had brought him to tears. "Yeah." He finally spoke, and the huskiness in his tone made the words sound as if they'd been put through a grinder. "Pussy of me, huh?" Luke laughed, but the noise grated on Cain's ears. "Crying like a girl because I got beat up in a bar."

"Not pussy at all." Cain hadn't forgotten what his fingers had touched just a few minutes ago -- *Christ, I don't think I'll ever forget* -- and he chose his words carefully. "But maybe it's the stress of lying about what really happened to you."

"What?" Luke whipped his focus up from the blanket, and Cain got the full eye contact he'd been hoping for. The terror within that gray stare sucker punched him in the gut.

"You have incredibly expressive eyes, Luke," Cain revealed, offering Luke a small smile. "And even if you didn't, and I couldn't see the panic of discovery in them right this second, I saw the scars on your back myself not five minutes ago."

"So?"

"So," Cain persisted, knowing with every fiber of his being he was doing the right thing here, even if he couldn't logically rationalize it. "I know what scars from a whip look and feel like. I know what cigar burns feel like too. You don't get whipped and burned like that in a bar fight. You can tell me what really happened to you, and I swear on my horses' lives that if you don't want me to tell another soul I never will."

Luke's elbows went to his raised knees, and he tunneled his fingers through his disheveled hair. The tears stopped, but his eyes were still bright with moisture. "Why do you want to know? What does it matter to you one way or another?"

"Because you're my employee, and you're good with my horses. I don't want to lose you to the weight of this burden, whatever it is." When Luke didn't look any less like a hunted animal without a safe place to hide, Cain exhaled carefully, and through an extra tightness in his chest, he let go of a little bit of his rigid control over his desires. "And because I like you, Luke," he added, although he kept it light. "You seem like a good guy to me, and I'm not usually wrong about stuff like that. That is why I want to know who in the hell did this to my friend."

Luke lifted his downturned head and settled his gaze on Cain's. "Justin MacLesten did this to me, and if word gets out around town, he'll grab up my sister and my mother and do the same thing to them."

Cain could barely stuff down the fiery, white-hot rage racing through his blood on Luke's behalf. His fists and arms ached with the need to go beat the living shit out of MacLesten himself. "What… why…how…I don't understand." Cain held up a hand before Luke could take offense. "I'm not saying I don't believe you; trust me on that. MacLesten is a bastard, and I believe him capable of just about any cruelty. But what kind of reason could he possibly have for justifying it, and how in the hell did he manage to do this to you without anyone stopping him?"

"I…I did something he didn't approve of." Luke's gaze shut Cain out completely, and it struck Cain that it was that same hooded look he'd seen just a few mornings ago on his porch when Luke had shown up to begin his job. "Anyway, a couple of days later, I was out riding fence when I got a call to meet MacLesten at one of the outer line cabins. I thought it was strange, but he's the boss. It's not like I could have refused."

"Just so you know," Cain cut in, needing with everything in him to separate what he was from Luke's old boss, "should I ever ask you to do something you don't approve of, or anything that doesn't seem right, you tell me. Clear?"

"Yeah." Luke nodded. "Thank you."

Silence reigned between them for awhile. Cain nudged again, saying gently, "Go on, Luke. Go ahead and get it all said."

"Okay." Luke paled, but unfathomable pride pricked Cain in the chest when Luke took a visible, deep breath and went on. "So I get to the cabin, and MacLesten is waiting for me outside. He tells me to let my horse roam and to join him inside. He goes in first, and when I step over the threshold to join him, a two-by-four swings out of nowhere and clips me across my gut. When I double over, it slams down on the back of my head, and then down my back, sending me into this blurry state of semi-consciousness. I'm kind of aware of what's happening, but I can't seem to make myself move. It's like I would imagine it feels to be drugged."

Luke stopped then, and to Cain it looked like the rest of the story would be even more painful to speak. Rage filled Cain to overflowing, and it warred with an almost desperate need to defend this man against anyone who would do him harm. The fact that Cain's hands were tied to exact revenge angered the hell out of him. He couldn't imagine how Luke functioned every day knowing the scum who'd done this to him had enough power to walk around town free. Cain understood Luke's need to protect his family -- and in truth he would do the same -- but it would be damned hard to live with, just the same.

"Anyway" -- Luke finally found his voice again -- "a blow to my temple knocked me out. When I came to, I was naked, stretched up, and hanging by my wrists. There was just enough give in the ropes that I could reach my toes to the floor and hold myself up."

"Son of a bitch," Cain swore viciously. It was impossible for him to show no emotion; to remain indifferent. Not when this man was involved. "Someone needs to take MacLesten up into the mountains and shoot him."

"Yeah." Luke actually chuckled at that, and the small sound of lightness tore right through Cain's heart. "Except he's not worth doing prison time for."

"I suppose you're right," Cain conceded, although he hated like hell doing it. "I'm sorry I interrupted. Go on."

"Right." Tightness pulled at Luke's mouth again, and it revealed the secret of how much this beating still tormented him. "When I came to, I was disoriented, and I panicked. The minute it became clear to MacLesten that I was conscious, he started punching me. I swayed off my toes with the force of the punches, swinging like one of those boxing bags you see in a gym. He seemed to find that amusing -- that I was basically doing all the work for him. He didn't even have to move in order to hit me. I twirled around so much with the power behind his blows that he was able to get me all over pretty good.

"After a while, his hands got tired, or maybe he got bored. I don't know." The words grew thicker, one by one, as they came out of

Luke. It appeared that each sentence was a challenge to get out. Cain waited, silently this time, praying Luke would trust him enough to speak the rest. "Anyway, that was when he switched to the whip." Luke turned away then, and in profile Cain could see him blinking rapidly as he tried to get control over his emotions. After a good five minutes that felt like forever, Luke finally settled his turbulent gray gaze back on Cain. "The fiery pain that ripped through my body with that first lash is something I'll never forget. It's something I'll feel for the rest of my life."

As Luke wiped beads of sweat off his upper lip, his hands shook. "For whatever reason, MacLesten stuck to my backside with the whip. Not that it felt like a blessing, though, because he made sure to leave some kind of mark from shoulder to ankle, with no space spared in between. When he finished, I was barely conscious, and I couldn't hold myself up anymore. I was just hanging from my arms, which were completely numb by that point anyway, so what did it matter. I thought for sure nothing could be worse than getting whipped, and that he was surely done with his sadistic punishment of me."

"But he wasn't." As if he were still touching Luke, Cain rubbed his fingertips together, but in his mind he remembered the round scars of flesh on Luke's back. The cigar burns.

"No, he wasn't." Luke shook his head, and his eyes filled with more moisture.

It killed Cain to see tears and fear in this man; without thinking, he reached out and wiped the wetness away with the pads of his thumbs. Luke jerked against the touch, but Cain understood that was just what an abused animal did. Luke had to relearn that human contact didn't automatically lead to pain.

Cain brushed Luke's hair away from his face and clasped his hand around his shoulder, holding it tight. "If you can't talk about this with somebody, then you will never be able to get past it." His fingers didn't want to release, but Cain forced himself to let Luke go and resume a respectable distance between them. "That person doesn't have to be me, but I think you'll find this a whole lot easier to live with if you can find someone to confide in and trust."

"I was assigned a counselor when I was in the hospital."

"Okay, that's good." It was exactly what Cain would have suggested if the subject hadn't come up. "Did you like him or her? Did you trust this person?"

"Her," Luke clarified. "And yes, I did. Cassie drove me into Billings twice a week to meet with her after I got out of the hospital."

"Okay. When's your next appointment?"

"It was yesterday."

Cain suddenly clenched his jaw so hard his teeth hurt. "But you didn't leave the property yesterday, Luke."

"That's because I canceled the session."

"Why in the hell would you do that?"

"Because I just started working for you, Cain." Streaks of life erupted in Luke's eyes. "I'm not going to start a job and less than one week into it start giving you times and days when I can't work. That's not right, and it's not fair to you."

"Good Christ, Luke," Cain uttered, along with another choice curse. "This is your well-being we're talking about here."

"And this is your *business*!" Luke yelled. "I'm not going to be some half-assed employee you can't count on!"

The fire in Luke's eyes excited the hell out of Cain. It turned him on, which was bad, but it also allowed him to lay into the guy, which was exactly what he needed. "You're not some half-assed employee, Luke! I already trust you with my horses, and let me tell you something, I don't trust very easily." Cain stood, towering his six-feet-two frame over the narrow bed. "But if you're going to be an idiot and ignore a vital part of your recovery, then I'm not sure you're the guy I want making decisions for my animals!"

Luke shot off the bed too, almost going chest to chest with Cain. His eyes swirled with all the colors of a rainstorm. "Are you saying I don't have the good sense God gave me to provide the best care for your horses?" He poked Cain in the chest, but then winced and reached for his back. "Ow."

"No, I'm not saying that at all! Wait." Cain narrowed his stare.

"What '*ow*? Luke, what's wrong?"

"Nothing." Wincing, Luke dropped back down to the bed. "Some of the deeper scars on my back still pull at the skin around them when I stretch or move quickly. That's all."

"And let me guess." Cain crossed his arms and raised a brow. "You're not taking care of them properly either. Right?"

Luke shot Cain one of the most stubborn, bullheaded sneers he'd ever witnessed. "I was taking very good care of them, but Cassie was helping me. They're not exactly in a place that is easy to reach, you know."

"Well then, let's solve one problem tonight," Cain said, so into the moment he couldn't back off. "Where is the cream you're supposed to be using?"

Luke's gaze went from fiery to wary in one blink of his eyes. He leaned back against the wall, but he never looked away. "Why, Cain?" he asked. "Why do you want to know?"

*No. No. No.* Ignoring the voice of reason in his head, Cain took a reckless step that might very well get him killed. "Because I'm taking over the job of looking out for you, Luke. And right now, that starts with me taking care of your back."

# Chapter Four

"You…you don't have to do that." Luke's gray eyes were as wide as Cain had ever seen them.

And now, even if it was just to save face and prove a point, there was no way Cain could turn tail and run.

"Actually, I do." Cain tried to project much more confidence than actually lived and breathed inside him. "If you're not feeling one hundred percent, then you can't do everything you need to do to gentle and train my horses. Go on -- lay down on your stomach." He gestured up the length of the small bed. "Tell me where to find this lotion or salve, and I'll get it myself."

"It's on the sink in the bathroom, but you really don't have to do this." Luke stretched out, face down, on the bed. "I would never slack off on the job over a little bit of discomfort."

"I know you wouldn't." Cain moved to the door at the foot of the bed, flipped the light on in the little white-tiled bathroom, and immediately spotted the bottle. Lotion in hand, he came back and sat down by Luke's hip. "Just like you don't have to worry about me."

Cain reached out and feathered his fingers over the small of Luke's back; a tremor rushed through the muscles under his touch. "I'm not MacLesten, Luke. I swear on my horses' lives I am not going to hurt you."

"I know." The pillow clutched in Luke's arms muffled his voice. He turned his head then, and Cain could see half of his face. His eyes were closed. "And you're right; I will feel better afterward. Go ahead."

As Cain squeezed a dollop of the lotion in his hands, he contemplated Luke's back. To warm the cool substance, he pressed it between his palms. But as he did, silently, on the inside, Cain wondered what kind of death wish he had, playing with fire like this. Scars or no scars, Luke had a beautiful body. It was an insane temptation Cain could ill afford. He wanted to touch in *play*, as well as in healing. *No.* A gutting pain sliced through Cain with a terrible finality. *You can't.* With as yet untapped strength of willpower, Cain forced himself to stick to the task at hand.

He shifted to his knees so he could lean in if needed, took a steadying breath, and gently pressed his hands against the top of Luke's back. Luke's muscles were sleek, sculpted, and well-defined beneath his golden tan flesh. Luke had been close to flawless before he'd been so brutally terrorized, Cain saw and felt it. As Cain rubbed the healing lotion into Luke's skin, the man's muscles contorted, tensed, and released beneath his fingers. Cain worked the warm flesh under his hands, kneading Luke's back with massage techniques he'd learned to use on animals, even as he knew full well this body he touched and learned right now was very much that of a man.

Nothing inappropriate would happen, but Christ, Cain could not deny the excitement in learning what another man felt like with his own two hands. The fact that it was this particular man, one whom Cain was already starting to like beyond mere sexual attraction, made what Cain did all the more potent. Luke murmured appreciatively beneath him, and it was all Cain could do not to lean down to kiss his cheek and nip at his ear.

With a supreme will he'd been employing all of his life, Cain paused, taking a moment to squeeze more lotion into his hands. "It feels good to get a rubdown every once in a while, huh?" he asked, doing his damnedest to convey only the smile on his face and not the hard-on tenting his sweats. He moved to the small of Luke's back and started again. "How are your injuries feeling? Is the lotion helping?"

"Yeah." Luke sounded drowsy. "The scars don't look it, but they really are pretty much healed. I feel good for the most part, even if it doesn't appear so."

"I can't even see the bruises on your face anymore," Cain shared. He dipped his hands down the sides of Luke's body and worked that flesh up to his furry armpits, reveling in the cuts of muscle that rippled under his touch. Good Christ, this man's body was beautiful. "As for the scars, my understanding is that women tend to think they're romantic and sexy." Heaven knew they weren't doing anything to turn Cain off.

"That's what Cassie sa…" A low, throaty moan suddenly purred out of Luke and his body undulated beneath Cain's hands. Cain stilled his fingers immediately. "Ohh, that feels so good. Don't stop. I've been trying to work out that twisting tension in my lower back for days and haven't been able to make it happen."

Cain shifted over Luke, straddling the man's thighs for better positioning. With fingers spread wide, he pressed his thumbs into the dip in Luke's back, working outward in small circles. He kept up on his knees so Luke wouldn't feel his erection. He didn't want to freak the hell out of the man and make him think he would be attacked.

*I can do this. I can take care of Luke, enjoy the discovery in learning his body, but not push it over a line to a place I can't take back.* He was strong. Cain told himself again, *I can do this.*

Silent pep talk now done, Cain worked Luke's hard muscles from top to bottom, all the way until he reached Luke's tailbone, to the barrier of navy blue sweatpants covering his lower body. Cain ran a fingertip along a thin ridge of scar tissue until he couldn't trace it anymore. The end of the faint line disappeared beneath Luke's clothes.

"You said he whipped you all the way down your back side,

right?" Cain murmured softly.

"Yeah." Luke nodded against his pillow. "He showed no mercy. I'm sure he was hoping I'd die when he cut me down and told me I could leave. I don't believe he thought I'd be able to get away and find help on my own."

Luke spoke of horrific things, but the panic seemed to be gone from his voice. He appeared merely to be sharing information now, and if nothing else, Cain felt better having talked with Luke for that alone. The new peace and calmness lulled Cain too, making him feel strangely at ease with what he was doing. Cain wanted Luke to feel safe and good, and the fact that the man let his body be touched was a huge step toward getting back his confidence.

"I'm going to do the rest of your scars now, Luke." Cain heard the huskiness in his own voice and discreetly cleared his throat. "All right?"

Luke just made an *"mmm"* sound, so Cain took that as consent. He hooked his fingers under the elastic waistband of the man's sweats and tugged gently. Luke lifted his hips just the slightest bit, and Cain slid the sweats down to the tops of Luke's thighs, revealing the glorious globes of his fit, tight ass. Luke tensed beneath Cain at the initial vulnerability that came with exposure, so Cain didn't touch while Luke adjusted to this step of renewed trust. Eventually, Luke settled back into the mattress and relaxed.

For which Cain was happy…for Luke. Cain himself, however, battled his entire frame pulling tauter than a drum. He'd certainly had many erotic dreams about looking at and touching another man's buttocks, but this was the first time he'd ever let himself get so close, even in innocence. He'd never seen or touched another man's body before, let alone be this close to an ass that he'd already had a couple of wet dreams about fucking. Cain was suddenly afraid that his excitement would flow through his hands and reveal what he was. Or rather, what he *would* be, if he could. Christ, he was nervous.

"If you're second-guessing your act of kindness, I totally understand." Luke's voice rumbled vibrations up through his body, forcing Cain to feel his words. "Guys slap each other on the butt all the time when they play sports and don't think anything of it. This is different. I get that. This would be kind of weird for anyone. I've made you feel sorry for me, and you feel like you have to help me, but you don't. I'm fine. You can go."

"Don't be an idiot." Cain slapped a palm against Luke's back when he made to get up. "I'm not so insecure with my own masculinity that I can't offer aid to another man." He squeezed lotion into his palms, rubbed them together, and laid his hands on Luke's ass cheeks.

*Motherfucking holy shit.* With one touch of Luke's ass, Cain immediately understood he'd been right to deny himself this in all of his years of life. This was too addictive. His cock reared like a stallion under his sweats, eager to get out and ride. This was too much of what Cain's untried, overeager body craved. *Just focus.* He kneaded the small, tight ass anyway, denting the firm flesh with the pressure of his fingers. He learned, agonizingly, that this particular ass, Luke's ass, fit just perfectly into his palms. Cain hated seeing the red scars, because he knew the pain Luke had suffered receiving them, but the thin crisscrosses didn't do a damn thing to dull Cain's desire to look and touch. He wanted to know this ass intimately. He wanted much, much more than was safe.

Cain pushed the taut orbs up and squeezed, inadvertently revealing Luke's puckered bud to his gaze. He did it again, unable not to. He had often imagined this small body part he'd coveted for so long, but he'd never actually seen anyone's asshole before. He'd never even looked at his own with a mirror. Hell, he'd never even touched his, other than to wipe his ass. He had figured that to do so would set fire to a need he couldn't quench.

He stared down at Luke's bud, watching as the little pink hole appeared briefly while Luke's ass cheeks were spread, and Cain actually felt his chest tighten with desire and need. He wanted that snug little ring like he wanted nothing else in life. He wanted to lean down and kiss it, to lick it, to know what it felt like inside. He itched to touch it with the tips of his fingers and then to push inside. He wanted to spread Luke open with his hands and plunge his raging cock deep inside, shafting that cavity again and again until he came and filled it with his cum.

Cain wanted Luke. He wanted the man in a lot of ways, not all of which were purely sexual. These wants were dangerous. *Life and death dangerous. Don't ever forget.* The sobering reminder snapped Cain out of his fantasy.

Crawling off of Luke in a shot, Cain became all business once again. He pushed Luke's sweats down to his ankles and quickly finished the job he'd so foolishly vowed to do. He made sure every scar on Luke's legs was massaged with lotion. Afterward, he pulled the pants back up, careful not to touch Luke's beautiful ass again.

"Okay, you're good to go," Cain said abruptly, hating the clinical detachment, but knowing it was necessary. Luke opened his eyes, and Cain turned his body so that his raging, painful erection wasn't visible to that wary, inquiring gaze. "Try to get some sleep. I'll see you tomorrow."

"Today."

"What?"

"It's already tomorrow," Luke corrected. "So I'll see you later today."

*Good God.* With a small shudder, Cain bit back his arousal, almost coming right where he stood. No one man had the right to be so damned cute.

"Whatever." Cain needed to get away. *Now.* "See you later. Good night." He shut the door before he had to hear Luke's rich, deep voice utter another word.


Luke waited until he heard the barn door slide closed. When he knew he was alone, he shoved his sweats down his legs, into a little bundle at the end of his small bed. His cock pointed straight up, red and long with popping veins. That hadn't been the body part Luke had imagined Cain touching while receiving the most insanely erotic, yet at the same time sweet rubdown of his life. It had been his ass. Luke hadn't been sure he would want to be intimate with a man again after what had happened to him, but tonight he had discovered that if he could share that closeness with Cain, even if it was just in a dream, then he still had the desire to be sexually vulnerable with a man.

Luke leaned over the edge of the bed, grabbed the handle of his duffel bag, and yanked it to his side. He unzipped the large compartment and foraged around its depths until he found the tube of lube he always kept hidden at the bottom of his gear. In the very few sexual relationships he'd had, going almost four years back since his last, he'd primarily been a top, much as was suited to his personality. But damn it, when Cain had squeezed his ass cheeks, desire had slammed through Luke. The desire to spread himself open and beg to be fucked hard and deep, taken completely, until they both roared with pleasure as they came.

His left hand lubed up, Luke rolled over, folded his legs beneath him, and pressed his shoulders and cheek into the thin mattress. Luke wanted it like this because Cain had been behind him, and Luke needed to keep this fantasy as close to the reality as possible. He was already so aroused he could almost come just by thinking about a taking. Luke reached around with one hand, pulled his cheek to reveal his crack, and with the other he delved between his legs to finger his asshole. His pucker automatically tightened. He grunted at first contact, but that was just because, in his mind, it was Cain touching him for the first time, Cain feeling around trying to get in.

*Please.* Luke flicked at his tight ring and rubbed at it with the tip of his finger. He imagined Cain would be gentle, just as he'd been while giving Luke the massage. Luke pictured himself tormented and sweating, crying for Cain to fuck him. Cain would tease and prolong the foreplay, making Luke so crazy he would spurt his cum all over his stomach with the first penetration of Cain's dick into his eager ass.

Luke's knees were spread so damn wide his prick touched the mattress. Between his arousal due to Cain's rubdown, and his own imagination, Luke slipped to a place of need that made him start to pump his hips against the mattress. He tickled his opening, yet denied himself the very thing he most wanted. He fucked the bed as if he were fucking Cain, repeatedly grinding his rigid cock into the soft blanket that had gotten bunched up and now cocooned his throbbing erection. Somehow, in his mind, Luke could take Cain and be taken by him at the same time. *So good.* Unable to hold off any longer, Luke shoved his prick into the mattress and at the same time plunged his finger deep into his ass.

"Oh God…" Luke quickly added another digit into his burning channel, and then a third, somehow just knowing Cain would be huge. Cain would stretch Luke beyond comfort and then let him learn to love it; that was just the kind of man he knew his Cain would be.

Luke fucked himself vigorously with his fingers, and fucked the bed enthusiastically too, all with the dream that it was Cain on both ends. He was so enthusiastic in his fantasy that the top of his head soon butted against the wall, preventing him from moving.

Luke was so damn close to coming anyway that a barrier to his writhing didn't matter. Rolling his head until he had his cheek pressed against the cool plaster, Luke gasped as the shot of cold sensation jolted through his scorching hot body. The wall was good. It held him in place, preventing any escape or retreat as he worked his fingers in his rectum, all the way in, until he couldn't get any deeper. He shoved his other hand between his body and the bed. One touch to the ultrasensitive nerve endings in his cock pushed him right over the edge.

"Cain, Cain," he whispered into the wall. "Fuck me…" Luke started shuddering, almost violently, as orgasm ripped through him like wildfire. His stuffed passage bore down and clenched, holding his buried fingers inside. In between each spasm, Luke jetted short, consecutive spurts of semen onto his bed.

*Shit.* Almost completely satisfied, Luke stayed in that cramped position for long minutes afterward, too exhausted to move.

Cᴀɪɴ ɴᴇᴠᴇʀ ᴍᴀᴅᴇ ɪᴛ ᴛᴏ the cabin. Halfway to the porch he had to stop and pull out his cock. Precum smeared the head of his rearing dick, and the earthy, acrid smell of his arousal quickly filled the air. With the picture of Luke's amazing body in his mind, and even more arousing, that closed-up little hole, Cain slipped to a place of no return quicker than he ever had gone before. Three drags of his fist up and down the length of his rock-hard cock and seed spewed from his slit, the power of his release leaving him weak and gasping for air.

Afterward, as Cain stumbled the rest of the way to his cabin, he wondered how it would feel to die.

# CHAPTER FIVE

A week and a half later, Cain ambled through the center of town to Nate's Bait and Saddle Shop, the place where he and Luke had agreed to meet up.

Yesterday, while mucking out the stalls together, Cain had bitched about having to drive into town to spend half the day searching for a birthday gift for Cassie. Luke had commented that if Cain didn't mind the company on the ride, he'd like to visit with his mother and sister.

Cain couldn't rightly refuse. Luke worked himself to the bone every day. Sometimes too hard, in Cain's opinion. There were some days Cain wanted to grab Luke and tell him he didn't have anything to prove; he could rest and take breaks when his body called for it. Intellectually, however, Cain knew Luke would immediately call him on the hypocrisy of the order, so he just kept his mouth shut and let Luke do the job for which he was being paid.

If there was any danger in allowing Luke to accompany him to town, it was that with every moment Cain spent in Luke's presence, he found more things adorable, kind, and sexy about Luke than he'd ever thought possible. It wasn't so much that they had everything in common and would be a perfect match if not for the obvious -- and not so obvious -- impossibilities of them ever being together. In point of fact, they didn't seem to have many of the little things in common at all. Other than their mutual love for horses and the vast Montana valley where they lived, Cain had discovered he and Luke were very different people.

Christ, the drive into town alone had set them to bickering about a radio station on which they could agree. Cain liked classical music. Hell, it wasn't that he was a snob or anything; it was just that he'd actually been around and living when it was commonplace to listen to people like Brahms and Debussy. Cain couldn't tell Luke that, of course, so he'd ended up looking like a pompous prig when he'd bitched about some speed metal song that had blared out of the radio when he'd turned the key in the ignition. Luke had used the truck last, so it had been on his favorite radio station. In Cain's grumbling comparison of the song to fingernails on a chalkboard, he'd inadvertently insulted Luke's favorite band. They'd finally settled on a bluegrass station that had an Alison Krauss music marathon going on, discovering they both appreciated the singer's haunting, sultry voice.

That had been a couple of hours ago, and damn it if Cain wasn't thinking about what it might take to pick a little fight with Luke again, if only so he could fantasize about what it would be like to make peace afterward. Cain immediately chided himself for even considering it, reminding himself of the futility -- not to mention very real danger -- in pursuing those desires.

Getting out of potentially arousing entanglements just like that was exactly why Cain had spent two hours in town searching for Cassie's perfect birthday present. He owed her an extra special gift this year for unknowingly helping him out of the very temptation he was dreaming about starting up all over again. Cain had to repay his sister-in-law for taking over the care of Luke's back again. Cain had subtly, deliberately, and with intent, led Cassie into putting herself back in charge of Luke's recovery. He'd casually mentioned that Luke's movements still looked a little tight to him; Cassie had drawn the conclusion Cain had wanted her to, and had immediately started coming over every morning to rub Luke down herself. Her instinct to help a person in need had gotten Cain out of a repeat performance of what had happened in Luke's bedroom ten days ago. For that, Cain was eternally grateful.

Reaching the shabby-looking storefront he wanted, Cain pushed the door open and let himself inside, smiling as the little bell attached to the inside handle jingled to announce his presence. This certainly wasn't the newest store in town, and in truth it was sometimes a challenge to sift through the racks until he found what he needed, but Cain was loyal to the place just the same. Loyal to the man who'd been fair in his dealings with him and his brothers for the dozen years they'd lived in the little dot-on-the-map town of Quinten, Montana.

"Hey there, Nate." Cain walked up to the counter and offered his hand to the grizzled man on the other side. "How's business treating you?"

"Like a cheap, lipstick-smeared hooker with her hand stretched out for payment," the old man grumbled, his white whiskers twitching on his upper lip.

Cain shook his head and chuckled. "I'm not sure if that's supposed to be good or bad."

Nate crooked his finger, and Cain leaned in closer. "Not sure myself," the old man admitted, with a mischievous twinkle in his rheumy brown eyes. "But it sure is fun keeping the folks guessing about my sanity, so I like to pull shit like that out of my ass as often as I can." Nate stepped back and winked. "Shoulda known better than to try and fool you."

"Hell, old man" -- Cain gave Nate's shoulder a good whack -- "you can be crazier than a loon for all I care." He raised an eyebrow knowingly. "Just so long as you can still make me a saddle to specs the next time I need it."

"I await your order." Nate settled his wiry, stooped body against the counter at his back. "In the meantime, what can I get for you today?"

"I'm good today." Cain smiled then. "Unless you've got an RC Cola in that cooler of yours, in which case I'll have one of them just to take the parch off."

"You know I do." Nate reached under the counter and seconds later produced a long-necked bottle of soda. Nate was the only person Cain knew who loved the RC brand like he did. With a grin, Cain watched the man pop off the cap on the edge of the counter. "Here you go." Nate handed it over, exchanging the dollar bill in Cain's hand for the beverage.

Cain took a long swig of the cool liquid, practically moaning with pleasure as the perfect combination of not too much sweetness and carbonation slid over his tongue and down his throat. This was the only time he ever drank soda, so Cain savored the drink for what it was, a special treat.

When he was finished, he handed the empty bottle over to Nate for recycling. Nate disappeared through a swinging door, and Cain called out, "Hey, Nate, has Luke Forrester been in yet today?"

"Haven't seen him," Nate replied. After reappearing, he settled his weight on a stool. "I heard that youngin's training horses for you these days. How's he doing?"

Cain stalled for a moment in order to moderate his voice. It would be second-guessed if he showed too much pride. "Real good," he finally answered. "I've got no complaints with his work ethic, and I can't say as I've had any trouble with him otherwise." He chuckled. "Of course, it's not like I have anyone for him to butt heads with, so that might have something to do with it." Even as he said it, Cain didn't believe that was the truth. A hundred coworkers wouldn't put Luke in any more danger of fighting than having just the one.

"You take good care of him," Nate ordered. The old man's voice held surprising command. "I got his little sister helping out here a couple days a week after school, and she's a real good girl. She's a hard worker, and there ain't no job she sneers at or says is beneath her. Brags on her big brother like nobody's business too. And from what I can figure, his paycheck is what keeps the family afloat."

Cain's cheeks burned, and shame filled his belly. "I didn't know that."

"Well, he probably don't like advertising it," Nate carried on. "A man has to protect the pride of his family, which is why I don't buy that shit that he started a fight in a bar, neither. Young man like that, so worried about keeping food on his momma and sister's table, that ain't a kid who's gonna do something stupid and risk taking that away. How's he doing, anyway? He healin' up all right?"

Visions of Luke's naked back and ass flashed through Cain's mind, sending hot blood to rushing all through his body. "Yep." He fiddled with the little paper bag that held Cassie's gift, unable to control the fidgeting. "Cassie officially gave him a clean bill of health yesterday and declared that he no longer needs her medical services."

"Shee-iittt." Nate guffawed. "Your brother got that little spitfire pregnant yet?"

Cain just shook his head. Sometimes old men were worse than old women. "Not yet," he shared, knowing it would make the old man happy. "But it is my understanding that he has turned the process into a religion."

"Ho boy." Nate slapped his hand on his knee. "To be young and in love again." The bell on the door tinkled, and Nate's bushy brows went halfway up his forehead. "Well, if it ain't Luke Forrester. Cain was just asking if you'd shown your face in here yet today."

Cain turned, and his blood burned even more as Luke's tall, lanky frame filled his line of sight. Christ, the man sure could wear a pair of jeans. Nobody ought to be able to cause another body to salivate over jeans, a blue plaid cotton shirt, and a tan cowboy hat riding low on a forehead. Shouldn't be able to. It wasn't right. But damn it if Luke did just that. Cain held his smile in check and nodded a greeting at Luke instead. He got the same back.

Nate was more vocal. "How you doing, boy?"

"I'm doing just fine, Mr. Palmer," Luke replied, smiling at Nate as he shook the old man's hand. It would have made Cain jealous if he weren't so damn warmed inside by Luke's natural kindness to the persnickety old fellow. "How is my sister working out for you?" Luke showed genuine interest and concern. "Is she showing up on time and doing everything you ask?"

"She is keeping me on my toes. She surely is." The brightness in the old man's eyes backed up his words. "I thank you for recommending her. She's working out real good."

"She's real grateful for the job, Mr. Palmer," Luke told him. "Thank you for taking a chance on her. I know a lot of the men around here thought it was a mistake to hire a girl."

"They tend to shut up about that real quick the first time she sticks her hand down into a bucket full of night crawlers without so much as twitching that pretty little face of hers. You don't need to worry about her none, Luke. You just do your job with Cain here without a lick of worryin'. I got my eye on her, and I look in on your mom every once in a while too. All right?"

Luke nodded, and Cain could tell the kindness from Nate meant a lot to him. Cain leaned in and touched Luke's shoulder. "Did you get everything done that you needed?"

"Yep." Luke nodded. "I'm ready."

Their gazes met and held. *Jesus.* Cain's breath caught. For just a split second, he understood how his brother often got lost in his wife's eyes. Suddenly remembering where he was and what he was doing, Cain broke the contact and cleared his throat. "Then let's go. We have horses that'll be wanting to eat by the time we get back. Nate" -- Cain reached across the counter -- "always good to shoot the breeze with you. I'll be seeing you soon."

"I ain't goin' nowhere. Keep safe." Nate dipped the brim of his John Deer ball cap. "Luke. Good to see you."

Luke touched the brim of his cowboy hat. "You have a good afternoon, Mr. Palmer."

Cain and Luke let themselves out, waving one last time at Nate through the storefront glass before heading down the sidewalk in the direction of the truck. Their silence was companionable, broken by the occasional nod or wave when a familiar face was seen.

Almost at the parking lot where Luke had parked the truck, Cain chewed on the inside of his cheek, a nervous habit he couldn't seem to break. Without shifting to look at Luke, he finally just spit out his thought before he could second-guess himself. "You know, Luke, it's all right with me if you want to invite your mom and sister out to the property. Family is important to both of us. I don't want you ever thinking yours is not welcome on my land. They are."

"I'll do that," Luke murmured. "Thank you."

"No problem."

They rounded off the main drag to the dirt parking lot and almost ran smack into another cowboy doing the reverse.

"Chris!" Luke exclaimed, clearly familiar with the big, barrel-chested dude. "How's it going, man?"

"Good," the thick-bodied man answered. "Just working."

"Oh, well, all right."

Cain watched Luke's easy smile lose some of its openness, and he wanted to slug this Chris guy in the gut for hurting Luke's feelings.

"Well, it's good to see you," Luke said. "Tell the other guys I said 'hey'."

The guy's nod was curt. "Will do." He moved around Luke, giving him his back. And then Cain heard the man mutter under his breath, "Queer freak, taking it up the --"

The guy didn't get the next word out. Cain shoved Cassie's gift at Luke's chest with one hand, and in less than two seconds slammed the stocky, ugly-minded fucker up against the side of the dry cleaners with the other.

Fingers digging into the man's jaw hard enough to make the beefy guy wince, Cain whispered with lethal softness, "What the hell was that you were snickering about that you didn't feel man enough to speak up and share with the whole class?"

The guy's eyes bugged out so big, and his face started sweating so profusely, Cain thought he might pass out. "N-nothing," the dude finally forced out through lips contorted by Cain's death grip on his jaw. "I didn't say nothing. I swear."

Cain squeezed harder, forcing the man's head back against the brick wall. "That's what I thought." He gave the guy's head a love tap against the brick at his back before letting him go, noting with pleasure the man's legs almost buckled when left to stand on his own. "Don't let it get back to me that I heard you saying *nothing* around town to other people. Got it?"

The dude nodded his head so vigorously it knocked his hat off kilter. "Yes, sir."

Cain made a snarling sound, and the guy took off like a shot, as fast as his tree-trunk legs would carry him. Turning back to Luke, his face the mask of rage that had terrified the other man, but unable to shake the volatile emotions quite yet, Cain grabbed his bag out of Luke's hand. He made quick work of getting to the truck.

Cain gave Luke only enough time to secure his seat belt before he tore out of town a whole lot faster than the local law allowed. He drove in silence, except for the damn radio. Only now, he couldn't give a shit what it was playing. He was strung up too tight with rage, and confusion, and -- worst of all to his way of thinking -- fear, to care about music.

When that guy had said *"queer"* every muscle in Cain's body had seized, terrified that somehow one of his secrets had gotten out. He had acted on pure instinct, the need to save himself taking complete and utter control of his actions. His only thought had been to shove enough fear of retribution down the guy's throat to make him stop speaking whatever the hell he'd been about to say. That was all Cain had wanted to do.

And he had.

Only now, Cain was afraid he'd done it so well he'd scared the shit out of Luke with his quick jump to violence. They were almost home, and Luke hadn't said one word the entire way. Instead, Luke had spent most of the ride picking at a tear in the leather seating, a fearful tick if Cain had ever seen one.

*Christ.* Just the thought of Luke being afraid of him sucker punched Cain hard enough to make him flinch. He had to fix this before it got out of hand.

"Listen, Luke." Cain paused just long enough to ease the truck to a stop in front of the barn, close enough for Luke to get his stuff out of the back. "We need to talk about what you saw back there."

"No, you don't have to say anything," Luke interrupted. The vehemence in his voice stopped Cain cold.

Shocked as hell, Cain turned in the seat. The fear he saw in Luke's darting gaze tore right at his heart.

Before Cain could insist on speaking his piece, Luke seemed to settle himself. He faced Cain head on. "Out of a sense of fair play," Luke said, "I should have disclosed everything that happened to me before I came to work for you. I owe you the respect of rectifying that right now." Luke's mouth tightened, trembled, and then he spoke again. "You need to know something that MacLesten found out about me." Luke's head lifted another notch. "Cain, you need to know I'm gay."

# Chapter Six

Luke chewed on his lip, and he waited for Cain to say something. He watched Cain shift from sitting forward to glancing out his side window and then back to looking out the front window again.

Still staring through the windshield, Cain finally spoke. "Tell me what you meant, about how you should have told me everything from the beginning. What does that mean?"

Luke dug his fingers into the ripped seat cushion in an effort to quell the tremor in his hands. He would have taken just the smallest sign -- anything -- from Cain that would give him an indication of what the man was thinking. Right now, Luke couldn't read his measured reaction to his confession at all.

Luke took a deep, steadying breath and began. "What I meant was that I should have told you why MacLesten did what he did to me." Luke's voice wavered only the slightest bit, and he was proud of that fact. "What I should have told you was that about three months ago, I was in Billings on my weekend off. While I was there, I ran into an old friend I hadn't seen in years. It was no big deal; we were just catching up over a meal. We had been intimate at one point a number of years ago, though, so I didn't think twice when he took my hand as we left the restaurant. And it wouldn't have been a big deal, if not for the fact that MacLesten was coming out of the hotel across the street and saw me holding hands with another man."

"Shit," Cain bit off sharply. He still wouldn't look Luke's way. "That was why he stripped you, tied you up like an animal, and then beat the crap out of you."

"Yeah." A shudder went through Luke as he recalled the afternoon. But he'd been talking about it with his counselor, and he really was all right. "MacLesten pretty much used every homosexual slur I've ever heard -- and some that I hadn't -- while beating me and then whipping me."

Cain's jaw clenched visibly. And repeatedly. "And then the burns from the cigar."

"No." As Luke remembered that day, his heart jumped fast enough to push through his sternum. "Not the cigar burns. Not then."

Cain's gaze snapped Luke's way then and it was like looking into the deepest waters of the ocean. "I felt them on your back, Luke. Don't pretend it didn't happen."

Trapped by his need to confess everything to Cain, Luke could not break away from a blue stare that felt as if it was drilling into his soul. "I'm not denying. I'm just saying they're not what came next." Luke looked away, needing to regain some control. He blinked a half dozen times and dug the heels of his hands into his thighs, forcing sensation to a part of his body other than his constricted chest. When composed, he found Cain's gaze still waiting for him. "He violated me, Hawk. He beat the shit out of me, and then he" -- Luke swallowed convulsively -- "he raped me."

The sea in Cain's eyes shifted to turbulent in a flash. "Motherfucking son of a bitch." That lethal softness Luke had seen Cain unleash on Chris back in town returned in his tone. It made Luke shiver, but much deeper than that, it made him feel safe.

Luke finished telling the rest quickly. "Not with his own person."

He desperately needed to be clear on that. "I thank God for that small blessing every day. I guess in MacLesten's warped mind that would have made him exactly what he was terrorizing me for. Instead, he used just about everything he could find in that line cabin to jam into me, starting with a toothbrush and getting progressively bigger while he taunted me about how much a faggot like me could take up the ass. After about the fourth or fifth thing he shoved into me, on top of the beating and whipping I had just suffered, I didn't have any pride left. I begged him to either finish it or kill me."

"Motherfucking son of a bitch," Cain swore viciously. "That motherfucking son of a bitch." He seemed to be stuck on that particular epithet.

As Luke listened to those words, his middle squeezed painfully, grateful beyond his ability to express that apparently Cain wasn't someone who thought Luke had gotten exactly what he deserved.

"Anyway, MacLesten either wanted to break me, or maybe he was bored by the fact that I'd stopped fighting back. Either way, that was when he cut me down. I just crumpled to the floor in a ball. I didn't have any strength left at all." Luke could still feel the stinging, agonizing, needlepoint pain that had suffused his arms and hands when the blood had come rushing back after hitting the floor. He remembered almost sobbing with gratitude for it, as this new hurt had taken away the focus of pain in other places. "For the longest time, he stood over me, admiring his handiwork, I guess. Then he pulled up a chair and sat almost right on top of me; that's when he lit the cigar. He just sat there smoking as easy as you please while he explained to me that if I told anyone what had happened, or tried to press charges against him, he would take my sister and my mother and do to them what he'd done to me. He ended it by burning the tip of his cigar repeatedly into my back.

"I believed his threat, Hawk," Luke told Cain. "I *do* believe him. He's a sick fuck, but he's one of the richest men in the state of Montana, and that means he has connections. He won't spend one night in jail before he makes bond, let alone do prison time for what he did to me. And even if he did, he'd have found a way and gotten to my family by then anyway. MacLesten doesn't make idle threats. He would retaliate quickly and severely were I to make any attempt to bring criminal charges against him for what happened. I won't risk my mom and my sister for a shot at justice. It's not worth it."

Cain nodded and then looked away. "It's a hard thing to swallow." His tone was thick and raspy. "Knowing there's a man out there you want to kill with your bare hands, but not being able to do anything about it. I can understand that it must sit in your craw, undigested enough to choke you, but I also understand why you don't act on it. No one will hear anything about it from me."

"Thank you," Luke murmured. Cain wouldn't look at him. Luke hated only getting Cain's profile; it made him so much less certain of where he stood when he couldn't see Cain's eyes. "I didn't tell you any of that so that you would feel sorry for me, but rather because MacLesten has obviously started telling people what he saw in Billings. Chris wouldn't have said what he did otherwise. We were friends while I was working for MacLesten, and I swear on a stack of Bibles that Chris never would have guessed I'm gay due to something I did while on the job or in the bunkhouse."

"No," Cain agreed, his tone low. "No one looking at you or working with you would ever suspect a damn thing."

Luke's stomach plummeted at that. Was Cain saying he wouldn't have hired Luke if he'd been able to tell at the outset that he was a homosexual? That if he'd seen something inherently gay in Luke from the start that he would have told his brother no? Forget righteous indignation, Luke couldn't give a rat's ass about feeling slighted on behalf of gay men everywhere. He was one man, and it stabbed him a whole lot deeper than he wanted to feel, thinking that Cain might respect him less now that he knew he was gay. Luke respected the work Cain did more than anything of which he'd ever been a part, and all he wanted was for Cain to respect him for his work too. It twisted at his chest to think he might not get that anymore.

Stubbornness prodded Luke to make his stand right then and finish what he'd intended to say. "My point in telling you all of this is that if MacLesten is starting to make whispers about me, then it won't be long before pretty much everyone knows. That would be an annoyance to you under normal circumstances, what with people telling you to get rid of the fag you have working for you. If you don't get rid of me, people are going to start wagging their tongues about you as well."

Sitting less than three feet away from Luke, with his hands gripping the wheel of the truck, Cain flinched as awareness of his new situation dawned. That was when Luke understood he needed to let go of hope and give Cain an easy out.

"You've been real nice to me, Hawk." Cain's nickname got caught in Luke's throat, cutting him deeply as he accepted that while he'd barely known this man, he was about to end their fragile, new friendship with his next words. "You gave me a fair shot when I was basically thrust upon you, and I thank you for that. But I don't want to cause you trouble, and having me here is gonna start doing that real damn soon; I can feel it. I guess I'm saying I'll understand if you ask me to pack my bag and go." Luke's breathing was unsteady, but he finished it. "And I just want to assure you that I won't kick up a fuss and cause you any trouble for choosing to do it."

Cain suddenly exploded and slammed his fists against the steering wheel, making Luke jerk back against the seat. Cain started cursing up a litany of foul phrases that would make a pimp blush. He cracked his hand against the door handle and kicked his way out of the truck. Through the windshield, Luke watched as Cain stormed the length of the hood, waving his arms wildly, all the while still blistering the air with an incredibly creative bevy of curses. Cain's hard, severely beautiful face was as dark as Luke had ever seen it, and Luke had the insane twin urges to run away *and* grab the man and kiss him, both at the same time. Obviously, Luke could only do one of those things without getting his head messily and painfully removed from his body.

Luke scrambled out of the truck and curved a wide arc around a still-raging Cain. "I'm just going to get my bag and go." He pointed at the barn as he edged his way toward it.

In a flash, Cain shoved Luke up against the side of the barn.

Luke's upper arms were imprisoned against the wall hard enough to leave bruises. A second later, Cain leaned his face right down into Luke's, his eyes flashing that midnight blue again. Then he hissed, "What the hell kind of monster do you think I am, Forrester? Or, just as bad, what kind of hideous combination of pussy and idiot all rolled into one do you take me for? You tell me, Luke. You tell me, damn it. You tell me right goddamned now."

"I…I don't know," Luke answered. Cain was only a little bit bigger than Luke, but right now strength and power radiated off him in droves. Luke sensed Cain's controlled restraint too, though, and so wasn't awash in panic or afraid for his safety. Luke wasn't scared. He was confused. "I don't think you're any of those things, Cain. I swear I don't."

Cain dropped Luke's arms and took a giant step back. Luke's attention caught on Cain's powerful hands as they curled in tight fists at his sides. Cain looked away from Luke, seemed to curse to himself some more, and then landed his blazing stare right back on Luke. "If you don't think I'm any of those jackass things," Cain delivered in that hushed voice Luke had come to learn meant Cain was royally pissed off, "then how in the hell can you come to such a jackass conclusion that I could ever be intimidated, by anyone, into firing my employee? Then you tell me how in fuck's sake you think I'd ever let someone who's as good with my horses as you are walk away from this ranch over the stupid ass fact that you're gay? Because I gotta tell you, Luke, I don't think I have ever been more insulted in my life than when you just assumed I was a homophobe and would fire you over the fact that you like to diddle with men."

"I…I…" Luke kept trying to make words come out, but he was too flabbergasted to speak. Cain was pissed as hell at him, and Luke's heart felt lighter than it had all day. "I…Damn it, Hawk, I'm sorry."

Cain pointed his finger right up in Luke's face and then hit it against his nose. He snarled, "Oh, no. No, no. I am so angry at you right now, don't you dare call me that name right now. That is a name I thought my friend called me, and right now you have not shown me anything to prove you know me at all. You know what? I can't even look at you right now because all I want to do is strangle you. And since you live in the barn, and I can't be in the barn with you right now, you're going to have to feed all of the horses yourself tonight. Don't screw it up. That is, unless you really *are* looking for a reason for me to fire you. That one will do it. Wanting to fuck other men won't."

Cain stomped off and stormed into his cabin across the yard, slamming the door so hard Luke felt the vibrations roll under his boots where he stood.

Luke had no earthly idea what had just happened, but he didn't really care. All that mattered was that he still had his job…and he got to stay close to Cain. Other than his mom and his sister, nothing else in the world mattered to him.

Whistling an Alison Krauss tune under his breath, Luke got to work.

The tirade of colorful language continued in Cain's mind once he got inside his cabin. He grabbed a beer out of the fridge and threw himself into a whole new level of Olympic caliber pacing, where upon he whittled a path into the pinewood flooring that covered the length of his small home. Cain could not believe Luke would even for a second think Cain would fire him for being gay. It was irrelevant that Cain was gay and now had to contend with an attraction that could be reciprocated; that wasn't what fueled Cain's anger so completely right now. Even if he were straight, he still would have wanted to slug Luke for having the thought that Cain was not only prejudiced, but that he would perpetrate an illegal act by firing someone for their sexual orientation. Luke's mistaken assumption had set a quick fire to Cain's temper even faster than hearing Luke's shocking, terrifying confession that he was gay.

*This is bad, bad, bad.* Cain didn't know what in the hell to do. It was one thing to be attracted to Luke with the safety barrier of knowing that nothing could ever come of it due to Luke's inability to reciprocate Cain's growing feelings. That kept Cain safe. Not being able to act on his attractions -- once he'd realized what they were so many years ago -- was what had kept Cain alive for over a hundred and fifty years. But now, to know there was even the possibility that Luke might return his desire was a torment and torture Cain had never had to deal with in his life. He wasn't sure he had the strength to see Luke every day, to work alongside him, to talk with him about the horses, to be so damn near him day and night, without getting dragged under the fierce tidal wave of like and lust he already felt for the younger man. Cain was very afraid he would stumble.

And for him, that would be the beginning of the end of his life.

"Shit."

# CHAPTER SEVEN

A week later, Cain pulled the truck to a stop by his cabin, weary but pleased by his trip. He'd driven to Bozeman the day before and spent the day at a horse welfare ranch run by a retired veterinarian friend of his, P.J., a phenomenal battle-ax of a woman. P.J. had called him a couple of days ago asking if he was ready to take on another horse. Cain knew that meant she'd been delivered a particularly abused, defensive animal with which Cain would immediately fall in love.

He'd been nearly right, except that P.J. didn't have one horse for him, she had two. They were pathetically malnourished and showed all the signs of repeated whippings and beatings, but Cain could tell by looking in a horse's eyes if he or she had a will to live and be strong again. Both of them did, and he'd spent the night at P.J.'s house getting clued in on their history and setting up a date to transport them to his property.

These horses, Esmeralda and Nightfire, would make ten animals in his stable. That was a lot of responsibility, even with Luke's help.

Four of them were trained and ready to be sold, but Cain still couldn't quite let them go. His facility was big enough to house all of them and many others. If he acquired too many more, though, without sending any of the retrained horses on their way to new homes, he would have to hire additional help. Cain would have to justify the expense to his brothers, all without being able to show them he had a clear timeline for when his work would eventually start showing a profit.

Cain's sincere intention when he'd started working exclusively with these abused horses had been to rehabilitate them and sell them at a profit. He was doing the first part very well; he found it impossibly difficult to do the second. Not even impossibly difficult, truthfully. Just impossible. He hadn't factored in how he would fall in love with them and not be able to let them go when their training and gentling was completed. That had been the one hiccup in his grand plan he hadn't anticipated.

Much in the way he hadn't anticipated how much he would miss Luke, even just being away from him for less than two days. While Cain had been at P.J.'s, he'd kept turning to say something to Luke, looking over his shoulder to give or ask an opinion about the new horses, only to find P.J. standing next to him instead of Luke. It had stunned Cain to realize how quickly he'd come to depend on Luke's thoughts and feelings about his animals. That instinct to seek Luke out and talk, one that apparently his brain had already categorized as familiar and necessary, had left Cain floored with a sense of rightness and contentedness he daily found harder and harder to keep at bay.

Cain hadn't just missed Luke's expertise and knowledge in regard to his horses, Cain had missed the man. In less than forty-eight hours, he'd missed sneaking looks at Luke when they were working together in the barn. He'd missed getting that first glimpse of him in the morning when they crossed paths, of having that first moment of sexual awareness, of appreciating all over again the cut of Luke's lean, hard body in a simple button-up shirt and a pair of well-worn jeans. He missed all of that. But most of all, Cain missed the friendship he'd been building with Luke.

Except losing that friendship didn't have anything to do with being separated by miles; it had everything to do with how Cain had chosen to cope with Luke's confession that he was gay. In between dealing with the animalistic need that festered within him to claw Justin MacLesten open with his bare hands and eat his innards for what he'd done to Luke, Cain had done a lot of hiding like a coward. He hated doing it, but he didn't see any other way of keeping an emotional distance.

Staying away was the only thing Cain could do. Since learning of Luke's homosexuality, Cain's sexual fantasies and erotic dreams had increased tenfold. It wasn't just the quantity of them that he couldn't ignore; it was the explicitness and details of them that scared Cain. It was no longer some random guy in some random place; it was Luke. *Luke with me, and no one else.* Not only was it specifically Luke, but Luke in places that were real in Cain's life. It wasn't fantasy Luke of one week ago, where Cain would dream of going down on him on a beach, or in a clandestine meeting on some faraway exotic island. In this last week, the dreams had shifted, becoming dramatically down-to-earth and real. Fantasy locations had been replaced by images of taking Luke in his bedroom, in Luke's bedroom, on the kitchen table, bent over the paddock fence under the stars, cramped in the cab of the truck but making it work.

The realistic nature of his dreams evoked all kinds of fear in Cain. He was terrified if he spent too much time around Luke the lines would blur so much he would act on them, and in doing so, set in motion a course that once started could not be changed. One that would end with his death.

"Shit." Cain got out of the truck and slammed the door. He did it so forcefully the vehicle shook, and that gave him a small measure of satisfaction. He'd take his small pleasures where he could get them, as so few other things were doing it for him these days.

"Hey, Cain, welcome back." That familiar, low, rich voice filled the air, interrupting Cain's foul mood. "I've been watching for you."

Cain turned to find Luke in his cowboy hat, a dark denim shirt, and faded jeans, looking as fucking sexy as Cain had ever seen him.

Need fueled the ornery temper Cain wallowed in. "Oh, yeah?" Cain snapped. "Why is that?"

Luke's stare switched from calm and easy to the gray clouds of a storm. He crossed his arms against his chest and widened his stance. "Because, *boss*, if you can pull your head out of your ass and stop being mad at me for five minutes, I have something to show you."

"I'm not fucking mad at you," Cain charged back, fired up. "Why the hell are you talking shit like that?"

"Oh, I don't know." Luke's tone was as dry as could be. "Maybe it has something to do with the fact that you've barely said two words to me all week. Or maybe it's the fact that you're cursing every other word these days. Or maybe, *just maybe*, it *might* have something to do with the fact that the last real conversation we had together you told me that you were so pissed at me that you couldn't even look at me. Now I am sorry about that, but if for just five minutes your fucking fragile ego can get over the fact that I woefully misjudged you, and if you could go saddle a horse and meet me in the main paddock, I think you'll see something that will drastically improve your mood. But hey" -- Luke threw his hands up -- "it's up to you. I'll be in the paddock with Fancy Face awaiting your illustrious presence. I don't know that I really give a shit one way or the other for myself, I just hope you don't disappoint Fancy."

With that scathing soliloquy, Luke left Cain standing in his dust, choking on a combination of kicked-up dirt and chagrin. *Shit.* Cain had just been unequivocally told to shove his cold-as-a-witch's-tit attitude where the sun don't shine. It rankled something fierce, but by all rights, Cain couldn't really blame the man for doing it. Cain had real, visceral personal fears about his attraction to the man, but that didn't mean Luke deserved to be handled with the distance of a ten-foot pole between them. Christ, it hadn't even occurred to Cain that Luke would think he'd been mad at him all this time. But of course Luke thought that. Luke didn't know Cain suffered an unhealthy amount of attraction and lust he had to deny. He only knew Cain had begun treating him differently since he'd revealed he was gay.

*Damn it.* It wasn't often Cain accepted being spoken to as Luke had just done. If there was one instance where Cain might deserve it, though, this was it. And damn it all if he didn't appreciate the fact and find it all the more attractive that Luke hadn't been afraid to give him a swift kick in the ass when he deserved it. It just made Cain like the sexy-as-hell son of a mother all the more.

"Fuck."

Cain was in trouble, and he knew it. He went and saddled up a horse anyway. He didn't want to keep Fancy Face -- or Luke -- waiting.

———

LUKE RUBBED FANCY'S MANE WITH encouragement as he watched Cain lead Laura's Love, or as Luke had affectionately dubbed the horse, L.L. Cool J, to the paddock. Relief swamped Luke. He hadn't been entirely sure he would still have a job after the way he'd spoken to Cain. Luke hadn't been able to help himself, though, not only on behalf of Fancy Face, but for himself. He had bitten his tongue all week, all the while hurting inside over Cain's sudden distance. The hurt had finally bubbled over when he hadn't been able to completely hide his excitement at seeing Cain back from his trip, after having missed him so much, only to get that curt and dismissive greeting when he'd had such good news to share. It was not as if Luke had been expecting a passionate kiss or anything -- not that he hadn't thought about it -- but he'd at least hoped for a handshake and a "How's everything going?" In the face of the terseness he'd gotten instead, Luke had not been able to keep his mouth shut.

*Oh well.* Work still had to matter the most, and boy had Luke worked while Cain had been away. *It's now or never.* This was why Cain had hired him. If Fancy Face could keep her cool, then there was no way Cain would let Luke go. And damn it, Luke did not want to go.

"Okay, sweetheart." Luke spoke gently to Fancy as he stroked her coat. "Time to show off your stuff to the big boss. You've behaved like a champ for me every step of the way; I know you can do it for Cain too. Make me proud."

Luke stroked the horse one last time and then hoisted himself onto her back from the ground, without the aid of a box step. It was a very small but successful first in a line of tasks Luke wanted Cain to witness. For these abused horses, for them to allow a body to swing up onto its back without a step to ease the weight, was a big deal. Once up and settled, Luke praised Fancy again and then guided her until they both faced Cain.

Cain gave him a small nod of approval -- the man fully understanding the small victory Luke had just shown him. Luke couldn't help it, he flushed with pleasure.

"Come in the paddock with L.L." Luke held Fancy steady in the middle of the ring. When Cain hesitated, Luke added, "It's okay, Hawk. She's ready for the company, I promise. Just give her a chance to prove it."

Cain did as told, and Luke's chest tightened in response. It meant Cain believed Luke's word, and there was nothing Luke wanted more than this man's full respect and trust.

Once inside the paddock, Cain mounted L.L. but kept a good ten feet of space between his horse and Fancy Face. "All right, Luke, this is your show. What now?"

"Don't soft foot her." Luke started to walk Fancy toward L.L. "Ride L.L. around the perimeter, make cuts across the ring as if you were in here with any well-trained animal. Otherwise, you're not going to be able to see that Fancy's not afraid of you and L.L."

Cain leveled his pure blue gaze on Luke from across the paddock. "Tell me you're sure, and look me in the eye while you're doing it."

Luke didn't hesitate. "I'm sure." His focus didn't waver one millimeter. "Do it."

Cain didn't hesitate either. He set L.L. off on a nice gallop around the paddock, let her cut back and forth across Fancy's path without slowing when he got close. Luke circled the horse away when needed, and sometimes Fancy Face did it herself, but she kept calm the whole time. She didn't rear, kick, or balk at the quick moves the other animal made in such close proximity to her. Luke praised her and touched her, just to let her know he was proud.

After crossing the space a dozen or so times, Cain reined L.L. to a stop in front of Luke and Fancy. "This is good work, for both of you. I'm incredibly impressed."

Luke smiled. He was so damn proud of this horse. "You ain't seen nothing yet." Luke slid off the horse. "Now it's time for you to ride her."

Watching like a proud father as Cain mounted Fancy without her shimmying or shying, Luke then took L.L.'s reins and led her back out of the paddock to give Cain some room to put Fancy through her paces. Luke rested his arms against the top rail of the paddock and relaxed, confident Fancy would not let him down.

Luke didn't focus on Fancy; he kept his attention on Cain instead. He watched layer after layer of surprise, satisfaction, and finally pleasure move over Cain's features as Fancy lived up to Luke's promises and obeyed every subtle command from the reins like a pro. Luke couldn't hold back his smile as he watched Cain's pride in the horse take over and eradicate any anger that might have been left in him from their turbulent week.

Anxious to show off one more piece of Fancy's progress, Luke called out, "I'll be back in a minute. Don't stop what you're doing. We have one more trick to show you." Then he took off in the direction of Cain's cabin.

Cain watched Luke until he disappeared around a bend in the path that accommodated a small copse of hundred-year-old trees. As he shook his head, he wondered what in the hell Luke was up to now. The progress he'd already shown with Fancy pleased Cain immensely. It was also plenty enough to kick Cain out of his funk and remind him of what his purpose was with his work. *Their work*, Cain amended, because Fancy's success was more than 75 percent Luke's doing. Cain had barely started handling her when Luke had come on board; she'd been Luke's first real assignment with gentling and retraining a horse, rather than just exercising the ones on which Cain had already completed the job.

Luke fit right into the little niche Cain was carving for himself on this small piece of Hawkins land. Cain didn't exactly know what the niche would become when everything was fleshed out and settled, but suddenly he knew Luke would be an important part of the end result. Somehow, without them really knowing each other, Luke filled in that empty spot Cain had so stubbornly refused to even acknowledge existed before his brother had requested he hire Luke a month ago.

*Damn it.* How in the hell had this one, still wet behind the ears, man gotten under his skin so fast? *Easily*, Cain answered his own question, that was how. How could he not? Luke was eager to prove himself, he was strong, he worked hard, and he had a mental toughness and ability to adapt and survive his circumstances. Most admirable to Cain, though, Luke was honest even when it was difficult and risky. Luke was all of those things. A man who wasn't couldn't have been so vulnerable while sharing a horrific, life-changing event as he'd done not too long ago and then, without fear, get right in Cain's face -- a man big enough to hurt him -- in order to tell Cain he was acting like an ass. That was why it was so hard to dismiss Luke, as Cain had been able to do with other men he'd been physically attracted to in his past. It was more than the physical that pulled Cain in and made him fantasize about what another life might be like. It was more than sexual with Luke.

It was… It was…everything.

Fancy Face suddenly danced a little side step beneath him, and the motion snapped Cain out of his wandering thoughts. He looked up in time to see Luke coming down the path with Whisky nipping at his heels. Cain immediately raised his hand and lifted one finger high in the air. Whisky came to an immediate stop.

Luke stopped too. "Don't command her to stay, not when I just unearthed her from her hiding spot and coaxed her down here with promises of a treat if she helps me out again."

Cain raised an eyebrow. "Again, Luke?"

"Yeah." Luke smiled, something big and beautiful and sincere. The sight of that grin grabbed at Cain hard, even from thirty feet away. "Whisky wants to visit with her new friend. Now, I don't want to override your command, so give her another signal and tell her it's okay to move."

Cain gave the signal, and Whisky darted off like a shot; she wiggled her wiry little body under the fence and bounded up to Fancy's side with a little yipping bark. Cain held his breath -- and the saddle horn. He mentally prepared himself to be bucked up and reared on, but it never happened. Whisky drew close to the horse, and Fancy just stepped back a little bit and then lowered her head. She sniffed Whisky's head and body and then nudged the dog with her muzzle. Whisky sat there and let herself be examined, all the while thumping her long tail against the packed dirt.

Cain lifted his gaze and found Luke's, knowing full well he wasn't doing a damn bit of good hiding the shock, admiration, and the thousand questions batting around in his mind.

"She's not afraid of Whisky?" Cain couldn't believe what Luke had done so quickly. The intelligence of the horse had a good bit to do with it, but there was no getting around that this was Luke's success too. "She's not afraid to have other horses near her, and she's learned to tolerate Whisky too?"

"More than tolerate," Luke shared. He led L.L. back into the paddock and mounted her. "Go ahead and give Whisky the okay to move around."

Cain didn't even question the suggestions anymore; he just did as Luke had instructed. He marveled at the medium-sized mutt trotting around the paddock, always coming back and forth to Fancy Face without the horse showing the slightest bit of fear. Luke added L.L. to the mix too, and started riding the other horse around the paddock, passing Fancy again and again as Whisky did the same. Cain set Fancy Face in motion, testing her ability to understand his rein and leg commands while dealing with the distraction of the other two animals in such close proximity. She did beautifully; after half an hour, Cain circled her to a stop and slid off the horse.

Luke did the same with L.L. With just a smile and a small, approving nod between them, they led the horses out of the paddock and back to the barn. They worked in silence, not only removing gear and rubbing down Fancy Face and L.L. but feeding them and the rest of the animals too. In between each task, Cain would find his attention wandering in Luke's direction, and he would chuckle and shake his head when he found Luke still smiling, so clearly puffed up with his own success. He didn't blame the man; Cain could hardly contain his own excitement at Luke's work.

Whisky had wandered back off to her hiding spot with a pat on her head and a scratch behind the ears, knowing without Cain having to scold her that she wasn't allowed in the barn. Just by looking at Luke, Cain could tell that if the man had to keep himself quiet for another minute he'd bust apart at the seams and scare the horses worse than Whisky ever could.

Normally when they finished their work for the day, Luke would head back to his room and Cain would go to his cabin. Tonight, when Luke made to move past him, Cain stopped the younger man with a look and beckoned him outside. Cain slid the door to the barn closed and without words led the way up the path to his cabin.

They neared the porch, and Cain turned to Luke with a knowing grin. "Okay. We're far enough away now. Go ahead." He dipped his head indulgently. "Let it out, Luke. Shout all the way up to the sky about how proud you are of what you've accomplished with Fancy Face. Go ahead; you deserve it."

"Me?" Luke's face lit up with life. "What about her?" He reached out and grabbed Cain's arms, but quickly let go, the touch of Luke's strong hands gone before Cain could savor it. "Sorry about that. Did you see how great she did?" Luke was a live wire, and it infected Cain's normally restrained demeanor like wine on an empty stomach. "God, she's so smart, Hawk. She wanted to show you how much she has learned. She was so eager to do well for you."

Cain pursed his lips. "I think she wanted to do well for you more than for me, but thanks for the thought."

"Us then," Luke quickly corrected. "She wants to excel for both of us. I know it sounds crazy" -- Luke grabbed Cain's arms again, only this time he was apparently too into sharing his thoughts to let go -- "but when I ride her, I can feel her intelligence. I can feel her desire to do well. And she did, Hawk. Damn it." He squeezed Cain's forearms, his touch so fucking firm and warm it went straight to Cain's cock. "She did so great. I want to celebrate." His gaze met Cain's and changed, darkened, heated. "I want…" Luke moved forward. "I wish…" He stepped back.

Cain reached out and snagged Luke by the shoulder, stopping him before he could retreat. He couldn't look away from that stormy stare. "You want what, Luke? You wish what?"

Luke's eyes changed again, this time to wary. "Nothing. I can't."

Cain squeezed Luke's shoulder. Hard. "Say it." Inside, he pleaded, although it came up through his throat more like an order. "Tell me. Now."

"I want…" Luke looked away, shook his head, but finally settled back on Cain. Stubborn fire mixed in with the trepidation in his stare now. "I swear to God, you son of a bitch, you can't fire me for this, because you're the one who asked." Luke stuck out his jaw and said, "What I want right now, more than anything in this world, is to kiss you until neither one of us can breathe."

Cain stepped forward. *Good Christ.* He trembled, but he slid his hand up Luke's arm until he cupped the man's warm, corded neck. "Then do it, Luke." Cain moved in until their chests touched, and for the first time, he knew what it was like to be truly alive. "Kiss me."

# CHAPTER EIGHT

Under his fingers, Cain felt Luke go taut as a drum.

"Wh-what…" Luke's gaze flew to Cain's. Confusion and uncertainty lived in Luke's eyes, but beneath that, the dimmest shimmer of hope shone too. The hope gave Cain the courage not to step away.

Luke cleared his throat and tried again. "What did you say?"

"You heard me." Cain stroked his hand down Luke's back, felt the shiver of awareness slide down Luke's spine. Cain knew, without ever having experienced it himself, that what he'd felt was desire. He stopped at Luke's waistband, but had to curl his hand into a fist to make it happen. Christ, he wanted to touch so damn much. Cain found Luke's stare again, even as he knew hardness must be filling his own eyes in an effort to cover the uncertainty of this course. "This is the biggest fucking move I've ever made in my life, damn it. Don't you dare make me beg. I --"

Cain didn't get another word out. Luke's eyes flashed with silver fire, and suddenly he crushed his mouth to Cain's and kissed the breath right out of him. For Cain, suddenly nothing beyond that hard mouth fused to his existed in the world. He'd never kissed anyone before, and he didn't know what to do. Luke started biting at Cain's lips, and Christ, Cain loved it. Luke clutched Cain's waist, pulling him closer, and suddenly Cain and Luke were cock to cock, and Cain ground himself against the man he wanted more than he wanted his own life.

The primal, instinctive need to mate took over, and Cain no longer cared if he did it right; he simply needed to possess. He bit back and licked at Luke's mouth, groaning when the man opened up and let him inside. Intellectually Cain knew he needed to slow down and find a rhythm, but the wet heat of Luke's mouth overrode that, and Cain wasn't able to focus on anything more than thrusting his tongue inside Luke's mouth to taste.

Cain hadn't even realized he'd been pulling at Luke's shirt until the tips of his fingers touched the hot, hard flesh of Luke's slim waist. The skin was taut and searing, and just feeling the muscles rippling beneath his hands was almost enough to make Cain come. In three steps, Cain had Luke against one of the support beams of the porch, slashing his mouth against Luke's again and again. Desire rushed through Cain so damn hard it frightened him. All he wanted to do was crawl inside Luke; even then he wasn't sure that would be enough.

"I want you," Cain muttered against Luke's lips. He pressed against Luke with almost all of his weight, searing them together from head to toe. Both of their hats had been knocked to the ground long ago. Chest heaving, Cain forced himself to meet Luke's gaze. The glazed passion he found there gave boldness to his words. "I want your cock. I want it in my mouth."

Luke took Cain's hand and slid it down his waist until they covered the bulge in his jeans. "It's yours, Hawk."

Cain shuddered at the gift. Luke left Cain's hand on his crotch, and he slid his palm around Cain's waist. Then he went lower, and Cain's breath caught when, even through his jeans, someone cupped his buttocks for the first time.

"What else do you want, Cain Hawkins?"

"I want your ass, Luke Forrester." The declaration was raw and as open as Cain had ever been. "I want you naked, on your stomach, somewhere, anywhere. I want my cock filling your hole so fucking deep and stretching through the tightness so fucking much neither one of us is sure I'm ever going to get out. I know you probably don't want that, what with what just happened to you --"

Luke shut Cain up with another kiss. Cain stopped and let himself be nipped and pecked. He let Luke take what he wanted, what he needed, and soon Cain slid under a tide of slow-burning lust that heated his body in a different way -- a deeper way. He let Luke edge his jaw open and slide his tongue deep inside, thrusting in and out in a way that drove Cain's untutored, innocent imagination wild. Christ, he had a feeling that for whatever time he had, he was going to love being kissed by this man.

Luke eventually pulled back, but he slid his arm around Cain's waist and kept him close. He leaned in and settled his forehead against Cain's. "Listen to me." Luke's voice was soft but insistent. "Not one damn thing about you reminds me of what that man did to me. You hear me?" He eased his hands under the back of Cain's shirt, and Cain trembled at the gentle, sensual fluttering of Luke's fingers at the small of his back. "Just like nothing MacLesten did to me made me second-guess what I am, or what I feel, or how I want to be with a man."

The pulse in Cain's neck skittered wildly, and damn it if he didn't feel lightheaded. "That's good" -- Cain started working open the snaps on Luke's shirt -- "because I have a feeling I'm going to be living inside you for the foreseeable future. Damn it." Frustration welled when Cain's hands fumbled on the cuffs of Luke's shirt. "Help me get this off you." Too impatient to wait, Cain left the shirt tangled at Luke's wrists and kissed his way down Luke's throat to his golden, hairless chest. "Christ, Luke, you are stunning." Cain settled his parted lips on Luke's little dime-sized brown nipple and started to suckle.

"Oh damn it, Hawk, I can't believe this is happening." Luke

tunneled his hands through Cain's hair and held him in place. Cain didn't need the incentive; he was already hungry as hell. He bit lightly and licked, satisfaction rolling through him when Luke twisted his fingers in Cain's hair and pulled. His voice raspy, Luke said, "God, that's so good...don't stop."

Cain loved the strength of Luke's arms holding him in place, reveled in the breadth of hot, male chest under his mouth and hands. He wanted to see all of Luke naked, and he wanted to be naked too. Cain wanted hairy thighs and sinewy calves and ugly callused feet. He wanted a big, hard dick most of all. He wanted everything, and he wanted it skin to skin, flesh to flesh, in glorious discovery of this maleness he'd coveted for so long.

He was so close to getting it too. Cain tugged on Luke's belt, working the buckle loose so he could find out exactly what that bulge would feel like in his hands. Suddenly, the cell phone on Cain's belt loop started to chime. He cursed foul, foul words in several languages as he dropped his head against Luke's sinewy shoulder.

"Go ahead," Luke prodded gently against Cain's ear. "It might be important."

Cain rolled his head and found Luke's gaze only inches away. Christ, he could get lost in those gray depths. "I could ignore it."

Luke smiled and touched the corner of Cain's mouth with the tip of one long, work-roughened finger. "No, you couldn't. Only your family has that cell number. You might be able to ignore it for five minutes, but then you'd have to check the message just to assure yourself everyone is okay."

Damn it, this man already knew him too well. Cain snatched the phone off his belt and flipped it open. "Hello?" he barked, not bothering to hide his annoyance. He slid his arm around Luke's waist and held him close, shaking his head when the man tried to discreetly slide away. "I'm busy. Someone had better be dying or I'm coming over there later and cracking skulls."

Cassie's voice greeted Cain's surliness. "Caleb has been gored by one of the bulls. I don't think he's near death's door, but you know how he is. He will be hellatious without you here to help Connor hold him down and stitch him up. Is that bloody enough for you?"

"Shit. You know the hell it is." Cain knew the drill. Caleb was a demon too, and so could not be taken to a doctor without the anomalies in his genetic makeup being detected. Cain couldn't either. Connor was human now, but he'd been of the same demon species as Caleb for two hundred years before Cassie's gift had turned him, so he knew what it took to care for his demon brothers. Demons were not susceptible to human diseases, but they did bleed and occasionally needed sewing up to begin the healing process. *Shit.* Cain muttered, "I'll be there in twenty minutes. Bye."

Cain tucked the phone back on his belt even as Luke tugged his shirt back up his arms. "Hell, I'm sorry," Cain said. Uncertainty about how to behave now that the fires of passion had been overrun by concern for his brother flared up in Cain. "I can't help it. Damn it." He stepped back in the direction of the truck, unable to tear his stare away from Luke. "I can't stay. I have to go."

"Forget about it." Luke quickly fastened his shirt, but left it hanging outside of his jeans. "It's your family. Of course you have to go."

"It's…yeah…it's my brother." Cain jerked his thumb in the direction of the main house, even though it was much too far away to be seen. He suddenly felt clumsy, as if he were in someone else's skin and head. "They're waiting for me."

"Of course." Luke waved his hand. "Go."

Shaking his head to clear the cobwebs, Cain opened the driver's-side door.

"Wait!" Luke called out, and was on Cain in four long strides. Cain held very still as Luke slid his hands around his waist. "Your shirt." Luke tucked the fabric back in for Cain, moving his hands all the way around until they met in the front. "Your hair." He used his fingers to comb through Cain's tousled locks, taming it down once again. Cain's heart thudded as Luke fussed over him. Other than his makeshift family, he'd never had this kind of treatment before. He didn't know how he was supposed to behave, so he just stood there stock-still. "There." Luke smoothed Cain's shirtfront. "Okay.

Everything looks put together again. Now you can go."

"Thanks." Cain couldn't push anything else past his lips. He wanted to say this wasn't over, that he'd find Luke when he got back, but the overriding thought that maybe fate had stepped in and stopped them for a reason held his tongue. Climbing in behind the wheel, Cain stifled the urge to grab Luke by his shirt and drag him close to kiss him goodbye. Cain nodded and drove away, hating himself for taking the coward's way out. Deep down inside, though, he just wasn't sure what the right move was. Not only for him, but for Luke too.

EIGHT HOURS LATER, CAIN STOOD under the spray of his shower and let the prickling hot spits of water wash the sweat from his body and the blood from his forearms and hands. It was going on three o'clock in the morning and he had just gotten home from dealing with his brother. The jokester had given them quite a scare for a few hours there when he'd slipped into a deep sleep and wouldn't wake up. On the one hand it had been a blessing, in that Cain and Con had been able to stitch up Caleb's wounds without any bitching and moaning. Underneath that, however, and much, much worse, was a fear that their brother was so far away from them that not even the pain of being sewn up had been enough to wake Caleb.

But a couple of hours ago, Caleb had finally opened his eyes. It wasn't long before he reverted back to his usual, stubborn pain-in-the-ass self, and Cain had decided it would be all right to head home. His gaze had naturally strayed to the barn when he'd pulled up, but the lateness of the hour was only one of a host of reasons why he'd forced his legs to the cabin rather than Luke's room.

Only now, without the fear for his brother's health taking up his thoughts, Cain's mind automatically drifted back to what he'd been doing when he'd gotten that call. The feel of Luke's hard body under his fingers ripped through Cain with a vengeance, leaving him weak in the knees, but rock hard someplace else. And the kiss. God, the kiss. Cain had witnessed Con and Cassie kissing many times. When he had, the sight had always dredged up a wistful sense of envy for what he would never have. He couldn't love a woman in that way, and since he'd always known the risk involved were he to love a man, he figured he would have to be content being on the outside looking in.

Cain had never factored in meeting a man like Luke. When he'd seen Luke looking at him earlier, with what he'd thought might be desire, the temptation had been too great, and Cain hadn't been able to walk away. While both of them had shared in the excitement over the success with Fancy Face, Cain had looked into Luke's eyes and intuitively known the man wanted to kiss him. In that moment Cain had wanted nothing more than to be kissed by Luke. Nothing. Not even his future.

Cain replayed that kiss in his mind -- the hot, searing, sometimes aggressive desperation of it -- and his hand automatically drifted down to his cock. Already hard beyond belief, he stroked himself, his moans echoing off the tiled walls as image after image of thrusting tongues and wet heat bombarded him, choked him, making him double over with need. He grabbed his balls, heavy with seed, and held them away from his body so he wouldn't come. He wanted to savor this, to make his memories of that one moment when he'd felt truly alive last for just a little bit longer. But just the *thought* of Luke had always been enough to catapult Cain to a fast orgasm; knowing now how the man felt in his arms made it more potent.

Cain fisted his thick, red, vein-swollen prick from tip to root hard enough to make it hurt. He grimaced, but didn't stop. He was green and uneducated but trying desperately to duplicate what he imagined the wicked tightness of Luke's ass channel would feel like wrapped around his cock. He wanted that so damn bad. The thought of sliding into Luke's ass, combined with that kiss from earlier, pushed Cain right over the edge.

"Oh…Oh…" Teeth clenched, Cain let go of his sac, added that hand to the first, and squeezed. Images of pounding into Luke from behind assaulted Cain's senses. He jerked, convulsed, and lost control of his faculties. His orgasm tore through his cock and he sprayed his release, covering the spigot of the tub with thick, dripping lengths of cum.

*Jesus.* Cain leaned against the shower wall afterward and let the water keep drumming down over his temporarily satiated body. The hot water turned to warm and then finally to so cold it sprouted goose bumps up and down his arms and legs. He cut off the water, shoved the shower curtain aside, and stepped over the rim of the tub.

As he toweled off and slipped into his sweats, he tried to ignore the low hum of life vibrating under his skin. He knew exactly what it was: the physical nagging of a body that had briefly accepted the relief of masturbation but hadn't been satisfied in the way it wanted. Cain had felt it before. Not anywhere near close to this depth, of course, but he had dealt with it. Two weeks ago, he would have let the demon out and gone flying. He would have tricked his body into finding satisfaction in another way, rather than with a man.

But Cain's body had never been given a taste of being with a man before. It had now. Cain knew, without having to do it, that flying wouldn't take care of the pain anymore. Only one thing would settle this thrumming going on inside him now.

*Luke.* He needed Luke.

Cain just didn't know if it was fair, or worse, ethical, to take what he needed.

Nevertheless, Cain left his cabin, crossed the expansive yard, and found himself moving down the almost dark barn to Luke's room; the loose hay and wood chips under his bare feet tickled his toes. He'd come out here under the false pretense of checking on Luke. He would look in on Luke, see that he slept like a baby, the events of earlier today already forgotten. Cain sold himself the flimsy excuse in order to get his body out the front door, but the closer he got, the less certain he was about what he hoped to find when he reached Luke's bedroom: someone waiting up for him or someone fast asleep.

Fact was, with that kiss, Cain had set a course for himself that could only end badly. Right now, that was all it still was. Cain was not yet in deep enough that he couldn't get away with acting as if today had never happened. Luke would end up believing Cain was the worst sort of rank bastard for the cut, but it could stop there if Cain wanted it to. He knew Luke well enough by now to know the younger man would not pursue him; he'd just let it go and pretend the kiss had never happened.

Therein lay the problem. Problems, really. Cain didn't want Luke thinking he was a jerk and that he didn't care. The absolute untruth of that would fester within Cain on a bone-deep level. Even more relevant than that, deep down, already burrowed further inside him than anything he'd ever denied himself, Cain didn't think he could fake that it hadn't happened. He couldn't forget the taste of Luke's kiss or the touch of his hands. And for all of Cain's ability to hide his emotions he wasn't sure he could conceal in his gaze the memory of what it had felt like to let go and act on his attraction to Luke.

Cain reached the door, strangely not surprised to find it open, almost in invitation. The little nightlight by the bed glowed again, and he had to wonder if his Luke was a little bit afraid of the dark. Cain lifted his focus to the bed itself, and his throat went dry at the image laid out before his greedy, wanting eyes: Luke, stretched out half on his side, half on his stomach. A little blue blanket rode low on his hips, so low it might as well not have been there. And his ass, God, his ass, just slightly paler than the upper half of his body, peeked out from the hemline of that blanket, his buttocks halfway on display. The sight sent Cain's thoughts straight back to that night when he'd touched Luke's ass for the first time.

Christ, Cain wanted to fuck Luke so much more now than he had just that short time ago. He more than wanted it. He hungered for it.

Suddenly Luke's voice rumbled across the shadows. "Are you gonna stand there all night, cowboy?" He rolled over in the semidarkness. "Or is there something else you want?"

Luke shifted the rest of the way over then. The blanket slipped behind him, exposing his fully erect cock.

Cain looked. Marveled. Wanted. Needed. Salivated, even.

As he did, all function left him, and he could not move.

# Chapter Nine

"I…I…" Words got trapped within the Sahara desert in Cain's mouth. And worse, embarrassingly, obviously, he could not take his eyes off Luke's erect penis. It was slender compared to his, but damn it if it wasn't at least ten long inches of perfection, curving up big and proud from a nest of inky black fur. The heavy, low-hanging balls resting between Luke's legs…*shit*. The sight of them was enough to make Cain's cock leak with excitement too.

"Good Christ," Cain finally muttered. He tore his gaze away from Luke's dick and made eye contact once more. "I don't know the right thing to say in a situation like this, but all I can think right now is that I want to make a meal out of you." He swallowed as Luke stood. Somehow, although he didn't know how, Cain found a way to make his legs move toward Luke. "I've got to tell you, Luke, right now I feel like a starving man."

Luke reached out and caressed Cain's cheek and mouth. Cain's eyes fell half closed as his skin fired to life under those rough fingers. An understanding pulsed through Cain's belly that he'd merely been breathing and existing until this day. Now, he would learn what it was like to be alive.

"And I've gotta tell *you*, Hawk" -- Luke mimicked, moving closer, making Cain break out in a sweat -- "I haven't been able to sleep a wink since you left, hoping you would come home and search me out. I heard your truck a little while ago. When you didn't come right away, I thought maybe I'd only dreamed what had happened, and that I was going a little crazy."

This was Cain's last out. There were no more chances to elude his fate beyond this point.

Luke traced the seam of Cain's lips with his fingers, and Cain couldn't help it, he darted his tongue out and licked.

"You're not crazy," Cain replied, and shut the door for good on the natural length of his demon life. "If this is a dream then I want us both to fall asleep so that we can have it together, again."

Cain couldn't wait any longer. He clamped Luke's head in his hands, dragged him close, and kissed him. He smashed his lips against the other man's, inexpertly, but with enthusiasm and passion. He bit and licked and sucked, and with a need unlike anything he'd ever experienced, he pried Luke's jaw open and pushed his way inside.

"I'm sorry, I'm sorry." Cain fed his apology into Luke's mouth, even as he moaned with pleasure at the warm, deep cavern he took with his tongue. "I'll do better next time, I promise. I just want you so much. I can't go slow."

"No, Hawk," Luke insisted between kisses. "No apologies between us." Luke gave as good as he got, and Cain found that he liked being on the receiving end of that kind of passionate aggression. He loved the feel of Luke's blunt fingertips digging into his face and the sensation of his hands twisting at tufts of Cain's hair, pulling at it until it stung.

Luke grabbed Cain's hand, dragged it down to his cock, and a tremor wracked Cain's body at first contact. Cain touched the velvety-hard flesh of another man's penis for the first time, and it was like coming home. His finger automatically traced the mushroom head, spreading the little bead of pre-ejaculate covering the tip. He squeezed, experimenting with the hot length, and Luke hissed a "yes, yes," breathing the words heavily against Cain's cheekbone.

Cain couldn't wait anymore. As much as he wanted to explore every inch of Luke's stunningly fit young body, Cain's life of denial made him crave the taste of Luke's cock more.

"I have to know," he muttered again, almost apologetically, as he dropped to his knees. Too impatient to even look all that closely this time, he just opened his mouth and took over half of Luke's burning cock inside -- and immediately proceeded to gag when the tip of it jammed the back of his throat.

"Slow down, baby, slow down." Luke tunneled his hands through Cain's hair and gently pulled him back.

Cain lifted his gaze to Luke's, embarrassment flooding his senses. "I'm sorry. I'm not doing it right."

"It's okay. You don't need to take me all the way down your throat our first time. Trust me." Luke brushed Cain's hair away from his forehead and shared a lopsided smile that pricked Cain's heart. "I like your big, capable hands all over me a whole hell of a lot too." Luke spread the spittle that had dribbled out of Cain's mouth all over his shaft. "Take what you want in your mouth."

"I want it all," Cain said from his position on his knees, his excitement almost to the point of overflowing.

Luke's chuckle from above was almost a groan. "And I hope to hell you give us a chance to get there. Tonight, though, take what you *can*, and use your hand on the rest. Here" -- Luke circled the base of his prick with his fingers -- "let me feed it to you, because I swear to God, I love watching it disappear through that O you form with those stern, hard lips of yours."

Cain took just the knobby head this time, to start. He swirled his tongue around the rim, and it drew a moan from Luke that sent a thrill of success shooting through his body. Needful once more, Cain batted Luke's hand away and replaced it with his own, shafting the smooth-as-silk, hot length with his fist. Quickly, Cain ventured a little bit deeper, sliding more of Luke into his mouth. Licking and sucking everywhere, tasting every delicious inch of Luke's cock, Cain then used the tip of his tongue to trace a thick vein running along the underside of Luke's dick. With a moan in response, Luke held Cain's head in place and thrust his hips forward and back just the slightest bit, creating an incredibly arousing visual for Cain of his mouth getting fucked by Luke's prick.

Christ, Cain loved this. He didn't know if it was just cock in general, or specifically Luke's cock; all Cain knew was that he would eat as much dick as he could for as long as he had left. Just sucking on Luke made Cain's prick strain and beg in his sweat pants. He stroked himself in time with the handjob he performed on half of Luke's length, and his tip leaked so much precum he could feel a big, wet circle on the soft fabric of his sweats. It was a damn good thing Cain had shot one off before coming down here or he was sure he would have already come in his clothes.

With one more rub to his own cock, Cain then let go of himself and pushed his hand up Luke's flat stomach to his chest. He searched for Luke's nipples as he took a deep drag on the pole in his mouth with as much suction as he could. *Fuck.* He groaned around a mouthful of Luke. *So good.* Finally, while still making a feast of Luke's dick, Cain found the man's hard nipples. He pinched and twisted, and Luke's cock jumped in Cain's mouth in response. Cain smiled around the appendage taking over his mouth and grazed his teeth along the length until only the tip was still housed inside.

"Oh God, Hawk…that feels so fucking good it almost hurts." Luke dug his fingers into Cain's scalp and almost doubled over.

Cain found the little slit at the tip of Luke's prick with the point of his tongue and licked its tiny opening.

"Don't stop…don't stop…" Luke moaned, and the breath whooshed audibly from his body. "Harder…harder… Oh God, you're gonna make me come."

Cain suddenly wanted nothing more than to make Luke lose it and force him to orgasm. He reached between Luke's legs and cupped his balls, rolling the heavy, hot weight over the wave of his undulating palm. Cain accidentally flicked his middle finger over a smooth patch of skin behind Luke's balls, and the man almost jumped out of his skin.

"Right there, right there, right there," Luke chanted, even going so far as to reach down and hold Cain's hand in place between his legs. "Don't stop sucking…"

Cain took as much of Luke's long prick as he could, dragged with deep suction, and then milked the rest with his hand. Luke pressed his finger over Cain's between his legs and applied pressure, and that seemed to be the hot button to push him over the edge.

"Oh God, baby, it's coming… Take it… Please…" Luke held Cain's head, but Cain didn't need to be forced, he wasn't going anywhere. One second, the member in his mouth seemed to swell, and in the next, wet salty heat spurted onto Cain's tongue, sparking his virgin taste buds to a whole new life. Luke jerked in front of Cain's face again and again as he came. Cain didn't let go of his grip as a second and third wave of semen overtook his mouth, some of it sliding down his throat before he could gather it up and swallow it in one big gulp. Christ, his body hummed with joy; he loved this. He loved drinking the seed of this man.

There was only one thing he thought he could love more.

Cain let Luke's still half-hard cock slide from his mouth and looked up the length of Luke's body. "I don't think I can wait," he admitted, his voice raspy and raw. "I want to play with you and learn you, but I don't know if I can. All I want to do is shove my dick inside you and fuck you, right now." Cain pressed his cheek against Luke's hard stomach and wrapped his arms around his sturdy, sleekly muscular thighs. When Luke cupped his head and face, holding Cain close, Cain almost choked on a wave of unfiltered emotion. "Please, Luke, tell me I can have you."

"You can." Luke pulled Cain to his feet. When Cain's legs were steady again, Luke let him go and stepped back. "I'll get myself ready." Luke reached under the bed and pulled out a duffel bag. Cain watched, rapt and fascinated, as Luke produced a tube of clear liquid. Luke paused, his stare finding Cain's from across the small space. "About before" -- he sucked his cheek between his teeth -- "I'm clean. What you did is okay."

"I believe you." Cain's heart thudded. "I am too."

"I believe you too." As he got to his feet, Luke offered a sweet smile. Uncapping the tube, he advised, "You know, Hawk, those sweatpants of yours might get in the way of you fucking me. You might want to think about taking them off."

Cain's cheeks burned with heat. "Smart-ass," he muttered. He started to do as told, but only got as far as slipping his hands under his waistband and then had to pause. Luke reached around to touch his own backside, and Cain froze in place. Christ, he knew just what was happening. "Show me," he told Luke. His heart suddenly in his throat, he lifted a gaze he knew must be filled with hunger to meet Luke's. "Turn around. I want to watch what you're doing."

With awareness of his own power, Luke shifted his stare from teasing to heated. He turned and presented his bare back and ass. The scars covering Luke's backside were still raised and angry looking, but Cain didn't care about the imperfections. As far as he was concerned, they only made Luke more human and beautiful.

Cain lowered his attention to Luke's tan hand as the man pulled one of his cheeks aside and exposed his crack. Watching, riveted, Cain stared as Luke flicked one long finger over the little winking hole a half dozen times, playing with his pucker, and then plunged his finger inside. Luke jerked, but he didn't pause. He moved his digit in and out of his ass in an abbreviated fucking motion. Cain salivated, thinking he couldn't stand to be on the sidelines just watching, when Luke pushed a second finger into his rectum to join the first.

Cain's legs went wobbly beneath him. "Christ, Luke, what are you doing to me?" His tone sounded almost like a reprimand. "That has got to be the hottest damn thing I've ever seen. I didn't think I could get any harder than I already was but, goddamn it" -- Cain touched himself and almost cried out at the sensitivity -- "looking at you right now somehow managed to do it."

"I want to be ready for you, Hawk." Luke pushed his ass back on his fingers, and Cain could swear the man almost purred at the self-invasion. "I have a feeling I'm gonna have to stretch a little bit more to accommodate you. But you tell me, baby" -- he glanced over his shoulder -- "do I need another finger?"

Cain never looked away. "Yeah." The word was barely more than an animal growl. "Stick another one in there and you'll almost be ready for me." Luke didn't hesitate, and the action had Cain shoving his sweats down his legs in one fumbling motion in order to get naked too. If he didn't get inside Luke's ass soon, he was pretty damn sure he was gonna die.

As Luke settled his focus on Cain's thick cock, his pupils dilated. Cain's shaft was maybe only seven inches when he was in his human form, but the shaft had a lot of girth, and he knew it. "Tell me you're ready," Cain pleaded as he took a step forward. He was needy, but right now he couldn't care how ashamed he might feel tomorrow about showing this weakness tonight. "Tell me I can have you right now."

"God, yes, right now." Luke slid his fingers out of his asshole and crawled on the bed, settling himself on his stomach. Christ, the man had positioned himself in exactly the way Cain had mentioned he wanted Luke earlier when they'd first kissed outside the cabin. Luke hadn't forgotten.

Luke shoved a folded-up blanket under his hips, and the simple, unaffected offering of his ass was the most purely sexual thing Cain had ever seen. "I want you inside me, Hawk," Luke whispered from the bed. For the third time since Cain had entered this room, his legs almost buckled. "Put on a condom and come take me."

Cain stopped, locked in place. "Shit. Damn. Fuck." His heart plummeted right into his stomach. "I didn't think, Luke." Damn it, he hadn't planned to do this, so he hadn't known. "I don't have any condoms."

"My bag." Luke pointed. "Look in my bag. Feel around. There must be one in there somewhere. Find it." Luke's frustration broke through in a rough chuckle. "I swear to everything holy, if you have to drive two counties over and find an all-night store that will sell you some, you are doing it. I'm all dressed up and ready for the dance." Luke had his head turned to the side, and Cain could see his gray gaze sparkling with a combination of mischief and desire. "I'm all dressed up in my best suit. Don't stand me up now."

Cain couldn't help it, he reached out and caressed Luke's ass. "Not a chance." He slid his fingers into Luke's crack, feeling the slippery lube that smeared his flesh. Cain's middle finger touched the promised land, and they gasped in unison. "I'm taking that in some way tonight." Cain rubbed the slicked-up, puckered little hole again. "Count on it."

With his other hand elbow deep in Luke's bag, digging around at the very bottom, Cain suddenly touched over the edge of something small and square. "Oh shit, I think I found one." He pulled up through clothing, almost passing out with relief when the press of his fingers confirmed the shape of a rolled-up condom inside the foil packet.

"Here." Luke tossed Cain the lube. "Use some of this too."

Cain clambered up on the narrow bed and straddled Luke's legs. Excitement shimmied through his muscles, making them quiver as he tore open the condom wrapper with shaking hands. He wasn't so much scared as he was overwhelmed. He worked the condom on his turgid prick, slicking it up with lube, as the image of Luke beneath him assaulted his vision and stole his breath away. Cain took in everything, from the turn of Luke's head, to the dark thickness of his inky hair pressed against the stark whiteness of the pillow. He admired the stretch of Luke's arms, elongated, sinewy muscles all the way up to his fingers, where they curled over the edge of the mattress and held on. Cain then dropped his gaze to the V of Luke's muscular, arrestingly beautiful back, stunning, battle scars and all. Cain looked down upon the man's thighs, pressed together beneath his own. Lastly, he settled his hungry gaze on Luke's firm buttocks, the thing for which it seemed he had waited all his life.

Sexy, hot, and welcoming; Luke in this position, giving Cain his ass, was the most basic offering, given freely from the one man Cain hadn't been able to ignore or walk away from. Luke Forrester. Somehow, from that first day, Cain had known that if given the chance, he wouldn't be able to pull back and remain indifferent when faced with this man.

He'd been right.

Christ, Cain couldn't wait another minute.

"Are you ready?" Cain asked, just to be sure, even as he pr..ed Luke's cheeks apart with his big palms.

"Yes." Luke nodded and somehow managed to lift his buttocks up in the air just a little bit more. With his legs pressed together, captured between Cain's, the sight was somehow masculine and demure at the same time.

Cain slid his legs down around Luke's, positioned himself, and pushed the head of his cock against Luke's exposed hole. Luke grunted and pushed up at the same time, and Cain's life changed forever. He pushed his body inside another man's.

*Oh Jesus. Jesus. Sweet Jesus.* Cain hissed with pleasure as tight heat enveloped his cock.

Beneath Cain, Luke's muscles seized up tight, and he cried out hoarsely, "Oh God…Hawk…"

Cain froze, the head of his cock clamped like a vise inside Luke's channel. He was excited beyond belief, and sexual pleasure unlike anything he'd experienced coursed through him, but at the same time, he was terrified to move. Maybe he was too big. Maybe he'd done it wrong. Maybe he was hurting Luke. Maybe he was tearing Luke apart with his penetration and this mating was bringing back memories of what MacLesten had done to him.

Cain braced himself on his hands on either side of Luke's back and then looked down at the connection, at his cock buried a few inches inside Luke's asshole. It was so beautiful, but he would cut off his penis in a second if it was terrorizing Luke in any way.

"Do you want me to stop?" Cain grimaced as he asked; dark, hot sensation swirled around his cock and tried to drag him under the tidal wave of pure, greedy, needful sex. "Do you want me to pull out?"

"Don't you dare!" Luke reached back and clawed at one of Cain's arms, holding him in place. "I'm not in that other place." Luke seemed to read Cain's fears intuitively and put them to rest.

"It has just been a long time, that's all. I need a minute to readjust." Luke's muscles melted beneath Cain then, and Cain hissed as the walls surrounding his penis gave way. The moment Luke relaxed completely, Cain slid all the way inside his passage, and they both moaned with the full connection.

Luke's ass channel gloved Cain from tip to base, and it felt so damn good Cain's eyes fluttered and rolled halfway back in his head. *Jesus God.* He pulled almost all the way out and then sank back in to the hilt. Christ, Cain thought he'd been kidding earlier about living inside Luke for the foreseeable future, but now that he was there he thought it might have been prophetic instead. Luke had a damned hot, tight tunnel; when he squeezed his anal muscles around Cain's overly sensitized cock, Cain knew Luke was okay and that the younger man was deliberately driving him insane.

Cain shook Luke's hand off his arm and shoved it back over the edge of the bed. Sliding his palms up Luke's sleek biceps and forearms until their fingers were entwined over the head of the bed, Cain lowered his weight down on Luke's back, covering him completely. He squeezed the man's thighs together with pressure from his, locking them together in every way imaginable.

Cain laid his mouth against Luke's ear, and made his voice deliberately soft. "You think I can't push every damn one of your buttons too?" The man beneath him had no idea how good Cain was at denying himself, at controlling his need for just about everything he'd ever desired. "You think I can't toy with what you want as much as you're doing to me?"

The corner of Luke's mouth shifted up in a half smile. "I'm counting on the fact that you can." Luke contracted his ass muscles around Cain's cock again.

Cain hissed and buried his face in Luke's mess of short, wavy hair. He inhaled the clean fragrance of honey shampoo, allowing all of his senses to have a piece of Luke first, to drag him into his being in every way. Once he did that, Cain started to rock his hips against Luke's ass, sliding his cock in and out of Luke's dark, glorious hole. Cain didn't want to lever up and pound away, at least not if he could control it. Instead, he reveled in his chest pressed against Luke's back, in feeling the shoulder blades beneath him shift and dig into his pectoral muscles. Cain loved being close enough to hear the small pants of breath Luke expelled in time with Cain's gentle, persistent thrusting. He loved feeling Luke's fingers curl into fists, clutching at the mattress just moments before he pushed himself up on Cain's impaling rod, working at getting him to move harder and get deeper inside.

Within moments, Luke started undulating back on Cain's cock in a bumping, clumsy wave, something so honest in its need it forced Cain near to the edge of what he could take. "Damn it, Hawk," Luke growled, "you're driving me nuts. Fuck me harder. Take me like I know you want to." The half of Luke's face Cain could see was contorted with a visible desperation that shot to hell Cain's suppressed longing. "Please, fuck me like you mean it. I'm so damn close to coming." Luke's next words dragged Cain under for good. "I want to feel you inside me as you lose it and come."

With that, Cain lost any sense of calm or control over the thrust of his hips -- or any other element of their coupling. A switch somewhere deep inside Cain flipped and he began to fuck Luke with a deep, hard rutting pattern, taking Luke like an animal on the scent of his mate. Cain's cock became a rooting snake inside Luke's channel, foraging its depths and then shying away, only to take the dark tunnel again with more arrogance and confidence the next time. Cain's sweat-slick torso slid back and forth over Luke's back, rubbing it raw with his chest hair. Cain couldn't make himself rear up and take the abrasiveness away, as he knew he should; he needed to feel every inch of his body possessing Luke's completely. He needed it on a bone-deep level he couldn't deny.

Cain squeezed Luke's hands hard enough to leave bruises, and he clamped his teeth onto the man's neck deep enough to leave a mark there too. Cain didn't know why he needed to take so roughly, but as he pounded away in Luke's ass, and as his balls drew up tight between his legs, he wasn't strong enough to deny this unfathomable need to put a physical claim on the man he was taking. Cain needed something to still be visible on Luke tomorrow when he had to go back to pretending Luke wasn't everything to him.

A rough growl escaping him, Cain unclamped his jaw and licked his way up to Luke's ear. "Christ, Luke, I…I never knew it could be this good." Cain dug the confession out from so deep inside it was barely cohesive.

Luke's lips were parted against his pillow, and his gaze shone bright in the night as he took Cain's hard fucking without flinching. "I've never wanted to be fucked by anyone the way I want it with you." Breathing became a tangible thing for Luke. "Oh God, Hawk…" The man's entire body convulsed beneath Cain. "I'm coming again…I'm coming again…"

Right then Luke's chute squeezed Cain's cock so damn tight, so fucking good, it bordered on painful. Luke suddenly jolted and shouted, and without ever having been with another man Cain knew Luke shot his load into the bedding beneath him, moaning Cain's name as it happened.

That was the end for Cain. "Ohhh…" Cain's entire body seized. "Oh damn…" Cain didn't even get in another thrust. He came right then and there, his orgasm shooting a wave of acute pleasure throughout his entire being. The deep, intense sensation worked its way into every extremity in Cain's body, making him cry out in the darkness of the small room. Cain shuddered and exploded, jetting hot cum into the condom sheathing his cock, buried deep in Luke Forrester's ass, again and again, until there was nothing left. Finally, he stilled.

Cain breathed heavily on top of Luke, and he could feel Luke doing the same beneath him. The unison motion lifted and swayed their bodies together in a way that felt far too intimate for Cain's safety.

Just as quickly as perfect joy had rocked through Cain, panic turned his sweating body cold. "Um, okay, thank you." He scrambled off Luke, biting back a groan as his cock pulled free of Luke's wonderful ass. "I…I…" He grabbed his sweats off the floor and bundled them in front of his dick like a shield, as if the ball of fabric could somehow hide what he'd done. His brain screamed that he'd just had sexual intercourse with another man, and in doing so he had put a gun to his own head. "Jesus, I'm sorry." He couldn't look Luke in the eyes. "I have to go."

Cain tore out of the little room, his heart pounding a million beats a minute. Christ, what had he just done? Sex with another male was more than taboo or forbidden within the Naverto demon species. It was a treasonous, criminal act that, when discovered, would result in his death. And not only had Cain just done that very thing, he'd gloried in it.

What in the hell was he supposed to do now?

# CHAPTER TEN

As Luke started the morning feedings, he hummed a happy little tune under his breath, unable to keep down how right everything suddenly felt with the world. He talked to the horses as he moved along, knowing they liked the connection of gentle, conversational speech. Luke knew he probably sounded extra chipper, and likely looked like a damned idiot to boot, but there wasn't anyone watching so he didn't much care. His mother and sister were coming to visit with him later this morning. It would ease their hearts to see him happy and upbeat, so he didn't try to censor himself. Even if, for Cain's sake, Luke couldn't tell his family why there was a small smile on his face that he couldn't quite wipe away.

Cain. Cain Hawkins. *Hawk.* Luke's cock stirred against his jeans just thinking the man's name. He couldn't be sure how Cain would act around him today, but the truth was that even if he was distant and pretended the previous night had never happened, Luke would be okay with it. Cain had obviously never been with another man before, and in the light of day, he might not be able to own what he'd done with Luke.

Heaven knew the man had been the very definition of awkward and fumbling as he'd cleared out of Luke's room last night. With someone else, Luke's feelings might have been hurt by the quick exit. With Cain, though, Luke couldn't take offense. Cain had just been so damn clumsy and almost unable to speak through his hasty retreat; the very naturalness and lack of artifice in his behavior proved the honesty in Cain's actions.

During Cain's bizarrely sweet exit, the only thought running in Luke's head had been that he wanted to tuck the bigger man in his pocket and promise him that the world wouldn't come to an end just because he'd fucked another man.

"Morning."

A curt voice broke through Luke's mental wanderings, and Luke snapped his focus up from filling L.L.'s feed bucket. His heart immediately started racing. Cain stood before him, and in Luke's eyes, he was breathtakingly handsome. Cain was as cleanly shaven as a man with his testosterone levels could be, and he had his short, chestnut-colored hair combed neat and close to his head. The man's long, powerful legs were encased in dark denim Levi's, and a tan, western-yoked shirt covered his wide chest. He looked good enough to eat. He also kept tapping his hand against his thigh and darting his attention around the barn. *He's nervous.* Cain's fear made Luke's chest ache. Luke had no interest in becoming aggressive and pushing Cain faster than he was able to go. As much as it went against Luke's style, he understood he had to hang back and let Cain dictate how this would play out.

"Morning, Hawk." Luke smiled in greeting and then got back to work, just as he would do on any other day.

*Your move.*

Cain felt like the world's biggest jackass. He stood in his barn, staring at Luke while Luke went about his job, while the man behaved as if the most intimate act two people can share had not just occurred between them less than four hours ago. On the one hand, Cain felt like growling over the fact that Luke had apparently written him off as a one-night stand. At the same time, fairness forced Cain to concede that he had been the one to run off like a coward after the deed had been done, not Luke.

Cain just hadn't known what to say or do during post-coital bliss, especially not while suffering the panic of knowing that said sexual satisfaction was further proof that he'd transgressed in a forbidden way. With an act that would end with his execution. The Naverto would find out what Cain had done with Luke; his aura wouldn't be able to hide the truth of his new sexuality. It was only a matter of time before one of his own visited and his secret life was discovered. *Shit.* Ice ran through Cain's veins.

"Hey, Hawk," Luke called out, breaking into Cain's disturbing thoughts.

Shaking his head to clear the clutter, Cain moved to help Luke feed the horses. Not that there were many left to feed; Luke was always on top of the job. Today, that was good. Cain had to leave soon and spend some time with Caleb.

As Cain passed Luke to get to the feed room, he determinedly kept his gaze off Luke's jeans-clad buttocks. Of course, that just meant Cain ate up the sight of Luke's strong back instead -- which as far as Cain's libido was concerned, was a stirring, finely sculpted piece of beauty too.

*Focus yourself, man.* Cain moved into the small room, cleared his throat, and called back casually through the open door, "What is it, Luke?"

"Is it still all right for my mother and sister to visit this morning?"

Cain came out of the room with a vitamin-enhanced bucket of oats, and a scowl on his face. "Of course it is." Christ, did the man think he intended to hold what happened between them against him? "Why in the hell wouldn't it be?" With one pointed glare, Cain dared Luke to mention what they'd done last night as a reason.

Luke glanced up at Cain from his bent position, catching Cain's gaze briefly before sliding down to feed the next animal. "No particular reason." Luke smiled easily in that way that snagged Cain in the chest and made him want to be dragged forcibly closer. "I just wanted to double-check that you didn't have a specific job you want me to do today that wouldn't allow me a visit with them, that's all."

*That fucking sexy smile.* A strange, new tingle ran down Cain's back. He jerked up straight, and his heart rate kicked up considerably. He wasn't used to this kind of thing, but if he didn't know any better, he'd think Luke was flirting with him. *Huh.*

"Come on, Luke." Cain mentally kicked himself back into work-mode and began moving. "I haven't had to tell you what to do from almost the first day you started working here. What makes you think today would be any different?"

"Nothing, I was just double-checking." The infernal man's lazy voice drifted out through the door with the goddamn most enticing drawl Cain had ever heard in another man. "My mom and sister are really excited to see what I'm doing now, and I just wanted to make sure I wasn't going to have to rescind my invitation."

*Well, hell.* Cain jerked up and narrowed his stare on Luke again. Confusion now scratched at Cain's earlier assessment of Luke's behavior. Luke sounded sincere. Maybe he hadn't been teasing Cain after all. A stab of disappointment knifed through Cain, but he ruthlessly stuffed it down, along with giving himself a silent reminder that pretending they hadn't been intimate was much better for Cain's wellbeing.

Clearing his throat softly, Cain asked, "What time are they coming?" He kept his voice soft in deference to the skittish horse he was getting ready to feed. Calliope wasn't quite ready to trust him yet, but he made a point to let her see him every day, and to touch her and talk to her. Slowly Cain would get her accustomed to human contact again.

"Around eleven," Luke said just as softly, having moved up on Cain so quietly Cain hadn't even known the man was there until Luke's answer brushed warm breath against Cain's ear. Just as whisper soft, Luke added, "Hi, baby."

For just a second, blood rushed straight to Cain's cock. *Fuck.* For a brief, heavenly moment, Cain had thought he was Luke's *"baby."* Then Luke reached across Cain and rubbed Calliope's muzzle in greeting. "How's my Calli doing this morning?" Luke said to the horse in a teasing, loving tone.

Luke continued to croon to the horse in the sweetest voice, and Cain swore he felt each kind, gentle word race through his body in tingling waves, as if Luke were intimately whispering the words to him.

*But he isn't, so stop wanting something you have no right to claim as your own.* Cain shook the foolishness from his brain and forced out a chuckle. "You do that with everybody, don't you?"

Luke shot him a sideways glance. "What?"

"Nicknames," Cain explained. "I swear to God you have one for every horse in this stable." He couldn't look away from Luke's silver-shot gaze. "And for me," Cain whispered, his voice a little scratchy. In response, Luke's pupils flared. Heatedly, Cain thought. Cain stepped back, suddenly nervous and unsure of himself. Clearing his throat, he shifted his focus to Fancy Face. "Of course, like you said before, you do it for everything."

"For everything I like," Luke corrected softly from beside Cain. He moved to pass Cain then, pausing for just a split second at Cain's back, and the man's natural heat seared Cain like sunburn through his shirt. "For everyone I care about."

A knife of need sliced right through Cain, something so deep and needful he could not ignore it. Before he even processed that he did it, Cain shot his hand out and grabbed Luke by the wrist, preventing him from getting any farther away. He clutched the strong, flesh-covered bone within his fingers tightly, maybe too tightly, but he couldn't let go.

Even holding Luke trapped, Cain couldn't make himself turn and face the man. It quite terrified him that he'd take one look and end up shoving Luke against one of the stall doors, losing all control once again.

"I might not get the chance to meet your mom and sister today." Cain babbled to cover the insecurity creating a fine sheen of perspiration across his upper lip. "I have a couple of things I need to do today away from the ranch, and I have to check in on my brother."

Luke rubbed his free hand against Cain's knuckles, where Cain still held Luke's arm, causing a shiver. "I know how tight you are with your siblings. How is Caleb doing this morning?" Such sincerity resonated in Luke's voice that it forced Cain's stare from his scuffed boots up to Luke's eyes to check for a sign that would back up the gentle, insightful tone. It was there in Luke's unwavering gaze, and it made Cain's breath catch, scratching deep in his throat.

"He'll live," Cain managed to force out through the tingling awareness moving through his upper body. "I never would have come home if he hadn't woken up and turned right back to his normal, ornery, smart-mouthed self." Cain's mind suddenly raced through the few words spoken between Luke and him last night that hadn't been of a base, sexual nature. His gaze narrowed. "How did you know it was Caleb that had been hurt?"

Luke's face shifted from golden tan to rosy red in a flash. His lower lip slipped between his teeth; he glanced away for a moment but it wasn't long before he once again faced Cain head-on. "You caught me." His cheeks somehow flushed even redder. "When midnight rolled around and you hadn't come home, I started to get worried about what might have happened to keep you away for so long. I didn't want you to know, though, so I called Cassie's cell phone and left a message. She called me back a little after that and told me what was going on. Don't get pissed at her; I told her not to tell you I called."

*Shit. He checked up on me.* Cain's breathing became so labored he was surprised he didn't pass out. He suddenly muttered, "I have to get going." After taking a step away, he realized he still had his hand manacled to Luke's wrist. He loosened his hold, but instead of letting go, he slid his palm down until his fingers entwined with Luke's. Christ, the small squeeze he received from Luke in return tore through Cain like wildfire. He was as scared as he'd ever been, but he made himself meet Luke's gaze like a man. "Maybe later…if you want to…damn it…" Cain shook his head and tried again. "I don't cook very much. I'm not that good at it, but I have food." Jesus, he was fucking this up, and it was humiliating. "Damn it. Come to the cabin tonight, Luke, if you want to, but not if you think I'm forcing you to or anything. Son of a bitch." Cain tugged his hand away before a puddle of sweat could form and give him away. "Never mind." He pushed past Luke to the open barn door, toward escape. "I'm running late. I'll see you later."

"Hawk!"

Cain froze as that pet name coiled an inferno of lust in his jeans. "Yeah?"

Luke suddenly stood in front of Cain. And for all that Luke's body was fit, and his face beautifully handsome, and his hair the thickest, richest, deepest brown Cain had ever seen, it was the twinkling light in Luke's gray eyes that grabbed at Cain the hardest and wouldn't let go.

The damn man had the cheeky audacity to smile at Cain. "I'll see you a little after seven, okay?"

"Okay," Cain parroted like an idiot.

Luke did something next that Cain had always thought impossible for him to experience with a man. Luke leaned in and pressed the sweetest, gentlest kiss to Cain's cheek, rolling a tremor through Cain he was sure was visible and revealing.

Luke settled his hand on Cain's hip and then leaned in again, whispering against Cain's ear, "I'll see you later. All right?" Luke then grazed his lips down the angle of Cain's cheek and planted another small kiss against the corner of Cain's mouth before stepping away.

Cain was gob-stopped. Overwhelmed. He could not force a single word out of his mouth.

Luke didn't have as much trouble. He, as easy as you please, added, "Have a good day, Hawk," before sliding past him, into the barn, to get back to work.

Cain didn't know what in the hell he was supposed to do in response on his end, so he just got the hell out of there before he did the wrong thing and screwed everything up.

A COUPLE OF HOURS LATER CAIN pulled the truck to a stop in front of his cabin. As he climbed out, he wondered to himself how in the hell people who had sex on a regular basis ever managed to get any work done. He'd been so damn flummoxed by Luke's little goodbye kisses this morning that he'd driven off without taking any of the paperwork he needed for his business in town.

If just this one interlude, along with a couple of kisses, already had Cain's brain addled this much, Cain had to ask himself how he would function if this thing with Luke went any further than it already had. And just as discomfiting, how in the hell would he be able to hide this relationship from anybody for more than five minutes?

Cain let himself inside the cabin and grabbed the accordion folder off his desk, just where he'd left it, with the intent to disappear before Luke noticed he'd returned. That would be embarrassing. It suddenly occurred to Cain that it was awfully quiet and that there wasn't an unfamiliar vehicle parked anywhere in sight that would indicate Luke's family was visiting. A quick glance at his watch showed the time to be well after eleven -- the time Luke had mentioned his mother and sister were coming.

Christ, Cain hoped everything was all right. *Well, hell.* Now that Cain had let that thought enter his mind, he wouldn't be satisfied until he checked on Luke. The man had just been too excited about his mother and sister visiting to be fine if they'd blown him off for a better deal.

Cursing himself for getting in too deep too fast, Cain climbed back out of the truck. He strode across the yard to the barn, where he could already see both doors pushed open wide. He fully expected to feel like an idiot when he found Luke doing something perfectly normal, like filing one of the horse's hooves. What Cain didn't expect, even in his wildest imaginings, was a dark-haired woman in a wheelchair sitting smack dab in the middle of his stable.

He paused just outside the entrance and clasped his hands

together behind his back. "Excuse me," Cain called out softly, not wanting to frighten her or the horses. When she turned to look at him, he added, "Can I help you with something?"

"Nope." The woman smiled, and even with the shadows of the interior of the barn there was something familiar about the tilt of the lips. "I'm just enjoying being around horses again. But don't tell my son. I don't want him or my daughter being sad about it. I'm Jean Forrester."

"Oh." Cain glanced over his shoulder in the direction of his truck. "I didn't see a car, so I figured you and your daughter hadn't been able to make it after all."

"Got a ride from a friend," Jean answered. "We don't have a car anymore."

"Oh." Heat flooded Cain's face. He felt like an absolute heel for mentioning a vehicle. "Sorry."

In the face of Cain's obvious embarrassment, Jean's features softened. "Don't worry about it." She held out her hand. "You must be Luke's boss. He absolutely raves about you."

Somehow Cain managed not to blush to the very tips of his hair follicles. "Cain Hawkins." Cain moved inside the barn, shaking the woman's hand as he introduced himself. "And yes, this place is mine, although Luke is giving me a run for my money with whom these horses are more devoted to."

"He always did love horses," Jean answered with a wistful smile. "And they always did seem to take to him too."

Those casually thrown out words opened up a whole new set of questions about Luke -- ones Cain would have to decide how much he was willing to know before his time ran out and he was unceremoniously snatched away from his life.

*But not right now. No sense in getting maudlin in front of Luke's mom.*

Now that Cain stood right in front of Jean Forrester, he could see Luke's coloring favored his mother very closely. No wonder the smile had immediately gotten Cain's full attention. The eyes, a darker version of Luke's, were very nearly the same too. Luke's mother was still a pretty woman, but in a way that had some tiredness to it that couldn't be hidden. Not that it mattered one damn bit to Cain, but he wondered why Luke hadn't mentioned his mother was in a wheelchair. It was another part of Luke and his family that Cain had to wonder if he would be given the chance to find out.

"Listen, I don't mind you sitting in the barn with the horses if that's what you want to do, but I can't believe Luke would just leave you here and take off."

"How right you are." Jean smiled. "You just missed him and his sister. I had to practically shove him out to get him to go. My daughter, Risa, she has the fever for horses too, just like I can see in you. She wore Luke down -- with my help -- and finally convinced him to let her exercise one of the horses. They just took off for a ride a few minutes before you showed up." She had the grace to look a little bit guilty. "Risa is a bit of a pistol but she has the same gentle touch with animals Luke has. You don't have to worry about the wellbeing of your horse, I promise you that."

"I'm not." Cain had already taken a quick scan of the barn and noted that Night Runner and Laura's Love were missing. "Luke knows better than to put a body on a horse that isn't ready to be ridden. The two he took out are well trained." Cain's brows drew together. "I'm just surprised he would leave you here alone to fend for yourself."

"Oh, I had to give him a good talking to, believe me." Jean chuckled, and the deep, feminine richness of it did something strangely soothing to Cain's insides he couldn't place or identify. "I had to remind him that I'm the momma, and he's the child, and that I can entertain myself for an hour without aid from him or his sister. Truth is" -- she slid a glance toward Cain -- "I wanted a little bit of time around the horses without my kids as an audience. They don't need to see how much I miss riding. It pains them enough that they can't give me more than they do, no matter how much I tell them it's not their responsibility to do so."

A stab of envy sliced through Cain's entire being. "I guess that just means you've been a great mother to them, and they want to return the gift. Can't find too much fault for that."

Jean's eyes twinkled with as much light as her smile. "My goodness, Luke told me so, but I couldn't quite let myself believe him. Now I see it for myself. You really aren't a thing like his old boss."

Blackness bubbled up inside Cain. He quickly stuffed the rage back down, else risk giving away Luke's secret. He forced out a wry smile instead. "Ms. Forrester, that's probably the nicest thing anyone has ever said to me."

The woman raised an eyebrow at him. "So then we're in agreement on the character of that one. Good." She started pushing her way down the length of the barn, moving along the horse's stalls, looking, staring. Cain stayed where he was, sensing she needed a moment to herself.

When she reached the last stall she wheeled to the other side and started back in his direction. "I'm not happy my son got fired from a job, but at the same time I think it's a blessing he's not working for Justin MacLesten anymore. I only met the man officially once, and believe me when I say it *wasn't* my pleasure. Luke wanted to show Risa and me where he was living, to show off the work he was doing. MacLesten got wind of it and ripped Luke a new one right in front of us and a half dozen other men, humiliating him, even though Luke wasn't officially on the clock at the time. The foreman gave him permission to have us there."

"That sounds like MacLesten," Cain murmured. The boiling desire to rearrange the bastard's body parts grew hotter and harder to ignore with every story he heard about the man. Even more significant to Cain's anger, how the son of a bitch had treated Luke. "My brothers and I have refused to do business with him for a number of years because of behavior just like that."

"I'm glad to hear somebody in Montana won't." Jean reached where Cain stood, putting herself back where she'd begun her trek. She looked up at Cain, almost defiantly showing off the sheen of moisture misting her deep gray eyes. "Luke signed on with MacLesten because we needed the money, for sure, but also because it was a job that let him work with horses. He was naïve, and he thought if he was working and living around horses then he'd be able to bring me to visit and be around them too. He was trying so hard to give me back a piece of our old life, but MacLesten snatched the gift away from him. It was still a job, though, and when there are bills to pay, you don't turn down the opportunity to work. Especially when the paycheck comes every two weeks like clockwork, and it doesn't bounce when you take it to the bank."

Suddenly, Cain completely understood Luke's repeated requests to make sure his family's visit was okay. It was such a small thing to ask for and so easy for a boss to grant. Yet for Luke, it had become something he hadn't been able to give to his mother, all because of Justin MacLesten.

Christ, Cain knew he couldn't offer Luke much in the way of a future. The truth was that the more time he spent with Luke, the less time he would end up having with him before he was taken away and killed. He could give Luke this time with his family, though, around these animals that they all loved so much, without any qualms or hesitation.

"Listen." Cain wanted to assure this woman, but he wasn't comfortable dealing with a lot of emotion. "I'm already running late for my meeting, so I really have to go. Please know that you and your daughter are welcome to come here whenever you want. Luke is a hard worker, and I don't have any concerns that his work will slip if he has company. If you want to sit and talk with my horses, then I say it can only do my animals good to get comfortable with another human voice. Just so long as you don't touch the ones I'm sure Luke warned you about, I have no problem with your presence on my property. Now, you have a good visit." He dipped his hat in her direction and backed away.

"Mr. Hawkins."

Cain immediately responded, stopping in midstride. He turned, but he didn't move closer. "Please, call me Cain."

"Cain, then." Jean smiled at him, and he sensed that somehow she could see straight into his uncertain heart. "Thank you," she said and left it at that.

Cain didn't know what to do, so he just nodded and left before he found another reason to want to be with Luke.

Like wanting his kind and insightful mother for himself.

Another on the list of things Cain Hawkins had always coveted, and yet for all his years of breathing had never known firsthand.

# CHAPTER ELEVEN

At 7:15 that night, Cain pulled the truck to a stop in front of his cabin. When he saw Luke already standing on the porch waiting for him, looking all gorgeous in boots, jeans, and a dark blue button-up shirt, he cringed. *Damn it.* Cain's mouth watered even as he cursed the man's punctuality. He'd hoped Luke would run a little bit late too and inadvertently save Cain from the embarrassment of being tardy for his first official date.

Christ, it had taken Cain almost half the day to accept this was a date and that he could not get out of it without being unspeakably cold-blooded. It didn't matter because, deep down, Cain knew he didn't want to wiggle out of this evening with Luke. The hot desire living inside Cain scared the shit out of him, but he wanted every minute he could get with Luke before his time came to an end.

Taking a deep breath to calm his sudden case of the jitters, Cain gave himself a silent pep talk to man up, and got out of the truck. "Sorry I'm late." As he shut the door, he added, "My schedule got unavoidably backed up. I should have called the phone line down in the barn to let you know. Obviously I haven't had time to cook anything, but I think there is some leftover spaghetti in the fridge." Once he reached the porch and got eye to eye with Luke, he rambled, "Or if you want something heartier, I have some steaks in the freezer, but you'd have to wait for me to defrost them in the microwave and then put them on the grill to cook. I have turkey and ham for sandwiches if you want something more casual. At least, I think I do."

In a flash Luke covered Cain's lips with his hand, effectively shutting him up. "Take a breath, Hawk." With a lopsided smile, he released Cain's mouth. "And let's start with something simple like 'hi.'"

The tips of Cain's ears burned with heat, but Luke's advice to breathe did indeed help. After exhaling, Cain murmured, "Hi." Nodding toward his front door, he added, "Would you like to come inside and have something to eat?" Christ, he'd never felt so in the dark and ill-prepared for anything in his life.

"I'd love to." Luke grabbed a rolled-up paper bag off the porch railing and tucked it under his arm. "Lead the way."

Cain opened the door and held it wide, granting Luke entry. He took in his place with fresh eyes, never having bothered to examine how it would look to another person. He'd created it for his comfort, and the truth was he'd never really considered himself a man who needed very much. The floor was top-of-the-line pine, as was the moss-colored suede couch and the black leather recliner he used to kick back and watch the occasional baseball game on a moderately sized flat-screen TV. The custom-built wall surrounding his small entertainment center was floor-to-ceiling shelves packed with books and a few small knickknacks that had meaning to him, pieces he'd collected over his lifetime.

A palm-sized, black marble gargoyle Cain had purchased some hundred and twenty years ago in Scotland -- when he'd been in a particularly bad place, and his humor had taken a dark turn -- sat in visible sight. As Cain flicked his gaze over it, he had the panicked hope the statue wouldn't stand out too much among the other animal sculptures and paintings of rural ranch life covering most of his walls. He would have no good answer if Luke commented on the gargoyle's presence.

The other half of the cabin's main room was the kitchen, bisected by a bar crafted from the body of a massive old tree from Hawkins Ranch land, toppled by the weight of a brutal storm a year ago. His home wasn't much, but it had everything he needed. *Christ,* Cain squeezed his eyes shut for a moment, *I hope it's good enough for him.*

Reminding himself of Luke's advice, Cain breathed. "Take a seat wherever you want." He switched on a lamp at his desk and then moved to the kitchen, flipping another light on in there.

As Luke pulled out a chair and sat down at the table, Cain couldn't help staring. Damn, Cain had to be careful with this man; something about him sitting at his dinner table just looked *right.* Clearing his throat, Cain turned to the fridge. "So, I promised you food. What would you like?"

"The leftover spaghetti is fine," Luke replied. "I can pretty much eat anything. My mom will be happy to rat me out on that the next time you see her. All you have to do is ask."

"Ahhhhh." As Cain popped the bowl of pasta in the microwave and got it heating, he glanced at the handsome man sitting at his table. "So she told you we met, huh?" He went back to the fridge. "You want a beer? I also have water, soy milk, and apple juice."

Luke chuckled. "Do you really have apple juice, Hawk?"

Cain braced his arm on the open door of the fridge and shot Luke an affronted stare. "I certainly do. Why? You want to call me out on it or something?"

"Shit, no." Luke laughed harder. "I think it's cute as hell. I'll take a glass with my spaghetti."

"Damn straight."

"And yes, my mom did tell me she met you. She also told me how generous you were with your offer to her to visit me whenever she liked. Thank you." Luke's tone turned somber. "You have no idea what you did for her spirit by giving her that gift."

Discomfort at being praised for something that was nothing

rolled through Cain once again. "It's not really a gift if it wasn't any kind of trouble to give."

"It is to her. And to me too."

Cain leaned across the bar to pass Luke his juice, a couple of forks, and a shaker of Parmesan cheese. Their gazes met and held, and Cain felt his breathing sync up with each inhale and exhale from Luke. *Shit.*

Shaking himself, Cain said, "Can I ask why your mother is in a wheelchair? Or would she say it's none of my business?" The microwave beeped then, pulling Cain away from Luke. *Fortuitous timing.* He figured doing something mundane like plating food took some of the pressure off the intimacy of the question.

"No, it's not rude to ask." Luke's voice held steady and even. "She would have told you if you'd asked. I was around twelve when she got hurt, so I guess that makes it almost fourteen years ago. She was shot by my father and thrown out of a second-story window."

"Jesus Christ." Cain staggered to a halt. He had their plates of food in his hands, and somehow forced himself to get to the table. Sliding one in front of Luke, he sat down, and grimaced. "How horrific. I'm so sorry I brought it up. I don't know what to say."

"It's all right." Luke lifted his focus fully to Cain, and Cain saw his eyes were as fiery as his words were bland. He'd clearly learned to control almost every bit of his emotions when sharing his story. "My mom survived, and that's all that matters. After my father attacked her, he climbed out onto the roof and jumped. I take comfort in the divine justice that she survived and he didn't."

"I'm so sorry."

Luke smiled but the lift of his lips held a cynical edge. "Insurance policies don't pay out on suicides, so our life got real basic after my father's death. The house, and the little piece of land, and the few horses we had that my mom loved so much…" Luke paused, visibly swallowing thickly. "Everything we owned had to be sold off to pay the bills, so that's what we did." Some of the hardness left Luke's face, and the sadness Cain had expected to see from the outset finally broke through. "My mother misses being with the horses and riding more than she misses her legs. She tries to hide it and pretend she doesn't, but I know the truth. It's the one thing I haven't been able to do for her, give her back that part of her life. Anyway" -- Luke rolled his shoulders and shook his head fiercely -- "I don't want to talk about that anymore." He caught Cain's gaze and smiled wickedly. "Why don't we talk about you instead?"

Cain reared back in his chair. "Me?" Fear, embarrassment, and inadequacy all warred inside for the top spot inside Cain. "What could you possibly want to know about me?"

"Let's start with something simple." Luke cut up his pasta into manageable pieces, like a little kid, causing Cain's stomach to flutter with attraction for the man. "How about, what's your favorite color?"

"Geez. I…I don't know." Cain's mind raced. "I don't think anyone has actually ever asked me that before."

Luke snorted. "You didn't go out on very many first dates in school then."

*You have no idea.* Cain scrambled; it was probably best he not let Luke think about him in relation to normal teenage things like school. "Green would be my favorite color, I guess. Yeah, I don't think anything is prettier than the valleys of Montana when they're covered with the fresh new grass of spring. I could look at it for hours and not get tired." Cain swirled some spaghetti on his fork. "How about you?" He stuffed his mouth with the tangy flavor of tomato sauce.

Luke finished chewing and took a swig of his juice. "Since you stole my answer" -- his gray gaze twinkled with silver -- "I would have to say that lately I'm partial to blue." He raised a brow pointedly at Cain. "Most particularly the clear blue of lake water. I've seen specific eyes deepen to that color very recently, and they do have the power to mesmerize me."

"Oh." Heat suffused Cain's entire being. "Oh." He didn't know if Luke's response was some sort of invitation with which he was supposed to know what to do, so he just stuffed his face with food.

Luke glanced to the right. "I see you have a television." Clearly, he was far more in control than Cain. "Do you have a favorite TV show?"

"I don't guess that I do." Relief flooded Cain. *We're back on ground I can handle.* "Do Toronto Blue Jays baseball games and Shark Week on the Discovery Channel count?"

Luke looked up from his food with a smile. "If that's what you like, then it counts just fine."

"Then that's what I like. So how about you? You got anything you just can't miss?"

"Well, along the lines of our massive difference in the kind of music we like" -- Luke pushed his empty plate away and leaned back in his chair -- "I prefer hockey to baseball. And if I had to pick a cable station I wouldn't want to be without, it would be the Sci-Fi Channel. That's kind of embarrassing, though, so don't spread it around."

Cain chuckled; he couldn't help it. The guy was gay, yet his primary worry was about people thinking he was a science fiction geek. "Don't worry; your secret is safe with me." As Cain got to his feet, he pointed at Luke's plate. "You done with that, or can I get you a second helping?"

"No, I'm good. Thank you."

"No problem." After rinsing out the plates, Cain turned and leaned against the counter, again, not sure what to do next. "Can I get you anything else? Dessert? I probably have a bag of cookies around here somewhere. Let me see if I can find them." In rapid order, he turned and started opening the small line of cabinets. Christ, he just needed to busy his hands and he would be fine in a minute.

"Hawk." Luke's strong tone broke into Cain's attempt to unearth the phantom bag of cookies, the command in the man's tone stilling him in place. "I'm not going to tell anyone what happened between us last night, okay? Your secrets are safe with me too."

"I know. I'm sorry." Cain couldn't let go of his death grip on the cabinet door to turn and face Luke again. "I don't know why I'm behaving like such an idiot."

"You're not being an idiot," Luke cajoled from the table. "But if you think you're embarrassed right now, come sit back down and tell me about the most humiliating moment of your life. That way, you'll know what feeling like a dork is really like."

*Christ.* Cain's most embarrassing moment hadn't happened all that long ago. The worst sort of envy and pain had filled him to the brim in those few minutes, but ultimately the greatest liberation had come as a result of it. That didn't, however, mean Cain was just willing to spill his guts *carte blanche.*

"*Quid pro quo?*" he asked, forcing himself to turn and meet Luke's gaze.

Luke nodded; he kicked Cain's chair out from under the table, sliding the soft felt tabs on its feet across the floor. "Of course." He jerked his head toward Cain's seat. "But you go first. Sit down."

"All right." Cain wiped his hands on his jeans before joining Luke at the table. Chewing on the inside of his cheek, he mentally sorted through where to begin. "Okay." He crossed his arms against his chest, settled his ankle on his knee, and forced himself to meet Luke's stare. He found something guileless, patient even, in those pretty gray eyes, and it gave Cain courage to speak the truth. "As you know, Connor and Cassie got married a couple of years ago. Anyway, being newlyweds, it's natural the mood strikes them sometimes in places other than their bedroom."

Luke's lips quirked up at the edges. "I would imagine were it up to your brother he'd keep Cassie naked and physically attached to him in some form or manner twenty-four hours a day, seven days a week."

"Oh?" Cain deadpanned. "So you *have* met my brother, have you?"

Luke's sharp bark of laughter, so very natural and welcoming, took away any tension left in the room. "Yes. I have sat in the same room with the two of them for five minutes. That's about all it takes to know the score."

"Yeah. So anyway, a little over a year and a half ago, I came home in the middle of the day. Even though I lived there, I wasn't expected at that time. I'd forgotten something; I don't even remember what it was now. But whatever it was, it was in the office, and that's right where I headed. I guess if I'd been listening rather than thinking about ten other things I had to do that day, I might have heard them and stopped before I got to the door. But I wasn't, so I didn't. And in fairness to me, the door was wide open. They didn't even bother to halfway close it."

"Point to you." Sweet indulgence twinkled in Luke's eyes. "Go on."

Only a little self-conscious now, Cain smiled too. "So I suddenly found myself standing in the open doorway, where I just managed to pull my feet up short and not go any farther into the room, with my vision full of my brother flat on his back, on his desk, with Cassie riding him in a full-on gallop they were both really, really enjoying."

"Oooh." Luke scrunched up his face. "That would be embarrassing."

Cain knew he could stop the story right there if he wanted to. Luke would easily think it was the end and not press for more. But with what Luke had told Cain about his family this evening, Cain fought through his gut instinct to keep his secrets hidden -- at least some of them -- and pressed on. "That wasn't why it was so embarrassing." Cain's skin heated from the inside, telling him to stop. "At least, not for me."

Luke didn't flinch. "Okay. So tell me the rest."

Cain rubbed at the back of his neck, tried to ease the tightness pulling at the tendons there. "So I saw them, but they were so into what they were doing they didn't see me. I wanted to turn around and walk away, but my brain rooted my feet to the spot. I couldn't look away from what they were doing. It wasn't the actual sex that mesmerized me, though, it was the way they were so totally into each other that the house could have fallen down around them and they wouldn't have known. That was what pulled me in. They stared into each other's eyes so intently that the look between them was as much a part of the sex act as their body parts that were connected in the middle."

"You were envious of what they had," Luke responded gently. "There's no crime in that."

"Yes, I was." As memories of how he had felt in that moment flooded his senses and left him ashamed, Cain nodded. "But it was more than that. I was more than envious. I was furious while watching them share something I knew I could never have myself. My whole being was consumed with anger. I just had this feeling fill me up, this sensation that if I couldn't have what they had, then nobody else should have it either. It wasn't fair that they were so damn happy and besotted with each other that they couldn't even tell when someone else was in the room with them violating their intimacy. I wanted to tear them apart, but I finally snapped myself out of the anger before it took me over. I stepped back to leave, but for a split second, Cassie pulled out of the moment, and she looked up at me. When she did, I knew she could see in my eyes everything I'd felt just moments before."

"Damn." Luke whistled low. "That must have been tough for both of you."

"Yeah." Cain looked down, needing a moment, and rubbed a pattern into the flecked, worn suede of his tan boot with the tip of his finger. "We never spoke of it. I know she knows I love her and Con together, that I wish them nothing but the best for the whole of their life, but things changed after that. I can't say she out and out pitied me, but after that I noticed when Con got all touchy feely with her, and I was around, she would get him to back off. My presence inhibited her comfort, hindered her ability to be freely affectionate with her new husband. What made me feel the shittiest, though, was that I knew she wasn't doing it for herself; she was acting that way for me. That was when I knew I had to get out of there, not only for my sake, but also for theirs. That's why this cabin went up in record time."

Cain lifted his gaze back to Luke's, knowing that hiding wasn't acceptable with this man. "I always wanted to work exclusively with horses, so I settled on rehabilitating abused ones." He smiled sheepishly. "And that brings us to where I am today. So" -- he raised a brow in challenge -- "can your most embarrassing and humiliating moment top mine?" As soon as Cain said it, he wanted to beat his own ass. "I am so sorry, Luke." The clammy hand of mortification filled Cain whole. "With what happened to you with MacLesten, of course it can."

"No." Luke shook his head. "What went down with MacLesten wasn't humiliating and embarrassing on my part. It was a criminal act. I had nothing to do with it other than being on the painful receiving end of someone else's bigotry."

"I'm glad to hear you say that." Cain knew sympathy flooded his gaze, something Luke didn't want, but he couldn't control the emotion. "When you first told me what that bastard did to you, I wasn't sure you weren't taking some blame on yourself that wasn't yours to own."

"The therapy is making a big difference." Luke expelled a breath, one that appeared as if it had come up through his entire being. He met Cain's gaze head-on, without flinching. "So is working here, doing something I love. Being around you helps more than anything else ever could."

The temperature in the open room raised at least ten degrees, and Cain's cock speared up against his jeans in immediate response. *Damn it.* He shifted in his chair.

"But that's not what you want to hear about right now." Luke changed the subject quickly, and Cain breathed easier once more. "You want a fair exchange for your most embarrassing and humiliating moment. And boy, let me tell you" -- Luke chuckled and shook his head -- "do I ever have one."

Cain slid down in his chair and got comfortable. "All right then. Lay it on me."

Luke's neck flushed rosy pink, but unfathomable light filled his eyes. "So, I'm gonna tell you about the time when I was fifteen years old, and I swore to anyone who would listen that I'd seen a great, winged man flying high in the night sky."

Across the span of the table, Cain gulped.

# CHAPTER TWELVE

Cain blinked and shoved his weight straight back against his chair. His gaze landed on Luke's, surely with more wildness than he wanted this man to see right now. "Wh-what…?" Cain cleared his throat of the thickness lodged there and tried again. "What did you say?"

Smirking, Luke pushed back in his chair and stretched his legs out long in front of him, crossing them at the ankles. "You look about like my mom did when I told her what I'd seen. She said I must have fallen asleep and been dreaming. Well, I probably did fall asleep, I will admit that, but when I woke up, I know what I saw skimming right above the trees in front of me."

Cain dug his fingers into his biceps, hard, painful enough to leave bruises. With a silent command to settle, he forced himself not to squirm any more than normal. Cocking his head a little bit to the side, he inquired, "What exactly did you see?"

"A man," Luke answered. "But at the same time, not a man. I have decent eyesight, and there was enough of a moon shining that night that I could see the richest looking, fresh-new-penny-colored skin covering a body that looked like an exaggerated, ultra-pumped-up shape of a man. But he had these massive wings; only not feathery like a bird, but more like a bat. His hair was long and dark, but he was definitely male." Luke's cheeks bloomed with color. "He was naked, and I could see that his...um...parts, were the same as mine, only bigger, and thicker, and erect."

Christ, Luke had just described Cain in his Naverto body to the detail -- even the hair; Cain had worn it long back then. He was so damned careful about where he flew, but somehow teenage Luke had seen him.

"Where exactly were you when you saw this *thing*?" Cain asked very carefully, throwing just a hint of skepticism into his tone.

"Two counties north of here. We moved around to a lot of the neighboring areas after my mom had her accident." Luke's jaw clenched just the slightest bit as he shared, the only action to betray that he cared. "You can only intrude on the generosity of neighbors for so long before they want their homes back. When the last welcome mat got pulled out from under us, we started moving. You should have seen me, Hawk. Thirteen years old, driving our car like I had every right to do it. Thank God I was big for my age, and we kept to back roads so I wouldn't be noticed."

"I bet that was terrifying for you." Empathy for Luke filled Cain. "Being behind the wheel with your mom and little sister as your passengers must have been scary. A kid can know the mechanics of a car well enough to operate it, but to have the instincts, experience, and confidence it takes to drive it safely is another thing entirely."

"Yeah." A world of responsibility weighed within the breath of that one word. Luke must have realized it, because he shook his head and wiped the moment of vulnerability off of his face, hiding it from Cain entirely. In a flash, a cocky grin took its place. "But that doesn't have anything to do with how embarrassed I was when I became the laughingstock of my ninth grade class. I went to school the next day and told everyone about this mythical thing I'd seen on my trip into the woods the night before. Man" -- Luke laughed -- "talk about shooting right up to the top of the geeky outcast list in one short day. Damn it, I was never so glad when six months rolled around and we moved again. A couple of years later we ended up here. Suffice it to say, I learned at that point not to speak about anything I wasn't prepared to be made fun of over."

*Like being gay.* Cain filled in the blank for Luke.

"But you never forgot what you saw that night," Cain said. "You remember the details of your subsequent embarrassment as equally as you recall the specifics of that flying beast."

"No." Luke lifted his attention from his fingers gliding back and forth over the wood grain of the table and made eye contact with Cain once more. "My memories of that flying beast in the woods are a thousand times more vivid than the other. You see, I hadn't really defined anything I was feeling at that point in my life; I just knew I didn't get excited at the thought of getting with a girl the way the other guys in my class did. But when I saw that body circling and soaring in the sky that night, so precisely sculpted and male in every way, I couldn't pretend I didn't know what I wanted anymore. I got more than excited by the thought of seeing some otherworldly creature. I got incredibly turned on by the fact that it was male. I got hard that night, Hawk, and for the first time it wasn't because I was touching and arousing myself; it was because I was responding to him."

"Shit." Cain immediately reacted to Luke's confession. His cock went stiff as a lead pipe, and he had a damn hard time hiding it. "Are you saying what I think you're saying?"

Luke nodded. "I wanted that powerful male being to take me, to do things to me." Luke's eyes were alight with memories in a way that stoked Cain's blood to furious, hot life. "I had explicit, sexual dreams of him and me together for a long time after -- of him arrogantly commanding me to pleasure him, of him showing me what it was going to be like to be had by a man."

*Fucking shit.* Cain's need went in one direction, and he no longer had the power to deny it. "Come here, Luke." He pushed his chair back and spread his legs. "Come stand right in front of me."

"What are you doing?"

"Uh-uh." Cain shook his head; he stared at Luke with unquenched, unfiltered desire showing in his eyes. "Would your flying beast let you ask questions like that?"

Acutely tuned in to every move Luke made, Cain stared, and he saw when the spark of understanding finally hit the other man. Saw the shiver roll through him too.

"No," Luke finally responded. "No, sir, he wouldn't."

Somewhere deep within himself, Cain found arrogance, and he let free a truly wicked smile. "Then don't ask me either. I'm your beast tonight." With leisurely slowness, Cain unbuckled his belt and opened the fly on his jeans. He reached inside his underwear and pulled his swollen, hard cock out in the open. "Suck me, Luke." He held his prick up for the taking. "Get down on your knees and suck me off until I come."

Luke didn't move on command, and heat immediately burned like fire through Cain. Swallowing through sudden nervousness, he met Luke's gaze. "It's... It's okay, you know." Discomfort slipped Cain out of the forceful beast character. "About...you know...taking my semen."

"I believe you." Luke bit his lip. "I'm okay too. What you did last night is fine."

"I know. You told me." As Cain captured Luke's gaze again, he spread his legs wide. The corner of his mouth once again lifted in a wickedly confident smile. "Now get the hell down here and take my cock."

"Yes, sir." Luke folded between Cain's knees, and Cain's dick wept heavy drops of precum. As Luke ran his tongue over his lips, clearly excited to play out a fantasy he didn't understand was reality, the sight of him mesmerized Cain. Cain hummed with life in a way he'd never experienced before Luke had come to work for him two months ago. He didn't know how this could possibly be happening, how they'd inadvertently found each other, but he took it as a sign that what they were doing together was supposed to happen. Cain couldn't tell Luke the full truth, of course, and his fate couldn't be changed, but he would take to his grave the belief that the small amount of time they had together was right, and that they were meant to be together.

Luke looked up, only inches away from Cain's jutting cock, his eyes all sultry in a way that somehow still seemed innocent. "Should I lick the drop of your seed off the tip first, sir, before I begin?"

Cain couldn't hold back the growl of anticipation that rumbled through his body. "Oh, yeah. Do it."

Luke darted out his tongue and caught the pearl of moisture, grazing Cain's slit as he did it. In reaction, Cain jerked his hips off the chair.

Uttering, "Good Christ," Cain forced himself to settle back in the chair. He knew his reaction was more a response of anticipation than actual sensation, but Cain swore he'd felt that nubby point shoot all the way down to his toes. "More. Please." He couldn't look away. "More."

Just like in his work, Luke was eager to please. He parted his lips around the bulbous head of Cain's thick penis and took him inside, surrounding Cain's nerve-sensitive flesh with moist, warm suction in a way that stole Cain's very breath from his lungs. Cain's response came from more than the tactile sensation of having his dick in another man's mouth -- although that was profoundly pleasurable in a way Cain never could have dreamed possible. More than that, what had Cain pumping his hips with each drag, was watching Luke's head bob up and down in his lap as the man eagerly took Cain's cock in his mouth. That sight, Luke so enthusiastically blowing him, aroused all of Cain's passions to the point of explosion.

"Oh Christ, that feels so good." Cain groaned, nearly breathless already. He wrapped his hands around the seat of the chair and held on, needing something to keep him from sliding right to the floor in a puddle of exquisite sensation. Everything happened much too fast; the tight tingling already crept closer inside Cain's body, pulling him toward ejaculation. "Do more, Luke. Fast. Eat my balls before I come."

It didn't get that far. Luke reached in Cain's underwear to pull out his heavy sac, and Cain could not stand to feel more than Luke's big, capable hand holding his nuts. "Never mind, never mind." Cain grabbed Luke's head and kept it buried in his crotch. "No… time…" Cain's legs suddenly stretched out taut and straight, seizing completely.

Cain let loose with his release, and he stabbed his cock deep down Luke's throat. His orgasm ripped through him with a force he could not control. The power practically lodged his nuts up in his body cavity as liquid life shot through his painfully hard cock and filled Luke's mouth to overflowing with seed. His entire body jerked, and he came so fucking much it didn't surprise him to feel wetness dribble down into his pubic hair.

In the aftermath, with Cain still trying to catch his breath, his penis slid from between Luke's lips. His shaft bounced, still half hard, against Luke's cheek.

"I'm sorry I couldn't take it all," Luke said as he wiped his chin clean. Christ, just seeing shiny spittle mixed with Cain's cum on Luke's chin was enough to start reheating Cain's blood.

"It has been awhile since I've given anyone a blowjob," Luke added, "and it was more than I expected. I'll do better next time."

A deep chuckle rumbled through Cain's system, a full bodied laugh he didn't try to hold back. He grabbed the back of Luke's neck and pulled the man up against his chest until they were eye to eye. Equals again. "Darlin'." Cain used his first endearment. Ever. Christ, he liked the way it felt tripping off his tongue. He pulled Luke to him, skated his lips across Luke's swollen mouth, and then nibbled at the edge for just a second before pulling away. Finding Luke's gaze again, he grinned. "That was the best damn blowjob I've ever had." No need to tell Luke it was the only blowjob he'd ever had. "Swallowing or not."

"I'm glad you liked it, sir." Luke leaned up and caught Cain's mouth in a lingering kiss, but pulled away and stood up before Cain could take Luke's mouth the way he craved.

Luke leaned back against the table, and a mischievous smile tilted his passion-reddened lips. "But I have something else I think you'll like even more." He kicked his leg up and settled his heel on Cain's knee. "Help me get my boots off."

Taking the worn leather of Luke's black cowboy boot in hand, Cain tugged, releasing the snug fit until the boot slid off and fell to the floor with a soft thud. Without looking away from Luke's powerful, steady gaze, Cain slid his hand under the hem of Luke's jeans, feeling up the heat of his calf until he touched the edge of Luke's sock and peeled that off too. Damn it, there was something about helping this man undress that had Cain's cock stirring and pushing against his stomach. *Already. Again.* Luke's big, bare foot curled around Cain's kneecap and then made a slapping sound as it hit the pine floor; he then quickly filled the vacated spot on Cain's knee with his other booted foot. Cain repeated the process.

By the time Luke started working open the buttons on his shirt, Cain's breathing had shifted to something shallow, filled with desire. He dug his own boots into the flooring and forced himself to remain seated while Luke shrugged his shirt off, revealing his stunning, smooth chest and finely hewn shoulders and arms.

As Cain dragged his focus down to Luke's crotch, where the man worked open his silver belt buckle, Cain said, "I'm channeling your beast right now, Luke. I hope you plan on getting fucked at the end of this little striptease, because that's where this show is heading. Just so you know."

"Patience, Hawk," Luke advised. He slid the zipper of his snug jeans down smoothly and parted the placket in a V, revealing a hint of the gray underwear. With a turn, Luke presented Cain with his backside and hooked his thumbs in the waistband of his jeans. "I think you're gonna like this."

Cain locked his gaze with laser precision on the tight jeans cupping Luke's firm buttocks. Memories of that ass split open and accepting his entry tore through Cain with the destructive power of a tornado. Sweat popped out on his forehead as a little river of pre-ejaculate streamed out of his dick. "I think you know how much I like your ass. I --" When the waistband of those jeans and underwear started sliding down, and the cleft of Luke's ass appeared, Cain staggered to a stop. Swallowing until he felt moisture in his mouth, Cain tried again. "I thought I proved that last ni…"

Right then Luke bent at the waist, pushed his jeans down over the hills of his scarred buttocks, and then down his legs, showing himself in all of his beautiful, naked glory. Words, comprehension, coherency -- hell, everything drained out of Cain. Cain fastened his gaze on one thing and one thing only: a two-inch, black plastic disc that sat covering right where Luke's asshole would be.

*Good Christ, he has a butt plug in his ass.* Cain had certainly heard of them, but in his quest not to give himself fake versions of what he hadn't thought he could have in real life, he definitely hadn't ever seen one. And he'd most assuredly never seen one in use, shoved up deep inside a body. Cain hadn't thought it possible to want to fuck a man more than he'd wanted to screw Luke last night, but he found that right then, at his kitchen table, he did.

*Holy hell.*

When Cain didn't say anything right away, nerves and insecurity got the better of Luke. He spun back to face Cain quickly, grabbing at the table behind him to steady himself. His backside hit the edge of the wood, bumping at the plug buried in his rectum. A little shot of pleasure rippled inside Luke's ass, and he gasped. Cain watched him, his blue, blue gaze wide open, clearly full of shock, and Luke scrambled to stand upright.

"I wanted to be ready for you in case you wanted me again," Luke explained quickly. "I wasn't trying to be presumptuous; it was just that you didn't want a lot of foreplay last ni --"

His voice rough and hard, Cain interrupted, "You've had that thing inside you all night. The entire time we've been sitting here eating and talking." Cain finally raised his gaze up from Luke's cock, and intensity burned fiery blue in his eyes. "During the entire time" -- Cain stood, and his big, wide, intimidating presence took over the room -- "when you did what you did to me?"

"Yes." Luke swallowed thickly. "I'm sorry if --"

"You son of a mother." Cain closed in on Luke, wrapped his arm around the younger man's waist, and jerked their bodies together. He tilted Luke's head until their faces touched. "Keeping this little secret to yourself" -- Cain delved down the small of Luke's back and rubbed his fingers over the base of the plug, jostling the toy torturously inside Luke's channel -- "when it has got to be one of the hottest damn things I've ever seen in my life."

In a shot, Cain lifted Luke in his strong arms and deposited him on the table. Seconds later, he had Luke flat on his back. As Luke stared up at Cain through heavy lids, watching as Cain tore off his clothes, his mouth watered.

"There's stuff," Luke shared, excitement already humming in his blood. "Condoms and lube in the bag I brought." He rolled over and slid across the table, stretching his arm over the side until he snagged the paper bag off the floor.

A strong hand wrapped around Luke's ankle, dragged him across the table, and then rolled him to his back once more. Cain locked his stare on Luke, and confidence shone so bright in the bigger man it made Luke shiver. Cain no longer seemed at all modest about his nudity or that his thick, heavy penis stuck straight out from his body.

"Now who's impatient?" Cain teased Luke with his own words. As Cain grabbed the bag and dumped the contents onto the table, snatching the box of condoms as it hit the wood, more fire flashed in his eyes.

Luke swallowed; his Adam's apple bobbed as he watched Cain roll a clear condom smoothly down his prick and tuck the end at the base. Good God, Luke hadn't done anything sexual in four years and now he was about to get fucked two nights in a row. Fucked by someone he liked on a gut level more than any other man with whom he'd had sex. Moisture pooled beneath Luke's back, his core temperature boiling as Cain squeezed lube on his hand and rubbed it all over his prick, covering the condom as if he'd been doing it forever. Man, the guy paid attention and learned quickly.

"I didn't buy the condoms in town," Luke quickly remembered to share. "I had them in my bag from before. When we need more

I'll drive to a little place about thirty miles north of here, just off the interstate. I would never be careless and give us away. Please know that."

Something dark passed through Cain's gaze right then, unsettling Luke. The shadows then disappeared before Luke could figure out what they meant.

"Uh-uh," Cain said instead, grinning that feral smile he'd worn right before he'd ordered Luke to go down on him. "The beast doesn't care about stuff like that. According to you, the beast cares about one thing." Cain wrapped his arms around Luke's thighs and yanked him to the edge of the table, until Luke's ass nearly hung over the edge. Cain arranged Luke's legs, splaying them out straight across the width of the table, and in the process split Luke open wide. The angle dislodged the plug buried in Luke's ass; Luke grunted and clenched his muscles around the toy, trying to keep it inside. With a whip fast move, Cain slid his hand up the back of Luke's thigh and deliberately pushed the plug back inside his ass until it could go no farther.

Cain then slid his wickedly passionate gaze from Luke's ass, to over his jutting cock, up his heaving chest, until he landed on Luke's eyes. Luke shivered in response. "What does the beast want, Luke?" Cain asked, his tone thick and heated. "What do you want your flying man to do to you?"

Luke licked his lips as anticipation, and maybe a little bit of fear, rolled through him. "He wants to fuck me." Sharing his fantasy of many years elicited another shiver. "And I want him to."

"With this?" Cain reached down and pulled at the plug, dislodging it almost all the way from Luke's fluttering passage, and then pushed the silicone back inside. "Or with this?" Cain stroked the length of his engorged cock, making the shaft rear even higher against his stomach.

"You, Hawk." Desire hit Luke like a bullet to his gut, bleeding him raw. "I want you."

Cain growled, bared his teeth, and pulled the plug out of Luke in a shot. The toy thudded as it hit the floor and rolled. Before Luke's ass even had time to recover and snap shut, Cain bore down on

Luke's opening and in one long drive shoved his prick deep inside Luke's ass, sending Luke straight to ecstasy.

Luke had prepared himself for Cain's thickness this time, but the intimacy of the invasion still shocked his senses and had him scrambling for something on which to hold. He reached out for the edge of the table, but grabbed onto his legs instead, and he tangled his fingers with Cain's, who still held Luke's thighs wide apart. Grasping for purchase, Luke moved his hands and grabbed tightly to Cain's strong wrists instead, while at the same time curled his tailbone up to receive the full measure of Cain's eager fucking. Goddamn, it was good, and Luke fought hard to keep his eyes from sliding closed in the throes of pleasure. He didn't want to miss a minute.

"Like this, Luke?" Cain pushed the words out roughly through clenched teeth. He pounded Luke's channel hard, vigorously, using enough force to rock the table. Even with the plug to prepare him, Luke knew Cain's taking was rough, the toy barely having stretched Luke enough to accommodate Cain's thickness and fierce thrusts. "Is this how your beast took you? Thoroughly enough to leave an imprint?" Cain drove in to the hilt, ground his pubes against Luke's flesh, and then dug his fingers into Luke's hips and held him still for a half-dozen sharp, knifing thrusts. Each slam from Cain's cock slapped his big balls against Luke's tender flesh and threw another layer of base sounds into the air. "Invasive enough to ruin you for any other man but him?"

"For you, Hawk, for you." Luke looked up into Cain's deep blue eyes, without any filters over whatever might be showing in his. He couldn't. To hide would feel like a lie. He grabbed Cain's forearms and held on tight. "Oh God, Hawk…" Luke tried to roll up to meet Cain's wonderful downward fucking every time it happened, needing to feel every possible piece of this man he could. "You're ruining me for anyone but you."

Something seemed to snap in Cain; he crawled up on the table, shoved Luke across the surface, and braced his knees on the surface. Suddenly Cain lifted Luke partially off the table, and only Luke's shoulders rested on the hard wood; Luke groaned and arched the rest of his body in sexual offering. Cain kept them connected with only a hard grip on Luke's thighs; he held Luke open for the repeated, erratic drive of his cock; each slam of his hips buried his shaft in Luke's ass to the root again and again.

Just as Luke groaned with pleasure, Cain ordered, in a guttural voice, "Play with your prick." Rivulets of sweat poured down his torso. "I want to see you come."

Luke's body provided all the slick moisture he needed. He quickly stroked his cock in compliance and started to pump his length in hard drags from base to tip. Luke's chest heaved, and he parted his lips to gather in breath another way, the culmination of everything his body was being forced to feel overwhelming him in every way. As Luke's cock screamed to life by his own hand, and his blistering hot ass took a physical coupling from Cain in a deep, primal way -- unlike anything Luke had ever experienced -- Luke whimpered with deep cries of pleasure.

"I'm close, Hawk...I'm so close." Luke reached down and grabbed his balls, pulling them away from his body so he couldn't come. His nuts were so fucking sensitive they hurt, but for him, this was only about what Cain wanted. "I'm coming for you... Oh God, you're fucking me good!" Luke stared into Cain's eyes as the tight edge of control slipped from his body. "Tell me what you want. Tell me right now."

"Straight up," Cain growled. He had Luke's thighs clamped in the vise of his forearms and biceps, the hold strong enough to cut off circulation. He manipulated Luke's body, jerking Luke's hole against his cock repeatedly. "Straight up, like a fountain." Cain pummeled Luke's tight chute like a battering ram; the aggression in the man threw Luke so deep into the fantasy they'd begun this mating with that he swore he saw hints of the beast living in Cain's eyes.

One more good pounding of Luke's tender channel, and Cain ordered, "Shoot right NOW!"

Luke let go of his sac and he pumped his fist up and down his dick fast, one, two, three times, and then howled like an animal as orgasm tore through his body. Fierce, physical pleasure, mixed with ejaculate, raced from Luke's balls up through his shaft, and he shot a jetting geyser of semen at least a foot into the air before his cum rained down in hot splashes onto his stomach, arm, and hand.

With a thick pole still buried in his clenching ass, Luke watched Cain take in what he'd asked for, watched the man's eyes brighten with pure light. Tan skin pulled taut over Cain's face, and his lips peeled back, baring his teeth. Luke observed every raw nuance Cain let show through his face and body; a split second later Cain cried out and slammed Luke's ass one last time. He then tucked his shaft in balls deep and warmed Luke's aching channel with the welcoming heat of his release, even through the barrier of a condom.

Rigid in the throes of coming, Cain then grunted and fell on top of Luke. The air between them was hot and humid; together they panted and struggled to get their breath back. Luke curled his arms around Cain's back and shifted them to their sides. He gasped as Cain's penis slid out of his body, causing a small frisson of pleasure to zing right through him. *Shit.* Luke jerked, out of his control, and then met Cain's knowing gaze as he spurted a second wave of cum. His seed landed on Cain's belly. *Oh God.* Heated burned through Luke's flesh and he wanted to bury his face in Cain's shoulder to hide.

In reaction, Cain reached down, smeared his fingers in the stuff, and brought his cum-smeared digits to his lips. "So" -- Cain sucked his fingers one at a time -- "I have what I want for dessert." He licked his last shiny digit clean. And Luke, watching how Cain took such pleasure in tasting Luke's essence, couldn't look away from the beauty and light shining in Cain's blue eyes. Then the man smiled and said to Luke, "But can I get you something?"

For the rest of his life, Luke would swear he'd never laughed so hard or felt so light and free as he did in that moment, entwined on the table with Cain.

# Chapter Thirteen

From a thousand feet in the air, Cain let the warm scent of ram fill his nostrils, and his muscles tensed in anticipation of the kill. His human mind might not like doing this but his demon instinct understood and savored the task, hungry almost to the point of starvation for a fresh kill.

Cain spotted the ram in the open valley under the cover of darkness; the animal surely thought the moonless night shielded his presence from predators above him on the food chain. Munching on rich, wild grass, intent upon his own meal, the ram had its guard down, and Cain took advantage of his distraction.

Shifting his Naverto wings from open and gliding to narrow and sleek, Cain became a missile as he dove for the earth and his unsuspecting prey. When he was mere feet away from the animal, he spread his wings full and wide, pulling up just short of the ground. The ram looked up, but it was too late, and Cain tore through its throat with his teeth.

The animal thrashed and tried to cry out, but Cain had already torn apart its gullet with the strength in his jaw, and now the ram only spewed blood from its neck whenever it tried to make a sound. Cain took the ram down quickly, wrapping his arms around its muscular body and ripping through its torso with the sharpness of his clawed nails, and pulled the animal's heart from its chest, ending its life fast so that it did not suffer.

When the ram's body no longer moved, Cain rolled it on its back and sliced it open from stem to stern with the razor precision of his claws, and then ripped back its skin and fur to reveal the muscle beneath. This was what Cain's demon body needed for survival; he tore off a piece of breast, digging in. Blood smeared his face as he gobbled, chewed, and swallowed, his taste buds hating the raw meat that was still warm with the vestiges of life, even as his body shrieked with joy at having the sustenance it needed to survive.

Cain crouched in the grass on his haunches and ate, acknowledging that with the distraction of Luke he'd put off a kill until it had become a searing pain in his gut not to have this fresh, raw meat. It wasn't that Luke was hovering and not allowing Cain a moment to slip away to take care of his demon needs; it was Cain's own neglect of this side of himself that had nearly done him in.

Luke didn't push for time with Cain, and a part of Cain was immensely grateful for that. Without words spoken between them, Luke seemed to understand that he was to go back to his room to sleep at night. The man appeared to harbor no hostility over the fact that they couldn't sleep together snuggled close and then rise in the morning and go to work as if they were a happily paired couple.

Even as Cain's need for secrecy clutched that gift from Luke close in fisted hands, another part of him wondered if Luke didn't press because he didn't consider them a real couple. A stabbing uncertainty about mating rituals ate at Cain when he was alone in bed after Luke's amiable departures. A lack of education about relationships made Cain second-guess whether or not Luke only considered them fucking partners. Maybe Luke didn't crave a whole night tucked in Cain's arms in the same way Cain already dreamed about holding Luke.

A lack of firsthand knowledge, and worry -- both distractions of a sort he'd never had to worry about in his past -- had taken over most of Cain's thoughts lately, and in doing so had pushed to the back of his mind that the time had grown near for his monthly kill. Sudden shooting pains in his stomach that night had reminded Cain that timing was vital in this feeding schedule, and that if he forgot it, his demon core would let him know painfully. In the valley now, Cain tore off another slab of meat and fed the beast -- half of himself -- satiating him at least for a little while longer.

As Cain pushed the blood-rich meat down his throat, he had the cynical thought that it was entirely possible he would be dead before another thirty days rolled around and he had to kill again. The Naverto Traveler would sense the change in Cain soon enough and come to investigate. At that point, Cain's transgression would be discovered. Then it was only a matter of being transported to Wales to stand before the Council of Twelve, followed by his execution for the crime of fornicating with a male.

The muscles in Cain's back started twitching, and without having to look, Cain knew he had company. His elongated ears picked up the subtlest rustling of grass. Just as quickly, though, his hackles settled, and he knew he was not in danger.

"Come closer," he told the newcomer. Rather than turn away from his meal, he used the nail on his pointer finger to cut off another piece of flesh for himself. "There's plenty enough to share."

Within seconds a large gray wolf approached from Cain's left. It moved closer on cautious paws and sniffed, starting at Cain's clawed feet, moving its wet nose up his naked leg until it apparently decided Cain did not pose a threat. Cain continued to eat, and he paid the wolf no direct attention. After a full minute of sizing him up, the animal tilted its head back and made a warbling sound in the back of its throat. Three gangly-legged pups joined it, eyeing the carcass of the ram with obvious hunger in their silver gazes.

The color of their eyes made Cain think of Luke's pale gray gaze. With a snort of disgust at his one-track mind, Cain wiped his bloody hands as best he could in the soft grass.

"He's all yours, Momma." Cain stood. "I'm full for another month."

Cain was used to the company of other critters in this situation. The scent of blood and death often brought an investigation by another animal to the site of his kill. Curiosity, hope of leftovers, scavenging, starvation -- all were motivating factors for an animal's search. Cain understood the survival instinct on a very basic level, and he always shared what was left after he'd taken his fill. There was no reason not to. Plus, on the rare chance that the remains of the body were discovered by humans, it had the added benefit of looking like a wild animal kill.

Cain gave the momma and her pups one last affectionate glance and then launched his body into the air, ready to leave this part of his life and get back to the other.

After all, Luke was in that one.

———

CAIN SOARED HIGH IN THE black night sky, absorbing all the smells and sights and sounds in existence far below him. The nutrients from his recent meal heightened his senses almost painfully. After a feeding a fireplace smelled like a forest fire and the sounds of a child's whimpering cry reached his ears with the volume of a tortured animal's screams.

Suddenly Cain's sharp gaze narrowed on a truck traveling down a solitary dirt road in the distance; a long private road Cain knew well. He knew the truck. Knew the man who owned it too.

*Justin MacLesten.*

Tonight, the man was alone.

Cain didn't think. His demon blood raced too close to the surface to be denied, and Cain was in too close agreement with what it wanted to try to fight it. He aimed toward earth, down through the cold, high atmosphere, without feeling the burn of the air as it raced over his flesh, much in the way he'd experienced when diving to take down that ram such a short time ago. Cain had one goal in mind and nothing would distract him from getting there.

He swooped down with arms stretched out and grabbed the back of the truck in his grip. At the same time, he spread his wings to their full, glorious breadth, using them as a parachute while he dug his heels into the dirt and dragged the big double cab truck to a jerking, tilting stop.

Cain then leaped over the length of the vehicle and down to the driver's side door in a flash. He shoved his hand through the open window and took hold of MacLesten's beefy neck before the man could move. "Don't even think about going for that shotgun," Cain warned. The tone of his demon voice registered much deeper than his human one; the sounds that came up through his throat were scratchy and gravelly in a way that proved that in this moment he was not human. Cain still had the ram's blood on the exaggerated mountain of his face and the unnatural thickness of his forearms, so he knew that on top of looking like a demon from hell, he looked like one who'd just come from a massacre.

MacLesten's watery brown eyes widened with absolute horror, and Cain knew a moment's understanding of the twisted pleasure his native clan received in frightening humans just for the sheer joy of it. By the time he was finished Cain wanted this man crapping his pants and believing with all of his being that he was being watched by forces bigger and more powerful than himself.

Cain tightened his hand around MacLesten's neck and hauled him out of his vehicle through the window, smiling when the man's shoulders and arms scraped against the tight space with enough force to make him cry out in pain. With that hint of satisfaction already burning in him, Cain dragged MacLesten's sorry carcass around to the front of the truck and pinned him there like a cockroach on a board, its little legs twitching as it struggled in futility to get away. *Good.* Let this bastard feel completely powerless about his situation and unable to do anything about it. Goddamn it, he'd done so much worse to Luke.

"Who…what…Who are you?" MacLesten's eyes bugged half out of his head; he gurgled, trying to breathe through the hold Cain had on his neck.

With great reluctance, Cain shifted his hand a little bit lower to hold MacLesten trapped to the truck by his sternum instead, not wanting the man to pass out before he'd gotten the message.

"What are you?" MacLesten whined. "What do you want with me?"

Cain chuckled, no trace of humor detected in the sound. "I'm the manifestation of the blackness of your soul, Justin MacLesten, and you've been a very, very bad man lately, haven't you?"

"No, no, I haven't. I swear." Spittle shot out of MacLesten's mouth along with his ridiculous denial. "I'm a good Christian who faithfully serves the Lord, I promise."

Cain just barely reined in the fierce need to tear the treacherous bastard to shreds for that galling untruth. He couldn't, however, overcome the need to knee MacLesten in the balls, and he smiled with grim satisfaction as the man shrieked in pain and his face paled considerably.

"Lie to yourself all you want, MacLesten." The need for vengeance sat heavy on Cain's heart. He jerked MacLesten up by his shirt until the man dangled in the air with his boots a foot off the ground. "But I see everything. I know everything. I know how you mistreat your employees. Behind your locked doors, where you think you're safe, I see how you abuse your wife."

MacLesten's jaw fell open -- clearly shocked at being discovered -- and Cain raised an eyebrow in a sad sort of empty triumph. The bastard was so stupid. Cain had gone on a hunch with the claim of spousal abuse, yet it didn't even occur to MacLesten that his people had lives of their own and knew how to talk. The man simply assumed that because Cain had pronounced these facts that he must have some sort of divine insight into MacLesten's private life.

Cain yanked MacLesten's ugly face close, let him get a good look at the ram's blood still marring his mutated demon face. Flashing MacLesten a cold grin, Cain showed the man the raw flesh from the dead animal still stuck between his teeth. "I'm watching you, Justin MacLesten." Cain's voice was deadly soft near the man's ear. "I am the avenging angel of someone to whom you did a great deal of damage." Cain slid his gaze to MacLesten's rheumy one and let the man see the fires of hatred and revenge burning in his blue, blue gaze. Cain's eyes would be the one thing that could give his identity away, but MacLesten was far too afraid that the beast before him had been sent up from the very depths of hell to think Cain could actually exist as a human. "I'm warning you right now, if you hurt him again, or anyone else he loves, I will be coming for you. And just so you know, what you did to him will look like a day at the beach compared to what I will do to you."

With that, Cain threw MacLesten against the hood of his truck, where the asshole bounced against the metal, denting it, before he fell to the ground in a heap. Cain stood above him with a sneer curling his lips. In another first in his life, Cain took sick satisfaction in another person's pain.

MacLesten rolled to his side, and the sharp, metallic smell of blood attacked Cain's heightened senses. He looked down through the beams of the truck's headlights, so bright in the wake of his ultra clear sight it pained his head, and saw blood seeping from a fresh cut on the man's lower lip.

Dropping to a crouch next to MacLesten, Cain whispered in a viciously soft tone, "Don't forget my warning. Because I swear to you, as *God* is *my* witness, I will make you regret it if you do."

"Wait, wait!" MacLesten called out, his voice pathetically weak, as Cain moved back to leave.

Cain merely glanced over his shoulder and wings.

"Who have I hurt to so offend you?" The man scrambled to his knees and clasped his hands together in front of his stomach. "I'm sure it's just a misunderstanding, and can be cleared up if you give me a name and tell me what he said I did wrong."

Cain growled fiercely, bared his teeth, and took a menacing step forward.

"Wait! Wait!" MacLesten threw up his hands, cowering in obvious fear. "I meant no disrespect. I'm sure it was an honest mistake on your friend's part. Perhaps I can make restitution."

The stupid, egotistical bastard did not know when to shut up. Every asinine word he uttered only incited Cain's anger more. Cain strode forward, grabbed a big hunk of MacLesten's gray hair, and snapped the man's neck back until those clueless brown eyes looked straight up at him. "Not everyone is for sale, you son of a bitch." Cain leaned down in the man's face. "If you've hurt so many people that you can't figure out who I'm talking about, then perhaps it's best I just end your life now and spare this town's residents another day in your presence." Cain moved his other hand to MacLesten's neck and let the claws there -- lethal weapons against any weak human body -- prick MacLesten's skin until four points of blood started to drip down the man's throat. "What do you say?"

"No, no." Through the hold Cain had around MacLesten's neck, MacLesten's voice barely held sound. "I heard you loud and clear. Model citizen." He darted his focus all around in the darkness, clearly searching for aid that didn't exist. He eventually looked back up at Cain and whispered brokenly, "I've got it."

The acrid, foul smell of urine assaulted Cain's nostrils right then. Cain threw Justin MacLesten to the ground, perversely pleased that at least one of his goals had been achieved this night. The man had soiled himself. Cain would take what he could get. Because seeing this man, but knowing he couldn't kill him on Luke's behalf, disturbed Cain's emotional balance in a way he wasn't prepared to feel. The deep, violent emotions frightened Cain all the way to his core.

Cain backed away from the man on the ground, suddenly knowing that every second spent in Justin MacLesten's presence imprinted a black mark on his soul he might not ever be able to wipe away. Even with that knowledge, Cain couldn't erase the memory of Luke curled against his stomach in the aftermath of a nightmare -- a nightmare this man had caused.

With another guttural growl, unable to control the savage sounds coming from deep inside him, Cain warned, "Don't forget what I said. If I hear that you've hurt anyone else in this town, I'm coming for you." He gave a pointed look to the markings on MacLesten's throat. "Next time, I won't be nice."

With one last snarl, Cain hurled himself into the air, flapped his wings to achieve flight, and got away from the pure ugliness of the scene. As he flew toward home, he couldn't shake the darkness from his thoughts -- from his very being. He abruptly veered course, not wanting to risk even the smallest chance that Luke would seek him out while in the throes of this blackness that had settled on his heart.

⸺

CAIN EMERGED FROM THE SHADOWS into the pool of soft light emanating from the back porch of the main house, knowing this secluded entrance to Hawkins Ranch house was designed for demon cover. It had been constructed to protect all three brothers from prying eyes. Even if Connor no longer needed it, he would never cut down the strangely placed copse of trees and brush that practically butted up against the back of his home. He would never leave his chosen brothers without a place to emerge from their demon outings; he would never turn his back on what Cain and Caleb still were.

It wasn't Connor sitting out on the back porch enjoying the cool night air in the wee hours of this morning, though, it was Cassie. Even more unsettling to Cain's already troubled feelings? Something in his heart told him this woman was exactly the person he wanted to see.

Without words, Cassie reached her hand out in welcome, offering softness and comfort in that slight touch. She guided Cain to the mudroom inside the screen door. "Here." She handed him a small stack of towels. "Clean yourself up while I go get some clothes."

Cain squeezed Cassie's fingers, stalling her before she could go. "Don't wake up Connor or Caleb." The tremor in his hand must have betrayed his vulnerability. "I don't want anyone but you to see me right now."

"Of course." She nodded and offered him a small smile. "You start on that" -- she pointed at his bloody forearms -- "and I'll be right back with something for you to wear."

Cain did as told, quickly and efficiently. He was used to cleaning himself up after a kill. After throwing the bloody towels in the washer he went back outside and began to pace the length of the porch, waiting for Cassie to return. The sound of her bare feet padding through the kitchen hit him first, the steps growing louder as she reached the mudroom; by the time she got to the back door, he was waiting for her.

Cassie handed him jeans, underwear, and an old black flannel shirt. As she looked him up and down, she said, "You might want to change that up a bit" -- she waved her arm up and down his massive length -- "otherwise the clothes are going to be a little bit snug."

The heat of complete embarrassment rose under Cain's demon skin. He immediately turned his thoughts inward, focused on his features, and coaxed the demon to slide away, leaving Cain in his human form in its wake.

Sliding a glance Cassie's way, Cain muttered, "I don't know if I'm more mortified that I'm standing here naked in front of you" -- he changed into some of his old clothes -- "or that I'm so messed up right now I didn't even think to change back to human before approaching you."

"Well, I've already seen you naked." Cassie waggled her eyebrows, and sat back down. "So don't sweat over that. As for the other" -- her voice softened in accordance with her features -- "you know I don't judge or fear what you are."

"Thank you."

"You're welcome." Cassie smiled in that unassuming yet beautiful way of hers that Cain was sure had been the beginning of this young woman stealing his big brother's heart.

Cain started moving the length of the porch again, his pattern straight and deliberate. So uncertain of the foreign feelings of rage, fear, and uncertainty coursing through his insides right now, he purposefully shifted the topic of conversation to her. "I won't ask when you possibly could have seen me naked," he commented as he raised a brow her way again. "I'll just assume it was accidental and happened in the six years we lived in the same house."

"Well" -- Cassie raised an eyebrow right back, chuckling as she did -- "you'd be right on at least one of those counts."

Cain shook his head and tried not to think of a teenage girl peeking on him in the shower or while he slept. "Saucy little wench."

"That's what your brother says. So" -- Cassie kicked her feet up on the porch railing, cutting off Cain's pacing path -- "Luke is doing a good job for you."

"Yep."

"And you like him."

"Of course I do." Cain shot Cassie a carefully orchestrated, exasperated look. "He's a helluva good worker. What's not to like?"

"Of course he is," Cassie replied, just as smoothly. "But that's not what I'm talking about, and you know it. I've seen you guys together many times, mostly when I came to your place to take care of Luke's back. You look at him with hunger and longing when you don't think he can see. You care about him, Cain. More than you thought you would. Perhaps even more than you thought you *could?* Yes?"

*Damn.* This young woman who'd invaded his and his brothers' lives nine years ago was a cunning and intelligent one. Damned insightful too. She had witnessed too much during her visits while caring for Luke's back. A task he had asked her to do. *Shit.* Cain loved Cassie, but he could only be grateful he wasn't the one married to her. He did not envy how often his brother must have to stay on his toes to keep up with her.

*Or maybe I do envy him.* Maybe that was the problem. A problem Cassie had been able to cut right through the bullshit bravado in Cain and see it for the truth it hid.

"Christ, Cassie," Cain confessed in a rush. "I care about Luke so damn much that I easily could have killed for him tonight." Cain recalled his hand automatically wrapping around MacLesten's thick neck and pricking with his claws until he drew blood. "Hell, I very nearly did."

Cassie's expression didn't change. Didn't register shock or horror at all. She merely said, "MacLesten, huh?"

Cain's jaw fell slack. "Luke told you what Justin MacLesten did to him?"

"Oh, honey." Pain etched Cassie's features in a way that gave everything she already knew about Luke's situation away. "I'm the one Luke called from that line cabin when he could finally move enough to get himself some help. I'm the one who drove him all the way to Billings because he refused to be taken to a hospital anywhere closer. He didn't want there to be a chance anyone could guess he'd basically been violated in his own backyard. Luke feared his mother and sister seeing him like that and then correctly guessing he hadn't gotten hurt in a bar fight. I've kept his secret, even from Connor. Luke told me he confided in you, though. You and I, and his councilor, are the only people who know what happened to him."

"No," Cain corrected, his blood heating to boiling again. "Justin MacLesten knows the truth too. And I have to tell you, Cassie, I have never felt such a desire to hurt and maim and kill as I did when I saw that bastard tonight. Nothing mattered to me more in that moment than scaring the hell out of him in retribution for what he did to Luke. Not discovery of who and what I am, not the prospect of being jailed for assault, not my own safety. I wanted to terrify him. And when I successfully did that, I wanted to hurt him in terrible ways, and then I wanted to end it by killing him."

"But you didn't." Cassie grabbed Cain's hand tightly in her smaller one. Tugging him down to his knees in front of her, she cupped his cheek gently. "You didn't, Cain. Instinctively, you knew when to pull back, and you did. You have the ultimate control over your actions, where a man like Justin MacLesten doesn't even accept that he should. When you get right down to it, that's what makes you a good man, and him one who has lost his humanity. That is the difference. Personal control and an inherent trust in yourself that you possess that control and humanity, no matter how tempting it is to let it go when you're angry. That's all that matters."

"Ohhh, man." Cain breathed out shakily. "I was so afraid to go home tonight. I couldn't risk Luke seeing me so rattled and unsettled like this. Even without the demon standing in front of him, I was afraid he would see the darkness and just *know*."

"So the question you have to ask yourself, my friend" -- Cassie drew Cain to his feet and kissed his cheek -- "is when are you going to start believing that you are good enough for Luke? When are you going to have enough faith in him to trust that he'll still like you back, even when he knows everything? Real love cannot grow in the shadow of secrets," she reminded him gently, with a little smile. "I seem to remember you and Caleb trying to get Connor to believe that not very long ago." She held up her ring finger and let her eternity wedding band twinkle in the porch light. "And look how that turned out."

"It's not the same thing." Christ, Cain had never told Cassie the consequences of acting on his attraction to men. His brothers would protect his fierce desire for privacy and never speak of it out of turn. Not even to Cassie. Cain could not break her heart and tell her the truth, not when she was so obviously happy that her brother-in-law and her best friend had hooked up. Not when it wouldn't matter anyway. The damage had already been done. Her knowing wouldn't change a damn thing. "It's just…it's just…" He shrugged, out of words. "It's different than you and Connor."

"No, it isn't," Cassie insisted. "But until you believe it, you will never have what you really want. You'll never really have Luke. But maybe I've said enough." She lifted on her tiptoes and pecked his cheek once more. "You know where the keys are, sweetie." With that, she opened the door and went inside. "Drive yourself home and get some sleep. Things will look better in the morning." She waved at him through the screen and then disappeared into the house.

Leaving Cain standing there alone, more confused and afraid than he'd ever been before. He *didn't* know that tomorrow would be better. No matter how much he wanted to, he couldn't believe everything would work out fine if he just had a little bit of faith.

His situation was not like his brother's and Cassie's.

It wasn't.

No amount of praying and believing would ever change it.

*Fuck.*

# Chapter Fourteen

A little after eight-thirty the next evening, a knock sounded at Cain's door.

"Come on in," Cain called out, having a better than decent idea of who it was. *Luke.* They had worked independent of each other today and hadn't really talked since Luke had gone back to his room two nights ago. Cain hated that Luke felt like he had to knock, even as gratitude for the unspoken respect for privacy flooded him. He just wished his life didn't make the small formality necessary. "It's not locked."

From where he stood at the bar, Cain glanced over his shoulder as the door opened. Upon seeing Luke enter, he automatically smiled. Christ, Cain had known it would be him, but just seeing him in that first moment after being apart still shot shivers down his spine. Tonight was no different, even with an inch of dust still covering Luke's jeans and shirt from his day of work.

"You got your mom home okay?" Cain asked as he went back to his task. "I only wonder because you left quite a while ago. Is everything all right?"

"She's fine." Luke came up behind Cain and peered around his shoulder. "But my sister was still at work, so Mom made me wash my face and hands and sit down to eat with her." Eying the roast beef sandwiches Cain was making, he added, "Which was about as adventurous as what you're fixing here." Sliding his arm around Cain's waist, Luke buried his face against the nape of Cain's neck. He planted a soft kiss there that turned Cain's knees to jelly. "Mmmm... You've just had a shower." Kissing his way past Cain's ear, he inhaled again, then purred, "You smell so good."

*Damn it.* Two minutes in Luke's presence and Cain's dick already stirred in his pants. "Just Ivory soap and Head and Shoulders."

As Luke settled his chin on Cain's shoulder, he chuckled. "That is so you, Hawk." Amusement laced Luke's words, and Cain didn't have to see the man's face to know he wore a smile. "Only you would admit you have a dandruff issue as part of a casual conversation." Luke caressed Cain's abdomen through his T-shirt in an easy, slow circle, and the sensation tingled through Cain so wonderfully it made his hands unsteady around the butter knife he held. "My mom wanted me to say thank you again, by the way. She really enjoyed spending the afternoon out here." Luke laughed, and loving warmth filled the sound. "She's going to send you a card in the mail and everything, telling you in written word how sweet you are. She's very sincere, and what you did meant a lot to her. I hope you don't think it's corny."

Whatever it was, it squeezed painfully at Cain's core. "I can't tell you the last time someone sent me a card in the mail." His heart thumped hard against his sternum. "For anything. It'll probably tickle me so damn much that I'll prop it up on top of the bookshelf and leave it there for the rest of the year. I like your mom, Luke. I like her a whole lot."

"That's good," Luke replied softly. He licked his way back to Cain's ear and nibbled on the ridiculously sensitive lobe. Luke also gathered Cain's T-shirt in a bunch and slipped his hand under the fabric to torment Cain's flesh. "That's real good."

Callused fingers danced over Cain's stomach. Luke then slowly moved his palm up, the movement fluttering the nerves in Cain's belly, and slowly lifted the T-shirt toward Cain's neck. With the fabric lifted, cool air teased Cain's nipples. Luke then scraped his fingertips over Cain's flesh with deliberate intent and teased the sensitive discs to life. Cain's eyes slid closed, and the knife slipped from his hand, clattering loudly against the counter.

"What…What…" Cain wrapped his fingers around the far edge of the bar, needing something with which to anchor himself. Delicious sensation raised goose pimples all over his body, and he gritted his teeth as Luke plucked his nipples to insane points of sensitivity. "What…" Cain gulped for breath and tried again. "What are you doing?"

"Playing with you, Hawk, just like you do with me."

Luke buried his face in the crook of Cain's neck. He bit and used suction, making Cain moan with pleasure. Cain knew what would show on his skin when Luke finished, and the thought that he would be marked by this man made Cain's cock push painfully against his jeans. Cain had left bites and burns in a lot of places over Luke's body in the last week and a half, but in his eagerness to touch and taste and learn, he rarely gave Luke a chance to do the same in return. In fact, hardly at all. The sudden realization of where this would inevitably progress shut down Cain's desire and left his stomach twisted in knots.

"Ohhh, Luke…" Cain suddenly groaned deep and low, stopping mid thought. Luke had slid his hand down to cover the bulge in Cain's jeans, and he rubbed Cain's rapidly thickening length through the fabric. When Luke moved to the snap on Cain's waistband, Cain blurted, "I've never done anything like this."

Luke didn't stop, but he did kiss the back of Cain's neck, so Cain knew the man had heard him.

Cain bit his lip, forcing himself to finish. "Except for the things I've done with you."

"I know, baby," Luke said against Cain's bare back.

Luke's lips brushed against Cain's shoulder, and Cain suddenly jerked to a halt. *How did Luke get my T-shirt off without me realizing it?*

Luke rubbed Cain's crotch again, shaping his length through his underwear, and Cain slipped under the tide of delicious sensation again. The man whispered, "You did give me enough clues to let me know you'd never been with another man."

"No," Cain confessed hoarsely. He reached down and stilled Luke's hands. "You don't understand." Cain blinked his way through the embarrassment and shame. Cassie had told Cain he had to start somewhere, and he figured this was that place. Cain leaned back against Luke, and when Luke automatically braced himself and cushioned Cain in his warmth, Cain's chest squeezed with unbearable tightness.

"What don't I understand?" Luke spoke against Cain's cheek and then kissed his temple with the softest caress. "You can tell me anything, and I won't judge. I promise."

Cain tipped his head back, resting against Luke's shoulder. He stared up at his beamed ceiling and forced himself to speak through the tightness of his fears. "It's more than just never having been with another man. I've never been with a woman either." Luke tightened his arm around Cain's chest, but he didn't speak, so Cain went on. "I've never kissed anyone who wasn't family, and no one who isn't family has ever kissed me. I've never made out with anyone, man or woman. I've never been on a date, so obviously I've never been in a relationship with anyone. I've never done anything sexual, other than rubbing my own cock with my own hand, until two weeks ago, when I started having sex with you."

Luke rocked Cain side to side in the enclosure of his arms, and it was so damn sweet and generous Cain had to blink and blink and blink so he didn't cry. "You want to tell me why?" Luke asked gently. He waited, holding Cain tucked against his chest, putting the choice in Cain's hands.

Cain took a shaky breath and slowly exhaled through the fear. "I didn't want to be a liar." It was a partial truth, and right now, it was the best he could give. "I always knew I wasn't attracted to women, so I made a vow a long time ago not to ever give a woman the hint that I was. Casually dating a woman as a cover for what I really wanted felt wrong to me. To give a woman the impression that she had the right to expect something from me seemed the height of cruelty. I'm a pretty private person anyway, introverted, so I don't think it really gave anyone pause to wonder why I never went out on dates. As for the other, not going out with men" -- Cain slid his hand down Luke's arm and threaded their fingers together -- "all I can say is that I had my reasons for not pursuing it. I did a damn good job too." He chuckled humorlessly. "Until you."

"Lucky me." Luke gave Cain a reassuring squeeze. "Lucky, lucky me."

Luke turned his face toward Cain's, and with Cain's head still tilted back against Luke's shoulder, the move put them very, very close. Luke started raining small kisses all over Cain's cheek, jaw, and brow. Each light touch, so full of everything Cain had ever wanted and dreamed for, lured Cain back to that place where, beneath the fear, he wanted to be.

Cain groaned and grazed his lips against Luke's face too. For just a moment, their gazes, completely unguarded, met and held. Then their mouths met in a fierce clashing of lips, tongues, and choppy breath. Luke's searching kiss worked as a drug on Cain, and he felt certain without the bands of Luke's arms around his middle, holding him upright, his legs would buckle, and he would fall. Luke took the deepest recesses of Cain's mouth, using sweeping licks with his nubby, wonderful tongue, only to then retreat and soften the caress. It was all Cain could do just to let go enough to receive everything Luke offered.

Cain felt ravished by Luke's barrage of continuous kisses, and he wondered if Luke felt the same when Cain so aggressively kissed him. He wondered if Luke loved it so much he would do anything for the man that gave him such pleasure. Cain's belly tightened as he wondered if receiving this much passion, in another way, from Luke, could be as desperately wonderful as it felt to give it.

Cain wondered if he was man enough to find out.

Luke slid his palms down the sides of Cain's torso and under the waistband of Cain's jeans, pushing until the fabric bunched around Cain's hips. Cain's flesh heated, and with every slight touch Luke delivered to Cain's shaft, Cain's cock screamed with nervous excitement. The thin layer of skin over Cain's jutting hipbones was a place of heightened sensitivity for him, and every time Luke rubbed his fingers there, Cain pressed himself back against Luke even more closely, working toward something he didn't quite yet understand.

"I love everything we do together, Hawk," Luke muttered raggedly against Cain's mouth. "And if that is all we can ever do, it is more than enough for me. But I won't lie to you, either." Their gazes met, shades and shapes blurry from their closeness. "I want you. I want inside. I want it so much it hurts just thinking about it. At the same time, I will not make it a condition of us being together. I would never push you to a place you're unwilling to go."

"I'm not unwilling." Cain reached down, covered Luke's hand, and guided him around until he cupped one globe of Cain's ass. Luke squeezed, and his pinky slid into the crease, making Cain's breath catch in response. "I'm just…" Heat crept up Cain's neck, and he wanted to look away, but he made himself stay and get it said. "I'm just scared about how it will feel. About how I will feel letting someone inside that part of my body."

Luke smiled, something full of understanding, and it reached all the way to his eyes, softening them to pale silver. "So we'll take it slow. Just as much as you want, and when it gets to where you don't think you can do any more, then we'll stop. Okay?"

Just hearing Luke say those words settled Cain's uncertainty so quickly it amazed him. He realized, with a lurch in the area of his heart, it happened because he believed Luke. He trusted this man's word. *I trust Luke.*

"Okay." Cain nodded. "Tell me what to do."

Luke chuckled. He guided Cain forward and helped him brace his hands against the bar. "Relax, baby. It's not a test. You can't do anything wrong." Sliding his arms around Cain's waist, Luke gave him a quick hug, and whispered against his shoulder, "At least not in my eyes."

"Ohhh, damn it." Cain's cock immediately started to leak precum. He dug his fingers into the wood of the bar until the tips turned white. "You keep saying stuff like that, and I'm going to come before you even start."

"And if you do" -- Luke licked and kissed his way to the base of Cain's neck -- "then that'll be all right."

Luke began drawing a line down Cain's spine with the tip of his tongue; in response Cain whimpered and his bare toes curl against the floor.

"God, Hawk." Luke's voice registered so low Cain almost couldn't hear it over the blood rushing through his veins, making it sound as if he had ocean waves crashing in his ears. "You have the sexiest damn back I have ever seen. Your skin is so smooth and hot, and the breadth of your shoulders, and good God, the little indentation at the small of your back…" Luke licked and kissed Cain in that small dip, then let the heat of his breath collide with the moisture. "God, it's insane. You're so damn beautiful."

Cain had never been accused of possessing beauty before; he knew his features were all just a bit too exaggerated and roughly hewn to be considered anything near beautiful or handsome. With Luke kissing and caressing him and telling him it was so, though, Cain wasn't stupid enough to try and correct the mistake.

Then Luke's comments didn't matter. He pushed his hands back inside Cain's jeans and underwear and slid them both off his body. Cain had been naked with Luke many times in the past eleven days, but he'd never felt as utterly exposed as he did right then.

Luke must have understood his fear. Right then, Luke immediately smoothed his palms up and down the outside of Cain's legs, then placed a gentle kiss against his left hip. "It's okay, Hawk. Remember, only as much as you want." All of that together completely calmed and soothed Cain, yet drove his arousal up a thousand fold.

"That's the problem." Cain pressed his forehead against the bar. "I want you to do everything. I just don't know if I can take everything."

"Well, let's find out," Luke said.

Within seconds Luke kissed and licked across Cain's buttocks, and even nibbled and gently bit the flesh. It was the most incredibly intimate thing. The feel of Luke's mouth on his ass, grazing there, curled Cain's toes into the floor. The raw sensation dragged Cain down into a place of intimacy he had never been before. He slid under the tide fast, even quicker than the times Luke had given him a blowjob. This was different. Nobody, not even himself, had ever played with his ass.

Cain squirmed against the tender assault. He rutted back against Luke's teeth and tongue, eager for this new, intimate touch. Luke nuzzled his nose against Cain's ass cheek, and Cain's muscles clenched. Luke grazed his stubbly cheek against Cain's buttocks, abrading the sensitive flesh, and Cain cried out with delight. Cain shamelessly bent down further and shoved his backside against Luke's face for more.

Everything felt so wonderful and right; Cain thought he had a great handle on everything happening to him. Then Luke spread Cain's ass cheeks apart, and Cain felt a very distinct *something* touch his pucker.

"Good Christ, Luke." Cain moaned as a wave of dark pleasure hit him like a baseball bat to his solar plexus. "What are you doing?"

"Tasting you, baby." Luke's voice rumbled right against Cain's asshole, sending a double tremor straight through Cain's body. *Holy hell.* Luke really was fluttering his tongue over Cain's bud. Just what Cain had thought when he'd felt the initial shock of moisture against his entrance. Luke licked and sucked some more, and then murmured, "It's something I've wanted to do for a long time."

Cain wanted to say something, or at the very least inquire as to why Luke had never asked him to do this to his ass, but Cain had no room inside him for words. He could only *feel.* He shot up onto his toes, shocked at the first probing contact. Luke's incredible tongue never let up; he kept up a constant combination of flickering and sucking pressure against Cain's rim. Very quickly, the sensation dragged Cain under to a place of raw need. He pushed back against that little instrument of pleasure -- Luke's goddamn wonderful tongue -- for more. Right then, Luke broke through, and something invaded Cain's ass for the first time.

"Oh…oh Christ," Cain gasped, stunned. At first, he couldn't process the sensation in his ass. "Oh Christ, Luke" -- Cain slammed his fist against the bar and then reached across to the far end to hold on -- "oh…oh, geez… You're inside me."

In answer, Luke somehow get his tongue in farther and then -- *Oh Christ, I can't believe it* -- Luke licked all around, just inside Cain's asshole. Before Cain even realized it was happening, a deep, jerking pleasure raced through his insides straight to his cock; he spurted hard, raining hot seed down onto the floor.

*Oh good Christ. I came like an adolescent boy discovering my cock for the first time.*

Luke slid his tongue out of Cain's ass, licked up his crack, and then back up his spine, in a reverse of what he'd done only a short while ago. When finished, he draped himself over Cain's slumped body. "So," he murmured against Cain's ear, "I guess you liked that, huh?"

Cain chuckled, and his cheeks slashed with heat. "Yeah, I guess I did." Damn it, he'd come all over his floor. It wasn't as if he could deny his enjoyment.

Luke snaked his hand around Cain's throat and drew Cain around until they could see into each other's eyes. Then, pulling Cain closer until their lips met, Luke pressed a soft, undemanding kiss to Cain's lips. Cain didn't know how the man so intuitively understood Cain's needs, but the gentle caress was exactly what Cain needed. Cain clung to the kiss, needing to maintain a connection between them desperately, although he didn't exactly know why. He just knew what they'd done had already moved well beyond sexual for Cain, and Cain showed Luke that through kissing. Perhaps it was naïve, but Cain hoped Luke felt the same way.

Luke took Cain's upper lip between his and sucked, and then shifted lower and nibbled on the other one. Before breaking away, he left Cain's mouth acutely sensitive and swollen, and the rest of Cain's body hungry for more.

Brushing the tips of his fingers through Cain's hair, Luke leaned up and planted a soft kiss high on Cain's forehead. "Have you had enough for tonight?" He grinned, something full of indulgence, and then went back to combing Cain's short hair away from his face. Christ, the touch was so tender and intimate it had Cain's cock stirring back to life. Rapid recovery was one of the benefits -- or curses -- of his demon DNA. His stare sparking, Luke smiled and asked, "Or do you think you can take something else?"

Pictures of Luke's face buried between his ass cheeks flashed through Cain's mind and gave him a quick answer. He couldn't look away from the sexual heat blazing in Luke's gaze either. "What's next?" Cain asked, his voice raw, revealing what his body wanted... no, what it needed.

Luke touched Cain's face gently, the fingertips flickering over his forehead, cheeks, and nose, before settling on his lips. "Open up, baby," he instructed, his eyes glazing with passion. Cain did, and Luke's fingers slipped inside. "Now suck. Get them all nice and wet, just like you do with my cock."

Cain did as told and worked Luke's fingers into his mouth one knuckle at a time until he hit the base. He licked the crease between Luke's digits before sucking his way back up the next one. Luke's hands were much like Cain's -- worker's hands. Callused in some places, blunt and squared off at the tips; every bit of Luke's body was proof of the physical labor that was such an integral part of his life. Right then, however, as Cain watched Luke's eyes flutter closed, and his breathing hitch, those hands became perfect in every way. Luke's hands were beautiful. Cain held Luke's palm and shoved three fingers into his mouth at the same time, treating them as a single appendage, and sucked on them with as much enthusiasm as he showed when he had Luke's cock in his mouth. Suddenly Luke pulled his hand away, his body shuddering.

"Enough of that." Luke snaked his hand around Cain's neck, holding him still for a biting, ravenous kiss. His eyes flashed with a heady combination of humor and hunger.

Cain grabbed at Luke too, unable to remain a completely passive partner. He clutched Luke's head, slanted his mouth across the other man's, and kissed him back with deep slides of his tongue into Luke's mouth, tangling with its counterpoint until neither one of them could breathe properly.

Barely sated, but accepting he needed to stop for breath, Cain broke the kiss, panting against Luke's mouth. "I want you. I mean, I want you" -- Cain guided Luke's hand around his waist, down his tailbone, and then pressed his index finger down into the crack of his ass -- "right where you are, right now, in every way."

Luke quickly delved his index finger down, found Cain's puckered hole, and started to rub. As he did, he drew Cain close and held him tight. In response, Cain burrowed his face in the crook of Luke's neck. Sliding his arms around Luke's waist, he held on too, wanting and excited, but scared as well.

Luke started to press against Cain's bud more insistently. When Luke slid his other hand down to split Cain open, Cain's muscles automatically contracted.

Cool air caressed Cain's completely exposed crack and asshole. Nerves took him over again. "What…what are you doing?"

"Shh, shh," Luke soothed softly. "I want to watch. I want to see what I'm doing."

"Okay." Cain nodded against Luke's neck. He remembered how insanely arousing he'd found it to watch a part of his body invade Luke's; he watched himself every single time he took Luke. Taking a breath, Cain added, "I'm okay."

The deliberate pressure on Cain's asshole continued, but then Luke started necking with him too. He sucked and nibbled on the tender skin where Cain's neck met his shoulder, driving the skin there crazy. Before Cain knew which way was up, Luke pulled him under so completely that Cain started humping Luke's upper thigh, rubbing his cock against the wonderful, hard muscle.

"There you go. There you go, baby," Luke murmured against Cain's neck. "Take what you need."

Cain did.

But so did Luke.

Suddenly, Luke's finger stretched Cain's hole, pushed in, and filled Cain's ass.

Cain cried out hoarsely, and he squeezed Luke hard enough cut off his breathing.

Because it *hurt*.

# Chapter Fifteen

*Oh Christ. Fucking Christ.* As Cain stood next to his bar, he could feel nothing more than the burning and stretching around his hole and in his ass channel. All of a sudden, he wasn't so sure he wanted to do this anymore.

Right away, Luke said, "Give yourself a minute to adjust." He let go of Cain's buttock and caressed upward to rub soothing circles against Cain's back. "You'll get used to what it feels like; when you can relax around my finger it won't hurt so much."

"It's okay," Cain lied. He wanted Luke to have this so damn bad, and if he had to deal with a little bit of pain…Well, he'd dealt with worse. "I'm okay."

Luke grabbed Cain's head and yanked him up until they faced each other. "You think you can lie to me, and I won't know? Baby, your ass is clenching so hard it has my finger in a vise. That's not relaxed, and that means it's hurting you."

"Please!" Cain begged, knowing he looked and sounded disgustingly desperate, but he didn't know how to play it cool. "Don't pull out. Don't stop."

Luke's stare softened, and the sight tore right through Cain's heart. "Then tell me what to do to help you. Tell me what will make you feel better."

"Kiss me," Cain said, his voice rough with a combination of discomfort and unchecked emotion too frightening to identify. "Just kiss me."

Luke did; he pressed his lips all over Cain's face, placing gentle pecks, sometimes using the barest flicks from the tip of his tongue, touching everywhere before landing on Cain's lips. He then settled in for a good, long session of mapping every nook and cranny of Cain's mouth with his tongue. Christ, Cain loved being kissed by this man. He loved just relaxing his jaw and letting Luke take over, loved sliding his fingers through Luke's thick, glossy hair and holding him close while Luke touched him in a way that was something as close to loving as Cain had ever experienced in his life. *Oh yes.* Cain started riding Luke's thigh again, just naturally undulating there. He gave his cock something to rub against and brought the shaft back to life again. Quickly.

The kisses and small gyrations also brought Cain's ass alive, in a way that allowed Luke to slide his finger within Cain's passage. *Holy shit.* "Oh…oh…" Cain bit his lip. As Luke took his channel with a deeper penetration, Cain clutched Luke's shirt. Everything around Cain's ass still felt incredibly tight -- and weird -- but just beneath those sensations a burgeoning, pleasurable bubble he couldn't identify erupted. He only knew a coiling in his lower belly told him that he liked it. *Mmm.* Cain started humping his dick against Luke's thigh once again as he became acquainted with something, anything, invading his ass.

"Better?" Luke murmured. He moved his finger in and out in slow, meticulous strokes, timing the small fucking to work in tandem with how Cain rocked his hips.

Before too long, Cain discovered he loved having something in his ass. "Uh-huh." As he worked his lower body off on both the front and the back end, he buried his face against Luke's neck. Something in Cain's rectum received good attention from the drag of Luke's finger, and each time Luke touched him there, it drove Cain nuts.

*Please.* Cain slid his leg up and around Luke's, locking it in place around the back of Luke's thigh. The move opened his body up in the rear and allowed Luke to ease his finger in a little farther. *Good Christ.* Cain's eyes practically rolled back in his head. "More, Luke…" Cain stuck his tongue in Luke's ear and fucked the small opening with the whole of his wet, hot mouth. "More."

The next time Cain pushed back, Luke worked another finger into his ass, right next to the first. This time, Cain breathed through the invasion rather than fighting it, and held on tight as the initial wave of pain and discomfort hit him. Within a minute, Cain's channel relaxed, and that second digit started rubbing right where the first one had been. *Jesus, fuck yes.* Cain craved getting into Luke's ass too, but since he couldn't, he went back to invading Luke's ear with his tongue.

Within seconds, while fighting his way through this new sensation of being stuffed and stretched, Cain uttered, "I think I'm gonna come again." He reached down and held his balls as a precaution. Luke's fingers weren't enough anymore. Cain wanted it all, and he confessed to Luke, "I want your cock buried all the way inside me when I do it."

Luke grabbed Cain around the neck with one hand and dragged their faces together. His breath heaved, washing over Cain with intimate warmth. Luke pulled Cain to him until their mouths were just touching, and growled back, "I've never wanted anything so much in my life." Closing his eyes for a moment, Luke took that beautiful silver gaze away. As he opened his eyes, he inhaled deeply. "Tell me you're sure."

Cain nodded, the words initially trapped in the emotion lodged in his throat. But he knew Luke needed them, so he forced out, "I'm sure."

Luke gently slid his fingers out of Cain's ass; Cain gasped, amazed at how quickly he'd become desirous of that presence and how incredibly bereft and empty he felt when it slipped away. Guiding

Cain into place once again, Luke positioned him against the bar. Cain grasped the edge, held on, and out of the corner of his eye he watched Luke walk to the desk and open the left-hand drawer. Lube and condoms were stored there -- as well as now in the drawer on the end table next to Cain's recliner. There were some in the bathroom and in Cain's nightstand too, along with a few of Luke's toys, just in case. If Cain weren't so damn turned on, and getting even more so as he watched Luke unzip his jeans and pull out his long, slender erection, Cain would have laughed at the way his life and home had been invaded in the past two weeks. Luke's presence had forced so many small changes in Cain's life, some done with an inner battle and some given up quite easily. It amazed Cain that nobody but Cassie seemed to notice.

As Cain once again thought about Luke taking him, more than just a bit of fear rolled through him. Once Luke fucked him, things would forever change. Cain was worried there would be a change in his face and demeanor that no amount of posturing would be able to hide. On top of that fear, though, he knew he wanted to take the risk anyway. He wanted this next stage in their mating too damned much to stop now.

He wanted to be fucked.

And he needed it to be Luke.

Luke moved into position behind Cain. Within seconds, the telltale click of the tube of lubricant opening filled Cain's ears. Moments later Luke fingered Cain's bud and slowly worked the cool, thick substance into Cain ass. Cain pushed back on Luke's finger, understanding now that the small motion helped ease the way in. His body didn't resist the invasion nearly as forcefully this time; as the cool lubricant warmed inside his channel and coated the walls of his rectum, Cain's heart rate kicked up in anticipation.

Fingers and slickness suddenly gone, this time something measurably thicker slid between Cain's split cheeks and kissed his hole. Good Christ. Cain's mind raced with nervousness and excitement. *This is really going to happen.*

"Push back against me, Hawk," Luke advised. "Just like you did before."

Cain breathed deeply, clutched the edge of the bar, and bore down and back on the pressure of the tip of Luke's cock lodged against the opening of his ass. As the pressure increased, Cain winced and squeezed his eyes closed, but didn't back off. Luke pressed forward against him, stretching, stretching, stretching Cain even more. And then, as if it wasn't worth the fight anymore, Cain's puckered hole released and gave up, and the distinct shape of the head of Luke's penis slipped, just barely, inside Cain's ass.

"Oh fuck…" Cain exhaled roughly. "You're there." The very enormity of what was happening almost overwhelmed Cain. He had let someone he cared desperately about inside his body. It was so very personal. And so much more intimate than he ever could have imagined.

Losing himself a bit, Cain dropped his head to the bar. His cheek hit the wood, and he dug the side of his face into the smoothly polished surface. He breathed choppily, the action creating little fog marks on the finished bar.

"Baby." Luke covered Cain. The motion pushed Luke deeper into Cain's ass, and they both grunted when his dick hit another barrier. Pressing his mouth against Cain's shoulder, Luke slid his arms around his torso. "Talk to me, Hawk. Are you all right?"

Cain nodded against the bar top, blinking against the rush of inexplicable pleasure and joy. Moisture he couldn't hold back filled his eyes. "It's so good, Luke," Cain shared. With his head on the bar for balance, Cain slid his arms over Luke's, where they held him tight around the middle. He needed the extra connection as he fought his way through the onslaught of feelings coursing through him. "You feel so damn good inside me."

"You're burning me up, baby." Luke pulled out slowly, and then pushed back in, bumping that inner wall again. Dark, forbidden sensation rolled through Cain in shimmering waves, and his knees almost gave out on him. Luke muttered, "Your ass is so damn hot it's going to set my cock on fire."

"Don't stop." Cain clutched the backs of Luke's rough hands

as Luke shafted his channel again. When Luke pushed harder and tried to get deeper, Cain gritted his teeth. Cain considered the small struggle his body put up against the deeper taking a part of the gift Luke gave him. Cain wanted everything. "Fuck me, Luke. Fuck me hard, the way I fuck you."

"God, baby." Luke's voice reverberated through Cain's body, and Cain shivered. "Your eagerness is killing me." Luke reared both of them upright, until they were two walls of muscle plastered against each other from head to ankle. Luke put his face over Cain's shoulder, putting them cheek to cheek. "Push back, Hawk." Luke tightened his hold around Cain's torso. "Right…" Cain felt the body against his back bracing to take the action. "…now."

Cain did. He bumped his hips backward and thrust his ass out, just as, with a grunt, Luke speared forward. Cain cried out, the sound guttural, from somewhere deep in his body, as Luke broke through and plunged deep into Cain's channel with the full length of his cock and took Cain to the furry hilt.

"Ohhhh…yes…yes…" The feel of being invaded took Cain over completely. He pulsed back against Luke again and again, instigating tiny slides along that long, long cock in his ass. *Luke's cock.* Cain keened with pleasure, the sound almost inaudible, as Luke started pushing into Cain's ass with little jabs too. Cain was finally being fucked, and good Christ, he loved it.

They moved in unison. Cain had never felt so acutely alive, not even when he'd been the one fucking Luke. It was the trust that rocked Cain to his core, and he knew it. He hadn't needed to trust Luke when he'd been the aggressor, but this reversal was wrought with vulnerability. As Cain realized how many times Luke had opened himself up to this position in the past two weeks, a tremor rolled through Cain.

"I have to have more, baby," Luke said against Cain's cheek. He pushed Cain forward against the bar again.

Cain automatically grabbed the edge. Just as he did, Luke dug his fingers into Cain's hips, his grip powerful enough to leave bruises, and started to move with a purpose. He withdrew almost all the way and then slammed back in with such ardor it lifted Cain to the balls of his feet. Cain's lips parted, and he choked on the shocking change of sensation. His body couldn't yet process the strangeness of the deep pull out before Luke refilled him with the hard, fast slide of his prick, torpedoing the sensitive tissues in Cain's channel again. Sensation after sensation, not all of them good, rushed through Cain, too much too fast, but he couldn't pause and process the quick shot of pleasure or the small pang of discomfort. Cain only cared that this fucking happened this way because Luke needed it to, and that knowledge pushed away anything but Cain's complete desire to take this act all the way to its inevitable conclusion.

Even though Luke wore a condom, Cain wanted to feel the heat of Luke's semen as it spilled out of his dick and warmed Cain's ass. "Are you close, Luke?" Cain uttered, barely getting the words out as Luke barraged his asshole with a rapid-fire shafting. Burning heat and soreness took over Cain's ass, but Christ, he wanted every damn thing Luke had in him to give. "You're moving like I do when I'm about to come."

Luke covered Cain from behind, and he whispered heatedly, "Oh yeah, baby?" He shoved into Cain's ass and lodged himself deep. He then reached around, grabbed Cain's half-hard cock, and started stroking the length back to full, raging life. "How is that?"

"Hard and fast and deep," Cain answered. When Luke swirled his fingers around the head of Cain's cock, Cain had to stop to gather himself before he could go on. *Two can play this game.* Baiting Luke shamelessly, Cain added, "Carnal and wicked and base, just the way you like it."

"No," Luke contradicted with a growl, "just the way I *love* it."

Cain moaned as he self-lubricated under the tutelage of Luke's deft fingers. Unable to hold himself back from the pleasure, he started pumping his cock into Luke's velvet fist. The muscles in his rectum started clenching involuntarily, and when Luke grunted against his ear and started moving again, Cain managed a small grin of victory.

With the dexterity of Luke's glove-tight hold on his cock, it didn't take long for Cain's balls to pull up, and for him to know the endgame was upon him. Again. "I'm so fucking close, Luke." As Luke milked a stream of pre-ejaculate out of Cain's cock, Cain threw his head back and clenched his jaw. He felt his skin pull taut over his face, and his breathing shifted to shallow pants. Right then Luke shoved in particularly hard and deep, and Cain grunted and said, "Make me come when you do. I want to come with you."

"Oh…oh, yes…damn it, Hawk." Luke bit down hard on Cain's shoulder blade. "I want more…longer…" He wrapped his arm around Cain's abdomen and anchored him in a clamp so tight that Cain gasped. "…can't, baby… Killing me…I'm coming right now…"

Just as Luke smashed Cain into the edge of the bar with one last, deep thrust, he bit into the muscled flesh on Cain's back hard enough to leave small cuts. Wet heat warmed Cain's ass, ejaculate Cain could feel -- even through the condom -- and in response Cain cried Luke's name into the sex-laden air. He rejoiced in Luke's final loss of control. Cain swore it felt as if Luke's hot semen filled him up to capacity and rolled through the entire length of his body, powerful enough to leave him weak. There was so much, and it felt so damn right, it seemed to shoot straight through Cain's ass to his own cock, demanding release. Seconds later Cain jerked his hips, dragging Luke forward with him as he came again. Cum shot from Cain's cock, landing on the side of the bar, and the pleasure nearly blinded him.

Both men fell against the counter, barely holding each other up as they fought to regulate their breathing. Luke recovered enough to speak first. "Good God, Hawk." He rubbed his cheek against Cain's sweat-slick back. "I hope to hell you liked that, because I just know that before too long I'm gonna want to do it again."

Cain chuckled. The sound, the very act, rumbled through him, and he let himself enjoy the swirling happiness curling inside his belly. He let himself love the way his laughter made Luke's chest shift against his back. Quietly, Cain acknowledged to himself that even though he was replete and satisfied, he still liked the feel of Luke's penis resting in his ass. Cain absorbed the brief fantasy of feeling like a real couple. He let go for a little while, knowing that too soon Luke would go back to his room and Cain would be forced to remember why that had to be.

As soon as Luke walked out the door, Cain would remember he was Naverto. With every minute he spent getting to know Luke, and every time they came together in this frantic mating, Cain sent out a flashing beacon of interest to the Traveler. This depth of feelings he experienced could not be hidden, or ignored, on the other end.

When investigated, Cain would be discovered.

And then he would be dead.

———

A WEEK LATER, CAIN HUMMED TO an Alison Krauss tune on the radio, one that he'd just had to stop on when checking the stations. The singer made him smile and think of Luke. As Cain realized how disgustingly saccharine it was of him to accept that lately everything reminded him of Luke, he rolled his eyes. If something -- whatever, it didn't matter what it was -- didn't immediately bring Luke to the forefront of Cain's thoughts, Cain just let himself think on it for a bit, and somehow he found a way to that inevitable end. It also amazed him that, still, somehow, nobody except Cassie seemed to notice he was a changed man.

He was changed too. Because of Luke, he was.

Cain drove home from a hard day of work on the main ranch property, something he hadn't done in almost eight months. A phone call from Connor had dragged him away from his own work, his brother spewing something vague about Caleb disappearing for a few days and that he needed some extra help rounding up cattle in the high country. Cain couldn't refuse, seeing as how his brothers still hadn't done anything other than make some light inquires about the future of Cain's horses. Connor and Caleb both knew full well it didn't take this long to retrain these horses for reselling.

Cain appreciated the time and quiet understanding. He loved his brothers, and he cared about regular Hawkins Ranch business too. His initial third of capitol twelve years ago had been equal to

Connor's and Caleb's, so a third of the property and all of its holdings still belonged to him. That didn't mean he didn't feel guilty about being a financial drain on ranch funds, though, especially without any clear idea of when he would be able to turn his work around and make it a flush business.

Maybe Cain would talk with Luke about the situation. If he could unburden just a little bit it might allow him to let go in a way he hadn't been able to thus far. For such a young man, Luke had a good, levelheaded way about him, and he might have a solution that would ease the way for Cain to let his horses go. Cain chuckled to himself, thinking Luke wouldn't have a solution so much as a chest to burrow against as Cain struggled with saying goodbye to his animals.

Cain eased his truck into view of the cabin, and his heart suddenly stopped beating. *Motherfucking shit.* Cassie and Luke stood not fifty feet away from where Cain screeched to a halt, still some twenty feet away from the cabin.

Only, Cassie and Luke were not alone. A very unassuming older man stood with them, chatting in that way people comfortable in their skin so easily do.

Cain's skin crawled with fear and icy coldness. He knew what the other two didn't.

It was time. The Traveler had come for him.

*Shit.*

# Chapter Sixteen

*No, no, no, no, no, no, no.* Cain's head, his heart, his entire being screamed that he couldn't do this yet. Not yet. He couldn't let Luke go. He couldn't, he couldn't, he couldn't. Not that he wouldn't, but that he could not.

Could. Not.

As Cain got out of the truck and headed for the small group, his heart raced. He had only one goal in his mind: buy more time with Luke.

With that thought in mind, Cain did the only thing he could. He completely ignored Luke, and moved right to Cassie's side. He didn't touch her, but he stood slightly in front of her, as if his only desire was to shield her from the gazes of the other men. The Traveler's gaze lit up with awareness, and Cain breathed his first silent sigh of relief.

This trickery wasn't over yet, though. Now came the truly hard part. Cain shifted his attention ever so briefly to Luke. "Aren't there still horses that need to be fed? I don't pay you to stand around yakking with my friends, Forrester. I pay you to work. Now go."

Luke blanched and then reddened. "Y-y-yes, of course." Cain could only thank a higher power that Luke's reaction could be mistaken for embarrassment due to a public dressing down, rather personal hurt. Cain's heart cracked, but he kept his face hard and didn't let how greatly it crushed him to hurt Luke show.

The Traveler didn't have the power to read Luke's emotions any more than he did Cassie's; he could only attune himself to other Naverto. And even with Naverto, the Traveler could not divine the individual name of the person for whom Cain had feelings, he could only detect the huge emotional and sexual change occurring within Cain. The Traveler only knew that Cain experienced those emotions *right now*, in a *big way*. It was up to Cain to convince the Traveler that the brightness in his aura existed for Cassie and not for Luke. Or at least, that was his plan.

"Well?" Cain narrowed his gaze on Luke. "Why are you still standing here gaping at us? For fuck's sake, man, go." He shooed Luke off with a flick of his hand. "Now."

"Yes, Mr. Hawkins." Luke backed away, his gaze a flat and dull gray Cain forced himself to ignore. "I'm sorry, sir. I'll go do that right now."

Then, just as painful, Cain turned his attention back to Cassie and the Traveler, dismissing Luke entirely, showing that Luke's departure to the barn held no interest for him whatsoever.

"So" -- Cain directed his full focus on the Traveler -- "you finally showed." Without looking behind him, Cain reached back and took Cassie's hand. He didn't bother to hide his disdain or impatience for the Traveler; he'd behaved the same on every other infrequent visit the Traveler had made to him in his life thus far. "I figured it wouldn't be too much longer before you were checking up on me."

The Traveler raised a thick, age-whitened eyebrow. "You didn't really expect that you'd be able to hide such a big shift in your celibate and solitary lifestyle, lad, now did you?"

"No." Cain figured the more he kept to the truth, the more believable he would be. He slid in front of Cassie once again, shielding her from the Traveler's scrutiny, much as he'd want to do if it were Luke. "But I was also hoping that when you came, Cassie wouldn't be on hand to make it so easy for you to figure out who it was."

"You always did like to butt your hard head against the Naverto ways," the Traveler said. The smugness in his tone clearly conveyed how fruitless he thought this effort to be. "But I have to say, boy, I never thought I'd see the day where you bucked this makeshift brotherhood you created with that inferior demon filth to cuckold your own brother." The Traveler's lip turned up in a sneer. "We may just get you back in the fold of the Naverto clan yet."

"I have no wish to hurt Connor." Cain's statement held an absolute, passionate truth the Traveler could not discount. "Neither does Cassie. But sometimes" -- the woman at the center of Cain's deception worked her way under his arm, so he used the opportunity to pull her to his chest and kiss the top of her dark hair -- "sometimes feelings and attraction grow so big they cannot be denied."

"Why do you pursue this?" the Traveler inquired. "I know all about your life, boy, so I know that this *human*" -- he shuddered visibly as he spoke the word -- "has already taken the seed of your brother under the full Halloween moon in order to make him human. She must have truly loved him at the time to allow the change to happen. That was only two years ago. Do you really think her feelings for you will last another seventeen years until another full Halloween moon occurs, and she can do the same for you?" His gaze swept down and then back up Cassie's form. "She seems a rather fickle sort to me."

"Hey!" Cassie broke through Cain's loose hold and charged the Traveler. "I don't know who the hell you are, sir" -- she poked him in the chest -- "but I will not have you calling my feelings fickle. I happen to love this man." She pointed back at Cain. "I happen to love every damn thing about him! So say what you want" -- she scrutinized the Traveler with a sneer of her own -- "but I guarantee you I will still be in his life in seventeen years when that next full moon comes around. And just so you know" -- she poked him again, and this time Cain couldn't hold back his chuckle, even as he pulled her away -- "I'll still be here in another nineteen after that, when the next one comes around. So put that in your pipe and smoke it." Cassie spit at the Traveler's feet, and even though Cain wasn't *in* love with Cassie, he had certainly never loved her more than he did in that moment. She stared at the Traveler with fire in her green eyes. "You certainly look like the type."

"Well." The Traveler smirked. "I can see where at least the sexual attraction comes from. She must be a wild animal when you get her on her back and slide between her legs."

Cassie didn't get the chance to defend herself this time; Cain took up the task in a flash. "You get the hell out of here, old man." He grabbed the Traveler by the lapels of his loose, mud-colored jacket. "You have what you need for your report. You already know I'm not going to invite you to dinner and kiss your ass the way other separatists try to do. Take your information back to the Council of Twelve and reassure them this separatist is not a threat to the clan now any more than he has been ever since he left. And just so you know" -- Cain twisted the Traveler's coat and lifted him off the ground -- "I know that demon law prevents you from going to my brother and telling him what you know about me and his wife. He is not Naverto, so he is not your concern. If you break the code and tell him about us, I will come for you." Cain let his gaze flash, freely revealing all of the hatred and fire he felt inside over not being able to be with Luke in the way that he wanted. He let the Traveler see his heightened emotions and believe it was for Cassie. "But I won't take you to the Council of Twelve; I'll just kill you myself and take whatever consequences follow." He lowered the Traveler to the ground, let go of his hold, and smoothed down the wrinkled fabric of the demon's jacket as he whispered, "Got it?"

"No need for dramatics, lad." The Traveler straightened himself up and smiled coolly. "I have no interest in lending aid to a former demon. If you want to self-destruct with deep bouts of unchecked emotions over his unfaithful wife, then that is what I will tell the council. I bid you good day." The Traveler bowed deeply, Cain thought a little dramatically himself. "I have others like you to check on before I'm due to make my report." He nodded and began to head in the direction of the mountains. He lifted his hand in a wave without turning around. "Goodbye."

"Wait, wait, wait," Cain chanted softly in Cassie's ear. He wrapped a forearm around her breasts and tucked her smaller height under his chin. "Give him time to reach an area of privacy. He'll want cover before he opens a portal that will take him to wherever he needs to go next."

"I presume there is a good reason for what I just did," Cassie hissed under her breath. "Because my husband wouldn't like it were he to find out. He won't care that none of it was true, and you know it."

"No, he wouldn't," Cain agreed. "And that is why I ask you not to tell him. At least not until I figure out what in the hell I'm going to do next."

"Sweetie" -- Cassie turned in Cain's arms -- "what is going on? This isn't like you. Not even close."

"I know." Cain nodded, but for the moment, whether out of prudence or paranoia, he maintained his embrace with Cassie. "I'll tell you all about it one day soon, I promise." Upon thinking about Luke, and what had happened, and possibly losing him, Cain's jaw clenched uncontrollably. "I ask that you don't demand answers right now. Please."

"You hurt Luke terribly." Cassie, as always, didn't pull her punches. "I saw it in his eyes, even if you didn't. You dismissed him like he didn't matter, as if he wasn't even a human being worthy of your acknowledgement."

Cain finally let the reality of what he'd done -- what he'd had to do -- hit him full force. It was akin to a sledgehammer ramming him in the gut. "I know." Just saying those two words made the situation more real, made the potential consequences that much more dire. "You'll just have to trust me when I say I did it for the greater good."

"I do trust you. I just hope for your sake that Luke can too."

"Me too, sis," Cain answered. He pecked a kiss to Cassie's head again, this time for the comfort it offered rather than as proof of the fragile lie he'd created. One that may have hurt Luke so badly it wouldn't end up mattering in the end if Cain had fooled the Traveler or not.

———

CAIN WAITED FOR OVER TWO hours, had made Cassie stick around too, before considering himself safe from the Traveler for at least a little while. Cain hadn't said much in that time. And thank God, Cassie hadn't pressed. Cain's thoughts had been too full of various apologies to Luke. For what he'd done. For how he'd treated the man. For doing the very thing he knew would have absolutely crushed his heart if Luke had done the same to him.

The time had come. Cain considered it safe enough to go find Luke and try to do some damage control. He stood in the slowly approaching darkness, his hand on the handle to the barn door, and gave himself one last pep talk about how he would successfully handle Luke. It would go well. Cain would stay calm and try to make sense. Luke would forgive him. That was how it would go.

That settled, Cain slid open the door to the barn…and came to a paralyzing state of motionlessness when he found Luke right on the other side stroking Fancy Face's muzzle.

"Sir." Luke barely nodded, and he definitely didn't look at Cain. "I've fed the horses, as instructed. I was just spending some time talking to them. I hope this meets with your approval."

Whatever sickness Cain had been feeling in his stomach quadrupled. "Don't do that, Luke," he said, his emotions from the day making his voice gravelly. "Please."

"Don't do what?" Luke carried on in a monotone Cain had never heard in this animated, openhearted man's voice. "Don't act like the lowly employee I am? Don't interact with you in the way that befits my station in your life? Don't behave in the way you made very clear earlier today I should? I saw you, you know." A small catch in Luke's voice betrayed that he felt something, and that small sound gave Cain hope. "I saw how you shielded Cassie. I saw you take her hand. Jesus Christ, Cain. You would rather have your friend think you're carrying on an affair with your sister-in-law than give a hint that you even think of me as a human being worthy of your attention or respect."

"Please, Luke" -- Cain took a step forward -- "don't do this."

Luke finally did turn. Watery brightness in his gaze betrayed his hurt and humiliation, rendering the flat tone of his voice a complete lie. The sight tore Cain up inside, killing him with the knowledge that he had been the one to put such pain there.

"Don't do *what*, Cain?" Luke asked again. "Don't act like you're only my boss, and not my friend? Don't act like we haven't spent the last two weeks fucking each other?" Luke's lower lip quivered, but he hardened his features and went on. "Don't act like the piece of shit nobody you treated me like earlier today?" Luke's gaze stormed, and he snarled, "You fucking bastard, don't you dare tell me not to act however the fuck I want to act after the way you treated me. Get the hell away from me. I can't even look at you anymore."

Cain pressed his hand to his chest, searching for the wetness of bleeding. There was no blood. His shirt was still dry. Luke's words hurt so damn much, though, that Cain checked again. He couldn't fathom that something could pain him this bad and not show up as a wound he could touch, see, and feel on the outside.

"No, Luke, no." Cain reached out, but Luke reared away from his touch. Cain let his hand fall to his side, listless and dead. "I... you...you don't understand. I didn't have a choice. I had to do it. I had to."

"Oh, no." Luke's voice registered so deep and soft it sounded otherworldly. "Don't you dare treat me like some battered wife and tell me that you just *had to* do it. My mother took my father's mood swings and abuse for years, so I know every goddamn rationalization in the book for forgiving someone who treats you like shit. I've heard them all. I swore I would never hurt another person that way, and I made sure my sister knew she was important and valuable, and to never take abuse from a boy she liked. So there is...*no*...*damn*... *way*...I am going to stand here and fucking take it from you."

Breathing became a challenge for Cain; each breath he took seized his insides. "I swear to you, Luke." Cain dredged each word from the depths of his soul. "I would not intentionally hurt you for the world. But that man" -- Cain pointed to the outside, behind him, as if the Traveler still stood there -- "if he knew what we were doing, he would take me away from you. Forever."

Luke snorted. "What, Cain, are there antigay police forces making their own laws now that I don't know about? Please, give me a break. It may not be a popular thing to be, and I admit it would be damn hard to be open in this little part of the world, but it is not illegal for us to be together."

"You just have to trust me, Luke. I couldn't have that man guessing at what we are doing. I couldn't."

"And fooling him entailed you treating me like a piece of crap that wasn't even worthy of being under your boot?" A hard line flattened Luke's lips to almost nothing, and his brow knitted with ferocity. "It's not like I was going to out us or anything. I didn't expect you to kiss me or hold my hand, or even admit I was your friend. But there is a huge gap between you introducing me politely as your employee and asking if I'd completed my work, to acknowledging my presence only to berate me and order me to do something you know *damn well* I would never neglect to do. You *damn well* did not have to treat me like you did today, and you and I both *damn well* know it. So don't you dare try to feed me that line of bullshit again, because if you do, I will walk out on your ass right now, and I will never come back. I swear to God I will be gone."

"No. Please, Luke. Listen to me. Please." Each word choked Cain's throat, his voice hoarse with fear. "If I had introduced you properly, or even just acknowledged you with a smile, that man would have known that everything I was feeling in that moment was for you, and not for Cassie. That man is intuitive. He sensed my emotions the minute I stepped out of the truck -- no, before that, even. I had to buy us some time. I had to make him think everything I felt was all for Cassie. I couldn't allow even so much as a hint to enter his thoughts that it was really for you. If I had treated you with any kind of respect or kindness, he would have figured us out before I even got your name past my lips. He would have known."

"So now your story is that he's psychic" -- Luke snorted and rolled his eyes -- "as well as being powerful enough to haul you away for being gay? Whoooaa." Luke waved his fingers spookily in front of Cain's face, and his lip lifted in a sneer. "Nice try. Too bad it's total bullshit." He looked Cain up and down with hard eyes. "Just like you." Luke bumped Cain's shoulder and shoved him aside. "I can't believe how proud I was to work for you, how proud I was to be with you, in every way. What a chump I was. You fooled me big time."

Luke paused just outside the barn door. His back stiffened, he shook his head, and then turned back around. He looked up at Cain, and the dead look in his eyes sucker punched Cain straight through his stomach and ripped out his spine. Then it got worse. "I never cared that we were in hiding," Luke shared, his tone strangely soft. "I understood it. Hell" -- he laughed humorlessly -- "if MacLesten hadn't seen me, I'd still be in the closet too. You treated me like trash in front of that man, though. Then when he leaves, you come running and pat me on head and tell me to just accept it." Luke clenched and unclenched his fists at his sides. "No fucking way. You may be my boss, but I am not your bitch." Night had almost completely fallen, but Cain could still see the taut lines ruling Luke's face. Luke flinched, but his back stiffened, and he didn't look away. "I've just discovered I can't be a man who works for someone who treats me like that." Luke's Adam's apple bobbed convulsively. "Goodbye, Cain." With that, Luke turned and started walking away.

Right then, Cain discovered he'd never dealt with real pain in his life before, not until that very moment. Or real panic, either. "Luke!" His voice came out harsh and guttural, even though he didn't feel either of those things. He couldn't help it. "Luke!"

Cain started unbuttoning his shirt.

From twenty feet away, Luke spun. His focus landed on Cain's fingers, already sliding his belt buckle out of the loops. "What, Cain? You think if we have sex everything will be all right? I love what we do, Hawkins, but I am not for sale." Luke started backing away again. "Not a chance."

"Wait!" Cain shouted again. He stripped off his boots and jeans more efficiently than he ever had before. "Wait, Luke." This time a plea filled his tone. "I'm trying here. Give me a chance. I want to show you something."

"What?" Luke stalled again and gave Cain's nudity a cursory once over. "Your erection?" Luke briefly fixed his gaze on Cain's cock, as if even though he didn't want to he couldn't quite ignore it. Luke's stare made Cain grow even harder, although that wasn't what he wanted right now. "It's beautiful. I love it, I admit that, but it doesn't change anything. It's no longer enough."

"No, I didn't think it was." A small grin actually tugged Cain's lips. When Luke shook his head and started to back away again, the smile left in a flash. *Fuck.* This was it. If Cain didn't do this, he would lose Luke for good, right here, right now. Cain found that when faced with the choice of Luke walking away, or continuing to hide himself, there was really no decision to make at all. "But I'm hoping this is enough," Cain added, and did something he had never wanted to do. He closed his eyes and concentrated on the demon living inside of him, the other half of himself. Once focused, Cain's body contorted and rearranged itself in a smooth, almost poetic way, until Cain the man was no more, and only the Naverto remained.

He revealed his secret, the only one that mattered. He showed the demon to Luke.

Cain opened his eyes, prepared for shock, revulsion, disdain, utter stupefaction, maybe even a little bit of titillation.

He wasn't prepared for what he got instead.

Luke's fist slamming into his mutated face.

Hard.

# Chapter Seventeen

Luke shook off the pain in his hand while trying desperately not to quake in the wake of the behemoth beast standing before him. *Good God.* He rubbed his neck and took an involuntary step back. *It's the fantastical beast of my dreams.*

The beast was real. It stood right in front of him. Naked and big and foreboding. A…a *thing* capable of snapping Luke in two with one hand. It was in no way, shape, or form human.

Luke swallowed down the lump of fear lodged in his throat and looked again.

The beast stepped forward and lifted its big hand. Luke flinched and stumbled back.

The beast moved away. Rejection sliced through its gaze, and shame filled Luke for his fearful response.

The beast lifted its hand to its own jaw and rubbed.

Luke remembered the punch.

"Sorry." Luke forced himself to move closer to the winged beast, deliberately stamping down the tremor in his voice.

176 | CAMERON DANE

"Why did you do it?" the beast asked, its voice scratchy, yet incredibly soft.

"I was scared." The words slipped out of Luke before he could think and pull them back in. He looked up at the giant beast before him and took another tentative step forward. "Your hand came up, and I thought you were going to hit me back for punching you."

Hurt flashed through the beast's eyes. Blue eyes. Cain's eyes. Before the flood of recognition washed through Luke, the beast stiffened, and the hint of vulnerability it had shown vanished. Flat, hard anger took its place. "I'm not talking about the fucking flinch, Luke." The beast... No, Cain. That was definitely Cain's tone beneath the roughened beast voice. The winged being sneered and bared his teeth. "Who wouldn't automatically want to run from this? I'm talking about the punch, damn it. Why in the hell did you hit me?"

Any hint of lingering fear thrumming through Luke's veins evaporated right then and there. This was Cain. *Shit.* Luke's blood boiled. This beast standing in front of him just became another lie between them.

*Son. Of. A. Bitch.* "You don't think almost a month of you deceiving me is an obvious enough reason for hitting you, Hawk?" Passion filled Luke's voice. He could not believe Cain's nerve, thinking it was *his* right to be the angry party here. "Longer than that, if you count back to the day I first started working for you. You think your miraculously showing me this *thing* you apparently are -- that you conveniently know I've fantasized about since I was a teenager, by the way -- is magically going to make me fall into your arms and forget about everything else that happened, Hawk? Because if you are so fucking arrogant to think it will, then I swear to God I will slug you a second time and not think twice about doing it."

"You called me Hawk just now," Cain replied in a near whisper, his eyes softening in a way Luke consciously had to harden himself against. "Twice. It's the first time you've done it since I found you in the barn."

"Don't change the subject," Luke snarled. Anger and confusion raged inside him, more than he'd ever experienced in his twenty-five years of life. And it was all this man's fault. "You hurt me today, Cain. You disrespected me in a way that hurt even more than what MacLesten did to me. I didn't expect anything more than what I got out of a soulless bastard like him, but you..." Luke pointed his finger, his entire arm shaking as he did it. "Your cruelty completely blindsided me because...because..." Luke fought desperately to keep at bay the wetness that wanted to spill down his cheeks. "...because from the moment I started working with you, I knew I had never met a man with more integrity in my life. I was honored just to know you. But you destroyed that today. In just a few short throwaway sentences, you killed what I thought for sure was an unshakable truth. You killed my belief that you are a good man who treats everyone with respect, no matter the discomfort it might cause you. And for what? To distance yourself from even just the hint, the whiff, of homosexuality? Well" -- Luke threw up his arms in surrender -- "congratulations. You've certainly distanced yourself from any future acts of it with me."

Cain's copper-skinned, roughly hewn jaw started to tick. "Are you finished?" Cain asked through gritted teeth. "Have you said all the hurtful things you need to say so that we're even? Because as much as I might like to, I can't stand here all night looking like this. Anyone could drive up to the property and see me, and from then on it wouldn't be much of a stretch to think I'd be strung up from the nearest branch. That is, if I'm not plugged full of buckshot right on the spot for being what I am."

*And what you are, Cain?* Luke didn't yet know, but damn, he was curious. He finally let himself take in the winged beast before him in a way he'd denied himself until then. He looked with curiosity rather than fear. Luke cataloged the hard, sharply angled face, the thickly muscled arms and legs, the talons that curled out past the tips of fingers and toes, the fully erect cock that was even thicker and longer than the one Luke knew so well already. Luke couldn't help himself; he walked around Cain, the body before him so stiff and upright, and looked in awe at the incredible length of folded wings that Luke knew had a mammoth span when stretched out in flight.

Now that Luke looked freely, and some of his immediate fear and anger had dissipated, he couldn't quite believe what his eyes were seeing. This beast had to be a trick of the light or a hallucination. This…this transformation from a man to a mythical creature didn't seem possible. Luke reached out and touched the pointed tip of a wing, drawing his hand along the outer edge of muscle. The entire body before him jerked with a start and shuddered visibly, unable to hide from Luke its uncertainty buried within.

Not *it*, Luke corrected himself immediately. *Him.* Somehow, in some fantastical way, the beast of his dreams and the man he'd been falling for were one and the same. Luke circled back around and looked up, for this body was measurably taller than the man who somehow lived in the same skin. Luke looked up into blue, blue eyes, searching them out and following until they stopped hiding and let Luke see inside. Those eyes, what they showed of the soul within, were the same. And they had so, so quickly become as familiar to Luke as his own.

*This is Cain.* No matter what else he was, living within, behind the truth of those deep blue eyes, was Luke's Cain.

Right then, Cain turned away, giving Luke only his rigid profile. "Are you done looking?" Cain breathed unevenly, and his voice registered low and harsh. Yet he held himself so stoic in his stillness Luke could barely see the rise and fall of his chest. "Have you scrutinized and stared enough to satisfy your curiosity?"

With that setdown, Luke remembered he was still mightily pissed at this man. "Listen, you jerk." He edged to Cain's side and got up as close in his face as he could. "You're the one who showed yourself to me. It's not like I was sneaking around spying on you and discovered this" -- he waved his hand the length of Cain's changed body -- "*whatever* this is, without your permission. So don't go getting all high and mighty with me. I'm taking a good, close look at something you obviously wanted me to see!"

"Needed you to see!" Cain roared back just as passionately. "Or else you were going to leave me!"

"And I still intend to do that!" They were face-to-face, right up in each other's personal space. "Because as fascinating and beautiful as this is, it doesn't have anything to do with how you treated me today."

"It has everything to do with how I treated you today!" Ferociousness filled Cain's tone. He actually took a large step backward, and Luke could swear he did it so that he didn't put hands to Luke and strangle him on the spot. "Everything, Luke." This time Cain's words weren't a bellowing shout; his voice held the hollowed-out sound of accepted defeat. "It has everything to do with you."

Suddenly afraid to move, frightened to reach out and offer comfort, Luke remained still. He was very afraid that if he touched Cain, Cain would somehow shatter into a million pieces right before his very eyes.

*Focus.* Luke forced himself to breathe and meet Cain's stare. "Then stop feeding me platitudes and bullshit, Hawk," Luke pleaded from his position of five long feet away, agony filling his throat up so tightly it almost strangled him. "Stop trying to take care of everything all by yourself. I don't claim to be the smartest guy around, but I am by no means stupid. I can see that something is wrong; terribly wrong. But if you won't trust me, then we have nothing, whether it is in secret or otherwise."

"I don't want us to be a secret," Cain admitted, his voice stripped bare. "I don't have any shame about what I feel for you, or about what we do together. I like you and respect you, and I care about you in a way I never imagined would be possible for me. Please." Looking away briefly, Cain appeared as if he talked himself down from jumping off a high cliff. Finally he lowered his gaze from the night sky and put it back on Luke. The raw openness in his eyes stole Luke's breath away. "Tell me you can see the truth in me when I say that."

"I do," Luke answered softly, his heart aching in a way it never had before. "But I can also see that you're scared, Hawk. Beneath this formidable beast body --"

"Demon," Cain corrected, his lips tightening to a thin line, as if it pained him to say the word aloud. "That is what I am, Luke. I am a demon."

"Okay," Luke answered, treading as softly as he could, for Cain's sake. "And some other time I'd like you to tell me what that means, for you. But right now, baby, all I care about is why this is relevant to the dismissive tone you took with me earlier tonight. All I care about is why you're so damn scared right now."

Cain's brows drew together, reshaping the unfamiliar map of his handsome face. "You really don't care about this, do you?" He gestured to his face and the line of his body. "You really aren't frightened by what I've shown you tonight, are you?"

"Frightened?" Luke scrunched up his face and shook his head. "For a couple of seconds, yeah, but not anymore. Shocked as hell. Curious, for sure. I do want answers, but I'm not scared of you." He actually snorted. "What did you think, Hawk? That I would run from you? That I would beg you not to kill me and eat me? That when faced with this magnificent beast who has lived in my dreams for ten years, I would turn away from it in horror when shown again in reality?"

Luke watched all kinds of layers of emotions get pushed up to the surface of Cain's gaze, only to be blinked away as soon as they appeared.

"What, baby? What?" Luke hated the clear confusion and agony clouding Cain's eyes. "Talk to me."

"I don't want to be taken away from you." The desolation in the scratchy demon voice stomped on Luke's core with the strength of a bull. "It hasn't been enough time. So...so...I...I did what I had to do to stay with you. That's all I wanted."

Luke watched, mesmerized, as a reversal of the previous magic happened again. First, the wings shrank down and disappeared entirely from view, presumably into Cain's back. Then, as his body started to shift back to its less bulky shape, the copper color of his skin almost seemed to swirl in iridescence over the surface of his body, until only olive-colored flesh remained. Too late, Luke realized the claws were already gone, and he had missed that, but he stared, transfixed, as the demon's harshly sculpted face receded and reshaped itself until his Cain stood before him once more.

As Cain got dressed, Luke realized that as much as that flying beast was a magnificent part of his fantasies, this being that stood before him now was the one he cared for more than any other. This was the being whose fears Luke wished, with every fiber of his being, he could chase away. This was the being who had to learn to trust him, else all was lost.

"Talk to me, Hawk," Luke pressed once Cain had dressed himself. "Who was that man who came to see you today? Who is he, and what could he possibly hold over you that allows him to dictate your life to such a terrible degree?"

"He is the Traveler," Cain shared, his voice so low Luke had to move closer in order to hear him. "He keeps tabs on the Naverto who choose to leave the clan. That is what I am, specifically." To Luke, it sounded like sharing these words was the hardest thing Cain had ever done in his life. "I am a Naverto demon."

"Okay." Luke still wasn't sure about the look in Cain's eyes. While before the fear had filled Luke with anger -- because Luke had assumed Cain had feared someone discovering their relationship -- that initial feeling now changed and slid down Luke's spine with the icy fingers of a different kind of fear. Something full of loss, or even death. Luke forced himself to continue anyway. "If this Traveler was just checking in on you, then why did his presence provoke such a strong reaction?"

"He wasn't just checking in on me," Cain said, his voice once again under control and steady. His eyes couldn't lie, though, and they were still wide and bleak. "He is special, and I didn't lie to you before. From wherever he is in the world, he has the ability to sense changes in my emotions and sexual activity. He can sense my aura. He can feel the shifts in my...my...well, energy, for a lack of a better word. He probably began sensing a small change when you started working for me, but it wasn't enough to garner his full attention. He is only one person doing this job, and there are many who choose to leave the clan. Some for a short time, and some, like me, who renounce and leave forever. When you and I had sex that first time, I knew his visit would only be a matter of time. Then we started to become closer" -- Cain's cheeks reddened -- "in other ways, and I knew the changes in me were something he would not be able to ignore. I tried to prepare myself to accept it like a man, but when I saw him today, I panicked. Then I saw Cassie, and the only thing I could think in that moment was to make him believe the brightness he could see surrounding me was for Cassie, and not for you. All I could think was that if I could fool him I'd be given a reprieve and that I could stay with you for a little while longer."

"So if he were to find out about us...what? He would drag you home? Is that what you're saying?" Luke tried to fit the pieces of this puzzle together. Cain's explanation jumped around so much Luke felt he was only getting jumbled bits and pieces. "Would he think he could take you home and cleanse you in some way? Is it so terribly frowned upon to be gay and a demon? I don't understand."

"Not all demon species," Cain answered. "But in mine, yes."

The short, vagueness of that answer, after the rambling Cain had done only moments before, raised the hairs on the back of Luke's neck to full attention. Pair that with the chill still working its way up his back, and Luke suddenly really didn't want to hear what Cain was clearly trying *not* to say.

Luke forced himself through the fear. It was the only thing he could do to help Cain through it too. "Trust me, Hawk." For the first time with this man, Luke made it an order, not a request. "I am young, but I am strong. If you want us to even have a shot, then you have got to trust me. With everything."

Cain's throat convulsed. "It is not only frowned upon to be gay within the Naverto species, it is illegal. Any discovery of homosexuality by the Council of Twelve or the Traveler can have only one end. You are found guilty of crimes against the procreation of the clan, and your execution is immediate. There is no jury process. There is no appeal. When I am discovered, for the Traveler *will* figure out my deception eventually, that is what will happen to me."

"No. Huh-uh. No." Luke shook his head vehemently. His mind

refused to process this. "No way. That can't be."

"Yes, Luke." Cain's voice was now solemn and resigned. "You wanted to know, and so now you must also accept. I have fooled the Traveler for a short while, but when he has a moment, perhaps when he gives his report, he will reflect upon my tale, and he will correctly assess that I could never carry on an affair with my brother's wife. He will realize I would never risk hurting Connor in that way. When he does, he will recall that you were the only other person here, and then he will know the truth. At that point, he will come for me, he will take me to Wales to stand before the Council of Twelve, and then I will be executed."

"No. No." Luke didn't want to believe it, but he looked into Cain's eyes and knew he spoke the truth. Luke staggered under the weight of this information, his legs suddenly very weak. Cain reached out and grabbed Luke's elbow, holding him until the world stopped spinning. "No, no, no. This can't be happening."

Cain's gaze softened in understanding -- a kinship that at this moment Luke desperately did not want. "That is exactly what was screaming in my head when I drove up earlier tonight and saw the Traveler standing there with you," Cain revealed with a small, stiffening shift to his lips. "That is why I did everything in my power to make you appear irrelevant and unimportant to me. I just wanted a little more time."

Luke's earlier anger at Cain's mean-spiritedness left him completely. He'd thought for sure there could be no explanation that would make him understand or justify Cain's behavior, but then again, he couldn't ever have anticipated this. "How can something like this still occur?" Righteous anger bubbled up in Luke and overtook the shock and disbelief. "It is completely barbaric."

"No." With that word, Cain shocked the hell out of Luke. "What it actually is, is practical."

Luke drew back and stared at Cain in horror. "How can you say that? It is a law that is going to end your life."

"I didn't say I liked it. What I said was that it was created for practical reasons. You see, for all the vigorous copulating in which

184 | CAMERON DANE

the Naverto species engages in, it is incredibly difficult to produce an offspring. The law was put into place to discourage same sex activity, male or female, whose activities would eliminate any chance of procreation."

"But you're not even living with those Naverto people anymore!" Luke exclaimed. "What does it matter to them what you do?"

"Because I'm relatively young within my species, and there's always the chance I could change my mind and rejoin the clan." Incredible calm filled Cain's voice, and with each logical point he made that put him one step closer to his own death, he killed Luke. "And even if I weren't young, as a Naverto male, I can produce a seed potent enough for conception all the way up until the year of my death."

"But you don't intend to do that!" Luke's ability to be big about this rapidly deserted him. After all, they were talking about the likelihood that this man would be ripped out of his arms very soon. He couldn't remain calm. "Can't you tell them you don't ever intend to mate with a Naverto female, no matter what?"


Now it was Cain's turn to have his heart split open.

"I can, and I will," he said gently. He reached out and brushed a tear from Luke's eyelash, a wetness it tore him up to see. "But it won't do any good, darlin'. It doesn't happen often, but every execution that takes place for this reason sends a powerful message among the Naverto who have the same kinds of feelings I do. It is effective in a way that nothing else can be. It encourages heterosexual activity even among those who do not feel it in their hearts, if only out of fear for their life if they do not perform what is considered their duty. This law very effectively does exactly what it sets out to do. It stamps down same sex coupling while at the same time promotes male/female unions, even if they are happening only out of fear for their lives."

"We'll run." Luke grabbed Cain's shirt and pulled him close. "We'll run away and hide you from this Traveler person. That is what we'll do."

"No." Cain let Luke down as gently as he could. He stroked Luke's glossy hair, taking this opportunity in case the end came quicker than he thought. "It doesn't work that way. The Traveler doesn't need my physical address in order to find me; he knows where I am because he can sense the location of my life force. Hiding won't make a difference. He'll find me, wherever I am, when he figures out the truth. Besides" -- Cain made an attempt at a smile -- "you could never leave your mother and sister, and I would never ask you to. You have a life here. And for as long as I have left on this earth, I have one too. I do not want to leave it."

"Then how could you do this?" Luke cried, suddenly battering Cain about the chest and shoulders with his fists. "How could you *let me* do it?" Luke's voice cracked in its agony. "Why did you let us keep having sex and getting to know each other? Why didn't you tell me the truth the first time we kissed? Why didn't you tell me what would happen to you if we continued? I never would have done it!" Luke jammed his knuckles into Cain's upper arm hard enough to make Cain wince. "I never would have risked you for sexual gratification! Not even for an intimate friendship. Never."

Luke jabbed Cain with a particularly hard punch, dead center in his chest. Cain reluctantly grabbed the arms pummeling at him, wrestling and subduing Luke until the man buried his face against Cain's throat. Luke seemed to crumple, and he locked his arms tightly around Cain's neck. Cain held Luke close, with his fingers linked at the base of Luke's spine. He remained silent and let Luke cope with all of the panic and fear that Cain himself had been dealing with slowly over the course of the last month. It was a lot for a body to absorb at one time, and Luke's sudden return to anger didn't hurt Cain. This was different. This came from the same place as Cain's panicked, flying leap into deception with the Traveler had.

This came from not wanting to lose one another.

Cain definitely understood that.

"I don't want you to die," Luke mumbled against Cain's throat, his voice fractured with the first stages of acceptance. "I don't want to let you go."

"I know." Cain pressed his lips to the top of Luke's head. He absorbed the scent of sweat and horses and underlying honey that was so distinctly this man. It was such a small pleasure, but just smelling Luke was something Cain now had to do. He had to get as much as he could as quickly as he could, for he would need Luke's inherent strength living deep inside him when it came time to face his death. "I know."

"I'll make you proud," Luke vowed, even as he clung to Cain harder. "Everything I do from now until your time to go will make you proud of me. And I promise --" Luke choked, unable to continue. His audible pain grabbed at Cain so hard that he tightened reflexively and lifted Luke right off the ground. Luke wound his legs around Cain's back and locked in tight. Cain had difficulty breathing through the tightness banding his chest, but he didn't care.

"I promise you, Hawk," Luke swore, "I won't" -- Cain felt the wetness of Luke's tears slide down the side of his neck, and in response, moisture pooled in his own gritty eyes -- "I promise I won't break after you go. I'll hold my head up. I'll make you proud even then."

Cain blinked hard and spoke through the thickness lodged in his throat. "You already make me proud, Luke. You make me happier and prouder than I ever thought I could be. And for the rest of the night" -- Cain started in the direction of the cabin with Luke still in his arms -- "I want to do something with you I've never done before."

"What?" Luke whispered against Cain's neck.

Cain and Luke were as safe as they were going to get, for now. The Traveler would still sense Cain's activity and emotions, but for now, and until he figured out the truth, he would believe Cain's feelings were for Cassie.

"I want to hold you in my arms all night long." Cain shared one of his dreams. Maneuvering his hold on Luke, he pushed the door open and then kicked it closed with his boot. "When I wake up in the morning, in *our* bed, I want your face to be the first thing I see. I want that from now on, for however long we have."

Luke squeezed Cain around the neck harder, giving Cain, without a lot of words, exactly what he needed. "I want that too."

They did just that. Whether it was cuddling close or shifting positions in their sleep, Cain and Luke never completely severed the physical connection between them, all night long.

———

CAIN WALKED OUT OF HIS bathroom the next morning, freshly showered. As he buttoned his shirt, he couldn't stop the warmth burgeoning within him, or a smile from taking him over as he looked upon the man sleeping so peacefully in his bed. *No*, he corrected himself immediately. *Not my bed. Our bed.*

He walked over to their bed and lowered himself on the edge next to where Luke slept. The man had one arm thrown wide and the other curled against his bare stomach. Leaning in, Cain braced his weight on the bed next to Luke's chest. He had work to get to, but he couldn't help himself. He leaned down and brushed a light kiss against Luke's pillow-creased cheek, his way of saying good morning, even if only he knew about it.

Luke stirred, blinking, seemingly still groggy, as he opened his eyes. He mumbled, "Morning," then stretched and yawned, still clearly exhausted. "What time is it?"

"Not quite early anymore," Cain replied as he brushed his fingertips across Luke's eyelids. "But not officially late yet either. Go back to sleep. I didn't mean to wake you. I'm going to feed the horses, and then I'll come back to make us some breakfast."

"Give me a minute." Luke tried to sit upright, but Cain held him down with an open palm to the center of his chest. "Hawk." Luke glared. "Let me up. I'll get dressed and help you."

"No." Cain shook his head and put a finger to Luke's lips before the sweet man could protest again. "You sleep in, just this once. I will take care of the morning feeding, and then" -- he smiled wickedly -- "I will come back. All right?"

Luke removed Cain's finger from his lips. "I really don't mind getting up to help you. I don't mind the work. I like the work. I get up and feed the horses every morning. It's part of why you pay me."

"I know," Cain agreed with an indulgent smile. "The fact that you work so hard is why I get such pleasure out of letting you relax in bed for just a little while longer, even if it's just for one day. Now…" As Cain got to his feet, he slid his hand across Luke's stomach. Luke's muscles contracted sharply, and a shiver rolled through his frame, pleasing Cain immensely. Hating to leave, he still said, "I'm going to go feed the horses," and started to move to the door, but then spun and laid his best "boss" stare on Luke. "I don't want to see you sneaking in the barn in five minutes to help me. Got it?"

"Okay." Luke stacked one folded arm behind his head and used his free hand to fiddle with the sheets, almost as if he had no clue what to do with free time. "Knock yourself out." He waved, almost pathetically. "Have fun."

"Okay," Cain mimicked, chuckling. He would get this young man to take a small breather from the hard routine of his life if it was the very last thing he did. Cain started for the door again. "I'll see you in a bit."

"Hawk!" The scratchiness in Luke's voice stopped Cain at the threshold of the bedroom door.

Cain turned and leaned his shoulder against the jamb. "Yes?"

Luke played with the sheets some more, his focus on his hands. "I woke up a couple of times last night." Then, finally, Luke lifted his gaze to Cain's. A perfect storm of silver and the deepest shade of gray colored his gaze; the power of its hold arrested Cain's heart. "Whenever I did, and I turned my head to find you, it felt good to always see you there. Safe. Right. I don't know." The fingers twisting in the sheets gathered more and more fabric in their path to wrinkling destruction. "I just wanted you to know that."

*Fuck, darlin'.* Cain's chest seized, and he moved back to the bed in three long strides. One move later, he was down on his knees.

Luke looked with wide eyes. "What?"

"Nothing." Cain didn't exactly know how to respond to Luke's honesty without losing his shit all over the place, so he did the next best thing. "I just want to give you a small preview of what's going to happen when I get back."

Luke's gaze deepened to mercury. "Oh." He licked his lips.

Cain slipped Luke's sweatpants down in the front, just enough for Luke's delicious, long cock to slip out; the shaft half hard already, due entirely to biology and nothing to do with Cain. "Mmm, one of my favorite flavors." Cain lowered his mouth to hover just above the mushroom head. "Morning wood."

Parting his lips, Cain took Luke's cock inside his mouth in one long drag, sucking, tasting, making wet slurping noises as he went almost all the way down to the base. The pungent smell of Luke's fur and the salty taste of his skin wrapped itself around Cain's senses. He bobbed up and down over Luke's rigid length three times and then circled the head with his tongue, licking the small drop of precum that had seeped free. Luke squirmed beneath him and let out a soft moan. With great reluctance Cain let Luke's cock slip from his mouth and then gave its tip one final, tiny kiss.

"Your wood could feed a man on the brink of starvation," Cain shared. He left Luke's cock and licked his way over the man's flat stomach, taking a moment to swirl his tongue in Luke's belly button before moving up to his chest. Settling his mouth over one of Luke's brown nipples, Cain darted his tongue out to flick just the pointy little tip. "But maybe for breakfast I want something a little lighter." Cain closed the distance to Luke's chest and started suckling on his nipple as if Luke could provide sustenance from the puckered, sensitive flesh.

With another moan, Luke wrapped his hand around the back of Cain's neck, holding him to his nipple. Grinning against Luke's chest, Cain gave Luke a little nip with his teeth and then moved on. He kissed his way up Luke's throat and under his chin, upward some more, to finally settle his mouth almost -- but not quite -- against Luke's. "Maybe that wasn't quite what I have a taste for right now either." Cain glanced up and met Luke's stare. Their gazes caught and held, and while he looked into Luke's eyes, Cain lowered his lips and took the man's mouth in a gentle, barely probing kiss. Luke's breath caught, and his lips parted. As soon as they did, Cain took advantage, sliding the tip of his tongue against Luke's, just allowing himself a hint of Luke's wet heat before pulling away. "That was perfect." Cain took Luke's hand in his. "That is what I always want. A small sip of the sweetest, most addictive taste I've ever experienced." Cain pressed a kiss to the center of Luke's palm, lingering for just a moment. "The taste of your kiss is what I love the most." After lowering Luke's hand back to the bed, Cain stood. His gaze never left Luke's, and with a grin, he took in Luke's slack jaw. "Like always, the taste of your kiss is just enough to make me want to come running back for more. I'll see you soon. When I come back I'll finish what I started."

Cain couldn't be quite sure, but he almost swore he heard Luke croak, "Hurry," before he left the cabin.

Cain smiled.

———

SLIDING OPEN THE BARN DOOR, Cain pushed the wood all the way into its pocket in order to let the morning sun shine in brightly through the big opening. He smiled and greeted each horse as he made his way to the feed room, making sure to tell each and every one of them how great they were and that it was going to be a wonderful day.

As Cain got to the final stall, Laura's Love, or -- Cain shook his head -- L.L. Cool J, as she also now answered to, the low-pitched ringing of the barn's landline phone drowned out his greeting.

"See," he told L.L. as he crossed to the white phone on the back wall, "everyone can tell it's going to be a beautiful day. That's probably Cassie calling to give Luke some insanely inappropriate gossip." Cain grabbed the receiver and put it to his ear. "Hello?" he greeted in an upbeat voice. "This is Cain speaking. How can I help you?"

"Oh, Cain, thank the heavens." A shrill, panicked voice -- definitely not Cassie's -- filled Cain's ear. "I've been trying to reach Luke for close to an hour."

"Ms. Forrester." Cain immediately recognized the voice, although, he had to say, he hadn't heard it used in quite this tone before. "Luke's not in the barn right now, but if you give me a minute, I can run and get him for you. Is everything all right?"

"I don't know. Maybe, maybe not. Is Risa out there with Luke by any chance?"

Dread suddenly fisted Cain's chest, sprouting beads of sweat on the outside of his skin, and fissures of cold on the inside. "No, she's not. Why? Isn't she at home?"

"No. She was supposed to go to work early today and help Mr. Palmer with inventory. When she didn't show up an hour after she was supposed to, he called me to find out if she was sick. Cain" -- Luke's mom's voice squeaked -- "Risa walks to work. It takes her close to an hour, and with her being an hour late before Mr. Palmer called me, that's two hours away from my house."

"I'm sure it's nothing, Ms. Forrester." Cain lied outright. He would not put this woman into a complete panic. "Maybe she forgot she was supposed to go in early and is hanging out with a friend."

"Yes, maybe." Ms. Forrester grabbed onto Cain's suggestion. "Maybe that's it."

"It probably is," Cain soothed as his mind raced. "Or maybe she is on her way to see us, but she's still walking. I'll get Luke, and we'll drive around and see if we can find her. I'm also going to get in touch with the sheriff --" Cain snapped his mouth closed and almost kicked himself when he said that. "As a precaution," he added. "I want you to start calling anyone who knows her and find out if she's with a friend. Then I want you to start calling neighbors one at a time, going successively further away from your home, and ask if they saw Risa pass by their house on her way to work. Okay?" Cain knew people needed things to do, otherwise they would go crazy. "You start doing that. I'll have my cell phone, so I'll keep checking in with you. All right?"

"Yes. Thank you." Cain could actually hear Ms. Forrester's relief through the phone line. "I'm going to get started on that right now."

"She'll be all right," Cain promised one last time. "I'll talk to you soon." He barely got the phone hung back up before he took off from the barn in a dead run.

# Chapter Eighteen

Cain tore open the door to the cabin and rushed inside. "Luke! Luke!" His voice filled the space. "Get up, Luke! Get dressed!"

Luke already had his sweats off and his legs slipped into his jeans when Cain reached the doorway. "What is it?" Luke dug his socks out of his boots and shoved them on his feet. "Is something wrong with one of the horses?"

"No." Cain couldn't think of a gentle way to share the information Luke needed to hear, so he didn't even try. "It's Risa." Luke paled to chalk white, and Cain's legs weakened as he watched. "Your mom just called the barn trying to find you. Risa was supposed to be at work over an hour ago, and she never showed. Your mom hasn't been able to locate her."

"MacLesten," Luke said. The single word was barely audible, but the fire beneath it was palpable. Luke's face changed to a cold mask unlike Cain had ever seen. Still putting on his shirt, Luke rushed past Cain to the outside.

Cain stayed close on his heels.

"MacLesten has her. That son of a bitch," Luke said, as if to himself, as he made his way to the barn. "He took her. I know it."

"I agree." Cain didn't bother to try and give another scenario. That was exactly where his mind had gone too.

Grabbing Luke's arm, Cain spun the man. He needed to see Luke's eyes, needed to be able to read his intentions. *Shit.* Cain didn't like the black rage he saw burning in Luke's mercury glare. "We have to get the sheriff, Luke." He shook the man. "We have to get the sheriff and tell him everything that happened to you. Then he'll believe us when we tell him MacLesten is most likely the one who has Risa."

"No." Luke shook his head so vehemently his neck made a snapping sound. "You go get the sheriff. *You* tell him about the line cabin on the far west end of MacLesten's property where I was held. That's where he has Risa. I know it. I don't care how much or little you tell the sheriff about what happened to me; none of that matters anymore. You just get him there as fast as you can. I'm going to take a horse and cut through Hawkins property to MacLesten land. That'll get me there a lot faster than a vehicle. I don't want that bastard to have one more minute alone with my sister. I'm taking a horse right now" -- he gave Cain a hard stare -- "and that's the end of it."

Cain nodded. He would never override Luke's need to ride to his sister's rescue. "Take Night Runner." He offered the best thing he could instead. Good advice. "He's the fastest horse I have. He'll take the push you give him and excel. Take the rifle with you. It's in the office; you know where the bullets are."

"Yeah, that's good." Luke turned and started running for the barn again.

Something primal and too powerful to ignore rushed through Cain; he raced after Luke until he was right on top of him. He whipped Luke around, grabbed the back of his neck, and hauled him in close. Plastering his forehead to Luke's, he said harshly, "You don't do anything stupid, you hear me?" He jerked Luke's head back and took the man's mouth in a quick, savage kiss. "Be careful." With a silent order, Cain forced himself to move away. One last look between them connected them as something far more intimate than merely a casual couple. "I'll be there with the cavalry soon."

Cain took off for his truck just as fast as Luke went for Night Runner. He did the smart thing for Risa, rather than the thing his heart wanted to do, which was stay right by Luke's side.

———

RISA GLARED UP AT THE disgusting animal; the scum who'd just backhanded her to the floor. Rubbing her throbbing cheek, she did the best she could to sooth the sharp sting of the hit. Strangely, she found it harder to control her anger than her fear, which, considering she was naked in a drafty cabin with a gross old man who clearly meant to do her harm, was something unexpected.

When MacLesten grabbed Risa by her long hair, dragged her to a cot in the corner of the cabin and threw her on it, his ability to do her harm finally sparked real fear in Risa. As her weight bounced on the thin mattress, flat from overuse, a half dozen sharp springs jabbed painfully into Risa's back.

Scrambling up into a crouching position against the wall, Risa made herself into as little a target as possible. Beneath this new fear, Risa's thoughts were just the same as they'd been since this man had chased her down with his truck and snatched her on her walk to work: make every hit and violation he took out on her body as difficult as possible to achieve. That was Risa's goal. No matter how many weapons Justin MacLesten had, or how many times he threatened to use them on her, or how he planned to hurt her in every conceivable way -- which he'd already told her in graphic detail -- she would not make it easy for him.

Risa wasn't stupid. She hadn't been raised in a vacuum or a bubble. She understood it was never smart to trust the word of someone who so clearly had every intention of doing her harm. Justin MacLesten was exactly that kind of man. Risa didn't for one second believe his occasional poor attempts to confuse her or charm her out of her absolute certainty of the horrors he was surely capable of committing.

Right then MacLesten wrapped his big, meaty hands around Risa's folded-up legs and yanked her down onto her back. She cried out as her head crashed into the wall; shooting lines of pain ran down her neck and arms. MacLesten covered her mouth with a slathering, sloppy kiss, pushed her legs apart, and shoved himself on top of her. His proximity made Risa sick, but she knew what she had to do. She let her body go lax, made MacLesten think she was backing off; she even pretended to kiss him back. As soon as he stopped smashing his slobbery lips against hers, she bared her teeth and bit him as hard as she could.

MacLesten howled. He reared up and cracked Risa across the cheek before she could get out of the way. "You little bitch." He fingered the edge of his mouth, touching where she'd drawn blood. "You might end up having more fight in you than your queer ass brother did. I didn't think I was going to have to tie you up like I did him" -- MacLesten looked down at her with a lecherous sneer -- "but maybe I will." He shoved down on her with his full weight, jamming her between the legs with his crotch, and Risa reminded herself to be grateful he still had his clothes on. "I think I'm gonna do it just for the fun of it." He covered her mouth with one hand and with the other twisted her breast brutally enough to spring tears to her eyes. All the while, his tone made it sound as if they were courting. "I think tying you to a bed will be a whole lot of fun."

Suddenly MacLesten shot upright and cocked his head to the side. Before Risa could even imagine what sickness had taken him over this time, he muttered, "Son of a bitch sissy prick," and hauled her out of the bed. "That little pussy doesn't have the good sense God gave him. Of course" -- he jerked Risa in front of him and jammed a gun under her jaw hard enough to make her teeth rattle -- "he renounced the qualities God gave him when he started begging other men to fuck him up the ass."

MacLesten dragged Risa to the center of the small cabin, right in line with the plank door. "Don't even try to sneak up on me, you fucking faggot!" he shouted at the top of his lungs. "Why don't you come in here and face me head-on, make me think you've got a little bit of manly pride left in your queer body!"

Risa stood still, attached to Justin MacLesten like the worst kind of body armor. She wasn't terribly surprised. She'd always thought her brother's old boss was nothing but a bully. Although MacLesten was big and nasty, Risa hadn't been completely terrified until this exact moment. She'd felt from the beginning she would do her best to keep alert and take the first chance to run, no matter what. But hearing MacLesten taunt her brother, and knowing with sick certainty Luke was indeed outside… In that moment, Risa's heart rate kicked into a whole new gear. She knew her brother, and she knew he'd let himself be killed without hesitation if it meant saving her.

*No.* Where Risa had burned hot with anger only moments earlier, she now shivered with cold, and her stomach quivered with fear. Pressure then hit her belly. She looked down as best she could, what with her head jammed up at an awkward angle due to the gun under her chin. She looked past the furry hand holding the gun beneath her chin, to MacLesten's other hand holding a four-inch skinning blade against her stomach. *Please, God. No.* Everything inside Risa pushed at her to scream at her brother to go away, but before she could squeak out a word, a shadow slid over the imperfections in the plank door. A split second later, the door exploded open, and her brother filled the space with a rifle braced against his shoulder.

"Let her go, you son of a bitch." Such seething emotion filled Luke's voice, he sounded almost inhuman. Risa did her best not to show her fear; she was very afraid that one move could push either of these men over the edge and get Luke killed.

"A tasty little morsel like this?" MacLesten sneered at Luke. When he licked the side of Risa's face with his disgusting, foul-smelling tongue, Risa counted to ten in her head and prayed not to vomit. "Maybe I'll have to tie you back up, boy, and let you watch. Show you what a real man is supposed to do with his dick."

Luke flinched visibly, and Risa could see how much it killed him not to be able to rush right to her rescue. "My sister has nothing to do with you and me, MacLesten." Luke took a couple of steps into the cabin. "So why don't you just let her go. Let her take my horse and get away from here. I'll let you work out your problems on me."

MacLesten's laugh lacked any trace of humanity. "I already did that with you, boy." The knife slid up Risa's stomach to her torso, and MacLesten started flicking the edge of the blade against the underside of Risa's bare breasts, like the scariest kind of loving caress. She watched as best she could, but MacLesten's hand holding the gun under her chin never even wavered. "And I say it's definitely time to play with this little gal now."

"Don't you touch her," Luke growled, his control clearly slipping. "I swear to God, you bastard, if you put even one more mark on her body, I'm going to put a bullet dead center through your skull."

"I'll do whatever the hell I want to her," MacLesten charged back. "I'll teach her every pleasure there is to know about her luscious young body. By the end, she'll be begging for it, just like you begged for your pathetic life when I got done teaching my lesson to you."

"I'm afraid I can't let you do that, Justin." Another voice cut through the air. Another body then filled the doorway, blocking out the morning sun with its height and width. A uniformed body, masculine in its frame, with a second weapon trained on MacLesten. Only this one was a Glock, not a rifle.

"Sheriff Boone." Justin greeted the newcomer as if he were having a party. "Can't say I was expecting to see you today."

"No, I don't imagine you were." The smooth, whisky voice of Sheriff Boone remained calm. "I was visiting with Connor Hawkins when I got a call that there might be something going on out here. Now I'm gonna need you to let that little girl go before someone gets hurt, Justin. All right?"

"Little girl? Hell, she's got to be almost eighteen," MacLesten scoffed. "Look at this stunning body here, Sheriff." The knife moved over Risa's breasts again, and then over the soft flesh of her belly, to finally rest at the V of her legs, against her nest of strawberry curls. "Look at the hair, Sheriff. Same on top as it is where it matters."

Risa looked away from her brother, forced herself to ignore the pain filling his stormy eyes. She concentrated her attention on the sheriff instead, on his steady hand and calm voice, as revulsion rolled through her every time the knife moved.

"She's got tits a world-class showgirl would kill for," MacLesten went on. "And shit, she's too poor for plastic surgery, so you know they're real. She ain't no little girl."

"I don't care about her age, Justin." The sheriff maintained his even tone, keeping cool, as his job surely dictated he must. "I care that you have her here against her will. I care that her cheek is red and swollen, which tells me you've hit her at least once. I care that you have a gun poised to shoot her and a knife where no knife should ever be. Now you need to let her go, right now, before this situation gets even worse for you than it is now."

"She's paying for her brother's sins," MacLesten replied. "Why don't you ask Luke Forrester why I have his sister, Sheriff? I think you'll find the answer real interesting."

"Luke Forrester is not my concern right now, Justin." Risa noticed the sheriff edge just a little bit to his left. "The only thing I care about is getting this girl back home safe to her mother without anybody getting hurt."

"He's a faggot, Sheriff!" MacLesten poked the gun under Risa's chin with a hard jab, the force making her teeth clink together painfully. "He's unnatural and sick. You want a queer like Luke Forrester hanging around town, hitting on your son? Your boy is an impressionable teenager, Boone. You want people like this sicko and his family living in our town trying to tell your son it's okay to want to fuck another man? You want your son even considering something like that? Because I don't think many around here do."

"I do not care about Luke Forrester right now." The sheriff edged to the left a little bit more. "Other than the fact that he's still holding a rifle on you." Sheriff Boone never took his eyes off MacLesten or Risa, as he added to Luke, "Which he should have stood down the second I got here."

Risa hoped Luke got the message. Maybe he did, but he still muttered, "Not a chance, Sheriff. Not until that bastard lets my sister out of this cabin."

Another presence suddenly cast more shadows over the floor of the cabin. "The numbers are starting to get stacked against you here, MacLesten," Cain said.

Risa noted that Cain had opted for a pistol similar to Sheriff Boone's.

Cain continued, "We have three guns trained on you and three bodies that are bigger than your one, ready to pounce on you."

"And yet I'm still standing because I still have the girl," MacLesten crowed to the growing crowd. "None of you is going to risk missing your target and putting a bullet in her pretty little body. Are you?"

Luke suddenly stepped back and raised his arm out to the side, holding his rifle away from his body. "You want me gone from this town, MacLesten?" he asked. One more step back, and he leaned the rifle against the cabin wall. "Will you let my sister go if I agree to leave your precious town and rid it of my gay presence? Is that what you want?" Luke's voice rose with each word. "You just tell me right now, and that is what I will do. You just give me the word. Right now."

"You think I'm gonna believe a single fucking word you say, you stinking faggot?" In a snap, MacLesten shifted the knife to Risa's throat; he now trained the gun on a defenseless Luke. "You promised me you were going to keep your fucking mouth shut, but then you went and sicced one of your queer friends on me and tried to make me think you got angels from hell watching out for you."

MacLesten's heart pounded like a drum against Risa's back, and she could smell the sweat pouring down his body. With his crazy talk, she suddenly knew without a single doubt he would soon snap. Her brother had already put his gun down, and she knew Cain would never risk her life. Risa knew it was up to her to do something. Now. Before it was too late.

*Think, girl.*

While MacLesten spouted off more hatred and ugliness, his attention remained focused solely on Luke. Risa swallowed and tested the closeness of the knife to her throat. The blade pressed hard enough to scare the hell out of her; she felt a small prick and then a line of slick wetness trickle down her neck. Even feeling that, she knew she had to take action. She only had one chance to end this well. If she let her weight go dead and dropped to the ground, MacLesten's hold on her would slice her throat right open. Instead, Risa strained her gaze as far as she could without moving her head, looking to the only other person in the room who might understand her plea and act on it. She looked up, up, out of the corner of her eye, and found an amber stare trained right on her and MacLesten. Sheriff Boone. He was Risa's only prayer for ending this before MacLesten's God complex took over and he shot her brother, no matter the consequences to himself.

Right then, just for a moment, Sheriff Boone dropped his gaze from MacLesten's face to hers. Risa took her chance. She held that amber focus, beseeching him with her stare to act. She nodded just the very slightest bit. Not enough for MacLesten to notice, but enough for that knife to kiss her neck once again. She then closed her eyes and prayed the sheriff understood what she asked for. She prayed Sheriff Boone trusted his shot.

Risa held herself as still as if death had already taken her, and she tried her damnedest not to flinch, no matter every slur and epithet MacLesten spewed, his spit spraying her cheek. Risa put her trust in Sheriff Boone.

Whether Risa's decision ended up coming a split second too late, or MacLesten's last grip with sanity just happened to crack right in that same moment, everything exploded in a cluster of gunfire in the span of a heartbeat.

Cain saw Sheriff Boone aim his weapon and fire, while at the same time MacLesten squeezed the trigger of his weapon aimed at Luke. As Cain screamed Luke's name, he took his own shot at MacLesten, backing up the sheriff's. Simultaneously, out of the corner of his eye, Cain saw MacLesten fall to the ground, as well as MacLesten's bullet slam into Luke, the force of the hit careening

Luke into the wall. Luke slid to the dirty floor in a heap.

"Luke!" Cain could do no more than register MacLesten hitting the ground, or Risa still standing in place as stiff as a statue. Sheriff Boone moved toward MacLesten, and Cain moved in on Luke. He dropped to Luke's side in a flash, pulling Luke into his arms. "Luke. Luke! Oh Christ, talk to me." Cain's voice was scraped raw. He laid Luke down and ripped his shirt open, sending buttons flying everywhere, and searched for the bullet wound.

Risa dropped to the other side of Luke and grabbed his lax hand. "Oh God, Cain" -- wet pools of green looked up at him for answers -- "is he still breathing?"

On the ground, Luke groaned, and a gray stare lifted up to Risa first. "Of course he's still breathing," Luke said, his tone a rather weak sounding grumble. "Just got…got the wind knocked out of me for a minute. That's all."

Risa leaned down and kissed her brother's forehead. "Thank God. I was so scared he would kill you."

Luke shifted his stare to Cain. Although pain filled Luke's eyes, the life still living there kick-started Cain's breathing again. "Thanks to Cain here yelling at me and shifting my position," Luke shared, "I'm pretty sure the bullet only clipped me near my shoulder." As Luke tried to move, he winced, and his face drained of all color.

Cain growled, making his displeasure known. "Don't even think about moving." Fear made his voice harsh and overbearing. He slipped his shirt off and used it to apply pressure to Luke's wound. To Cain's untrained eye, the bullet hole was a little too far away from Luke's shoulder, and a little too close to his heart for comfort. The blood, the entrance wound, all of it, made Cain's heart seize terribly. "You just took a bullet." He had to look away for a few seconds; he didn't want Luke to see the wetness filling his eyes. "You stubborn jerk. I could kill you myself for scaring me like that."

Right then, cowboy boots and jeans-clad legs came into view. Sheriff Boone leaned down and draped his uniform shirt around Risa's shoulders, shielding her nudity from view. "We'll have paramedics and deputies here in a matter of minutes," he told them.

"But I need your help, Cain." The Sheriff walked back over to Justin MacLesten's prone body. "He has two bullet wounds, one of them yours. I need you to help me stanch the flow of one of them until help arrives."

"Not a chance." Cain had no intention of moving from Luke's side. "You can put me in jail if you want, but that bastard can die right there for all I care."

"I'll do it," Risa offered, shocking the hell out of Cain. "Let Cain help my brother." After getting to her feet, she closed the sheriff's shirt up all the way to the very top button, and in doing so covered herself from neck to knees. She then walked the small distance to help the very man who'd terrorized her only moments ago. "I'll help you keep him alive."

Sheriff Boone nodded and handed Risa a towel; Cain figured he must have found it in the bathroom. "Good girl. Brave girl."

"No…" A familiar tenacity filled Risa's voice, one that reminded Cain of Luke. "I just want him to live long enough to have to face the looks of everyone in town when they find out what he did to me."

Luke shifted his attention from his sister back to Cain. "She *is* brave." A catch in his voice roughened his words. He then started coughing, a horrible hacking sound Cain couldn't bear to hear.

"Shh, shh." Leaning down, Cain kissed Luke's brow, cheek, and temple. "Save your strength," he ordered while combing his fingers through Luke's hair. "You can talk all you want later when you're all patched up. Okay?"

Luke held Cain's gaze, and even with the blur of their proximity, Cain absorbed the effects of physical pain starting to take over his partner. "I can't feel my arm anymore, Hawk." Luke's voice became so soft Cain had to stay close in order to hear it. "Is it still there?"

Cain's chest burned with terrible tightness, he was stunned he could still breathe. "Of course it is, sweetheart. It's just numb, but you're going to be fine." Shifting, he pressed a kiss against Luke's lips; such powerful emotion for this man slammed through him, Cain had to close his eyes against the tears threatening to start up again. Steeling himself, Cain kissed Luke again, and then tried to smile.

Christ, he didn't want Luke sensing his fear. "It's just a flesh wound. I swear."

"Liar." After he said that, Luke tried to twist his lips into a smile. Cain could tell.

Luke turned his head just a little bit, shifting his gaze to his sister, MacLesten, and Sheriff Boone. When he came back to Cain, clouds, more than just filled with physical pain, filled his gaze. "You have to back off, Cain," Luke stated, strength suddenly infusing his voice. "You might be able to trust the sheriff not to say he saw you kissing and holding me, but when those deputies and paramedics get here, you've gotta not be looking at me like you are right now, or else MacLesten's going to end up outing more than just me today."

Cain let go of the pressure he applied to Luke's wound and grabbed the man's face. He lowered himself until their foreheads touched; fire rushed through his being. "You listen to me, you stubborn, heroic jackass. I don't give a shit how many people see how I look at you, you got me? They're going to see my ugly mug looking just like this when they come in here and cart you away from this cabin. They're going to see it full of worry when I'm sitting at the hospital while you're in surgery. And they're going to see it determined to take care of you when I pick you up from that hospital and take you home. So don't tell me to pretend not to feel the way I feel about you, Luke. After today, I don't know how to do that anymore." Abruptly, Cain let go and went back to pressing his hands against Luke's wound, but he looked up and added, "You got that?"

Luke just nodded, but Cain thought he saw a new resolve settle in the man's stare, one that hadn't been there just a moment before. *Good.* It was about damn time to come out of hiding. For both of them.

With that decision made, Cain snapped his attention up to the other triage unit some four feet away. "What about the two of you?" he challenged, knowing full well his impassioned speech to Luke had carried through the small cabin. "Either one of you got a problem with us?"

"I already knew about my brother," Risa said without turning

204 | Cameron Dane

around. "And I kinda already figured out the rest when I watched the two of you working together."

Cain shifted his attention to Sheriff Boone and met that knowing, amber gaze. "And what about you?"

"Like I told MacLesten earlier," Sheriff Boone answered with that smooth, even tone of his, "I don't care about Luke Forrester's sexual orientation. If it doesn't relate to me protecting this town, then it does not concern me. I don't care about you being gay either, Cain Hawkins." And damn it if the man almost made it sound like the worst sort of offense that Cain had even questioned him on the matter.

The sheriff's words barely had thirty seconds to resonate before the sounds of tires and breaks squealing to a halt outside distracted everyone in the cabin.

Sheriff Boone had Risa temporarily take over holding both towels over Justin MacLesten's wounds. "That'll be the cavalry," he said as he made his way to the open door.

"Hey." Luke managed to reach up and caress Cain's cheek, drawing Cain's attention back down to him. Luke's smile was weak, but he murmured, "That's what you said you would bring me. A cavalry."

"That's right." Cain drew Luke's hand to his lips and kissed his palm. His eyes wet again, he said, "That's what I promised, and I know how to deliver."

"You do." Luke nodded, his gaze slipping and becoming heavy. "You really do."

All sorts of voices shattered the strange stillness in the cabin then. A multitude of blue uniformed paramedics -- along with the local volunteer firefighter crew -- filled the small space, all of them directed by Sheriff Boone.

As two men came Cain's way, Cain squeezed Luke's hand tight and leaned down until they were face-to-face. "Now you make me a promise, Luke Forrester."

Luke eyelids fluttered, but he met and held Cain's stare. "Anything," he whispered.

"Don't you dare die on me." Cain pressed his lips to Luke's, clinging there one last time, before one of the paramedics pulled Luke away. As one of the uniformed men transferred Luke to a stretcher, Cain took back his bloody shirt and slipped it on. "Don't you dare die on me," he whispered again.

Luke was already being carried away, though, so if he answered, Cain didn't hear it.

A smaller hand slid into Cain's much bigger one then, forcing Cain to focus. He did the thing he knew Luke would want him to do above all else. He plastered himself to Risa's side; he knew Luke wouldn't want his sister to be alone. Rather than follow on the fender of the paramedic van that held Luke, as his heart screamed for him to do, Cain stayed with Risa.

# CHAPTER NINETEEN

The clock ticked past one in the afternoon, and, considering the bitch of a day they'd gone through, Cain couldn't believe it wasn't nightfall already. He now sat by Luke's bedside, watching the man's chest rise and fall with steady, even breaths. Each time it moved, the sight reinforced to him that Luke was still alive.

Ten minutes ago, in the care of Connor and Cassie, Risa had gone home, at Cain's request. Risa would have to wait to give her statement to the sheriff anyway; Duke Boone was out breaking the news of MacLesten's actions to the bastard's wife.

Finally, right now, these were the first minutes Cain had been allowed with Luke since the paramedics had taken him away from the cabin on a stretcher. Cain couldn't imagine going through this day again, thinking even for a second he might lose Luke in a cruel blink of an eye. Yet Cain knew Luke would have to deal with so much worse when the Traveler came to take Cain away; that truth had not escaped him. There would be no hospital bed with a chair next to it where Luke could sit and pray for Cain's recovery; Cain would just be gone.

Christ, Cain had never really understood, had not truly had any sense of the depth of what Luke would have to deal with after he was gone, until earlier today when Justin MacLesten had put a bullet much too close to Luke's heart for Cain's wellbeing. For that split second, when Cain hadn't known where the bullet had hit Luke, he'd experienced what it would feel like to lose Luke. His heart had stopped; his insides had grown bleak and cold, as if he were living an eternal lifetime in the coldest, cruelest Montana winter night. Christ, the vision had been desperately lonely. Cain wiped his eyes and shivered.

"Here." A deep, familiar voice filled the room. A big, strong hand then lowered a paper cup of coffee over his shoulder. It was Connor. "I thought you might need this."

As Connor moved into view, Cain took the steaming cup of coffee. "Shouldn't you be on the road delivering Risa to her mother?" Cain asked as he slid the cup of coffee on the stand beside Luke's bed. His stomach couldn't handle the stuff right now.

Connor pulled a chair over and plopped down in it next to Cain. "I thought that might be better suited to just Cassandra's presence." Connor kept his voice soft in deference to Luke. "Just in case the girl wanted to say something about what happened to her. You know" -- Connor's jaw hardened -- "about what that son of bitch did to her before Luke got there."

"Cassie does have a way of getting people to share their innermost secrets." Cain shot his brother a sympathetic look. "Only in this instance, we don't have to worry about that. Risa wants everyone to know the details of what that bastard did to her." Cain's smile was that of a man who truly relished the thought. "She wants everyone to know what a twisted bastard Justin MacLesten is. MacLesten is going to pay for what he did to Risa" -- Cain swallowed against the rise of pain and anger threatening to take him over once again -- "and he'll pay for what he did to Luke too."

"That matters a great deal to you, doesn't it?"

"Ye --" Cain's voice hitched on the answer, so he nodded instead.

He made himself find his brother's dark, almost black gaze, and didn't look away. "Luke and I are together, Con, together in the way I can see right now you're thinking we are...in every way. Like you and Cassie are, but without the paperwork."

"Goddamn fucking shit, Cain." Connor's eyes slid closed briefly. "I never would have pushed you to take Luke on at your stable if I'd known he was gay." Swiping his hand over his face, Connor didn't succeed in smoothing the hard, flinty line compressing his lips. "I never would have put you at risk like that. You have to know that."

"It's okay." Cain let his protective brother off the hook. "He calls me Hawk, you know." Cain shared something intimate in a way he never could before, because he hadn't ever let himself feel softness or passion for another man. "Kind of like how you're the only one that calls Cassie Cassandra. It makes me feel special when he says it, and I love hearing it more than just about anything else in the world."

With his elbow propped on the arm of the chair, Connor dropped his chin into his hand. "Do you love hearing him call you Hawk more than your very life?"

Cain nodded. He didn't even hesitate. "In the same way I know you'd give up your last breath in order to be with Cassie." Cain knew exactly what he was telling his brother, without saying all the words. "I understand how you feel about Cassie in a way I never did before. Now I don't just *know* that you'd die for her, I *understand* why you would."

"Shit. With one big difference; you actually will have to die. Damn it, I won't lie to you. Part of me wishes you still didn't understand it. You're the brother of my heart, and I don't want to lose you."

Sadness filled Connor's gaze, and Cain knew his stare reflected the same. "I know."

"On the other hand" -- Connor offered a wicked, knowing smile -- "if I have to let you go, at least you're not going out for some back alley, experimentation, late night, slam-bam, thank you man. Luke actually means something to you. Just sitting here with you I can see that. I don't know how I didn't realize it before. He is a good man.

I've always liked him."

Cain threw back his head, and a sharp bark of laughter rang through the hospital room. "You are so full of shit, Con. You wanted Luke out of your house because you were sure he was hitting on your wife. You didn't like him so much back then." Cain met his brother's chastised stare. "You can't go getting convenient amnesia about that fact now."

"Well, it's like you said, I think every man is hitting on my wife." Connor looked briefly to Luke and then back to Cain. "I'm bound to be wrong once or twice."

Cain shook his head and rolled his eyes. "If you say so."

Cain shifted his gaze to Luke. Just seeing Luke lying there, waiting for the anesthesia to wear off enough to wake up, Cain re-experienced the pain of how close he'd come to losing Luke today. The rush of feeling, and the panic, drove home the knowledge that, either way, in a very short time, the inevitable separation would be a permanent one that no amount of praying could ever change. If Cain had realized one thing today, it was that he could do at least one thing to prepare for his separation from Luke.

"Listen, Con" -- Cain pulled his focus from Luke and put it back on his brother -- "I need to talk to you about something important."

"Always," Connor assured. "About anything."

This request was strangely the hardest and easiest thing Cain had ever needed to make in his life. Hard because he was finally, truly accepting he would one day be separated from Luke forever. Easy because making sure Luke's financial future was taken care of wasn't something Cain even had to think about twice. "When I die, I'd like you and Caleb to settle a percentage of my stake in Hawkins Ranch holdings on Luke. I don't expect you to give him my full third, but I want you and Caleb to discuss it and come up with a fair percentage. He is to have the cabin and the horses too. Please assure him he can do whatever he wants with them."

Connor blinked repeatedly, and Cain knew he worked hard to keep the moisture out of his eyes. Connor didn't interrupt, though, for that Cain was grateful. He just let Cain get it said.

"I don't need paperwork to be drawn up," Cain shared, "and I don't even need to know the number you and Caleb come up with. I trust you both, and I trust that you understand my feelings for Luke well enough that you will not forget this conversation or choose to ignore it after I'm gone. You take care of it, and don't let Luke turn it down. He's such a hard worker, and he's so proud. I know he'll feel like he's being given a handout. Make him understand that it is not. He comes first now in my life, just as much as Cassie comes first in yours."

Luke stirred just then, and for Cain, nothing else mattered. He shot up and over to Luke's side, taking Luke's hand and holding it against his chest. Luke blinked heavily, drowsily, until gray eyes finally appeared.

"Hey there, darlin'." Cain fingered Luke's locks away from his forehead, meeting his gaze. "Welcome back."

"Risa?" Luke asked. The effects of the anesthesia made his voice scratchy. "How is she?"

"She's fine." Cain lifted Luke's hand and kissed his fingers. "She's just fine. Cassie took her home for a little bit. I'm sure she'll be back with your mom in a while."

"Okay." Luke's eyelids fluttered and fell closed again. "So tired..." His head lolled to the side. "Arm hurts."

"You just rest." Cain leaned down, kissed Luke's furrowed brow, and then tried to smooth the worry lines out with his fingers. He settled on the edge of the bed and didn't let go of Luke's hand. "You just go to sleep, and I'll be here when you wake up."

Luke didn't open his eyes again, but he did twine his fingers within Cain's and squeeze. The hold was strong and sure, and Cain needed no other proof that he was right where he was supposed to be.

A soft sound made Cain glance up. He found his brother standing at the hospital door, already holding it halfway open, clearly in an attempt to escape undetected. When Cain caught his gaze, Connor mouthed the words *"It's done"* before slipping away.

With those two not even fully spoken words, Cain had complete faith that his wishes would be met, and that Luke would be cared for long after he was gone.

———

"OH GOD, HAWK." LUKE GRITTED his teeth as Cain's wet, eager mouth enveloped his cock. He pumped up his hips, offering Cain the rest of his length. "Don't stop, baby. I missed this so damn much." Sucking in a deep, hissing breath, Luke fell back against the headboard as pleasure coursed through his shaft. "Yeah...that's so good."

Right then Cain let Luke's painfully erect penis slip from between his lips. Cain looked over his shoulder to where Luke lay propped up against the bed, and his blue eyes darkened with obvious concern. "You all right?" Cain's gaze slid to Luke's bandaged shoulder and upper arm. "This isn't putting too much strain on you your first night home?"

*Home. In Cain's bed. In Cain's cabin.* Warmth spread right though Luke's insides. *I'm home.* A rightness of his place in the world filled Luke, a sensation he'd never even come close to feeling before. "I'm fine," Luke promised. He chuckled and slapped Cain's bare ass. The man had himself straddled on Luke's chest, and his lovely buttocks were right in touching and viewing distance. "Hell, you're the one doing all the strenuous work." Luke glanced back down to his rigid dick, so close to Cain's mouth. "I'm just lying here enjoying myself."

"That's all I want." With a grin, Cain went back to focusing on Luke's cock. "I just want you to relax." Cain then licked the length of Luke's prick up one side and down the other, as if it were a giant Popsicle and he didn't want any of it to melt away before he had a chance to savor it all. *Yes.* Luke reveled in the pleasure; he purred deep in his throat, loving the feel of Cain's tongue working over his extremely sensitive flesh. He could only love one thing more: being able to better see Cain while the man took his cock with those deep strokes. Thinking about how he could achieve that without moving, Luke instead found something he knew he would love even more than staring at his dick disappearing into Cain's mouth.

*Cain's ass.* Luke lifted his hands, ignoring the sharp tug of tightness the motion pulled in his shoulder. He cupped Cain's bare buttocks in his palms, then squeezed and spread his lusciously firm cheeks apart. *Yes.* "Oh, baby" -- Luke slid a thumb up and down Cain's crack -- "your pretty rose hole is practically winking at me. I think its begging me to put something in it. Do you want to be fucked?" Teasing, Luke fingered Cain's pulsing bud. "Is that what your sweet ass is trying to tell me?"

Cain made a strangled kind of moaning sound around Luke's cock, and in doing so created a strange, wonderful vibration through Luke's dick. Luke jerked his hips off bed in response.

Cain let Luke's cock slip from between his lips once more. "Do it, Luke." He burrowed between Luke's legs and licked at his heavy balls. "Fuck me with one of your toys." Hooking his arms around Luke's legs, he drew them up into a bent position. "Fuck me with one that can get deep. A long one that can fuck me hard and make me think it's you. I want you inside me, but I'm not giving this cock up tonight for anything."

With that said, Cain dived right back into his task. He took Luke's shaft deep into his mouth, and Luke knew he wouldn't give up that delicious feeling either. At the same time, he did so want his Hawk to lose his mind. Luke managed to shift his upper body far enough to the side to reach Cain's nightstand, slide open the drawer, and reach inside for toys and lube that had only ever seen the inside of a locked chest in Luke's old bedroom at his mother's house. Luke felt around for the toy he wanted, one that was a ridiculous pink in color, but had a long, thin length, with a knob positioned right in the place he knew would make Cain's toes curl when he felt it inside him.

*Got it.* Dropping the wand on the bed, Luke grabbed the tube of lube first. "Get your teeth away from my particulars for a minute there, baby." Luke squeezed a generous amount of lube onto his fingers.

After pulling off from Luke's cock, Cain twisted his body, and smiled something wickedly evil. "Worried?"

"You've only taken my cock twice," Luke reminded him, grinning back. Lightness filled Luke's heart; he hadn't felt this free since MacLesten had attacked him almost three months ago. "You bet your ass I'm worried."

"Chicken." Cain hugged Luke's thigh, rested his cheek against the muscles there, and slid his eyes closed with what could only be pure contentment. Luke liked what he saw, the picture of Cain content in his presence; trusting, as well. It was how Luke felt too.

Luke slipped his lubed fingers between the hills of Cain's ass cheeks and rubbed at the man's puckered hole. He felt the automatic tightening against the pad of his finger, but after a few seconds the squeezing eased. Cain slid his legs slid farther apart, pushing his cock against Luke's chest. Luke pressed Cain's entrance with a firmer touch, Cain rocked back against the contact, and Luke's finger slipped inside his lover's heated channel. Cain hissed, but his cock jerked against Luke, so Luke knew Cain was okay. After easing another finger in to work the lubrication into Cain's tight, hot passage, Luke then teased Cain's sweet spot with just a few tantalizing strokes, to the man's soft moans of delight, and then pulled the invasion away. His fingers weren't what Cain wanted tonight, and Luke knew it. Luke found it was his goal in life to give Cain Hawkins everything he wanted for as long as he could. *Tonight, it's some fun with a toy.* Luke lubed up the pink wand, wrapped the string bracelet around his wrist to anchor it, and then he slowly worked the slender, rounded tip into Cain's rectum.

"Oh Christ." As the slender probe penetrated Cain by slowly inching degrees, Cain moaned against Luke's leg. The man didn't stop making sexy little noises until Luke had more than half of the toy buried in his ass. "Damn it, it's not you" -- Cain squeezed Luke's thighs with python strength -- "but it's still so good. Fuck me... oh Christ, yes...just like that." Luke started shafting Cain with the wand, working Cain's sweet ass with more speed and vigor. "Ram it all the way in, just like when you take me." Cain bit at Luke's leg as Luke did just that. "Make me think it's you."

Riveted, Luke stared at where the toy took Cain's channel with deep, teasingly tormenting strokes, and he smiled along with every little whimpering noise Cain made. Cain rubbed his stiffening cock against Luke's chest, as clear an indication as anything that he got off on what Luke did to him. Luke slid the fake cock deep into Cain's channel again, and Cain moaned and writhed with the full penetration of his ass.

Luke loved how quickly Cain had taken to being fucked, just as much as he so clearly loved being the one doing the fucking. This pairing felt like the perfect fit for Luke, who had found within Cain's embrace a true love for being on the receiving end of his partner's cock just as much as he wanted to be the one taking his man. Relationships hadn't always been like this for Luke. With the two other men Luke had been in relationships with, he had not been as comfortable, or gotten as much pleasure, out of the other guy taking him. Luke had always preferred being in charge and being the one doing the fucking. With Cain, it was different. Luke didn't feel as if there was anything he could do wrong with this man. He trusted Cain so completely, in every way, that he felt no fear letting go in the path of Cain's fierce sexual desires. Luke knew Cain wouldn't abuse him or hurt him in any way -- which was why that whole incident with the Traveler had cut him so deeply. That hadn't been the real Cain. And in the end, Cain had found a way to trust Luke enough to tell him why. Luke wouldn't yet put voice or a label on their relationship, but damn it, when he thought about being with Cain, his heart already told him what the label would be. *The L one.*

Good God, how had Luke gotten so lucky to have found it with this man? And how long would he have Cain before the Traveler returned and took Cain away?

Right then, Cain pushed his ass back on the anal probe, uttering, "Oh yeah...fuck me." He fucked himself off with such raw honesty the sight and sound of it sucked Luke back down into a shared carnal place of pleasure. Luke didn't care that Cain had forgotten to reciprocate the pleasure of this mating; Luke only cared about making Cain lose his cool and for him to let go completely as his needs overtook him. Knowing now what pleased Cain, Luke shoved the wand all the way inside his ass, giving him the entire nine inches, nearly his own length. Cain howled in response and bit Luke's leg. He then started pumping his hips against Luke and sliding his cock all over Luke's chest.

*So beautiful.* "That's it, baby," Luke said. With one hand, he guided Cain's body against his chest; with the other he worked the probe in and out of Cain's ass in time with every jerking motion of Cain's hips. "Fuck my chest with your cock, take what you need. Come for me, baby."

Cain's erratic thrusting grew even more vigorous and out of control, but Luke kept up with the constant shifting. Every time Cain came down to grind his cock against Luke's chest his rectum tightened around the wand but Luke never let the toy slip free of his hold or control. He continued the hard, deep fucking Cain so clearly wanted this night. Maybe even needed. Luke slipped the probe past Cain's fluttering entrance once again and took his channel to the hilt.

Cain lifted his head right then, just the slightest bit. Sweat and redness took over the hard lines and angles, showing a man fully in the throes of sexual desire. "Oh Christ, Luke." Cain squeezed his eyes closed. "It's so good...I'm so close..."

Luke jammed the probe in deep one last time, and then started pulsing the length in short, lightning-fast strokes, barely moving the wand at all, in a way he knew would drive Cain wild. "Don't fight it," Luke ordered. Sticky, wet precum coated Luke's torso, proving Cain's extreme desire and needs; the man had fucking produced a lake's worth of early seed. "Don't fight the feeling. Come for me, baby." Luke withdrew the long wand completely from Cain's rectum. "Fucking come all over me." He then forced the fake dick back in, all the way home, and ordered, "Right now."

In rapid response, Cain fucked Luke's chest in earnest, smearing his dick all through the slick wetness, clearly looking for anything to give himself relief. Luke held the probe deep in Cain's ass, watching, loving the sight as much as anything he'd ever done with Cain. In mere seconds, Cain exploded before Luke's very eyes. His entire body shuddered, and sweat poured off him in droves as he came all over Luke, covering both of their middles with his scorching cum.

Minutes later, when Cain starting showing signs of returning to earth, Luke gently pulled the toy out of the man's ass and laid it on the nightstand. Cain shivered, and Luke couldn't help it, he leaned forward to press a tender, loving kiss to the small of Cain's back. His shoulder stabbed him with pain as he did it, but he only winced a little bit. He then took a moment to rub Cain's hole until the muscle settled and closed, and finally whispered, "Are you okay?" He kept his voice soft in deference to the overwhelmingly intimate feeling in the room.

Cain rose up on his hands and knees and looked back at Luke. "I'm all right." His mouth twisted into a harsh, almost angry-looking line, though, and he added, "It's just wasn't exactly what I had planned for your first night home. I got distracted, and I didn't mean to do that."

Nothing could have cut Luke up inside more than Cain's anger at himself. "Come here, baby." He reached for Cain, pulling and shifting him until he reversed Cain's position and he and Cain were face to face. With a tug in his chest, Luke noted that Cain made particular care not to put any weight near Luke's wound.

Luke reached up and combed his fingers through Cain's short, chestnut hair, and smiled gently. "What happened may not have been what you planned, Hawk, but it was exactly what I needed."

Cain's pupils flared, nearly drowning out the blue. "Really?"

Luke nodded. "Really."

A smile started to tug at the corner of Cain's mouth, and a blush stole over the slashes of his cheeks. Leaning down until their noses touched, yet still holding himself up on his hands so as not to put any weight on Luke's shoulder, Cain whispered, "Then I have just one thing to say." He closed the distance between them and pecked Luke's lips with a light, teasing kiss. "Welcome home, darlin'." He then lifted up, and Luke found the man's ocean gaze again.

It was about the best damn greeting Luke had ever heard.

He pulled Cain down on top of him, injury and all, and made sure Cain knew it.

# CHAPTER TWENTY

"I swear to God, Cassie" -- Luke sat shotgun as Cassie drove -- "between you and Cain, you'd think I don't know how to do anything for myself anymore." Luke gave Cassie a pointed look, much as he had Cain earlier that morning over breakfast. Cassie had her focus on the road and not on him, and thus his glare wasn't any more effective on this woman than it had been on Cain. "I have been driving since before it was legal for me to be behind the wheel, you know. I can take myself to and from my therapy sessions without any help from either one of you. I know it's shocking to hear, but I promise I can do it."

"Can the sarcasm, Forrester," Cassie replied. "You're almost home, and you're still breathing, so obviously it didn't kill you to let me help out. Aside from that" -- she took her attention off the dirt road for a second and sent him a knowing glance -- "you know you're eating up the way Cain is fretting over you, so don't try to pretend to me that you're not. I know you too well."

Luke had the grace to blush. "I did. I do. Because of this damn shoulder" -- Luke rolled the sore appendage, cursing the limitations his injury created -- "he's not letting me do nearly the work I need to in order to feel useful. He's giving me orders to keep it light and to stay clear of the more finicky animals right now, and it's pissing me off, because he knows I can't fight him on it. He's right, and we're both fully aware of it. I shouldn't be working with Calliope right now, even though I want to. I'm not yet fully healed enough to handle her if she throws me or fights me. He'd never forgive himself if I exacerbated my injury due to something he knew I wasn't ready for. Trust me, it's frustrating as hell."

"Yeah," Cassie agreed. "But that's just the way marriage is sometimes." As she pulled into view of the cabin, she reached out and quickly squeezed his forearm. "You just have to roll with the punches and save your frustration for a battle you have a prayer of winning. Because this one, my friend" -- she rolled the truck to a stop just past the cabin -- "you don't."

Luke had started sputtering, and his chest began to pound in earnest, the moment Cassie had so casually mentioned the word marriage in connection to what he had with Cain. Before Luke could get too scared about the connotation and repercussions, not to mention everything the word marriage meant to him, something in the distance grabbed his complete attention. *What is that?* In the path to the main paddock, a huge blue tarp covered only God knew what. In addition, just to get Luke's heart pumping again, because apparently it wasn't thumping hard enough already, he noticed Cain working in the corral beyond. Completely transfixed, Luke watched Cain circle Fancy Face in a canter around the perimeter of the paddock. Cain then left the structure, riding her, and headed right for them. *Good God.* Luke gulped. The man knew how to sit a horse with authority. And God help him, but Luke could only think he did it with incredible sex appeal.

Before he'd even realized he'd done it, Luke got out of the truck and strode toward Cain, meeting him at the halfway point, just as Cain slid off the horse.

"I've been watching for you," Cain shared. His voice was laced with an energy Luke had never heard before. Not nervous exactly, but more like contained excitement. "I didn't think you were ever going to get here." Strangely, Cain handed Fancy Face's reins over to Cassie, and then grabbed Luke's hand, dragging him across the yard. "I missed you. I have something I want to show you."

"I missed you too," Luke answered, confused as hell. He let Cain pull him to the tarp anyway. "Cassie slowed us down." He threw the woman a meaningful glance over his shoulder. "I swear to all that is sacred that she had to stop and pee four times between here and Billings."

"Hey!" Cassie drew up straight and threw her shoulders back. "I was instructed to slow us down." She pointed at Cain. "By him. That's all I'm saying." She led Fancy Face in the direction of the barn. "Bye."

Luke turned back to Cain, finding the light and extra brightness in the man's gaze even more of a puzzle now. "What is she talking about?"

"Nothing. Never mind." With a quick kiss to Luke's hand, Cain then let him go and circled around to the back of the long tarp. "It doesn't matter anymore, because it came today, just like it was supposed to. It's for you. Well, it's not really for you, but I want you to see it first. Because it's kind of for you --"

"Hawk." Luke raised his hand and cut Cain off. "What are you talking about?"

"This," Cain said. Then, like a magician, he took hold of the tarp and snapped its length back with a flick of his wrists, unveiling the item that had, up until then, been completely hidden.

*Holy. Fucking. Shit.* Luke couldn't believe his eyes. He was amazed his knees didn't buckle under the weight of overwhelming emotion flooding his body and shooting adrenaline straight to his heart. His hand went to his mouth, covering it, wiping away words he couldn't yet speak aloud. He looked, and looked, and still couldn't believe his eyes. What this gift meant to him. What it meant about the kind of man Cain was to have done something so beautiful and kind. *Shit.* In front of Luke sat a mobile wheelchair ramp used for paraplegics and quadriplegics to get on a level with a horse's back, thus making it easier to be lifted and transferred to a horse. Sitting there like a king's crown, at the top of the ramp, was a specially designed saddle with back support and a chest harness so that someone like his mother could ride.

"Well?" Cain prompted from the other side of the ramp. "What do you think?"

"You --" Luke finally managed to find his voice, but just barely. He pointed at Cain but then paced away from him, unable to even look at the man just then. This gift… Luke's feelings… Everything was just too much to fathom right now. "You --" Luke turned and stalked back over to Cain, pointing again. "You can't do something like this overnight. Those saddles are custom-made, and they don't come cheap. You must have been planning this from the moment you met my mother." God, Luke could barely comprehend such information. He knew these two items alone had to have run Cain between three and four thousand dollars, and it would have taken longer than just a few days to put a gift like this together. "You must have been planning this ever since you saw her in that wheelchair." Luke paced away again. God, he had to. His heart squeezed with unbearable tightness. For this one man. "Haven't you?"

"Since that night actually," Cain admitted. Luke didn't face Cain, but he heard the change in the man's voice. The barely checked excitement that had filled Cain before now held a trace of hesitation, uncertainty. The crack broke Luke's heart to hear, but he still couldn't gather himself enough to respond. "When you told me riding was what your mom missed the most after she had her accident," Cain rushed on, "I remembered reading something about special saddles. The ramp I found on the Internet. That night, I could see in your eyes how much it tore you up not to be able to give your mother a way to ride. Don't you understand?" A plea filled Cain's voice, and the sound sliced Luke open once again. "Now you can give her a way to ride. This gift is for you, so that you can give it to her. So that you can ride with her again."

Luke shook his head, trying with the last vestiges of his will to hold his feelings inside. The emotions coursing through him had come too much too fast, and they would scare Cain if he understood the depth to which Luke already felt them. Still… *Fuck.* Feelings Luke could barely control pushed inside him to be free. "I can't believe you did this," Luke breathed, knowing and believing, but still not quite able to process the information. "I can't believe you fucking did this and managed to keep it a complete secret from me."

"Cassie knew, and Risa helped me too. I needed someone who could custom fit the saddle to your mother. Do you not like it?"

From across the dozen feet separating them, Luke could hear the scratch in Cain's throat, and the sound created more cracks in Luke's resolve to hold everything bubbling within inside.

Finally turning to face Cain, Luke assessed that Cain no longer stared at the ramp and saddle. The man fidgeted, and he shifted between taking fleeting glances at Luke and then dropping his gaze to the ground. The sight tore Luke up inside even more. *Oh God. Please help me.*

No longer able to stamp down the fierce emotions living inside him, Luke strode over to Cain in big steps. He grabbed Cain's shirt, twisting it in his fists, and shook the man. Cain finally lifted his gaze up from the ground, and Luke was right there waiting for him. The insecurity in Cain's blue eyes pushed Luke over the top, past the point of no return.

*He's too wonderful.* As Luke stood there on Cain's property -- a place that felt more like home to him than any other in his life -- Luke fell. He knew there was no turning back. *He has to know.*

*Man up, Hawkins.* Cain's gut twisted, and he wished like hell it didn't hurt so much to have his gift rejected. He'd never experienced anything quite so acutely, pointedly painful before. "Did I overstep my bounds, Luke?" Cain knew he sounded weak, broken, but he found himself unable to stop the flow of blood. "Is this going to insult your mother? Do you think I'm trying to buy --"

Right then Luke yanked Cain down with the hold on his shirt

and shut him up with a hot, searing, openmouthed kiss. Luke took Cain's mouth in a way that felt like possession. But just as fast as Luke had taken Cain's mouth, he broke the kiss. Luke pulled away, his gray eyes glittering silver in the sunlight, and he growled, "I'm not mad, damn it. I'm overwhelmed by your kindness, your thoughtfulness, and your generous heart. Don't you get it, Hawk? I'm not very good at hiding it anymore. I'm in love with you. There, I've said it. I'm insanely, madly in love with you."

Cain's entire world crashed to a standstill. "Wh-what?" His heart stopped. He actually felt the muscle contract and squeeze against his chest, stopping his breathing. Then it started pounding so hard and fast his ears rang too loudly, and he couldn't be sure he'd heard what he thought he'd heard. What he desperately wanted to have heard correctly. Cain forced his lips to move. "What did you say?"

"You heard me." Luke held onto Cain's shirt with a death grip, his eyes glittering like mercury in the sunlight. "You make me feel so much, all of the time, and it has become so big inside me that I can't not speak of it any longer. I love you, Cain Hawkins. I am desperately *in* love with you. Lord knows, I tried not to be. From way back on that first day when you came out on your porch without a shirt on and had me immediately hard for you, I told myself not to fall. But you --"

Luke pulled Cain to him with sure, incredible strength, and Cain went willingly. Their faces were only inches apart, their breaths mingled, as Luke added, "This is all your fault. How I feel, how I can't make myself *not* feel, is all your fault. It wasn't inevitable. If you hadn't been so wonderful right from the very beginning, this wouldn't have happened. If you hadn't comforted me that night in my old room, or hadn't gotten pissed off at me for doubting that you would keep me when I told you I was gay, or if you hadn't praised me so much every time I did something good with the horses, or dared me to kiss you that first time when you were so obviously uncertain, or if you hadn't had the bravery to come to me that first night we were together, or later on when you took a chance and showed me the other side of what you are --"

"Shut up." Cain's voice was thick and raspy. He covered Luke's mouth with his hand and started walking him backward toward the cabin. Cain had a powerful need, and it couldn't be denied. "You're going to have to stop talking, Luke, because right now, I need you naked more than I ever have before."

"Wha-what?" Now it was Luke's turn to look like a deer caught in the headlights.

"You heard me." Cain's heart raced so fast he almost couldn't breathe, and he was very afraid a river of tears sat right behind his eyes, pressing to get free. It was all because this man had given Cain words that only his brothers and Cassie had ever given him before. More than that, even more staggering for Cain's soul to understand, was that he knew that Luke meant them. Luke wasn't his family -- people who in a sense were obligated to have affection for him. Luke had picked Cain all on his own and had given his love because he wanted to. Not because he had to. *Shit.*

Cain wasn't the type of man who could feel a gift like that and not react. But he also wasn't nearly so eloquent nor softly spoken as Luke. "You don't say something like that, Luke Forrester, and not expect to have to deal with consequences. If you really thought you could say…" Cain stopped, overwhelmed. He grabbed Luke's face in his hands, drawing their heads together until their lips touched, just barely clinging together, but still conveying a swelling depth of feeling in a touch so light it almost wasn't a kiss. Cain let the kiss end and started guiding Luke in the direction of the cabin again. "If you think you can say those words and not believe I'm going to need to be inside you within five minutes of hearing them, then you don't know me at all."

"Wait." Countering Cain's strength, Luke forced them to a stop. But not for long.

"Nah uh, darlin'." Cain jerked Luke to him and rubbed himself against the sexy, sweet man. "Feel that?" He slid his cock against Luke's, loving the feel of his man, even through his jeans. "It's already crying because it needs to go home. Home is inside you, Luke. It's where I need to be."

Luke's chuckle sounded half as much like a groan. "Believe me, Hawk, I want you there too." He leaned up and kissed Cain on the cheek. And damn it if the gesture didn't make Cain feel as if Luke were masterfully handling an indulged, randy husband on the hunt. "Just give me a minute to get something out of Cassie's truck. It's something important I want you to see."

Christ, Cain had totally forgotten about Cassie. "All right, Luke, go get what you want to show me, but make it fast."

Luke grinned and ran for Cassie's truck.

While Luke did that, Cain turned in a circle and found Cassie trying to slip from the barn to her truck unnoticed. "Hey!" Cain jogged and caught up to her.

"Yes?" Cassie cheeks blossomed with color, and Cain knew she'd heard at least some of his conversation with Luke.

Cain blushed himself. "Thanks." He dug his hands into the back pockets of his jeans. "You know, for all your help."

"No problem."

Luke came around the front of Cassie's truck as she climbed in behind the wheel.

"I'll talk to you soon." Cassie blew them both a kiss, and drove away.

Five seconds later, Cassie no longer existed in Cain's thoughts. Luke stood beside him, so beautiful and alluring without even trying to be, and stole Cain's entire focus. The mere sight of the man made Cain groan, and he dragged Luke the rest of the way to the cabin. After getting them inside and shutting the door, Cain pressed Luke up against the wood and plastered his mouth to the other man's for a long, drugging kiss. He held Luke's head in a powerful grip and rubbed his thumbs against the outer seam of Luke's lips. The moment Luke opened up for air, Cain took full advantage and slid his tongue inside for a deeper taste. With a moan, Luke returned Cain's kiss in full force. Luke slid his hands up Cain's chest and around his neck. Suddenly the pointy corner of whatever Luke held poked Cain in the cheek. Cain tried to pull the thing out of Luke's hand to drop it to the floor, but Luke suddenly broke their kiss and strong-armed Cain a pace away.

"Here." Luke handed Cain a brown folder. He slipped past Cain, moving across the small space, until he stood in front of the TV. "Sit down." Luke gestured to the couch. "Take a few minutes to look through that and then I'll tell you what it means to me." A flush crept up Luke's face. "What I want because of it."

"All right." Clueless, Cain walked to the couch and sat down. He wasn't worried, though. If Luke needed something, Cain would give it to him without question. He wasn't suspicious. He wasn't distracted either. His dick pressing against his jeans wouldn't let him be. "But seriously, darlin'" -- Cain opened the folder -- "go ahead and start taking your clothes off, because I'm going to need you naked and ready for me by the time I'm done flipping through this."

"I won't argue with that." Luke started unbuttoning his shirt. "I want that too."

Luke moved to work his belt out of the loops. With extreme difficulty, Cain forced his hungry stare away from the enticing image of Luke's flat, hard stomach, and he opened the file instead. This file was obviously very important to Luke, and in Cain's mind that made it important to him too. It didn't take Cain but a few minutes to care in earnest.

And then to be terrified.

"Why are you showing me this?" Cain held up the file. *Luke's fucking medical records.* "Is something wrong with your wound, and you didn't want to tell me about it before? Are you hurt? Are you sick?" Cain's voice rose with panic, but he could not control the squeeze in his throat. "Damn it, Luke, tell me what it is, and I will find a way to make it better. I will not lose you. Do you understand me?"

"No, Hawk, no." Luke held up his hands, and he was already beautiful in his nudity. To Cain's uneducated eye, with the exception of the bandage still on his shoulder and upper arm, Luke looked healthy. Luke rushed to Cain and knelt on the rug in front of him. "I'm sorry, I didn't think. I didn't mean to scare you. God, that was stupid of me, what with everything that has happened recently."

Pushing his way in between Cain's legs, Luke reached up and stroked Cain's cheek. "I'm fine, health-wise. I promise."

Cain dragged Luke's hand down and pressed it against his mouth. "You swear?" His heart thudded so loudly he felt certain Luke could hear it. "You're really fine?"

Luke nodded. "In fact, that's what I wanted you to see in the file. I am healthy in every way."

"Okay." Setting the files aside, Cain then pulled Luke up on his lap until the sexiest -- healthiest -- man he'd ever known straddled his lap. "But you didn't have to offer proof of how well you are doing." Cain circled his arms around Luke's waist and pulled him forward, putting Luke's golden chest right in line with his mouth. "I believe you." With one dip down, Cain pressed his parted lips against Luke's nipple. From teasing the man often during their time together, he knew the small disc was incredibly sensitive. Flicking out his tongue, Cain licked the little tip. Luke inhaled sharply in response; Cain felt the intake of air against his lips. After licking Luke's chest one more time Cain pulled back and looked into Luke's eyes. "That doesn't mean I'm letting you back on an untrained horse yet, darlin'. Doctor's okay or not." Cain then kissed his way across to Luke's other nipple, desperate to taste it too. "Because you don't yet have mine."

"You don't understand…" As Cain slid his palms down Luke's back to cup his ass, Luke's protest changed to a low groan.

When Cain grazed the tips of his fingers over the slick substance coating Luke's crease, Cain groaned too. Christ, the man had worked fast while Cain had been looking over the medical file. Cain's prick couldn't be more pleased. The only thing deterring his pleasure was his own cock still sat trapped inside his jeans.

"What don't I understand?" Cain kneaded Luke's muscular buttocks, loving the firm flesh. "Tell me while you get my cock out for me. I don't want to let go of your ass."

Luke rose up on his knees to get at Cain's belt buckle and zipper. Moving too, Cain slid his middle digit along Luke's crack until he reached the man's bud. Luke automatically gyrated into the touch, but Cain didn't give him what he wanted. He didn't penetrate the snug barrier with his finger. Today, after hearing Luke declare is love, Cain wanted to breach that hole with his cock first.

Air suddenly caressed Cain's heated penis. As Luke took Cain in his capable hands and started stroking his thick, rigid length, Cain cried out with the shock of fast pleasure. "Get me ready." Cain pumped his thickening length up into the tight glove of Luke's hands. "Get a condom and the lube...oh Christ, that's good." Luke manipulated Cain's tip and his testicles at the same time. *Shit. No time.* Cain grabbed for the side table drawer himself. "I need to be inside you right now."

Luke reached out and stilled Cain's hand over the box of condoms. "I already have the lube." He slicked Cain's cock up with the clear liquid. "That's why I wanted you to see my file. For as long as we have together" -- Luke squeezed Cain's hand until Cain released the box of condoms and it dropped to the floor -- "I want it to just be us. I don't want a condom between us anymore."

With the speed of a bullet, Cain shot his complete attention up to Luke. "Wh-wh-what?" Stunned did not even begin to describe Cain's feelings. This man -- with his beautiful heartfelt confessions -- had turned Cain into an idiot incapable of speech twice in one afternoon. With what Luke had just confessed to wanting, Cain was surprised he hadn't lost it and come right in Luke's hand. "Wh-what did you say?"

"That's why I wanted you to see the file," Luke shared. He leaned forward, letting their chests press together. He tipped Cain's head back and gently combed his fingers through Cain's hair. A storm of emotion swirled in Luke's gaze, and the sight mesmerized Cain. He could not look away. "I've only ever been with two men in my life before I met you, and those relationships were short-lived and well-ended over four years ago. I've been celibate since then. I continue to get tested, and I just wanted to give you physical proof that I am clean, in every way. Before you are taken away from me..." Luke's words were stripped from him for a minute then, but Cain could see everything he tried to say in his eyes. "Before you go" -- Luke grazed Cain's face with feather soft touches -- "I want to know what it feels like to have you inside me without so much as a thin latex barrier between us." Luke's face almost crumbled then, but Cain's throat constricted far too tightly to offer any kind of verbal comfort. "Please, I know I'm the only one you've been with, and I trust you. Make love to me, Hawk. Right now. Just you and me. Please."

Cain didn't have words, and he couldn't tear his gaze away from Luke's. Instead, he tried to say everything in his heart through actions. He tilted Luke's hips forward, against him, with one hand, held his cock steady in the other, and gave them what they both needed. Using the head of his cock, Cain rubbed, teased, and settled that naturally nervous muscle between Luke's cheeks, relaxing the man with light contact, and then nudged his way inside. *Oh Christ, yes.* Cain pushed his cock deeper inside Luke's ass, and scorching heat seared his length. Tightness, such wonderful goddamn tightness, immediately had Cain's shaft begging for full, fast friction. Instead of pounding away, though, Cain watched Luke, staring as the beautiful man gasped at that first invasion. As Cain continued to ease Luke's weight down on his cock, Luke breathed through clenched teeth, but Cain didn't stop, couldn't, until he'd fully seated himself deep inside Luke's glorious ass.

Then Cain didn't move. With a hand to the small of Luke's back, Cain held him in place, and never once pulled his stare away. "Tell me again." He broke his silence with his request. Something that came out more like an order. He couldn't help his tone, though. "Tell me again."

Luke's eyes flashed, and he brushed his thumbs over Cain's open mouth. He clearly knew exactly which words Cain wanted to hear. "I love you."

In response, Cain's cock swelled and pulsed deep inside Luke's rectum. "Again." He darted his tongue out and licked the pad of Luke's thumb.

"I love you."

Cain caressed Luke's lean hips, and he rocked the man just a little bit, hardly a fraction, but that small motion was enough to make the nerve endings in Cain's cock scream with need. "Again." Cain pulled

Luke down until their faces touched.

This time Luke spoke against Cain's mouth. "I love you." He held Cain's face and pressed a kiss to his lips. He seemed to understand what Cain needed, and gave it to him again on his own. "I love you."

Cain felt the words race all the way through his body, like gasoline on a fire. "Don't stop." He started them moving faster, unable to deny them what their bodies needed.

Smiling against Cain's mouth, Luke whispered, "I love you. I love you. I love you," again and again.

Just then Cain shafted Luke particularly deep, and Luke squeezed his eyes closed as he took the full, hard penetration. Seconds later, though, Luke opened his eyes again, and their gazes locked. Cain didn't want Luke to ever look away. He needed the truth of the love he saw reflected in Luke's eyes as much as he needed the words.

*Even more than I need his body.*

The shock of that truth spearheaded Cain's physical response. He knifed his hips up, taking Luke's ass as deep as he could. Holding them merged together, Cain clamped his arms around Luke's waist, linking them completely, like a lock and a key. "Tell me one more time." His voice so terribly ragged, Cain feared his plea came out more as a sob, but he could not hold back his need. "Please."

Luke tunneled his fingers through Cain's hair, held his head steady, and clamped his ass like a vise on Cain's cock. "I love you, Hawk." He made it a vow. A pledge. The emotion burned deep in his bright stare. "I will love you always."

Right then, no movement, no friction, going on pure emotion, Cain lost what was left of his soul. He spilled deep inside Luke's body, spurting a slow, continuous stream of his seed, coating Luke with everything he felt that he couldn't bring himself to say.

Luke cried out as the scorching wet heat of Cain's essence filled his channel -- the only man to come inside him without a layer of protection between them. The insanely intimate feel of Cain's cum, paired with the almost agonized, trapped emotion locked behind

Cain's blue eyes, pushed Luke over the edge too. With his cock trapped between their stomachs, Luke shuddered and spilled himself on Cain's belly.

Neither man said a word afterward. They just held each other in silence for long minutes, but they both felt the change in what they meant to each other right then.

They both knew, for better or for worse, there was no going back.

# CHAPTER TWENTY-ONE

"Remind me to thank Cassie again for giving us this glider," Cain said, his voice rumbling against Luke's back. Cain kept them in a slow, rocking motion with the heel of his boot on the porch floor. "It's nice to sit out here in the evening and enjoy the breeze after we're done taking care of the horses."

Luke liked being stretched out across the glider's slatted wooden length while tucked between Cain's legs, with his head resting against Cain's chest. Luke wasn't sure Cassie had intended for them to snuggle when she'd brought the glider over -- along with instructions to use it as a part of Luke's recuperation process -- but it was working out rather nicely for that purpose anyway. Cain had already ordered a new one to fill the empty space on Cassie's back porch; he'd told Luke there wasn't a chance in hell he was ever giving this one back. The glider was a nice place to just sit and be, or to think. Or, like right now, to broach a subject Luke had hoped Cain would have mentioned since Luke's shooting, but had not.

"So, Hawk." Luke drew little circles on Cain's jeans-covered knee. "Do you want to tell me about the angel from hell I apparently have watching out for me?"

Cain tensed against Luke's back. "Damn it," Cain said softly. "I was hoping you hadn't heard that. I'm so sorry."

After that apology, Cain finally admitted to Luke, in his own words, what he'd done to Justin MacLesten that terrible night. Luke paid close attention to Cain's story as it unfolded, but mostly he listened to the raw anguish in Cain's voice.

"I'm so damn sorry, Luke," Cain said again. "When I was out flying and saw MacLesten, I didn't think about the consequences. I reacted on pure rage. Christ, he was sure I was a dark angel sent up from hell to put him in his place for all the wrongs he'd done in his miserable life. I don't like admitting it, but that's exactly what I felt like that night."

"Is that where you're from?" Luke asked. So many things had happened since the night Cain had shown Luke what he was, so much that they'd never gotten back to talking about it. "I mean I know you're not an angel; you told me that you are a demon. But what does that mean? Are you just borrowing this body I'm with right now, and will you take another one when its life span is over?"

"No, it doesn't work like that." His tone even -- careful sounding -- Cain set the glider moving again. "I'm corporeal, Luke, flesh and blood, originating on this planet, just like any other sentient being. No species of demon can look human all of the time, but nor are any of us from hell, or henchmen of the devil either. I can't possess your body. Well" -- he squeezed Luke around the middle -- "not in the context you're thinking of anyway. My mother and father are both Naverto demons -- which are actually what you might consider a shifter, if you were ever to read those kinds of novels or watch those sorts of movies. We're not part of religion or the devil or anything inherently evil, such as exists in religious texts or films or any kind of lore like that -- although there is a natural bent toward mischievousness and mind-play demons use with humans; I will own up to that. That is probably where all the underworld associations originated. But in truth, were I to live my natural life, I would die at the end of my five hundredth year of life, as that is the end of a Naverto demon's life cycle."

"Shit." Luke tried to look up at Cain's face, but he'd slid so comfortably down Cain's chest that all he got was the stubbly underside of his chin. "How old are you right now?"

"One hundred and seventy-five."

"God, you sure do age well."

"Thank you. Err, I think anyway."

Luke didn't bother to try and look, but if he did he would bet Cain was in full blush. This man endlessly fascinated Luke. Because he did, that meant the other half of his being was equally intriguing, and it filled Luke with curiosity. "So the only reason you left your Naverto people behind is because you were trying to hide your homosexuality from them?"

"Actually, being attracted to men really had nothing to do with my leaving. My defection had more to do with not liking the underlying cruelty I just mentioned; I didn't like the way it is encouraged in the demon world to play with the minds of vulnerable human beings. From the time I was an adolescent and conscious of the trickery, and worse, the delight in the trickery, I knew I could have no part of it. When I became a teenager and outright refused to participate, the male and female who gave me life disowned me and kicked me out of their home."

"Oh, Hawk, I'm so sorry." Luke twisted in the circle of Cain's arms, until he was face-to-face with a pair of blue eyes unsuccessfully trying to hide old pain. He slid his arms around Cain's neck and hugged him close. "I'm so sorry that happened to you."

"It's okay." Cain squeezed his arms tighter around Luke's back, though, and spoke softly against Luke's shirt. "Turned out to be the best thing that ever happened to me. After toiling away on my own, moving from place to place all over Wales and England and Scotland, I eventually met Connor and Caleb, who had each separated from their demon clan for similar reasons. We helped each other survive, and we formed a strong brotherhood. Beneath the demon skin we occasionally have to wear, all we really want is to be decent, hardworking people. We don't want trouble or mischief; we just want to be good neighbors and not bother anyone with what we are while we're trying to do it."

"You've managed to achieve all of that, right here," Luke assured Cain, sensing somehow the man needed to hear it. He pulled back and cupped Cain's face gently. "You are a good man. I don't care that inside that man also happens to be something else quite magnificent. First and foremost, what you are, what people in this town will remember you as, is a strong, straight-shooting guy they could always depend upon when help was needed."

"Well…" Cain fingered Luke's lips, his eyes suddenly twinkling. "…maybe not exactly a *straight* shooter. Otherwise, I wouldn't be lying here right now wishing you would kiss me."

"Funny" -- Luke lowered his mouth to Cain's -- "because I was thinking about just how damn kissable you look right now."

"Mmm, I think you should act on that thought." Cain parted his lips, and Luke happily accommodated his wishes.

Luke dug his fingers in the short tufts of Cain's chestnut hair, mussing up the neatness Cain seemed so insistent upon trying to maintain. He loved to ruffle this man's starched feathers. Nothing seemed to do that more than exploring the depths of his mouth and the unique softness of the hard line of his lips with long, endless kisses combined with short, darting pecks that went on forever. Luke started by teasing the outer edge of Cain's mouth, nipping and sucking and tugging until Cain writhed beneath him, begging for more through a hard grip on Luke's back. When Luke couldn't stand the deprivation anymore either, he gave Cain what he wanted and slowly sank his tongue all the way inside for a deeper taste. Cain moaned beneath him, and suddenly, Cain wasn't only crushing Luke with his arms; Cain wrapped his legs around Luke's thighs as well. Luke felt as if he were a fly being cocooned in a spider's web, except Luke had no interest in getting himself untangled and running away; he wanted just the opposite. When Cain took hold of Luke's tongue and sucked it hard -- the first sign Cain was about to change things up and become the aggressor once again -- anticipation rushed through Luke's entire being. He loved when Cain took charge.

Just then a distinct clearing of the throat hit Luke's ears. Cain stiffened beneath him, proving he'd heard the sound too. *Shit. Company.* Luke shot off Cain in a flash. As soon as he lifted his weight, Cain rose to his feet right by Luke's side.

The intimidating, large stature of Sheriff Duke Boone stood before them, and Luke automatically straightened with respect. "Sheriff." Luke dipped his head in greeting. "I apologize. We apologize." He turned to include Cain, who nodded. Luke figured it would be a hard bet to guess who blushed a deeper red, him or Cain. "We weren't expecting you."

"No problem." Sheriff Boone waved his hand negligently. "And don't worry; seeing you together isn't exactly a shock to my senses. After all, it can't be all that surprising to hear you two are the talk of the town right now. Everyone is whispering in each other's ears about the two of you being together."

"Oh?" Cain's voice rose in challenge. "How exactly would you assess what they're saying? Don't be shy; lay it on us."

"You both have surprise and sympathy working on your side right now," the sheriff answered. "Finding out what Justin was going to do to Luke's sister, and then hearing what he'd already done to Luke… Well, let's just say, right now, it's hard to feel scorn for someone who's been through as much as Luke has."

"I guess that's nice to hear," Luke murmured. "But I can't imagine you drove all the way out to our home to tell us that." Cain rubbed Luke right then, right over where the bullet had hit Luke, and Luke knew he'd said the right thing. *Our home.* They were a pair from this point forward. "Not that you're not welcome, Sheriff, but why are you here?"

"I have some news to share." The sheriff cut right to it, his amber gaze landing steadily on Luke. "Justin MacLesten is dead."

Luke staggered, and he thanked God he had Cain behind him to hold him up. "What? How?"

"Infection set in after the surgery," Duke explained. "It's not relevant except insofar as you don't have to worry about testifying in a trial anymore. I know you weren't looking forward to that. That whole nightmare is over, Luke. For good."

"What about Cain?" Luke would not rest easy yet. He couldn't. "He took one of those shots that hit MacLesten, and now the man's dead. What will happen to him?"

The sheriff's lips thinned. "There will be an official investigation, of course. But I don't believe you need to be overly concerned. We both had just cause to shoot, so I don't think charges will be brought against anyone for what happened. Try not to worry. I believe Cain is in the clear."

"Thank God." Luke slumped against Cain. He felt the tension leave Cain too. "Thank you for telling us right away. We will sleep easier. Thank you." Reaching out, Luke shook Duke Boone's hand. "Thank you."

"No problem." As Duke backed up to his sheriff-emblazoned SUV, he chuckled and shook his head. "I'll let you tell your little sister, though. She was really looking forward to putting that bastard on trial. I half think she might be disappointed that he died."

Cain lifted his hand in a small wave, laughing too. "Wise man. You run and hide. We'll take care of Risa," he promised. "You have a good day, Duke. We'll talk to you soon."

Luke stared into the distance until the sheriff's truck was no longer in sight. Then he turned in Cain's arms and hugged him tight around the waist. He burrowed close to the safety he always felt with this man. In response, Cain tucked Luke into a protective embrace and settled his chin on top of Luke's head.

"It's over." Luke spoke against Cain's shoulder. "I can't believe I don't have to think about him anymore. I can't believe it's really over."

"You will, sweetheart." Cain smoothed his hands over Luke's hair in a soothing caress. "Give yourself a few days to process the information and let it sink in." Cain's cell phone started vibrating right then, alerting them both to the call. "Damn it. My family is uncanny about calling and interrupting me when I'm about to kiss you."

Luke chuckled. After pecking a kiss to Cain's cheek, he stepped back to lean against the porch railing, and he watched the glorious oranges and reds fill the sky as the sun slowly set on another Montana day. He was quiet while Cain took his call.

A few minutes later, with some terse "I'm busy's" on Cain's end, Cain captured Luke's hand in his and started pulling him toward the truck.

"What is it?" Luke asked. They parted at the hood of the truck; Cain got behind the wheel while Luke went the other way. Once he slid in on the passenger side, he met Cain's gaze. "What's up? Is everyone okay?"

"Everyone is fine." Cain's tone rang just a little tersely as he started up the truck and got them going. He shot Luke a brief, frustrated glance. "But other than that, all Connor would say was that it was damned important, and that we needed to get our asses to the main house ASAP."

"Oh," Luke muttered, sliding down in his seat. "A mystery. Great, because we so totally need one more thing to worry about."

"Exactly," Cain replied, his tone bone dry.

They exchanged a worried glance and then shared the rest of the twenty-minute drive in silence.

———

"ALL RIGHT, WE'RE HERE!" As Cain and Luke entered the front door hand in hand, Cain shouted at the top of his lungs. His words and tone briefly flashed him back to that morning when he'd come to see Connor so innocently, and had ended up with Luke. "Where in the hell is the fire; the one we just had to come and help you put out right goddamned now!"

It wasn't Connor's face Cain saw first, but rather Caleb's starkly handsome, patrician one. As Caleb popped his head out of the office, he coolly said, "We're in here," and then took a couple of steps toward them. His eyes flashed a welcome, a rich blue so similar in color to Cain's it was hard to believe they weren't really related. Caleb then turned that gaze on Luke, and a smile joined the twinkling. "Hey,

Luke. Welcome."

"Hey." Luke waved and smiled. "It's good to see you again. I understand you've been away. It must be good to be back."

Caleb's eyes practically sparkled blue diamonds. "It's always good to come home. Today, it's especially good."

Cain squeezed Luke's hand harder, suddenly completely aware of why Connor always felt as if everyone was hitting on Cassie. Cain knew Caleb had no sexual interest in men whatsoever, but he still couldn't help the wave of possession that washed over him when his brother turned his natural charm on to Luke.

"Is that why we're here?" Cain snapped, a little peevishly, he knew. Right in that moment, though, he couldn't hold the pettiness in. "To welcome you home from your latest vacation?"

Caleb's pure blue stare slid from Luke to Cain. "Better be nice to me about that vacation, brother." The teasing tone of a moment ago completely disappeared.

"Oh?" Cain lifted a brow. "And why is that?"

"Because," Caleb shared, dropping a bomb, "on that little vacation you just mocked, I think I found a way to save your life."

# Chapter Twenty-Two

This time Cain stumbled, and Luke grabbed hold of his arm to hold him up.

Cain recovered quickly, though. *Son of a bitch.* The fire raging through him made him want to lunge at his brother and strangle him.

"Don't you dare tease me about this, Caleb." Harsh roughness ruled Cain's voice. "Don't you dare be flip and witty about this." He clutched Luke's hand, desperate for a life with this man. "Not about this."

"Jesus Christ, you're dramatic these days." Caleb rolled his eyes. "It's just as well I'm here. Neither you nor Connor would have had a shot at a life with the mate of your dreams if it weren't for my interference. Follow me." Caleb beckoned them into the office. "Connor and Cassie are waiting."

Cain went, but reluctantly. Luke had to tug him to get him moving. Shooting Cain a pleading stare, Luke said, "Let's hear them out, Hawk," and pulled Cain into the office. "They're your brothers.

It's the least you can do."

"Thank you, Luke," Caleb replied before Cain could. Caleb then took up a casual stance, leaning his hip against a low bookshelf. Connor sat behind a massive mahogany desk, and he had Cassie leaning against him, his arm around her waist. Cain and Luke took the pair of seats in front of the desk.

"I always knew you were a smart guy," Caleb told Luke, his smile mischievous. "When I first met you, I also knew right away that you had absolutely no interest in hitting on Cassie. I never thought you were a threat to Connor's undying love for her." The smooth-talking brother shot his married sibling a sly look. "Of course, that didn't stop him from wanting to break your arms at a certain Halloween party two years ago when you danced with her just a little too close for his comfort."

"Shut it, Caleb," Connor ordered in a clipped tone. "No one is interested in your peanut gallery comments."

"Oh, I certainly am." Cassie wore a triumphant smile, and it lit up her pretty, girl-next-door face. "Were you jealous over me?" She poked Connor in the arm. "That's soooo sweeeetttt."

"You can zip it too, wife," Connor grumbled, even as Cassie tousled his dark hair. In a flash, he grabbed her around the waist and dragged her down on his lap. "It's not like you don't already know perfectly well that I see red when just about any guy in this town takes a second look at you. Don't pretend as if you don't."

"I do." She pecked a kiss to his cheek. "The only reason it doesn't bother me is because I know you know you have nothing to worry about in that regard. I've never had eyes for anyone else or ever loved anyone else. You were my first, and you will forever be my one and only."

Caleb rolled his eyes at Cain and Luke and pretended to throw up.

"I tried to tell him that very thing," Caleb shared with everyone. "Thank God Connor eventually broke down and decided to believe it. I never could quite convince him you were not a threat though, Luke. That night, when I told him he had absolutely nothing to worry about, he just wouldn't see it. Of course, neither did my other stubborn brother see the truth right away." Caleb raised his eyebrows at Cain. "But I knew. I saw our young Luke that night, and I noticed right away that it wasn't Cassie he was sneaking peeks at; it was Cain. That was when I knew I had to do something." Caleb shifted his focus fully to Cain and it held steady and sure. "That was when I knew I had to dig and find a way to set you free."

"What in the hell are you talking about?" Cain shook his head and rolled his eyes at his irritating, playboy brother. "You don't know shit about relationships -- except how to sweet-talk your way into too many women's beds."

"Maybe, maybe not." Caleb's voice came across flippant in a way that made Cain think that, beneath the charming façade, Cain's insensitive comment had wounded him. "But you should thank your lucky stars I do know how to charm just about every kind of female, dear brother, because getting a number of your Naverto ones in bed when I was in Wales led me to your path to humanity."

*Becoming human. Always. Forever.* Cain could not even contemplate such a notion. To foster a small amount of hope that he could be human, only to lose it, would kill Cain. He couldn't bear to have hope and then be ripped from Luke's arms. "No." Cain shook his head, his throat terribly dry. "That's not possible."

"Hear him out." Connor spoke, using Luke's same words of advice. "Caleb has been working relentlessly on this for the last two years. He didn't want to say anything because he didn't want to give you false hope if nothing came of his search. But this time, this time, he found something." Connor's dark brown stare shifted to almost black with the depth of his emotions. "He found something secret, something the Naverto don't want anyone to know exists. Caleb is almost certain he found another way out for you. Another way to being human, another way that can end only one of two ways: with you walking away human, or you not walking away at all."

Cain's heart started pumping fast, making him dizzy, and his field of vision narrowed to a tunnel. In his hand, he felt Luke's fingers turn to ice. "What do you mean?" Cain uttered, but he spoke so

242 | CAMERON DANE

softly he wasn't certain he'd even said the words out loud. It was almost as if saying them would make his brother's words real, and in doing so, leave Cain that much more fragile to breaking apart if the hope turned out to be false. "What other way? There is no other way."

"No, Cain, that's not true." Caleb shook his head to back up his claim. Even more terrifying for Cain, the lighthearted jokester always living in his brother was completely gone. Sitting before Cain was a man 100 percent, absolutely, serious. "That is what the Council of Twelve wants you to think. That is what almost every blessed Naverto in creation does believe, but it is not true. I found someone, a Naverto woman very near the end of her life cycle, whose great-grandfather, to the quiet shame of his entire family, went to the Council of Twelve and asked for something called the Changing Gauntlet. It is a ritual that is little known, but when requested cannot be refused. That is why the Council of Twelve works so hard to make sure no one knows it even exists. Because when you request it, and if you can survive it, you will come out the other end human. In doing so, they lose another potential breeder."

"The Changing Gauntlet?" Cain searched through his memories of the first fifteen years of his life he'd spent in Wales, near the bulk of the Naverto community, but his mind was a virtual blank. What little he recalled was an insane amount of clan pride about how wonderful and superior it was to be Naverto, even among the other demon species. "Are you sure this is real?" It scared Cain to hear about hope, but more frightening than that was to let himself *feel* it, even just for a short while, and then have it snatched away. "How can it exist and there not be even the slightest hint of it in Naverto lore? How can there not be rumors of it? It doesn't seem possible. I think someone was pulling your chain."

"No, this is no lie." Caleb pulled a handful of folded papers out of his pocket, handed them to Luke, who passed them to Cain. As Cain read the transcript, he trembled with the words. Caleb continued to explain. "That woman I met had her grandmother's journal -- the daughter of the man who requested the Changing Gauntlet. I copied certain passages. This woman speaks of the silent shame her family is suffering for what her father has done. She speaks of hiding what he really did from anyone outside the immediate family -- meaning her, her mother, and her older brother. She speaks of her mother concocting a lie that her husband was taken down by a band of rogue demons and killed in order to cover the fact that he was there one day and gone the next. She speaks of how humiliating that story was to tell her friends, but that her mother said it was better to do that than to spin a tale of a hero's death that would be scrutinized more closely for cracks in the lie. They feared rejection from others if what the father had really done ever became public; that truth would be a thousand times worse. You know that is correct, Cain," Caleb said gently, offering terrible, terrible hope. "You know that for a proud demon the greatest shame that can be delivered upon him is for one of his own to reject his demon half and successfully find a way to become fully human."

Cain's throat constricted painfully, making it hard to breathe. "I don't understand." He tried to push down the rising panic mixing itself with a terrible kind of longing, of hope -- something he'd never thought to feel in his life. Cain leaned forward, pressing his face to his knees, and sucked in heaving gulps of air. The papers offering the tantalizing dream of a way out of being a demon fell to the floor. "It's not possible. I don't understand how this can be."

"Hawk?" Quickly lowering himself to his knees in front of Cain, Luke began rubbing Cain's shoulders and back in a circular pattern. "Are you okay, baby? Do you need water? A whisky? Tell me what you need, and I'll get it for you."

Luke's touch acted as an immediate balm for Cain's anxiety. He looked up, found Luke's stormy gaze full of worry, and wanted nothing more than to soothe him in return. "I'm okay." Reaching out, Cain brushed a lock of dark hair from Luke's forehead. Luke's answering smile was small but filled with support and deep understanding. The sight of Luke, so full of love, made Cain realize this little pebble of hope was as potentially devastating to Luke as it was to him. They were both going to lose the same thing. Each other.

244 | CAMERON DANE

"It's just a lot to hear," Cain admitted. "It's a lot to take in, learning that something I never thought possible for me might have some great, secret answer" -- Cain let the first little grain of hope be spoken aloud -- "and that it's the council's greatest hope that I never hear about it."

Caleb cleared his throat. "Are you ready to hear the rest of what I dug up, or do you need a few more minutes to digest what I've already told you?"

Cain pulled Luke up from the floor and settled the man against his chest, needing to feel this person he so cherished close to him while they learned their fate. Cain then settled his gaze on Caleb, and no discomfort lived in Caleb's eyes or manner as a result of the intimacy he'd just witnessed between his up until now theoretically gay brother and another man. Pride filled Cain's entire being. It was one thing for Caleb to say he didn't care about Cain's sexuality when Cain had never actually acted upon it; it was quite another for Caleb to back his statement up with action when he witnessed his brother's homosexuality in play for the first time.

Cain's heart filled up to the brim, but he managed to say to Caleb, "Tell us the rest. Tell us what you know."

"Okay." Caleb nodded. "Here's what I was eventually able to figure out, not only through that journal, but by digging into the personal writings of many a deceased Naverto, until I was able to piece everything together. It seems as though this Changing Gauntlet has been kept a very, very good secret, as it has been requested less than a dozen times in the entire history of your people."

"Christ." In spite of himself, awe filled Cain. "That's insane."

"Yeah, your higher-ups are definitely the masters of the cover-up," Caleb responded wryly. "Your women's lips do not loosen easily, even in the throes of fantastic sex."

Cain chuckled. He couldn't believe that he could, but he did. That was another gift of this particular brother, something Cain had forgotten just how much he appreciated: his wonderful sense of humor. "Well, you'll understand if I just take your word for it on that bit about the loose lips, or lack there of, of Naverto women."

"Yeah." Caleb openly slid his gaze up and down Luke and Cain wrapped in a tangle together. "I can see that."

"Go on." Cain sobered once more. "Tell me what you discovered."

"Okay." Caleb lost his smile too. "I can open up a portal that will put you right in front of the Council of Twelve. You'll be naked, looking as you want to be permanently, like this, in your human form. You inform them that you want to face the Changing Gauntlet. I imagine they will try to pretend ignorance, but you must simply hold your ground because in the end, they cannot refuse you."

"That is the easy part," Connor offered from behind his desk, his voice weary. The exhausted, almost sad look on Connor's face was enough to send shivers of fear down Cain's back. "The gauntlet itself is the thing you must determine whether or not you can face and survive."

"Connor is absolutely right about that." A similar expression pushed through the normal lightheartedness in Caleb. In his stare, Caleb almost seemed to be saying goodbye. "From what I have been able to decipher, the gauntlet is horrific. When the council agrees to your request, you will suffer through twelve hours of torture, one hour at the hand of each council member. They may beat you, humiliate you, do whatever they choose in order to mar and harm your mind and your physical body. They can do anything they wish, short of an act that will bring about your immediate death."

Luke tensed in front of Cain. He wrapped his fingers around Cain's forearm with a death grip unlike anything Cain had ever felt in his life. "What do you mean by 'short of bringing about his immediate death'?" Luke's voice wavered in a way that hurt Cain's heart to hear.

"It means they cannot pull out a gun and shoot Cain in the head, or the heart, or the gut," Caleb told Luke. "It means they cannot use the length of a sword or a knife and stab him repeatedly until death. It means that they can beat him as much as they like, but it is my understanding that there are restrictions on what kind of devices can be used in order to do that. Cain may fight back if given an opening, but it is my understanding he will rarely find a place to do so. As long as Cain doesn't say 'I quit' or 'I give up,' the torture will continue. The point is not to kill Cain outright, but to damage him to within an inch of his life and then throw him back out of the portal to see if his human body can survive what it has chosen to become. The beating is not the end of the gauntlet. The end is Cain surviving it and rejoining the living on his own. You may put him in bed and get him out of sight of prying eyes, but other than that we cannot aid him in his recovery. We cannot clean his wounds or bandage him or administer medication; he must save himself. If we give him so much as one painkiller from our own hands then the process of the Changing Gauntlet is null and void. He will have suffered the torture for nothing, for he will revert back to being Naverto."

Caleb let out a long, slow breath and then he met Cain's stare over Luke's shoulder. "So that is what you must decide if you are capable of surviving. If you think you can do this, I would recommend doing it quickly, for if the council discovers that you have acted on your feelings for another man before the choice is made, then it will not matter. They will take you and execute you in front of the masses, and any request at that point for the gauntlet will be superseded by the law you broke by engaging in homosexual acts with Luke."

"What?" Cassie screeched. She shot off Connor's lap, and her lovely face quickly drained of all color, so much so her lips were barely discernible. She turned and whacked Connor on the shoulder. "You just said that because he was gay he could never become human; you never told me he would be killed for acting on it." Tears filled Cassie's eyes. "That is vital information. How could you not tell me that?"

Connor pulled Cassie back down to him. "Cain has a right to his privacy. It was not my place to tell you." He gently wiped her cheeks. "Also, I knew it would devastate you. I knew it would break your heart to lose him."

"But if I'd known..." Cassie insisted. "I wouldn't have...I shouldn't have..."

Luke shifted and shot Cain a puzzled look. As he did, Connor narrowed his gaze on Cassie. "If you'd known, you wouldn't have done what, sweetheart?"

Cassie's mouth gaped open and then snapped shut, once, twice. Finally, she waved her arms haphazardly, as if reaching for words. "I...I...I wouldn't have said a prayer for them to get together, all right? I'm in pretty damn good with God, you know. He answers all of my prayers. It's a very powerful connection, and I just wouldn't have done it if I'd known Cain could be killed for it. No offense, Luke." She offered him a teary smile. "But when losing Cain is the result, I wouldn't have wished for you to be together."

"No offense taken," Luke answered. "Truth is, I yelled at Cain for the exact same thing when he told me what he was and what would happen to him as a result of being with me. I would have done everything in my power not to succumb to what was going on between us that first time. I don't want to lose him any more than the three of you do." Luke slid his gaze over each one of them, his eyes never wavering or showing an ounce of embarrassment or shame. "I love him just as much as all of you do, and I would never put his life at risk intentionally."

"*He* is sitting right here," Cain interjected. He squeezed Luke's side and got them both to their feet. "And *he* is an adult, who made a fully informed adult decision, for adult reasons. *He* will decide what is to come next, and when *he* does, *he* will share it with the rest of you."

Cain reached across the desk, extended his hand out to Connor, and got a good, firm, heartfelt tug in the clasp of Connor's hand. After offering Cassie a small wave, Cain made his way over to Caleb, who he still leaned so-very casually against the bookshelf.

Cain pulled Caleb into a tight bear hug and whispered against his brother's ear, "Thank you for doing this for me. I didn't give you nearly enough credit for the wealth of selfless love you have inside you. That was my grievous error. I only pray we end up with enough time together for you to forgive me."

Caleb braced his hand around Cain's neck and held him at arm's length, looking him right in the eyes. "You listen to me. You are my brother and I would do anything in the world to bring you closer to happiness. As I would do the same for Connor or Cassie, and as I will now do for Luke. You are my family, and I love you, and that means I would go to the ends of the earth for you. And let me tell you something" -- Caleb's lips quirked up in his familiar, throwaway smile -- "there were moments in Wales when I felt like I very nearly did."

Cain wanted to laugh, but he was very afraid if he did the sound would catch and turn into a sob, so he just bit the inside of his cheek and tried to keep his gaze from becoming too bright with moisture.

Caleb seemed to understand. He pulled Cain in and kissed him on the temple. "Now go home with your man, think about what you've learned tonight, and make your choice. I have the spell to open the portal when you decide. Let us know, either way."

Cain nodded. Without words spoken between them, Luke took the keys dangling in Cain's hand and drove them home.

# CHAPTER TWENTY-THREE

Cain rolled over in bed and reached out for Luke, only to find the space beside him a rumple of cool sheets rather than a warm, solid man. Lifting his head, he glanced at the digital alarm clock on Luke's nightstand; it was just past one thirty in the morning. Cain sighed, got out of bed, and padded to the darkened living room, knowing exactly where Luke would be.

"You have to stop doing this, darlin'." Cain found Luke in front of the TV, the volume so low it could barely be heard. He leaned over the back of the couch, kissed the top of Luke's mussed hair, then crawled over the couch and joined him, bumping their shoulders together. "You've hardly slept in two days. If you don't let go, you're going to drop from exhaustion."

"Look." Pointing at the flickering TV, Luke said, "I found sharks on the National Geographic Channel. They're your favorite. Right?"

*Christ, this man breaks my heart.* "I do like them." Cain slid his arm around Luke's shoulders and tucked him into his body. Without hesitation Luke burrowed closer, slid his arms around Cain's waist.

and held on tight. "It's sweet that you remembered, Luke. I like them a lot."

"I don't want you to go tomorrow." Cain's chest muffled Luke's voice. "I don't want you to do this gauntlet thing after all."

With his arms around Luke, Cain held the man close, offering what little comfort he could. "Oh, Luke, darlin', you know this wasn't really even a choice. I have to do this. It's the only chance we have."

"But maybe not." Luke sat up on folded legs, his face so painful in its need it tore Cain up inside to see. "Maybe you're wrong. Maybe the Traveler doesn't know you very well at all. Cassie's a beautiful woman, so why wouldn't he logically think you're attracted to her? Maybe we can have a human lifetime together before you are figured out. By doing this Changing Gauntlet, it doesn't even matter. We'll have less than seventeen hours. Have you really thought about that? Potentially saying goodbye tomorrow, for good?"

Cain had done nothing but think on this matter, and the choice had been agonizing, a choice that had torn through his very soul. "Damn it" -- Cain shot up from the couch and pointed a dagger of a finger at Luke -- "of course I've thought about it. Don't fight me on this, damn it. Christ, I'm begging you, don't make this harder for me than it has to be. I'm trying to do the right thing here. I'm trying to give us a chance at a life together. You said you understood that. Why are you changing your mind now?"

Luke exploded off the couch too, moving until they stood chest to chest, face-to-face. "Because I'm the one who has to keep on living if you don't make it, Hawk!" The words sounded as if they'd been put through a blender and ripped up from Luke's gut. "I'm the one who has to stay here and figure out a way to go on if you don't come back to me. So you'll just have to excuse me for scrambling in any way I can to give myself as many memories of you as possible before you're taken from me. You'll just have to forgive me for wanting as much time with you as I can get, soaking up as much of you as I can with every second we have, before you absolutely have to go. Don't make me apologize for wanting that, because I won't."

"You make it sound like you have no faith in my coming back!" Hurt rocketed through Cain hard enough to rear him backward. "Do you not believe I'll have any chance at surviving this thing? Do you think I won't be fighting with every fiber of my being, using every ounce of will I have? The picture of you waiting for me on the other end is the thing that will get me through this, damn it. Christ, Luke, I need to know you believe in me. When I go in there, I need to feel in my blood that you are right there with me, cheering me on. I need your faith in me. I need it. Otherwise, you're right. I won't get through it."

"I have every faith that you fully believe every word you just uttered." Luke didn't back down one inch. "Don't you dare question that or make my fears about what is going to happen to you seem trivial. Justin MacLesten tortured me for four hours, so I know damn well what it can do to a body. You're talking about taking three times that amount of stress with God only knows what kind of weaponry; the kinds of things MacLesten never even imagined. Plus, I can't take you to a hospital afterward the way Cassie did for me. All I can do is put you in bed and wait, wait to see if you can rouse your beaten body enough to tend to it and give it what it needs to survive."

"But --"

"No." Luke cut Cain off with a point of his finger. "You challenged my feelings about this, so now you have to stand there and listen to them. You have to face what is going to happen to you, Hawk. You have to face it before you go; otherwise, the shock of that first blow is going to do you in. The pain will far surpass what you think you can take. But I can see it in your eyes, baby." Luke's gray gaze softened to the color of early storm clouds. "All you're thinking right now is that if you're noble enough, you'll live through it. Well, let me tell you something. Nobility ain't worth shit when you're getting your ass kicked with no end in sight."

Cain opened his mouth, but Luke went on before he could get a word in edgewise. "There will be moments, probably most of the time, where the pain will be unbearable. You have to know that right now, you must, so that you can give yourself permission to do anything you need to do in order to survive. Nothing is sacred when someone is torturing you with the intent to break your spirit. I need to know right now that you will be ready to do anything and everything to get yourself through that torture and back to me. You need to tell yourself it's okay to do whatever it takes before you go, or else you won't do it, and then you will surely die. That" -- Luke finished with a quiver in his lower lip -- "is why I am afraid. You are incredibly brave, but you haven't taken five minutes to sit down and be with the truth of what will happen to you tomorrow."

Cain's legs trembled, and his chest squeezed so tight he thought he would pass out. He fell to the recliner behind him, and sank his face into his hands. Good Christ, all he could think was that Luke knew him too well. Luke was absolutely, 100 percent right. Cain *had* been thinking that because his cause was just and noble he would have the extra strength to battle in those moments when he wanted to give up. He *had* told himself he only needed a picture of Luke in his mind, and that image would be enough to get him through the pain. He'd been thinking in an entirely romantic fashion when, in reality, he needed to prepare himself to behave like a jackal or a hyena, an animal that was willing to be scorned and looked down upon in order to survive. He had to care about one thing and one thing only while he suffered through the Changing Gauntlet: getting back to Luke.

Dropping to kneel in front of Cain, Luke took Cain's head into his strong hands. He pressed a lingering kiss against the crown of Cain's head, sending shivers down Cain's spine. Then he whispered, "I love you," and Cain felt the heated rush of fever race through his body, chased by a shiver of icy coldness. Lingering behind in the aftermath lived a newfound depth of respect for Luke, something he'd not known it was possible to feel.

Cain lifted his gaze and met Luke's waiting, wary one. "It took a lot of guts for you to say what you did." Cain's voice sounded shaky to his own ears. He wiped a trembling hand over his mouth, over the perspiration that had popped out on his upper lip. "It took a lot to face my ego and anger, and to tell me the truth about what you saw in me." He cupped Luke's cheek, and when Luke turned his head and pressed a kiss into his hand, Cain's stomach flip-flopped. "Or more accurately, what you didn't see in me. What I know now, that maybe I didn't fully want to know before, is that you must have gone through a hell of a lot more at the hands of Justin MacLesten than you've let on about."

Luke's gaze was dark and stormy; with a nod, his eyes glazed with moisture. "I've told you everything that happened, but now I'm trying to make you understand how you're going to *feel* about what's going to happen. You need to know so that you can prepare yourself and have an advantage. Because, please don't misunderstand me, I do believe you can survive this -- but not if you go in there like a gentleman of honor facing a foe who is equally upstanding. Mentally, you have to become that feral, hungry dog in the alley that will hurt whoever it has to in order to grab a piece of meat. You are a starving, selfish animal, do you understand me? The only meal available to you is on the other side of that gauntlet. You want that meal, baby, because that meal is me. Do you understand the concept in here?" He tapped Cain's head with his finger. "And in here?" He put his hand over Cain's heart. "For twelve hours tomorrow, there is nothing noble or good about Cain Hawkins; there is only an animal that must survive. Do you get that? Do you *really* get that?"

"I didn't before," Cain admitted, his face heating. Christ, he'd been so arrogant and ignorant. "But I do now. I promise I do." He pulled Luke to him and pressed their lips together, letting them stay attached for a long stretch of minutes. Cain closed his eyes and savored the connection -- one that had become the dearest thing in his life. "I will fight for us, Luke." Cain felt a change deep in his body, in a way he hadn't in the last forty-eight hours. "I will fight to get back to you with everything I have in my being. When I run out of that, I will dig deeper and find something more. That is the one promise I can make to you, and I make it from the bottom of my soul."

With a soft cry, Luke wrapped his arms around Cain's shoulders and tugged him into a tight, suffocating embrace. "I know you will."

His tightly closed fists dug into Cain's bare back. "I know you will."

Cain held Luke close, tucked between his spread legs. He rolled back over Luke's explosion of words in his mind, feeling them all, until one early admission snagged at his brain and wouldn't let go. Within Luke's words was a request for a gift Cain could give him right now. One that if successful in his task tomorrow, he would no longer be able to grant.

"I want to give you a memory" -- Cain drew Luke to his feet -- "near and dear to me, that you're not likely to ever forget."

Luke blushed, and Cain read Luke's intent as his stare slid toward the bedroom door. "Not that." Cain swatted Luke's ass with a playful smack. "But something I used to do to alleviate my desire for *that* before you came along." Cain shucked off his sweats and dragged Luke outside through the back door.

"Hawk, wait." Luke dragged his feet. "What are you doing? Where are we going?"

"Darlin'" -- Cain rolled his neck and began the mental direction his body needed to bring about the change -- "close your mouth and prepare to be swept off your feet, because we are going flying."

---

"OH, CAIN, THIS IS SO beautiful!" Luke gaped. Awe filled him, just as Cain had promised it would. He and Cain soared through the midnight blue sky, stars twinkling in clusters above. Luke felt as if he could reach out and touch every bright light. "The mountains, and trees, and the valleys are breathtaking from this high in the sky. More than I ever could have imagined."

"Are you sure you're all right?" Cain called back over his shoulder. "We're not too high?"

"Are you kidding?" Luke smacked a joyous, exuberant kiss to Cain's ear. "Don't you dare treat me with kid gloves. Show me everything you like to do when you're flying this high in the sky."

Throwing back his head, Cain roared with the most beautiful laughter. He grabbed onto Luke's legs and swooped them down from a great height, skimming so low they almost grazed the tops of a line of great pine trees on a mountainside. Every time Cain sent them in a different direction on this journey in flight, Luke shrieked with delight, uncaring of how he sounded.

Riding piggyback on Cain's demon body, with his arms wrapped around Cain's neck and his legs around his waist, Luke soared on the inside and in the sky. He was tucked in between Cain's beating wings, and he loved it, loved feeling those appendages brush against the sides of his body each time they flapped together and kept them in flight.

Luke now understood why Cain had used flying as a distraction from his body's sexual needs. When arcing and diving through the crisp, biting air, an incredible rush raced through the system, making one feel completely alive -- much as the body feels as it builds up to a fierce, sexual climax. Luke experienced the thrum of pleasure flying created just by being Cain's passenger; he couldn't imagine the scope it must bring to be the one with the wings, actually experiencing the natural high as a result of the work his body did.

Cain suddenly shifted the bulk of his frame from gliding to working his wings as a bird would in order to keep them suspended in the sky. Feeling Cain's body work beneath him, experiencing the sensation of the muscles in his back bunching and releasing in efficient harmony with his wings as they sliced through the air, whooshing and flapping, brought about insane arousal in Luke. Cain in this form was a thing of true beauty. As much as Luke had barely gotten to know this part of Cain, and as much as he understood the necessity that it could no longer exist in order for them to be together, Luke knew with a certainty he would miss this Naverto beast, this fantasy of his teen years that had somehow become the man with whom he had fallen in love.

"I'd keep you up here all night if I could," Cain called back to him, breaking Luke from his amorous thoughts. "But I try not to push it and risk detection. We're going to have to head home now."

"It's okay." Luke squeezed his thighs against Cain's thick, muscular waist, giving him a makeshift hug. "Even just this little bit was wonderful."

Cain nodded, and he gave an answering squeeze to Luke's legs. Luke closed his eyes and held onto Cain, absorbing as much as he could in ways other than with the visual. This moment became less about looking at the beauty of the Montana landscape beneath him or of noticing a nocturnal animal out scavenging for food in the night, and more about paying close attention to all the subtle nuances of Cain's demon body at work.

Luke picked up on the demon's breathing -- something steady, but audible in its vigor as he worked his wings to keep his body airborne. There was great effort involved in flying, and although the task didn't make Cain wheeze or pant with breathlessness, it clearly required a great deal of work from his lungs and heart to get the job done. Which made absolute sense, as the body attached to those wings consisted of ripped, hulking muscles Cain did not possess in his human form. There was nothing sleek about the demon -- nothing streamlined for efficiency. This form was built to overwhelm and intimidate, and Luke imagined if the individual within had mischief or troublemaking in his thoughts, it would be quite frightening to come face-to-face with it in the dead of the night.

Luke knew Cain didn't have intimidation on his mind, though, so rather than scaring Luke, this stunning form in flight aroused his desires and sent his senses into overload. The pungent musk of hard-working male emanated from Cain's body, tickling Luke's olfactory senses, and sent desire straight to his brain and then right down to his cock, rousing him to life against Cain's back, with only his sweatpants as a barrier between them.

Through the rest of the short flight back to the cabin, Luke battled the desire to lick the back of Cain's copper-skinned neck. He fought not to purr with pleasure every time Cain's wings grazed his hips, sides, and arms -- each touch like a gossamer kiss to the flesh trapped beneath Luke's clothes. Luke gritted his teeth against the need to shift his body and hump his cock along the deep indentation of the demon's lower back, not stopping until he came with an overabundance of carnal gratification. As much as Luke wanted to, he didn't do any of that. He wasn't willing to risk distracting Cain and possibly putting their safety at risk.

When Cain put them on the ground, however, when the talons of his feet sank into the lush grass in the small, open space behind the cabin, when he let go of his hold on Luke's calves so that Luke could slide to the ground, all bets were off. *You're all mine now.* Luke trailed the tips of his fingers over Cain's muscular buttocks, smiling when the great beast before him shivered. He circled Cain's big body, letting his hand run along the bare hip and hollow at the top of the beast's thigh, to finally settle on the nest of curls at the base of an enormous cock, the shaft just as erect as Luke's. Luke then looked up, up over a chest that was so much thicker and bulkier than the one he knew so well, up over a mountainous, copper-toned face, to the purest set of blue eyes -- eyes belonging to the man he loved.

The intensity of that familiar gaze gave Luke the courage to speak his desires. "This is your last night in this body, Cain." Luke wrapped his hand around a very different prick and squeezed the thickened shaft. "More than anything, I want the beast of my fevered dreams to fuck me before he is gone forever."

# Chapter Twenty-Four

Just after Luke's declaration, Cain's misshapen, exaggerated demon face held a look of complete horror. "No, Luke, no." Cain shoved Luke's hand away from his cock and then stepped back until he bumped up against the log siding of the cabin and could get away no farther. "I'm too big like this." He reached down, as if with one hand he could cover himself from Luke's eyes. "I'll hurt you."

"You won't hurt me." Luke advanced with purpose, not stopping until he pressed himself against Cain's large, hard body. Reaching down, he freed Cain's cock from the cover of that big hand and let the jutting length spring free until the tip pressed against Luke's stomach. "Don't ever hide any of yourself from me; I won't tolerate it."

Darting his gaze all around, Cain refused to settle on Luke. "It's too big for me to put inside you like this." Cain pushed his cock up against his stomach, as if trying to make his member blend in with the rest of his coppery skin and thus disappear. "If we have sex like this, I'll surely rip you in two." Stark nobility mapped Cain's demon face in a manner similar to Cain in his human form, and the sight of it twisted at Luke's heart.

"No, baby," Luke insisted, "you won't. I've taken that big dildo we now keep in your nightstand drawer inside my body -- the one you're too afraid to use on me. You're not that much bigger than that fake dick, and I've been using that thing on myself since I was seventeen years old. Every time I used it, before I found you, I thought about this very demon before me right now, who is now shaking with emotion because you know you want to take me just as much as I want to be taken."

"Ohhh Christ." Cain slumped against the cabin wall, his blue eyes glazed with passion as he finally gave in and looked at Luke. "You could tempt a saint, Luke, and the good Lord knows I'm not one of those. I'm as hard as I've ever been, and I want to know what it feels like to have sex in this body" -- Cain lifted his hand and fingered Luke's cheek and mouth -- "but even just the thought of bringing you pain scares the shit out of me."

"No pain," Luke promised. The thrill of a new discovery raced through his body. "Just pleasure. All pleasure." Leaning in, Luke pressed his face against this different, thickly-muscled chest. He inhaled, glorying in the layers of simple clean-smelling soap that still clung to Cain's body beneath the sweat that, although evaporated, still exuded a musky fragrance. Luke licked and kissed his way over a broad expanse of pectoral muscles, smiling in victory when he reached a richly textured nipple with a tiny, jutting tip. He circled the disc with his tongue and then bit the puckering skin, then cheered on the inside when Cain gasped and jammed his hips forward, automatically looking for that connection he was so afraid to give.

*So close.* Luke didn't let up. Instead he started suckling like a bear cub getting nourishment from his momma's teat. He gave succor to Cain's neglected nipple with flicks from his nonexistent fingernail and tweaks from his thumb and index finger. Cain squirmed against Luke, clearly so needy of a firmer touch, so Luke slid the tips of his fingers down over the wide, hard demon torso and stomach to wrap his hands around the thick, turgid cock poking up proudly from between this beast's thighs. He wrapped the thick length tightly in his fists and dragged his hands down Cain's enormous length to the rounded tip, taking a moment to wipe across the slit and gather the fat beads of precum already forming there.

"Christ." Sucking in a breath, Cain uttered, "I just told you I'm not a saint." He strong-armed Luke and put some distance between them, shooting the man a quick glare. "I'm discovering I'm not very patient with foreplay in this body either. Go get the lube right now or else I'm going to come and end this before I get anywhere near your gorgeous, tight ass."

Luke smiled in triumph. "I'll be right back." With a quick lean in, he stole a kiss from Cain's wide, demon mouth, shocking the hell out of Cain if the widening of his gaze was any indication. Luke knew that it was.

Luke shot into the cabin anyway, scrambling in the dark while scanning his memory for the location of the closest tube of lube. He went straight for the end table next to the couch, the area lit by the flickering of the TV. Ever the economist, bred into him through years of miserly living, Luke took a minute to grab the remote from the couch and flick the television off. Only then could he, in good conscience, yank open the drawer of the end table and search for the tube of lube. When he found it, he held it aloft like a trophy. Racing back outside, Luke found Cain standing in the center of the lush, small field, returned to his human form.

Before Luke could utter a word, before his spirit truly plummeted, Cain held up a hand. "Don't be upset. I haven't changed my mind." He leveled a pointed, unwavering stare on Luke, one that from working with Cain twenty-four/seven for almost three months meant Cain would not budge from his position. "I will give you the demon once I'm inside you, but I cannot force myself into you while I am engorged in that form. Please understand me." Cain stood, forlorn, some ten feet away. "I cannot allow myself to give him to you in any other way."

Luke tossed the tube of lube across the space between them. Cain exhibited lightning-fast reflexes and snatched the bottle out of the sky with barely a glance in its direction. In response Luke grew painfully hard. *Shit, he's insanely magnificent.* Luke's body heated rapidly, and he made the first step toward Cain. With the next, he raised his arms above his head and slipped out of his T-shirt. Cain's gaze darkened with obvious appreciation, and the look of hunger hastened Luke's hands to his waist. At half the distance to Cain, Luke paused to lower his sweats, kicking out of them and leaving them in the grass. He then stalked his prey, naked, the rest of the way. Right now Luke felt like the one in charge. He had a sense that once Cain let his demon loose, though, that Cain -- the beast -- would be in full control of their encounter. Luke shuddered. He could not wait.

When just a foot separated Luke and Cain, Luke turned and folded in half at the waist, offering himself without embarrassment or shame. "Get me ready." Reaching back, Luke spread his cheeks, offering his quivering hole to the man he loved -- to the demon he'd dreamed about in such a carnal manner for ten years. "Make my ass slick for your cock."

A strong hand settled on Luke's back. Warm fingers traced down his spine, making him shiver. "No, Luke." Cain guided Luke to face him, drawing him upright as he did. "Not like that."

Confusion and pain lanced through Luke, but before he could question Cain's rejection, Cain's blue gaze flashed and a naughty smile altered his serious stare. With a wicked whisper, he said, "Not like that. Like this," and swooped Luke up in his arms, like a man fully in charge of the memory he wanted to create.

With barely a second to fear that wolfish look from Cain -- something he unleashed very rarely -- Cain took Luke with a ferocious, wet kiss, and swept the inside of Luke's mouth from back to front with his masterful tongue. Whimpering, Luke threw his arms around Cain's neck and shifted his body to get at the heat sweltering in Cain. He met the full measure of Cain's kiss head-on. Luke rubbed his tongue along the nubby length of Cain's, tangling and kissing him back with equal fervor; Cain's answering growl of approval vibrated all the way through Luke's body down to his toes.

"I have to have you." Cain lowered them both to the cool bed of grass. "One touch from you and my head empties of anything but visions of us coming together."

"I feel the same way." Pulling Cain down on top of him, Luke wrapped his legs around the man's waist, then gasped as Cain's cock slid against the crease of his ass. Luke blinked up at Cain, his need surely shining in his stare, but unable to care enough to try and hide it. "Fuck me, Cain." He grabbed the tube of lube that had fallen to the grass next to them, popped the top, and upended a generous bubble of the stuff straight onto his chest. "Use what you need. Don't be gentle, and don't be afraid. Fuck me the way you want to. Don't hold anything back."

As Cain scooped up most of the clear liquid, his blue eyes glittered. "You give a man license to lose his mind --" Cain unwound Luke's legs and folded them up until his feet were braced against Cain's chest -- "and you just might end up with a lust-filled demon, out of control."

Luke's cock jumped painfully against his stomach. "That's exactly what I want."

Cain rocked over Luke right then, bearing his weight down on the soles of Luke's feet, and Luke held his breath, the rest of his thought trapped in his throat. Cain pressed until Luke's knees were up over his shoulders, effectively splitting his ass in half. The cool breeze caressed Luke's exposed crack, making him shiver. But then Cain slid his slick fingers along the length of Luke's crease, applied ever increasing pressure to Luke's pulsating bud, and Luke shuddered. Luke's pucker and channel contracted in anticipation, eagerness even. And then Luke didn't have to anticipate the sensation of being filled; Cain pushed two long, blunt fingers inside Luke's ass, started to work his snug hole, and sent Luke to heaven.

"Oh God, Cain." Luke worked his entrance as best he could against Cain's wonderful invasion. "That's so good, but I want more."

In response, Cain gave Luke another finger. *Yes.* Luke grunted and worked to relax his muscles and accept the stretching of the thicker penetration. Watching openly, Cain twisted that triple taking, touching all along Luke's anal walls with his big fingers.

Greedy and desperate for his fantasy to become reality, Luke found that Cain's partial taking with his fingers wasn't nearly enough. Luke wanted the fucking of his life. "Give me more. I want more." He locked his gaze on Cain's and wouldn't let the man stray away. "I want you. Give me you."

Without words, Cain slid his digits from Luke's channel. Before Luke could miss the attention, Cain guided his erection to Luke's pulsing, needy entrance. Through the sliver of space that separated their bodies, Luke stared, watching with an overwhelming swell of emotion as Cain pushed the head of his penis through Luke's fluttering hole, and then more of his length very slowly started to disappear into Luke's body too. *Oh God, yes.* Another thick inch took Luke's sensitive channel, stretching him so incredibly already. Luke bit his lip, and he -- feeling the mating through his whole goddamn body -- couldn't tear his stare from Cain's eyes to look down. Cain couldn't get terribly deep yet. With each pull back, then push forward again to try to get deeper into Luke's ass, Cain revealed the forbidden pleasure he so needed on every inch of his face. The man's stark beauty -- his goddamn gentle humanity -- tore through Luke's soul. As if Luke's body understood the love, the next time Cain pushed his length inside, Luke settled completely, and Cain finally buried himself deep inside Luke's dark tunnel.

*Oh Jesus God.* Luke couldn't say a word or look away. Cain began to slowly move, and his face contorted with pleasure each time he stroked his cock in and out of Luke's tight chute. Luke could see something else in Cain's eyes too; the man hadn't forgotten his promise to make the transformation, and he didn't intend to reneg on the deal.

Suddenly, in a shot, Cain shifted Luke's legs back around his waist, and then planted his hands in the grass over Luke's shoulders. *Oh yes.* Luke shivered as the change in position stretched him open in a different way and Cain's shaft slid deeper inside. Less confined now, Luke began to lift his hips to help slide his pulsing, narrow passage up against Cain's shaft.

In response Cain gritted his teeth, clearly working close to the edge of what he could stand to feel. He lowered his weight onto Luke, and when their faces were so close their features were blurred, a thick, guttural moan escaped him. "Get ready for it." He plastered a hard, searing kiss against Luke's lips, one of promise that tasted of an apology too. "Now."

With that, Cain threw back his head, his eyes slid closed, and his facial features started twisting. Luke watched, fascinated, as the man he loved started to change. At first Luke was transfixed by Cain's magnificent wings, the great width unfurling from within Cain's back and opening to fill the star lit sky, not stopping until they spanned the width of the small clearing, glorious in their mammoth, extended beauty.

Quickly though, watching the beauty of Cain's wings and the rest of the changes took a backseat to the wild intensity in Cain's stare. Cain clenched his jaw, repeatedly, as if he were working with everything in him to maintain control. Luke knew why. Buried deep inside Luke's ass, Cain's cock suddenly started to grow and push against the walls of Luke's rectum, stretching him with the breadth of new girth, and forced the limits of what Luke could take. Of what he could stand to feel for this man and the great passion he was capable of giving.

*Everything I wanted.*

The new length of Cain's cock pushed its way deeper inside Luke's passage, taking him fully, just as Luke had requested. Almost unbearably possessed, Luke grunted with the massive taking. Uncertainty immediately lived in Cain's gaze -- within the beast's fierce face -- showing the human within fighting against the beast's clear need to own this mating ritual in a fundamental way.

His heart cracking, Luke pulled Cain down until their foreheads touched. "You are so beautiful." He lifted up and pressed his mouth to Cain's, his chest squeezing when Cain clung to him and lowered Luke back down to the grass. Breaking the kiss, Luke instead grazed his lips over Cain's jagged demon face, kissing every inch, and didn't stop until he had his mouth pressed against the shell of Cain's elongated, pointy ear. Luke licked, delighting in the answering shiver that slid through Cain. He then uttered into Cain's ear, "But if you don't start fucking me like you mean it, I'm going to scream so loud the noise will bring the entire state of Montana rushing to our backyard to see what's going on."

Rearing back, Cain narrowed his stare, his pupil's flaring. Right away he withdrew, taking almost his entire length from Luke's ass, and left only the giant mushroom inside the tight ring of Luke's asshole. Cain then growled, baring magnificent teeth, and shifted downward, slowly pushed his way back inside, and sent Luke's channel into a frenzy of confused, excited sensations. A second time, Cain -- the demon -- penetrated Luke with agonizing slowness, and once again withdrew to leave just his cockhead resting inside Luke's channel.

*Shit. Shit Shit.* Luke exhaled shakily. On the one hand, because it was Cain, Luke loved everything; it felt damned good to be penetrated so precisely, so completely, by someone who demanded perfection in everything he did. On the flip side, the agonizingly slow teasing -- along with the immense size of Cain's demon cock -- sent Luke to a place of such desperate need he wasn't sure if everything he was experiencing was rooted in pleasure or pain. He only knew he wanted everything this demon body that housed the man he loved could stand to give him.

"Please, Cain." Luke didn't care if Cain detected or pitied Luke begging. "Harder…" The moment Luke begged, Cain pushed back inside Luke and pressed them both into the ground. "Ohhhh, yes…" Luke reveled in Cain pushing him into the rich earth. Cain then shafted Luke yet again, still torturously controlled, but with a little more of the force Luke so craved. "Take me." Luke wrapped his arms around Cain's neck, tightened his thigh muscles against Cain's waist, and began to pump himself up against Cain's cock, the action repeatedly lifting him straight off the ground. He locked his limbs around Cain's hard body and held on. "Take me…please…"

Cain suddenly clutched Luke's ass cheeks with his giant demon hands. Seconds later Cain rose to his feet, and Luke was in the air with him. As Cain strode in the direction of the cabin, he kept Luke attached to his prick. Once Cain reached the cabin he slammed Luke against the log wall, sandwiching him there. Cain pushed Luke down on his penetration and speared up deeply at the same time, powerfully joining them deeply as one. Luke cried out, and he clutched Cain's shoulders, his ass screaming with unparalleled delight as Cain finally began to fuck him in earnest.

"You've awakened the demon within me," Cain said against Luke's shoulder. As he jammed his enormous erection in deep once more, grinding Luke's body against the cabin as he did, he bit down on Luke's shoulder. "You should be careful what you dream about" -- Cain licked and bit his way to Luke's mouth -- "for some dreams, when granted, will surely leave you with a sore ass come the morning." Cain clutched Luke's thighs hard enough to leave bruises, certainly leaving nicks and scratches from his talons, as he started a steady shafting of Luke's ass -- a fierce pace that set Luke on fire inside.

"I know," Luke whispered back roughly, holding on as tightly as he could. Cain had finally reached a place where he'd let go so completely that he didn't seem to comprehend that he would leave clear marks of his desire on Luke's body -- and Luke was fiercely glad. He loved it. "But it'll be worth it." Luke knew that with each word he spoke, he provoked a harder fucking, a deeper loss of Cain's control. "It'll be worth not being able to sit for a week when I feel you lose it and fill me up deep inside with your demon cum."

"Sooner than you think." His voice stripped bare, Cain was so far gone his gaze burned bright with a need too intimate to speak. "Sooner than you think." He took Luke with an openmouthed, carnal kiss. He groaned with the rough kiss, and Luke did too. Their tongues dueled for dominance, each one knowing that neither one would give up the battle this time.

Luke worked his hips and thighs as best he could, trying to make Cain more a part of his body, needing the connection like an itch just out of his reach. The force of Cain's kiss jammed Luke's head against the cabin wall; each rough thrust from Cain's fucking shoved Luke's body into the wood, scraping his skin raw with each thrust from

Cain's powerful demon body. With each pounding, Cain's fucking became less purposeful and more erratic, and his kisses turned into a mapping of Luke's entire face. It seemed as if Cain tasted Luke all over because he couldn't make himself break the connection. Luke didn't care why Cain tasted and ate at him so completely; he just knew he loved it. He craved this trust, this loss of control Cain so rarely let himself have. And if Cain only gave in because he thought the demon within him demanded it then Luke was getting exactly what he wanted in this encounter.

His mouth against Luke's cheek, Cain raggedly whispered, "I'm close, Luke. I'm so fucking close." Somehow, Cain's breathing turned even harsher and choppier. He buried his face in Luke's scalp, licking and biting Luke's head, and hammered Luke's ass with a half dozen vigorous thrusts. The man fell completely under the power of his passions, and the powerful mating burned Luke up inside.

Luke had been waiting, so hungry and desperate, for Cain's complete loss of control. With it now upon them, Luke wrapped his arms around Cain's broad shoulders, and he squeezed tight with his thighs, not letting up or pulling away from the connection one little bit. "Let me have it, Cain," he whispered against Cain's long, demon ear. He clenched the muscles in his ass as tight as he could, clamping down like a vise on Cain's thick cock. "Let it go and give it all to me."

Cain's entire being vibrated like a live wire. "Ohh Christ, this body is so fucking sensitive..." For a split second, Cain stuttered to a complete stop. Then, before Luke's eyes, Cain started flapping his enormous coppery wings in great sweeping arcs. Their immense power lifted them both more than a foot off the ground, suspending them higher and higher in midair for long seconds, before Cain catapulted them back against the cabin hard enough to rattle Luke's teeth. Cain had Luke pinned to the wood at least five feet off the ground, with his demon wings flapping and beating hard on either side of Luke, the strength and power in those wings keeping them hanging above the earth. The beast inside Cain then rammed Luke again and again, pounding Luke's ass relentlessly. Both men were raw from the intensity of the fucking -- Luke physically, and Cain so clearly ripped open emotionally, surely in a way he'd never let himself be before.

Taking -- stealing -- everything Cain had to give, Luke gave back as best he could from his disadvantaged position. He steadied Cain's frantic licking and biting of his face and head, and he dragged their mouths together once more. Luke shoved his tongue past Cain's lips, mating and sucking and licking, taking complete control of the kiss. Cain shuddered and moaned, his entire body seizing as his too bright gaze found Luke in the night. The coppery skin over Cain's mountainous face pulled taut, and his lips slid back, exposing the brightness of his strong, white teeth.

*So fucking beautiful.* At the sight of this Cain, this wonderful piece of him, Luke lost his heart all over again. "Cain…"

"Oh…oh…oh Christ." Cain suddenly looked scared. "It's happening." His lips parted, almost as if he had to gasp for breath. With his blue eyes darkening to match the night sky, he slammed Luke into the cabin wall one more time, shoved his demon cock up deep inside Luke's ass, tucking it farther than it had ever gone before, and practically tore Luke in two.

Luke moaned and gasped. Biting his lip, he struggled to take the thick, deep, powerful invasion without crying out. Then, in a flash, the searing pain no longer mattered. Before him, Cain keened a wailing noise that sounded as if it had originated high in the back of his throat. A second later, Cain threw back his head, howling in the most basic form of release. Cain's massive beast body jerked and seized, and then he flooded Luke abused passage with demon seed. Luke wrapped his arms around Cain and held on, struggling to breathe. He clamped his thighs and took the burning hot ejaculate into his body, as every spurt seemed to go on longer than the last. With his eyes squeezed shut, Luke forced his weight down on Cain's cock, to better accept the cum marking his tender ass channel and coating him deep inside -- steaming wet proof of Cain's ownership. *In exactly the way I wanted.*

In that moment, Luke had never experienced anything more right or perfect than Cain branding him inside. He was, without a doubt, desperately in love with this man.

Eventually, after Luke's squeezing passage had drained Cain's cock of every drop of seed, Cain's mind opened back up to things other than his own fierce sexual desire. As he processed that he had Luke pressed against the cabin some six feet off the ground, shock rolled through him. Cain couldn't remember lifting Luke into the air. After he'd changed into the demon, he couldn't remember doing or feeling anything other than fucking Luke with everything in him.

In exactly the way he'd been so terrified to do.

"Are you all right?" Cain asked. Goose bumps suddenly popped up all over his body. The silence became deafening, causing him to shiver.

Luke nodded, his cheek rubbing against Cain's ear. "Yeah. I'm okay."

Slowly, Cain lowered them back to the ground. Once his feet hit solid earth, he released the death grip he had on the backs of Luke's thighs, but then cringed when his fingertips grazed over angry, deep indentations covering Luke's flesh. Christ, Cain's demon fingernails had gripped Luke with a less than gentle hand. Cain untangled Luke from his waist, holding Luke steady as he withdrew his cock as gently as he could and then set Luke back on his own feet. Cain watched Luke with each step, and he listened intently. As Cain slid his too large demon cock from Luke's all too human body, Luke gasped and then winced.

*Oh Christ. No.* "You're not all right." Cain's soul shrank with shame. "Damn it, I hurt you. I was too aggressive, and I hurt you with my size and strength. I knew I would. Why didn't you tell me? Why didn't you stop me?"

"Shh, shh." Luke covered Cain's demon mouth with his hand. "You didn't hurt me, baby. Get that out of your head right now."

"But..." Cain mumbled around Luke's hand.

"But nothing," Luke insisted. "I'm fine." He took Cain's hand and pulled him to the center of the clearing. This time Luke did the guiding, and Cain followed him to their grassy bed. Cain let himself be led willingly, and even let himself be laid on his back -- although with the protrusion of his wings it wasn't the most comfortable position. Following, Luke stretched himself out on top of Cain. For some reason, when Luke was draped over him like this, Cain felt the most cherished and loved by him. The complete, warm contact settled Cain inside in a way nothing else could.

Leaning down until their noses touched, Luke pecked a kiss to Cain's lips. "You let the demon inside you out tonight, and you allowed him to live in a way you have never before." Shifting Cain's legs for him, Luke then settled in the V of his parted thighs. "What we did was insanely perfect in every way."

Cain wasn't so sure about that. Indisputable hard evidence proved the contrary. "But you didn't even come." It wasn't as if Cain couldn't feel Luke's erection pushing against the crease of his thigh. "Crawl up on my chest and at least let me take care of your hard-on."

"Oh, it's going to get taken care of." Luke traced Cain's hard lips with his index finger. His tone was full of purpose, and his gray gaze remained open with a strength and calm Cain envied. "You're going to be the one to do it too. I wanted the beast of my dreams to fuck me with everything he had in him, and he did. It was powerful, and lustful, and everything I fantasized about from the time I was fifteen years old."

Luke caressed the ridges of Cain's demon face lovingly, and then he leaned down and pressed a light kiss to the crooked nose. Luke's stare didn't waver, and the sight filled Cain with so much longing it tore straight through his gut, leaving a gaping wound in its wake. Luke's next words ripped up through Cain's chest and finished the job. "I loved my experience with the demon, but now I want my Hawk back. I want to make love to him under the stars until the sun comes up and we are forced to stop. Give me my Hawk back, Cain of the Naverto demons, and let me see the handsome face of the man I love."

# CHAPTER TWENTY-FIVE

*Oh my. The way he speaks to me.* Cain shifted his internal and external body without hesitation. Immediately, the demon sucked back inside Cain, jostling him and Luke when his wings dragged along the grass as they retracted into his back. Cain quickly made the change and let his other, more familiar, more comfortable body, free once again.

As Cain changed, pressure began to build against the back of his eyes, threatening to spill over with tears, and he felt like the worst sort of pussy. Cain couldn't help it though. The truth of Luke's love was the most powerful thing he'd ever experienced in his life. Hating the exposure and feeling weak, Cain turned his head and stared off into the stillness of the night, trying to recoup some of the demon prowess he'd temporarily lost.

Luke wasn't having any of it though. He cupped his hand under Cain's cheek and turned him until they were face-to-face once more. "Oh, baby," Luke soothed as awareness lit up his silver gaze. "There was a part of you that really thought I might love being with the demon more than I love being with you, wasn't there?"

Cain was being completely ridiculous, and he knew it, but with everything going on, he couldn't seem to keep that stiff upper lip he'd perfected over the course of his one hundred and seventy-five years of life. "He was your first crush." Cain owned up to his fear -- a buried one he hadn't even realized existed until Luke had so casually stated that he wanted Hawk back. Then all of the emotions and insecurities had bubbled up irrationally, making Cain feel emotionally raw and exposed. "I guess I thought somewhere, deep down, there might be a part of you that wouldn't be quite as excited by me after you'd been with him."

"Oh, Hawk, no...no." Luke tunneled his fingers through Cain's hair and leaned down until their lips met in a soft touch. He kissed Cain's mouth, and his nose, and his rough hewn, human cheeks, and his strong forehead. Then he ended by settling his forehead against Cain's. "If it were not a matter of choice, I'd take you both in a heartbeat. But, honey, when it's a matter of losing you, of losing this man who hired me, this man who comforted me during my nightmares about MacLesten, this man who holds his head up high when people openly stare at us when we go into town, baby, that's not even a contest. I love you. I love everything you are without the demon, but the reverse is not true. I would not love the demon half so well without the knowledge that you are inside him when he appears. I can give up the demon, but I could never give up the man I call Hawk. Not ever."

"I'm sorry; I'm sorry." Cain blinked and blinked and blinked, directing his focus toward the cabin. He worked like the very devil to stamp down this emotional flood consuming him whole. "When you say stuff like that...I'm not used to it...Not used to how it makes me feel."

"Shh, it's all right." With the softest touch, Luke brushed Cain's cheeks with his fingers. He didn't force Cain to face him this time, but instead, merely placed a gentle kiss against his temple, and let the soft touch linger. "You do such a good job taking care of me. For once, let me take care of you and make it all better. All right?"

Cain nodded, his cheek pressed against the pungent grass, too choked up speak through the clog jamming his throat. His eyes fell closed, and he just let himself *feel* as Luke slid his mouth down his neck, one small kiss at a time, leaving a trail of simmering undercurrents in his wake. When Luke's exploration reached Cain's chest, he slid his hands down and cupped Cain's hips at the same time, and he began an assault on Cain on multiple levels. Luke alternated sucking on Cain's sensitized nipples, keeping them both in a constant state of puckered delight. At the same time, he rubbed his callused palms against the bare skin of Cain's hips, outer thighs, and around to the outer slope of his buttocks. The fleeting yet continuous contact felt so unbearably good Cain automatically bent his legs and dug his heels into the soft earth, searching for a way to anchor the slow, sensual burn rapidly returning to his mind and body.

Luke did a million things extremely well. In that moment, Cain realized Luke was already a master at knowing exactly how to take care of Cain.

Pressing light kisses down Cain's middle, Luke nipped small love bites against Cain's stomach, making Cain quiver. Cain didn't feel anything for a moment, and he thought Luke had gone away, but then with a soft touch Cain's cock stirred to gentle life, and he knew Luke had only paused in order to make everything perfect for them. Luke wiped Cain's penis clean with something soft -- Cain guessed Luke's discarded sweats. Cain didn't want to open his eyes and look, but wherever the fabric had come from, contact with it teased Cain's prick to aching life. Cain floated within the spell of Luke's loving touch, and when Luke swirled his tongue around the head of Cain's ultrasensitive cock, he moaned low in his throat. The wonderful, wet heat then moved lower, surrounding Cain's turgid prick, inch by agonizing inch, until Cain's tip kissed the back of Luke's throat. Cain knifed his hips off the ground in response, but Luke didn't let go; he sucked and dragged on Cain's shaft again and again, working to make Cain's cock raging hard and thick. Cain wanted to open his eyes; he ached to watch Luke's mouth working his cock, but he was afraid that if he did his emotions would swell out of control. Cain couldn't bear such a loss again, so he kept his eyes closed and allowed Luke to have his way with him.

He let Luke take care of him.

*He's perfect.*

Eventually Luke abandoned Cain's member, leaving Cain spike-stiff and leaking a steady stream of precum. Pressing the back of Cain's thighs upward, Luke forced Cain's legs against his chest. Cain's asshole was then greeted by the gift of Luke's mouth, and Cain could not hold back the fierce groan of pleasure.

"Ohhh Christ, Luke…" Cain clenched his teeth. The moist tip of Luke's tongue flickered over Cain's pulsating hole a dozen times. Then he sucked the tightly-closed entrance a little bit to relax him, and Cain swallowed back a scream. Right then Luke jammed his tongue through and invaded the burning hot tightness of Cain's ass. Cain pushed up on Luke's questing, fucking tongue, reveling in the feel of the man wickedly teasing his ring and just inside his channel. "You know how much I love when you do that to me." Forbidden sensation slammed through Cain. Christ, full-on shock still slammed through Cain every damn time Luke rimmed him. "You drive me insane when you make a feast of my ass."

Luke didn't say anything, he just kept spearing Cain's hole with his tongue, pushing Cain right to the brink of coming. Then, just as with Cain's nipples and his cock, Luke took the teasing foreplay away. *No. Please.* Cain couldn't remain disconnected any longer. He whipped his head up, opened his eyes, and found Luke, his silver gaze stunning, above him, waiting.

"That's what I've been waiting to see," Luke whispered. Reaching down between their bodies, he guided his slicked-up, lubricated cock to Cain's opening. Cain gasped as Luke pushed the head of his penis into Cain's rectum, taking him with a slow, persistent pressure. "Those pure blue eyes that show me everything you feel. That's my Hawk. That's who I've been waiting to show himself ever since I asked you to come back to me."

Luke shifted against Cain's stretched entrance, easing his way in deeper. And in a way that had never happened before, Cain relaxed completely, instantly, and he took Luke without the slightest resistance. Luke slipped inside and embedded the entire length of his cock all the way inside Cain's scorching ass. Nothing had ever felt quite so right, nor quite so terrifying, in Cain's life.

"That's it, baby." Luke rocked inside Cain gently, barely moving. The gentle fucking was the sweetest, scariest sensation Cain had ever known. "Wrap your legs around mine, get us all tangled up from top to bottom." Luke didn't wait for Cain; he guided Cain's left thigh around the side of his and hooked Cain's ankle behind his knee.

*Oh yes.* Cain immediately knew why. The coarse hairs on Cain's legs brushed and mingled with the finer, darker ones sparsely covering Luke's, ratcheting up the intimacy of everything they did together another notch. Somehow, experiencing that new layer to their mating, and finding himself trapped in the quiet intensity of Luke's open gaze -- even more than the fact that he had Luke's penis buried in his ass -- made Cain want to turn his face and hide. His heart pounded wildly, nearly out of control, but Cain forced himself to stay present. He wrapped his other leg around Luke's. Blinking, Cain tried to hold back a depth of overwhelmingly powerful emotions he couldn't afford to feel, couldn't afford to commit to right now, even as Luke held him bound in the gentlest shackles of passion Cain had ever experienced.

With his elbows resting against Cain's shoulders, Luke bracketed Cain's head in his arms and tunneled his fingers through Cain's hair, soothing Cain with a light caress. Luke blanketed Cain; hard stomach to hard stomach, chest to chest, gray eyes latched to blue. Yet, still, always, Luke maintained that incredibly safe, insanely arousing, undulation between cock and ass, fucking Cain so very softly, yet in a deeper manner than Cain had ever known. Every pump of Luke's hips gently slapped his balls against Cain's buttocks and incited each nerve in Cain's ass channel to glorious life.

"This is what I want you to take with you when you go away, Hawk." The fiery passion in Luke's gaze belied the languorous, torturous lovemaking he delivered to Cain's sensitized body and battered senses. "You are a quiet man, and you have a hard time trusting in words. I want you to take what we're doing and transcribe it in your mind. I want you to know what it means when you're far away from me tomorrow, fighting for your life."

"Uh-huh." Cain nodded, his eyes sparkling bright, he was sure, as breathlessness filled him to the brim. Too much feeling swelled in Cain and made him squirm. He pushed up against Luke's cock for a faster union -- one he'd become familiar with and could handle. "I will."

In a flash, Luke reached down and slowed Cain's hips back down; he wouldn't let Cain hide behind dizzying lust. "What does it mean?" Luke asked, unrelenting in the strength of his convictions and feelings. Letting go of Cain's hips, Luke grazed his fingers up the sides of Cain's body, not stopping until he took hold of Cain's hands and pressed them into the damp grass. Luke linked them together in every way, palm against palm, fingers intertwined, as well as the rest of their bodies. Still, he would not let Cain look away. "Tell me what it means."

Cain was very afraid wetness did leak out the corners of his eyes, but he could not stop the flow. "It…It means…that…that you… love me." His voice was so raspy, it barely sounded like English, but he spoke of Luke's feelings aloud for the first time, let himself hear the truth coming from his own mouth, and finally let himself believe it. Staggered by the avalanche of emotions, Cain tried to lift his head to touch his mouth to Luke's, but a smashing of their lips remained just out of his reach. So Cain *felt* the kiss instead, as Luke so clearly wanted, and conveyed the press of their lips as best as he could with words. "That somehow the kind, sweet, loyal, funny, honest, beautiful Luke Forrester loves me. Loves me, Cain Hawkins."

"That's right." Luke nodded. He then closed the distance between them and gave Cain his kiss, tender and clinging at first, and then slid his tongue inside for a teasing, fleeting flick of connection before pulling away. "I do love you, Hawk. And nothing, *nothing*, will ever change that. Ever."

Cain choked on the storm of emotions filling the night air; any further words got locked deep inside his chest, unspoken.

Luke didn't have the same trouble. He pushed up deep inside Cain's ass, reminded him of the connection of their bodies, and then he leaned down, his lips a sliver of a breath away from Cain's. He held Cain's gaze under the moonlight and whispered again, "I love you, Cain Hawkins. I love you with all of my heart, and you can trust in it and depend on it forever."

Luke pressed his lips softly to Cain's again, and Cain lost what little control he had left. He came with a small cry, his cock pressed against Luke's stomach. Seed spilled from within, onto Luke, claiming Luke with the mark of his seed in a way he couldn't yet say with words.

When the first spurt of wet warmth hit Luke's belly, Luke gasped into Cain's mouth. Squeezing Cain's hands in a death grip, Luke pressed them into the rich, moist grass with one final thrust into Cain's body. Just as quickly as Cain had come, Luke swelled inside Cain, pushing at his passage so wonderfully, and he filled Cain's ass with his hot, wet release.

Luke had been right. Cain could feel the truth. Luke's essence was filled with love.

———

AT SIX THE NEXT NIGHT, CAIN watched as Caleb drew a series of symbols on the floor of his cabin with a thick piece of chalk. Earlier in the day Cain and Luke had moved the table and desk to Luke's old room in the stable, as they'd been unsure of exactly how much room Caleb would need to open a portal -- not to mention the kind of mess it might create. They'd shoved the couch, coffee table, and recliner up against the wall of bookshelves, covering as much as they could with bed sheets. The thin fabric was a silly, ineffectual barrier, and both men knew it, but without words, they had both understood the need to do something that would give them a little bit of power and control over what was about to occur, even if it was false.

Caleb said a few words Cain didn't understand -- probably Gaelic since it was a Naverto ritual. Caleb then sliced his forearm open, and everyone in the room gasped. Drops of blood from Caleb's small wound sprinkled down over the symbols he'd created, spotting each one of them with his blood. Within moments of Caleb's chant, the flooring in the diameter of the four-foot circle disappeared and a fog of pale blue that seemed to hover just above the floor took its place. Caleb reached his arm into the fog, all the way up to his shoulder, proving to the group that nothing solid remained below the mist.

With that done, Caleb turned to the small group gathered, and the man's solemn blue gaze collided with Cain's. "The portal is set," Caleb said as he got to his feet. "It will remain open until I close it, so you need not worry about that. You can go through and confront the council whenever you're ready."

For Cain, ready was a relative term. Whether or not Cain was *ready* would be determined on the other end of twelve hours. Right now, though, with a sickness in his belly, he understood he could no longer delay the inevitable.

*It's time to say goodbye.*

Cain turned to his oldest brother first, and he tried not to get caught up in the checked, restrained emotion pushing up through the darkness of Connor's black gaze. This brother was the one who'd held the three of them together, the one with the strongest will of them all, the one who already had what Cain was heading into hell to attain for himself. Cain could only say, "Don't forget what I asked you for." *The gift of property to Luke, should I not return.* More than anything, Cain knew that Connor respected responsibility and commitment to loved ones, and so he knew the man would respect Cain's request.

"Already been done," Connor replied, his voice gruff. Suddenly clasping Cain's hand, Connor pulled him into a strong hug. He squeezed Cain tight and then let him go, adding, almost like an order, "But none of that matters because you're coming back to us. Right?"

"Right," Cain agreed, his heart aching to see the need for that confirmation in his brother's dark gaze. This moment had cracked Connor's formidable armor a little bit, and it killed Cain to see it.

"I'll be seeing you soon."

Cassie grabbed Cain next and threw her arms around his neck, before Cain could even say the word goodbye. "You just concentrate on taking care of yourself," she whispered into his ear. "As long as you're still breathing, you're winning. That's all we need you to be doing when you get back. That's all it takes to beat them. Got it?"

"Got it, boss." Cain couldn't help chuckling as he pictured this fiery, dark-haired woman on the sidelines of a football field browbeating a team of fifty-four hulking men to victory. His chest constricted, though, and he said softy, for her ears only, "Take care of Connor for me, okay? Just in case. He needs you more than he lets show. All right?"

Nodding, Cassie pulled away, her green gaze filled with moisture. "He loves you back just as much. I won't let him pull away, no matter what. I promise."

Cain leaned down and pecked Cassie's cheek. He should have known she'd see her husband's vulnerability and need; she never missed anything. "Good girl." He tugged her ever-present braid one more time.

Then, finally, Cain locked his stare on eyes that looked so much like his own.

"You don't have to get mushy with me," Caleb said, his smile wide and magnificent in his devil-may-care way. "I'm not worried one bit. I know you're coming back."

Cain studied the teasing face and eyes before him, but he also absorbed the palms that rubbed relentlessly against a pair of faded jeans -- one hand covered in streams of blood from his own sacrifice in this endeavor. Cain knew what his brother wasn't saying, beneath the jokes. "You listen to me," Cain uttered, his gaze locked on Caleb's. "You are a fine man."

"Well" -- Caleb flashed a truly wicked grin -- "that's what the ladies tell me."

"Shut up, you jackass," Cain growled. He grabbed his brother's head in his hands and wouldn't let him joke his way out of the hold. "You listen to me, because you need to hear this. You are every bit as responsible for my survival and sanity through all these years as Connor is. You deserve true happiness, and you deserve the love of someone who sees how wonderful you are. Don't ever sell yourself short on that, or else I will come back, if only to kick your ass until you open your eyes and start to see it yourself."

Caleb's stoic visage started to crumble. "I'm gonna hold you to that." He pointed his finger at Cain and shook it. "I'm gonna damn well hold you to that." Then Caleb seemed to shake the vulnerability off, and he replaced the look with his more familiar and comfortable façade. Maybe he needed a lighthearted moment in order to get through what he felt, Cain didn't know, but Caleb suddenly grabbed Cain and kissed him full on the mouth. He even slid his tongue past Cain's lips, grazing the tips of their tongues together, before pulling away.

Cain stood there, processing Caleb's kiss, too stunned to react.

"There," Caleb declared triumphantly. He slapped Cain on the rear and smiled. "Just a little something to remember me by. Now, if you don't come back, you won't be able to kick my ass for doing that, and I'll just notch you up as another satisfied customer."

"Christ." Cain shook his head and tried like hell not to focus on the flames burning up his face. "You will do anything to avoid a truly intimate moment, Caleb, won't you?"

Caleb did sober then, completely. "I just can't stand the thought of losing you, really losing you, so I'm choosing not to think about it. That's how I'm getting through this, okay?"

"I care about you too," Cain admitted right back. "Jackass." The smile they shared was full of history, both painful and wonderful, but always side by side. The three of them.

Now, Cain had to deliberately step into harm's way for the man he loved the best -- the one he'd put off saying goodbye to for long enough. The one who would be just as shattered by Cain's failure as he himself would be.

*Luke.*

Cain slid his focus over his makeshift family, a surrogate one of two brothers and a sister to whom he could not feel more attached were they actually blood kin. He saw they were waiting for the final farewell just as much as he was. "Geez, guys." Cain gave them each a hard, pointed stare. "Could you at least pretend not to pay attention here for five minutes, and act like you're not going to listen in on every word I say?"

Surprisingly, they actually gave him the courtesy of moving to his bedroom door and pretending to engage in soft conversation. Knowing that was as much as he would get, Cain turned, and without looking, slipped his hand in Luke's. Cain pulled Luke away until they were right beside the portal.

Luke covered Cain's mouth with his hand before Cain could utter his first word. "I'll see you soon," Luke whispered, his voice almost -- *almost* -- sounding as if he believed what he said. Cain had come to know this man very well over the past three months, though, so the slight, ragged thickness beneath Luke's words stabbed him in the heart.

Quickly, Cain grabbed Luke and pulled him into a tight embrace. "Listen to me." Each word Cain spoke sliced his throat open. "I have to tell you something. I wasn't going to at first; I didn't think it was my right. I see now I was wrong. All this time I've been thinking I should wait until afterward, and tell you when I knew for certain we could be together."

"Then wait." Luke dug his fingers into Cain's back and clung to him so hard it brought tears to Cain's eyes. "Wait, Cain. Save it. Tell me when you get back."

"No, darlin', I won't do that." It killed him, but Cain denied Luke that little bit of extra hope. Instead he pulled from a powerful will inside himself -- something he'd never even known he had until Luke had shown him and gifted him with it last night. "I can't risk never speaking this." Cain clutched Luke's face in the palms of his hands, wiping away a matching wetness with the pads of his thumbs. Cain looked into Luke's eyes, finding a dark storm within that betrayed the spine he held so stiff and straight. "You mean the world to me, and with just the chance that I might not come back...and the thought of you never knowing --"

"Please." Luke tangled his hands in Cain's T-shirt, twisting the fabric in his fingers. "Please, wait. Tell me when you get ba --"

"I love you, Luke."

Luke's face crumbled. He threw himself into Cain's arms and buried his face against Cain's chest.

Pressing a kiss to the top of Luke's head, Cain rubbed his hands up and down Luke's back. Then he tucked his mouth against Luke's ear and made himself say the rest. "I love you so much. No matter what happens, I need you to know I don't regret a single second of the time I spent falling in love with you. If the cost is my life, then it was worth it, worth every drop of blood in exchange for the time I got to spend with you. I needed you to hear me say it, Luke. I have to tell you something else too. Of the one hundred and seventy-five years I've been alive, the single most profound and humbling moment in my life was when you said those same words to me. Don't ever forget that. No matter what happens, never question whether I went out regretting the choice to enter the Changing Gauntlet. Never think for one second while I'm in there I doubted my choice. I would do anything, and *will* do anything, to spend the rest of my life with you. Never forget it, Luke. Never. Never forget that I love you with all of my heart, and you can trust in that and depend on it forever." Cain repeated Luke's very words back to him, knowing the intuitive nature of this man. He would pick up on them and understand how very much it had meant to Cain to hear them last night.

Cain then slid his palm up Luke's back, wrapped his hand around Luke's neck, and tilted up his face. Cain took a moment to commit to memory this gorgeous face that had an even more beautiful person beneath the physical beauty. Cain mapped the lines at the corners of Luke's eyes with his fingertips, lines that had to be from laughter, for he was too young to be sporting wrinkles. Then he touched over the dark brows, as glossy as the thick hair on top of his head. Cain feathered his fingers down the bridge of Luke's nose -- a nose that sported a bump from the beating he'd taken at MacLesten's hands. Cain grazed the pads of his fingers down to the strong jaw already growing a soft, sexy shadow, and finally ended on Luke's strong lips.

Luke possessed a fine mouth; it was a mouth for which Cain would give up everything to possess, just so long as in exchange he could feel Luke's kisses for the rest of his days. Cain tucked the image of Luke's face in his pocket, for he undoubtedly would need to draw from the memory and use the strength of this moment to get himself through the next dozen hours of his life.

"It's time for me to go, darlin'," Cain finally said. He made himself smile, even though he wanted to wail, scream, and cry. "Can you give me just one last thing before I leave?"

Rather than answering, Luke took the edge of Cain's T-shirt in his hands. He raised the fabric up over Cain's head, proving to Cain with action that he was all right now and would be the strong companion he'd promised to be. Cain let Luke undress him, enjoyed the ritualistic feel of it -- of feeling like his love was sending him off to battle. Cain knew that was fancifully romantic, and he wasn't supposed to be thinking that way, but he would take these potentially last moments with Luke and view them however he wanted.

In whatever way got him through to the other side and back to Luke again.

Luke helped Cain off with his boots, jeans, underwear, and socks, folding them neatly in a pile and setting them aside. As Luke slid his gaze up the length of Cain's nude body, not stopping until they made eye contact, Cain shivered.

"What do you need, Hawk?" Luke finally questioned, his smile almost matching the stoic nature of the one Cain did his damndest to give Luke. "I'll do anything you need."

Cain slid his arm around Luke's waist and pulled him in close. Christ, he loved how this man felt in his arms. "I just need a kiss for luck." Cain closed the distance between them. When he hovered above Luke, he added, "I need one last memory to carry me into the fight of my life."

"You got it."

Luke settled his focus on Cain's mouth. He let his thumb tease the edges and then snagged the pad on Cain's lower lip, dragging it down. Cain darted out his tongue, licking Luke's finger, just as Luke leaned in and took possession of Cain's lip, tugging it between his teeth. Suddenly their mouths were slanted wide over each other's, taking and giving with equal fervor, tongues fighting in desperation and fear of what this kiss might mean. It was a kiss violent in its intensity, with fingers digging deep into the flesh of cheeks and hands tugging at great fists of hair, each trying with all of his might to impossibly convey in one kiss the depth of love they felt for each other.

Just as quickly, with a strangled cry, Cain tore his lips away from Luke and stepped to the edge of the portal. The great pressure behind his eyes almost blinded him, but he managed to find Luke's face, streaming with wetness, one more time. "I love you, Luke." As Cain let his heel slip over the edge of the circle, he could not feel anything beneath his foot. He locked his stare on Luke as fear started to take him over and steal his breath. Cain wheezed again, "I love you…"

And with an ocean of fear crashing in his ears, deafening him, Cain saw Luke's mouth form the words, "I love you too," just as he stepped over the edge.

---

THE PORTAL HAD NOT BEEN the wild, endless, water-park slide ride through a rift in time and space Cain had expected. In fact, he'd almost been disappointed when in actuality the portal ended up being as simple as the sensation of stepping through a doorway from one room to another.

If the portal hadn't ended up being the movie cliché Cain had anticipated, the room where he now stood more than made up for it. From the cavernous, candle-lit chamber, right down to the twelve somber-looking Naverto sitting in a row behind an ornate, thick-legged table, this was exactly what Cain had imagined he would face. The lineup of the Council of Twelve made Cain think of the Supreme Court, except there were no women on this panel. And, unlike going before the highest court in the land, in this instance, Cain had to remind himself his fate was in his own hands, not theirs.

Cain saw no need to hold off the eventual conclusion of that any longer. He was as ready as he would ever be. "My name is Cain Hawkins," he declared in a loud, clear voice. He held his head high and set his chin at a defiant angle. "And I demand the right to be put through the Changing Gauntlet."

# CHAPTER TWENTY-SIX

"Who do you think you are, you whelp?" The leader of the Council, a particularly tall Naverto, at least seven feet by Cain's estimate, rose from his glorified throne. "You have no right to interrupt a council meeting in this manner."

Cain's heart pumped blood through his veins much too fast for comfort, but his chin didn't waver. "I am a member of the Naverto, just as you are. As a member of this clan, I have the right to demand the Changing Gauntlet. You cannot deny me."

"You are speaking in nonsensical riddles, boy," the spokesman for the council accused. He circled around the table and moved to stand in front of Cain, his demon body covered only by a loincloth. Cain tilted his head back and looked up, up into the blackest eyes he'd ever seen. "You have no appointment to be seen by the Council. Your insolence is intolerable." He flicked his wrist. "Go away now, before I have you removed forcibly."

"You can try." Cain held his ground and tried not to focus on how badly this giant would pummel his six-feet-two human form.

"But I know my rights. Give me the Changing Gauntlet right now, or else I walk out of here and tell every Naverto demon across this land of the great secret you are keeping from them." Cain let his gaze drift from the mammoth Naverto before him to the others, and he didn't finish his thought until he'd looked every one of them in the eyes. "I don't imagine this Changing Gauntlet is the only secret the twelve of you are trying to hide. This is my right," Cain reiterated strongly. "So I ask you now, which one of you will challenge me for the first hour, for I am ready."

A door suddenly groaned open from somewhere deep in the shadows behind Cain. Cain whirled just in time to see the tall, scruffy mess of the Traveler entering the chamber. Before the man had fully entered the room, he said, "Council members, I am returned from my journey, and I have news of the utmost importance to tell you."

"It no longer matters." Cain made his presence known. The Traveler whipped his head up and his focus shot to Cain; each one read the truth in the other immediately. Christ, Cain really had not been a minute too soon. "I have already demanded the Changing Gauntlet. Nothing else matters now; they cannot deny me. Your information is no longer relevant."

The Traveler held Cain's gaze, and although Cain could see he'd figured out the truth, Cain also could swear grudging respect, and maybe even pleasure, lived in that stare. The Traveler merely nodded. "Of course." He bowed, and added to the council, "I will return to give my report tomorrow."

Cain smiled as he watched the Traveler withdraw from the chamber. Satisfied, confident he'd just dodged a fatal bullet, Cain turned to demand his rights once again. Just as he did, he was backhanded across the cheek so hard it knocked him to the ground.

Stars and blotches of light filled Cain's vision. As he fought to regain his sight, the behemoth Naverto kicked him in the gut and robbed the breath right from his body. With a low, vicious growl, the demon swore, "How dare you give orders in this chamber? How dare you come in here as if you are the one in charge?"

Cain rolled to his knees and elbows, coughing and gasping as he tried to gain his feet. Right then another swift kick jammed up under his body, deep into the flesh of his belly, and lifted him clear off the ground. In the air for just a moment, Cain then crashed back down to the stone floor in a jarring, mind-numbing thud.

Rolling his head, Cain looked up at the giant Naverto, the demon a blur. Cain's eyesight was already out of focus from the pain. Cain rasped, "So you have chosen to go first." The demon's eyes widened with understanding. As Cain tried to match that frightening stare with one of his own, he wiped his split lip and rose up to his knees -- as far as he could go right now. "Start the clock," Cain demanded. He then reached out, grabbed the demon's ankle, and yanked him off his feet, getting his first lick in. "The Changing Gauntlet has begun."

---

"AHHHHHH!" CAIN SCREAMED AS FIRE lanced through his back. Another wave of torture had begun. He didn't know who or what inflicted the torture anymore; long ago one of the Naverto council had hooded him and tied him up. This time, white-hot pain sliced through Cain's flesh. The searing precision of a thousand tiny razor blades, sewn into a punishing, leather strop, cut into his back.

Cain no longer had any idea of the length of time he'd actually been able to hold out in a fight against that first Naverto council member -- or how long ago that had been. He just knew he'd blacked out at least three times since that first crushing blow to his skull from the demon with the softball-sized fists. For every second he'd been conscious since then, everything else had become one big, fiery ball of pain. Only, to his horror, the punishment hadn't stopped during the times when he was barely aware of his surrounding or unable to open his mouth and yell for the beatings to stop. Always, always, the torture continued. The battered state of Cain's body shrieked at him to bring this to an end, even when he wasn't conscious and begging his wardens to put an end to this nightmare.

During those moments when Cain had wanted to cry uncle, he had demanded his mind conjure up every image of Luke he'd ever stored in his brain. He pictured Luke riding a horse, playing with Whisky, watching TV, eating, showering, making love to Cain -- anything Cain could think of that would make him grit his teeth and keep those words *"I give up"* stuffed down inside him.

Once again, the leather belt ripped across Cain's shoulder blades and set his flesh ablaze with fire. "Ahhhhh, please…please stop!" Cain cried, his voice hoarse. Instead, one of the Naverto -- he didn't know which -- sliced the bladed strop across the small of Cain's back, landing another bloody blow, and licked more fire through Cain's flesh. The excruciating sensation was akin to a thousand paper cuts slicing into his skin again and again. Slick wetness slid down Cain's body and he knew it was his own blood dripping in tiny rivulets onto the slab of stone to which he'd been tied.

The razor-encrusted leather in the hand of his attacker kept up its attack, cutting across the back of Cain's thighs with a stinging slap. "Ahh…please." Cain screamed as the strop whipped down on him in a crushing slice across his buttocks. "Please! You're killing me."

Someone suddenly loosened the rope holding the hood in place around Cain's neck, and half the black material was pulled away from his face. A blinding brightness assaulted Cain in the one eye the demon had uncovered, but then a shadow quickly darkened the space. When the bleary waves subsided, a Naverto face filled Cain's line of sight. The incessant pounding in Cain's skull was hard enough to make him blurry and nauseous, but once he could see, he took comfort in the knowledge that this was not the same demon who'd delivered the first hit. *I know I made it through one hour, at least.*

"Do you give up, traitor?" Seductive menace laced the demon's voice. "Do you admit your folly and rescind your foolish request for this process?"

Cain struggled against the restraints holding him facedown in an X across a frigid-cold stone slab. A resurgence of adrenaline arced through him, and he wrenched his shoulders and neck until his face nearly touched his captor's. "Never," Cain growled, the sound emitting from low in his throat. "Never." Then he reared back and spit in the demon's face.

Blood lust fired in the demon's eyes. He grabbed the back of Cain's head and slammed his face into the stone bed, jarring Cain's brain in his skull, and Cain's world once again faded to black.

———

As SOMETHING JERKED CAIN BACK INTO awareness, he gasped and choked. He didn't know how long he'd been out, but he now had his sight back -- if only possibly to make him aware that a new form of abuse had begun. Water flowed in a continuous stream over Cain's face, running up his nose and into his mouth, effectively drowning him without ever dunking his head under water. He coughed and thrashed his head from side to side but nothing eased the burning in his nose and lungs. The force of Cain's coughing stung tears to his eyes, and he choked so badly his throat clogged up, rendering him unable to breathe through his mouth. A waterfall poured over his face, and his nasal cavity burned with a sharp, stinging pain. He knew he couldn't let this particular torture continue; he needed some way to breathe or he would die.

Like an animal moving purely on survival instinct, Cain rammed his body upright and head-butted the Naverto demon dumping water on his face. This was not the face of his previous tormentor, and the knowledge that he'd moved to another level in the gauntlet surged a renewal of hope through Cain.

Clearly unprepared for the fight in his captive, the demon stumbled backward. The hose dropped from his hand and clattered against the floor, putting Cain's hell on hold -- at least for a few seconds. With the water no longer filling him with panic, Cain took a moment to process that he was no longer tied to the slab of stone. At least for the moment, he was free to fight. *Luke! I'm winning.* A great roar of love erupted from Cain's gut, reaching every corner of this new torture chamber. He rushed the demon before him and threw them both to the hard floor.

*Luke! Luke! Luke!* With his love in his head, Cain punched and clawed and hit like a madman, his only goal to inflict as much pain as he could before he was defeated and taken under the demon's control once again. A great club of a hand circled Cain's neck and squeezed, but rather than cowering in fear, Cain rolled into a tumble with the demon, stopping when he was on top, temporarily in the position of power. The demon struggled mightily, but with a burst of superhuman energy, Cain forced his weight down until he was right on top of the demon, their hot breath mingling. With eyes certainly flashing victory -- or maybe insanity -- Cain bared his teeth and bit down, tearing a hunk of flesh right out of the demon's face.

The demon howled, and with a strength very natural to his body, he flung Cain across the room, right into the wall. Barely processing the slam through his body, shaking every bone within, Cain could only watch as the demon -- with the use of his Naverto wings -- flew on top of Cain in a flash. "You are going to regret that." With that vow made, the demon dragged Cain to his feet and cracked him across the face with his hand.

*Oh Christ.* As Cain wiped the blood from his mouth, he didn't feel the slightest bit human. Like an animal, he'd drawn blood from his opponent's face with his teeth, and he reveled in it. "I don't think so," Cain uttered, his voice so soft it was frightening. With his lips pulled back over his teeth, in a sick kind of glee, Cain jammed his knee up in between the Naverto's legs, using enough force to shove the beast's balls back into his body.

The demon cried out and doubled over in obvious pain. With the wind temporarily knocked out of his opponent, Cain got in a few more hits, but his reprieve didn't last long. The demon hauled Cain off his feet and shoved him against the wall, one hand holding him up around his neck and the other jamming punches into his torso with unrelenting force, knocking the wind from Cain's lungs. Hatred and disgust filled the demon's eyes, and he gave Cain a punishing beating for gaining that small upper hand. Blow after blow rained down on Cain, so hard and heinous the crushing pain sent Cain spiraling into darkness once again.

———

CAIN CAME TO, BACK IN the confines of the hood again. This time he could process nothing more than the bone-crushing pain that had taken over every inch of his body. Every muscle in his battered frame ached, bruises one on top of the next, so tender and sensitive that just breathing brought tears to his eyes. Under the stifling material of the hood, Cain's face felt puffy and swollen from the countless hits he'd taken in this twisted madness of a gang jump out.

Cain's skin felt slippery from top to bottom. He knew the wet sensation came from a combination of his own sweat and blood, as well as the piss and feces of at least two Naverto demons relieving themselves on him during his ordeal. Both Naverto had made a point of forcing Cain to watch them urinate and defecate as it happened, so Cain supposed that was part of the humiliation process. They'd made sure Cain was cognizant and alert as they'd waved their dicks in front of him, peeing all over him while spouting off that if Cain wanted to be human then it was their right as the superior species to defile him whenever and however they wished. Only problem was, by that point, Cain could do nothing more than focus on the physical pain consuming his body, so any efforts to shame him into giving up the gauntlet had fallen on deaf ears.

The air in the room suddenly changed, and without a doubt, Cain knew someone had entered the torture chamber. Cain became very still, pressing his bare back into the unforgiving stone beneath him. His hands were tied to spikes above his head and he cautiously unwrapped his fingers from the metal and settled them on the stone slab once again. He had no earthly idea where he was in the timeline of his torture, and any efforts to question his tormentors had fallen to guffaws of laughter. Cain thought for sure he must be near the end of his twelve hours -- if completed them already -- when without the slightest hint of warning a molten-hot length of metal came down on his stomach and seared his flesh, fusing his skin to what he could only assume was a branding iron.

*Ahhhh!* Pain hit Cain so brutally, with such excruciating fire, he couldn't even scream aloud; he could only open his mouth beneath the hood and experience the terror in silence, as not a single sound came out of his throat. His body could not produce a noise adequate enough to offset the deliberate burning of his flesh, and he knew it. Tears streamed down Cain's temples into his hair. As he sat there with his flesh being burned, he thought for sure nothing could be worse than this nightmare level of suffering.

Cain quickly found out how wrong he could be. When the Naverto pulled the scalding metal from Cain's flesh, his skin remained attached. As Cain's mangled skin stretched unbearably, bile rose in his throat. His flesh finally ripped free of the metal, and Cain turned his head just in time to escape choking on his own vomit. He threw up into the hood still covering his face; the smell of burnt skin and puke filled his nostrils, so powerful in its stench it threatened to make him sick all over again.

Quickly the next wave of torture began, and Cain realized the burning of his skin wouldn't be the worst pain he suffered from this particular demon's torture. Liquid fire rained down upon Cain's open wound like acid. Some kind of alcohol flayed him open with such heat his entire body arced off the stone slab. Cain twisted and pulled against his restraints, trying desperately to get away from the hurt. He yanked himself so hard he cut deep welts into the tender skin on his ankles and wrists; those scraped-raw areas quickly received a liberal dousing of the liquid fire too. The fiery waterfall on his open wounds became more than Cain could handle, and he slipped away again, his bloody hands wrapped so tightly around the spikes holding him prisoner that he bent them in half. As Cain went under this time, he could only thank God the blackness would -- at least for a few minutes -- take away the pain.

———

"PLEASE. PLEASE." As DELIRIUM AND mania battled for supremacy in Cain's confused brain -- an organ that could no longer process any more harm being done to his body -- he cried beneath the hood. The latest demon delivered a crushing blow to Cain's kidney, and Cain didn't know how much more he could withstand and remain alive. This demon had him tied in an X, on his stomach again, although Cain had no earthly clue when that had happened. He had no idea what time it was, what day it was, or if he'd been in this room for twelve hours or twelve years. He only knew that somehow, someway, he had to bring this to an end.

"Please...please, stop." Cain couldn't be sure he spoke out loud or if he begged only in his nightmares. Or, if his pleas were real, could anyone hear him through the hood and the scrape of what was left of his voice.

A fist slammed dead center into Cain's back right then and shot to the surface what was left of Cain's sanity. "Ohhhh... Christ... Please, help me..." He mewled and dug his forehead into the stone beneath him, desperate to find some way to focus himself. "Stop this." Desperation filled his voice. He could hear it, and he didn't care. "Please, help me... Stop this..."

The battering ram of fists against Cain's back came to a halt. "You can end this," a voice suddenly whispered against Cain's ear. A gentle hand caressed his beaten head through the hood. "All you have to do is say you made a mistake. Tell me you don't want to do this anymore. Tell me you give up, and it will all be over."

*Yes, yes. That sounds so good.* Cain opened his mouth to say those exact words, to cease this madness, when another voice, one he couldn't be sure lived in his head or was outside of his body, overrode him. "Whatever it takes, Hawk. You have to let go and do whatever it takes to survive."

*Luke. My Luke.*

Within the darkness of the hood, Cain strained his eyes, searching for a face to go with the loving voice murmuring encouragement in his ear. He found nothing, but the voice said again, "Whatever it takes, Hawk. Whatever it takes."

"I promise," Cain vowed raggedly. Tears leaked out of his eyes and snot ran down his nose, mingling with everything else that had gathered on his face during the course of his ordeal. "I promise I won't quit."

"Your choice." The other, trickster voice sounded at Cain's ear, not nearly as friendly as it had been a moment before. "I'll get back to my work then."

Two seconds later, something cold and hard and thick was jammed into Cain's rectum, and Cain howled. "Ahhhh!" The pain of the invasion ripped Cain in two, and an assault on everything he held dear with Luke began.

Cain had been urinated and defecated on, beaten to surely within an inch of his life, all without breaking, but the theft of this beautiful act he so loved tore through what remained of Cain's fighting spirit in a way nothing else could. The abuse from his other torturers had not been an abomination of what he and Luke did together in the bonds of love; this terrible, repeated penetration into his body, so brutally, from this Naverto was. The demon used the hard, cold object on Cain with a relentless ramming force into Cain's passage. Along with each deep shove from the device into his ass, Cain screamed, and his demon attacker asked, "Do you give up?"

Each time Cain yelled "No!" the rod dug harder into his channel and tore Cain anew.

Within a half-dozen strokes, Cain sobbed and begged for help -- from fate, from God, from he didn't know whom. Yet, somehow, with each awful taking of his body, and question from his torturer, Cain managed to choke out a refusal to quit. Each time pain consumed his rectum, though, Cain found it harder to say no, and his voice grew softer, with less conviction, with each word. Cain knew, deep in his soul, he would soon give up the fight. *Please.* Cain whimpered. *It has to stop.*

Suddenly, Cain didn't know how, Luke stood in front of him. The handsome cowboy bent down and squatted in front of Cain, and Cain could see Luke smiling that beautiful smile of his, no matter that a hood remained over his head.

"Remember, baby." Luke stroked Cain's face. "Whatever it takes. Whatever it takes to win. Nothing you do is wrong. Remember that."

As the rod took Cain deeply once again, Cain kept his focus

completely Luke. "It's better now..." -- he winced, and he cried out his refusal to the demon, but then picked right back up with Luke -- "...now that you're here."

"I am here," Luke promised. Rising from his crouching position, he leaned over Cain and kissed the crown of his head. "So put me where you need me to help you get through this."

Suddenly, a granite rod didn't rape Cain anymore; instead Luke made vigorous love to Cain. Cain no longer heard the demon's voice demanding he quit; Luke filled every corner of Cain's mind and senses; Luke told Cain how good it felt to take Cain like this, and that he was sorry, but that pain was part of his passion. And because it was Luke, Cain didn't resist the assault. Instead, he became aroused.

A small, tiny part of Cain's brain still rooted in reality panicked and resisted, screamed in his mind that this was not Luke, and that it was wrong to think otherwise. The voice of reason grew, and Cain began to struggle against the assault and his bindings once again, pain filling his rectal cavity anew. Sweat poured off his body in droves, and he fought and cried against the assault. Once again, though, Luke returned to Cain's ear, whispering that it was okay and to breathe. His voice calmed and soothed Cain enough to stop struggling, to save himself from suffocating under the hood. Cain slowed down; his breathing remained heavy but he was no longer hyperventilating.

At his ear, inside his brain -- everywhere -- Cain heard Luke's voice. Luke promised him that everything was all right, if Cain would just let Luke take care of him. Luke's familiar weight suddenly pressed down on Cain's back, perfect and loving, even as a small part of sanity left inside Cain's brain questioned whether this was what happened when people snapped and lost their minds for good. If true insanity was Luke's voice talking dirty behind him, giving Cain the fucking of his life, then Cain fell and embraced the break in his mind with every cell in his being. He needed to believe that only Luke was inside him, fucking him, right now. The drugging, soothing voice inside Cain's head continued, full of every cadence and nuance of Luke, taking Cain to a place of safety. In that moment, fantasy became reality and took over Cain's desire for survival. Luke whispering in Cain's head; Luke making love to him, became Cain's only reality. Cain had no need to hide his immense love for Luke from any Naverto demon anymore, because Luke was the only thing that mattered. There were no more secrets, and there was nothing worse that could be done to him than what had already happened. Cain needed nothing more than to be sheltered and made love to by Luke, for Luke to take all of his pain away and magically turn it into pleasure.

"Luke, Luke…oh, yes, Luke…" Cain chanted through the hood as, in his mind, his lover's cock took him in place of some violence-filled demon Cain had never even seen. How could something Cain had never set eyes on hurt him? The reality had to be Luke fucking him; the demon assault was the bad dream, and Luke would make it go away. Cain loved nothing more than the sensation of his man filling him with his great, long cock, and Cain knew Luke understood his desires. So for Cain's sake, Luke took care of him, and did just that. "I want my Luke…just my Luke…just my Luke…" Cain moaned as his man took him with the force of his vigorous passions behind every thrust.

The fucking was hard, but filled with love, and soon Cain humped the hard bed beneath him in time with the thrusts. His cock quickly pressed up against his stomach in rigid, hard formation. Luke's voice remained so close it filled Cain's head; soon Cain could only hear Luke's declarations of love and devotion, over and over again. Nothing else mattered. *Luke. Luke. Luke.* The chant became a voice in Cain's head and a flashing neon sign in front of his blind eyes -- his lover's name consuming and swallowing him whole, to the point that nothing else existed. Luke filled Cain up inside, as he always did. With Luke all around him, in him, Cain's balls drew up tight, and he gasped with pleasure inside the hood. Cain then erupted with a fierce orgasm, spilling his seed between his body and the hard bed, coming to the fierce fucking from his man.

"Oh Christ." Cain shuddered as Luke shafted him roughly again. "I love everything you do to me."

"That is good." A menacing voice, not Luke's, slipped into Cain's

298 | CAMERON DANE

head. "For you still have five hours at the hands of our brand of *love*."

Cain panicked and jerked, but suddenly Luke was there again, his voice steady and strong. "Don't worry, love, there's no need to be scared. I'm the only one here." A gentle kiss flickered against Cain's battered back. Then, a bruising hit rammed his body again. All the while, Luke remained at Cain's side, soothing him, whispering, "Don't fight. It's only me, and I'm not ever leaving you."

This time, when oblivion took Cain once again, he knew everything would be okay. As he slid into the blackness, Cain understood that Luke had taken over beating him, and all the while he promised Cain that everything would be all right.

———

CASSIE APPROACHED LUKE, EASED DOWN next to him, and made herself as comfortable as she could against the cold wall at her back. Almost two hours ago, the sun had peeked up over the mountains, and a new day had begun. Luke hadn't taken his eyes off the portal in the thirteen hours Cain had been away, other than to ask Connor and Caleb to go feed the horses for him. His very stillness and silence began to worry her.

"Honey." Cassie slid her arm around Luke's hunched shoulders and kept her voice gentle. "We don't know how long it took Cain to convince the council to put him through the Changing Gauntlet, or, for that matter, if he has even managed to convince them yet. It could be hours, or even days, before he comes back. You need to take a break and get some sleep. You worked all day yesterday before Cain went through the portal, and you haven't so much as closed your eyes for ten minutes since he left. Sweetie, you're going to break if you don't bend a little bit, and that won't do Cain any good."

Luke flicked his gaze to Cassie for just a few seconds, but then went right back to staring at the simmering portal. The newly etched, desperate fear and pain Cassie saw in Luke stole her breath away.

"*Bending*," Luke said, his voice raw with unchecked emotion, "was eating, because I knew I needed to in order to keep up my strength. *Bending* is sitting here quietly, when it's all I can do not to tear this cabin apart from end to end to release some of my fear. *Bending*" -- the word got caught in Luke's throat and came out as more of a croak -- "is staring at that portal for over thirteen hours and *not* diving in after the man I love, when that is the only thing I've wanted to do from the second he disappeared. So don't tell me about *bending*, Cassie, because *bending* is the only damn thing I've been doing since this whole fucking thing started. It's how I'm surviving, and if you don't like the way I happen to be doing it, then you can go the hell away."

"Hey!" Connor swooped in. With a fistful of the front of Luke's shirt, Connor hauled Luke to his feet. "You watch your tone with my wife, or else I will knock you into unconsciousness and keep you that way until this ordeal is finished. Got it?"

Cassie reached in and uncurled her husband's hand from Luke's shirt. "It's okay." She separated the two of them. "I'm a big girl, and I can take a little bit of rough language."

"Not when I'm standing within hearing distance, you won't," Connor told her. He turned back to Luke with a protective fire burning in his dark eyes. "My wife brought you food so that you didn't have to take your eyes off this damned portal for even one minute. She brought you a blanket and covered you up in the cold hours of night. She sat next to you and kept you company without a word spoken between you. And, at your obsessive request, she went to the bedroom countless times and checked Cain's medical supplies, assuring you again and again that everything is there. Now, I think it's damn well time you snapped out of your funk and gave her a thank you and an apology, or else I'm damn tempted to beat it out of you."

"Connor Hawkins!" Cassie shoved her way in between the two men and glared at her giant, angry husband. "Don't you dare threaten to hit this man; Cain would never forgive you. You know damn well Luke is terrified, and that is the basis of his insensitivity. You know this because you are just as scared yourself. So the both of you" -- she put a hand to each man's chest and shoved them apart -- "ease off the testosterone for five minutes and remember the reason we are here."

"I --"

"But --"

Then, neither man's protest mattered. Every hard word and threat evaporated when the portal swirled and gurgled; the mist hovering above it drew up in a column straight to the ceiling. Like a great geyser of oil, the portal spat out a bloody mess and hurled it through the air, where it hit the roof and then the wall, finally landing in a motionless heap on the floor.

Cain had been returned.

# CHAPTER TWENTY-SEVEN

Blood, cuts, and swelling body parts covered the naked bundle slumped on the floor so completely that it was barely recognizable as human, let alone as Cain.

Connor was the closest, and he reached Cain first. But like an animal, Luke shoved him away and bent over the curled-up form of Cain. "You don't touch him," Luke snarled. "He's mine. I'll be the one to carry him to our bedroom."

Cassie grabbed Connor, holding him back as the big man reached for Luke. "No, let him do it." She wrapped her arm around Connor and hugged him to her side. When he shot her an incredulous, dangerous glance, she added, "You would demand the same right if it were me."

Connor nodded and backed off.

With hands shaking like a palsied old woman's, Luke rolled Cain over as gently as he could. As he took in the damage Cain had suffered at the hands of his torturers, tears filled his eyes and splashed onto Cain's bloodied body. Every inch of Cain's body was covered with some element of physical abuse -- proof of his horrific torture. With a stifled, choking cry, Luke reached out to Cain's neck and felt for a pulse beneath remnants of blood, excrement, and vomit. A faint, jittery, feathery skittering caressed against Luke's fingertips, and the soft sensation was the most wonderful thing Luke had ever experienced in his twenty-five years of life. *Yes. Bless you, baby.*

Sparing a glance for the others, Luke said, "He's alive." He then flitted his fingers over the misshapen mess of Cain's face, afraid to touch with any kind of strength. "He's alive." Luke couldn't help it; he leaned down, and with drops leaking from his eyes, pressed a soft, loving kiss on Cain's swollen, split lips. It was the only time in their short, passionate relationship that Luke didn't get even the slightest echo of a response back from Cain.

After wiping his eyes, Luke stiffened his spine, knowing that falling apart right now wouldn't do Cain a damn bit of good. "I'm taking him to bed." He slid his arms under Cain's body, one beneath his back and the other under his knees.

"Do you need a hand?" Connor asked.

"No, I've got him." Luke rolled Cain against his chest, got him in a secure hold, and rose to his feet. Cain was completely unconscious -- dead weight -- and his head lolled over Luke's arm like a rag doll. Luke didn't feel the weight of the burden, though. He didn't stagger, and he didn't process the strain on his muscles. He did turn to Connor, though. Dark eyes met his; Connor looked as helpless as Luke had felt from the moment Cain had disappeared through the portal. "But if you could shift him," Luke offered, "and adjust his head to rest against my shoulder while I hold him, I would apprec --"

Connor flew to Luke's side before Luke could finish his request. With the gentle hands of a parent, Connor tilted Cain's upper body and tucked his head in the crook of Luke's neck. Luke shifted his hold, rounding his arm around Cain's shoulders more fully, and enfolded Cain more completely into his chest.

At the same time, Caleb moved to the portal.

"Close that thing up," Luke ordered as he carried Cain to bed. "No matter what happens, Cain is never going through that thing again."

"Put him in bed," Caleb called out. "But for God's sake, Luke, no matter how much it hurts to look at him, don't you dare do anything else."

"I won't," Luke promised. That vow was the hardest Luke had ever spoken, but he made himself speak it aloud. Saying it made it real. "Don't worry, Caleb. I won't."

————

THIRTY-SIX HOURS LATER, LUKE SAT beside his and Cain's bed and watched the slow, shallow rise and fall of Cain's bruised and bloodied chest. All the while, each time he saw a small sign of life, he reminded himself it was proof that Cain still lived. Cain's shallow breathing was the only hopeful sign Luke had to hold onto; the man had yet to open his eyes and do anything to help himself in his recovery.

It killed Luke to stare at the card table on the other side of the bed, full of medical supplies Cain had set up with his own hands two and a half days ago, and not be able to take care of the man himself. Cain had left aspirin in a bowl, like some narcotic candy, not because he had intentions of consuming mass quantities of them, but because he'd had the forethought that it would be easier for him to grab a few whenever he was able to rouse himself than wrestle with the bottle. Antibacterial liquid had been transferred into a number of squeeze bottles for the very same reason. Cain had also laid out liquid stitch, gauze, and ice packs. Additionally, he had bananas and Gatorade in a cooler by the bed… The list went on and on.

Everything Cain had purchased to help himself was top grade, but none of it would do a damn bit of good if it remained untouched, gathering a layer of dust. The supplies sat there, organized in neat lines like good little soldiers. Their very presence taunted Luke, drawing his gaze with each hour that went by where Cain didn't open his eyes and reach out to begin the process of healing himself.

If only Luke could clean Cain's wounds, it would make a difference. Tending to him would surely bring about an end to this coma into which Cain seemed to have slipped. The longer Luke sat here, helpless, the more tempting it became to wet down a towel and clean Cain himself. In those moments, Luke had to get up and leave the room in order to talk himself down. He had to lecture himself out loud so that he could hear the words, reminding himself in no uncertain terms that Cain would not want him to assist in his recovery. While looking Cain in the eyes before he'd gone through the portal, Luke had promised that he wouldn't crack.

But God, it was hard. It was so, so very hard to sit back and do nothing while the man he loved lay practically lifeless just inches away from him, while Luke's hands were tied to do anything about it. Rubbing his hands over his haggard face, Luke pushed up to the edge of his seat. Yesterday Caleb had dragged the leather recliner to the bedroom for Luke. Caleb had commented that it was clear to him Luke had no intention of leaving until Cain woke up, so he might as well not have a numb ass while he kept his vigil. Too much fear still lived in Luke to laugh, but he had appreciated Caleb's attempt at humor. He'd said so too, along with another thank you to him and Connor and Cassie, who were taking care of the horses while Luke kept watch over Cain.

Luke exhaled a shaky, uneven breath, trying desperately to gather himself. He picked up Cain's lax hand and pressed it between his, kissed the blood-encrusted fingertips one at a time, and then tucked it under his chin. It terrified Luke all the way to his core to think there was a very real possibility that Cain would never hold Luke's hand again; merely thinking such a thing crushed Luke's chest with debilitating tightness and pain.

To Luke's mind, thirty-six hours was a long time to go without any kind of treatment for the vicious torture through which Cain had so obviously survived. Luke knew nothing of how bad Cain's injuries truly were, of how, beyond the visible cuts, welts, burns, and bruises, there could be dozens of other things killing Cain that Luke couldn't see. The very real potential for internal hemorrhaging existed, or even possibly bruising and swelling in his brain, something hidden that could kill him.

Luke's focus strayed to the medical supplies again, and then beyond them to the truck outside, just beyond the bedroom window. The glow of the porch light illuminated the vehicle, and the sight of it beckoned Luke to pick Cain up and take him to get help.

*No. You can't.* Luke's heart told him to rush him to get help; his head said to remember the rules of the gauntlet and his vow to Cain. Luke didn't know what in the hell to do. "Please, God." He prayed, the only thing he knew to do, as tightness filled his chest. "I don't know if you even help people like me, or if other people are right, and you see me as an abomination. But if you listen when I talk to you, then I'm asking for your help right now." Luke looked to the well-lit truck again. "Is that some kind of sign?" He blinked through the heavy moisture of unshed tears. "Or am I just going crazy while I sit here helplessly and watch the man I love die? Am I looking for outside help that isn't there because I can't bear the thought of him in pain for one minute longer? I want to trust in what Cain told me to do, God. I do trust in him." Luke kissed Cain's fingers again. He moved Cain's bloody hand up his jaw and rested Cain's knuckles against his cheek. Luke turned his focus to Cain's bruised, mangled face. A face that had yet to come back to life and let Luke see those beautiful blue eyes that would tell him his Cain was back. "I do trust you, Hawk," he promised the unconscious man. "But please…" The heaviness pressing behind Luke's eyes spilled over, streaming wetness down his cheeks. "Please come back to me. I love you so much, and I don't want to be in this world without you.

"Please." Luke turned back to God, in this moment letting nothing stay trapped inside. "Give me the strength to get through this. I need you. I need you just as much as I need him."

Right then, something happened. *What? Please.* Luke stopped, his breath trapped in his lungs. He closed his eyes and waited; he prayed. *There.* It happened again. Barely a movement, barely a sign of life, but Luke felt the truth of it shoot straight to his heart and give him hope. Cain slid the backs of his fingers against Luke's face, barely moving an inch over Luke's cheek, but it had happened. Luke would swear Cain had felt the wetness on Luke's face and tried to wipe his tears away. The movement wasn't much, but it was something, and Luke needed nothing more in order to go on.

"Thank you." His voice scratched so raspy it barely came out as a whisper, but he knew he'd been heard.

By both of them.

—

FROM THE PLUSH CONFINES OF the recliner, Luke jerked awake to the sound of Cain's injured, animalistic moaning. His eyesight quickly adjusted to the darkness and immediately landed on the broken man in bed. He stared as Cain tried desperately to roll onto his side and claw his way to the meds.

Luke's heart raced so fast that when he shot to his feet his head swam and he had to grab the edge of the bed for support. Uncaring of the spots dancing before his eyes, Luke ran around the bed and dropped to his knees in order to see Cain, awake, for the first time in almost forty-two hours.

Cain's eyes *were* finally open. The blue was as familiar to Luke as the gray in his own when looking into a mirror. But any familiarity ended there. These were not the eyes of a human being. These eyes, with enormous pupils, and desperate, wild darting all over the room, looked everywhere, but clearly didn't see anything beyond a litany of things of which to be afraid. More than the wildness in Cain's stare, a deep, ragged breathing pushed in and out through the man's open mouth, and his nostrils flared as if he struggled to remain alive. This was not yet Cain. Right now, this was just an animal trying to survive.

Nevertheless, Luke had never seen a more beautiful sight. Somewhere beneath that panic and pain, Cain breathed and existed, and nothing else mattered to Luke. With great force, Luke shoved his hands between his folded legs and determinedly sat on them. He could think of no other way to stop himself from shifting Cain's head to the side and putting his focus directly on the table of medical aids. Once again, Luke reminded himself that Cain had to recover by himself.

Now that Cain had regained some form of consciousness, he struggled just to breathe, so much more so than when he'd been unconscious. The man was clearly terrified to even move, and Luke could only guess that somewhere in Cain's brain he waited for the next wave of punishing blows to land on his battered body. *Oh God, baby. What they must have done to you.* Remaining still killed Luke, but with will he'd never known he possessed, he waited and watched with his breath trapped in his chest. After long, agonizing minutes, Cain managed to roll over and shift himself in the direction of his medicines, but he seemed so whipped by the small step that his eyes slid closed and he fell into a bout of restless sleep.

Luke stayed on his knees, though, unmoving, waiting. Less than an hour later, Cain rewarded him for his patience. The man's eyes fluttered open again. His gaze still appeared wildly lost, and he didn't appear to notice Luke, but he did manage to focus on the table beside his bed. Something of its importance must have registered in Cain's memory, because he dragged himself closer, whimpering and struggling the entire way.

Luke held his breath once more, his heart skittering just as hard as Cain's must be, and watched Cain struggle over a distance of less than two feet. With victory, Cain finally clawed his fingers around the edge of the bowl of aspirin. He knocked it off the table with clumsy, stilted movements, but thank God, everything spilled on the bed rather than the floor. Biting his lip, Luke also crossed his fingers under his legs, waiting again. When Cain managed to get his stiff fingers to open, to then grasp some pills and shove them in his mouth, Luke started breathing again. Luke couldn't tell how many painkillers Cain had taken, but right now, he didn't much care. One, two, five -- as long as Cain hadn't consumed the whole bottle then Luke imagined at this point maximum pain relief could only do Cain a world of good.

Right then Cain struggled, reaching for the table again. Luke shot to his knees, shock rocking through him. He'd thought for sure just getting the aspirin would wipe Cain out for the rest of the night.

But no, still in a visible daze, Cain continued to work to heal himself.

Pressing his hands together, Luke prayed. He watched with bated breath as Cain wrapped his hand around one of the squeeze bottles and dragged it to his side. That action finally brought on the exhaustion, and Cain lay there motionless for long minutes afterward, the only movement the deep rise and fall of his chest, proof of just how much these little actions taxed his body and mind. Then, in a shot, Cain lifted his arm, upended the bottle over his torso, and started to squeeze. As the stream of antibiotic liquid reached his flesh and rolled over the first of his wounds, a deep, agonized roar erupted from Cain's entire being. His agony filled the room with sounds of excruciating pain. And Luke, so completely helpless on the sidelines, silently shrieked in accompanying pain for the man he loved. Cain cried out with each splash of liquid that touched his flesh. His deep, crushing pain was clear, yet he continued to wave the bottle all up and down the front of his body, squirting his chest, his stomach, and his thighs with the cleansing liquid. Cain didn't let up until every drop from the bottle covered his blood-crusted flesh. When finished, the empty bottle fell from his hand, landing on top of the smattering of aspirin on the bedspread. Luke didn't want to move the pills out of Cain's reach, just in case he reached for them later. Finally, Cain went limp, and he slipped into a deep, motionless sleep once again.

Only then, when Cain had slid back into unconsciousness, did Luke stand. On unsteady legs, he went back to his chair, understanding now that Cain would be out for hours. The little he'd just done had to feel like a marathon to him. Luke could only wish exhaustion would swamp him too. Adrenaline pumped through his body, too heavily to allow him sleep. Watching Cain in pain, but unable to lift a finger to help, pressed on Luke's psyche. His sense of helplessness put a constant strain on his muscles; the tension he had to put on his body in order to keep from jumping to action to help Cain lived on the surface of Luke's soul, in his very being. All of that turmoil should make it difficult for him to keep his eyes open but Luke found it hard to close his eyes, even just to get a little rest.

In order to keep up his strength, Luke occasionally forced

himself to take short naps, but God, he hated to do it. He was so afraid he would miss something important if he succumbed to sleep. Or worse, in his deepest fears, in his nightmares, he would close his eyes for five minutes to wake up and find Cain dead. Something was especially horrific about sleeping peacefully while someone who'd just gone through twelve hours of torture died all alone, so Luke settled his focus on Cain once again, fixated on the steady rise and fall of his chest. He tried to summon some cautious optimism that Cain was slowly on the mend -- even if the sight of him with antibacterial liquid streaking through the blood caking his skin, leaving stains all over his flesh, made Cain somehow appear even more fucked up than before.

How Cain looked right now didn't matter. Whatever physical scarring lingered in the aftermath of his ordeal didn't matter either. Luke didn't care what Cain looked like. As long as he was breathing, and he was able to successfully recover from the internal damage done to his body, Luke would be happy.

If only he could have that. If only.

Luke let his gaze linger on Cain's swollen, bruised face and started to pray once again.

———

BLINKING, BLINKING, BLINKING, CAIN SLOWLY opened his eyes. Bright shafts of light attacked his eyeballs and shot a piercing pain straight into his head. He rolled to get away from the light, but froze mid-motion as the rest of his body screamed to life too, each part fighting for dominance in what hurt the most.

*Pills.* A memory of pills laying somewhere close by tickled his brain. Those pills would help ease the terrible, throbbing pain attacking every inch of his body. Cain rolled again, back to his starting position, and gritted his teeth against the stabbing pain assaulting his skull as a result of the sunlight pouring in through the bedroom window.

Little pebbles pressed against Cain's hip. He ran his hand in the mess of bedding, searching for the offenders. Unearthing some of the dirty little stones, Cain almost shoved them off the bed. Something scratched at the back of his brain again, though, and made him bring the round things up close to his eyes. Squinting, he held the pebbles away from his face a bit to hopefully clear the blur from his eyes. Once he zeroed in on the white, mechanically shaped rocks, it finally hit him that they weren't gravel at all but the aspirin for which he was looking. *Not enough.* A sharp, lancing pain stabbed at Cain's lower quadrant, prompting him to try to move with more urgency. Feeling around in the bedding, he managed to come up with a handful more of the dirty pills. With a grimace that made his sore jaw ache, he shoved them into his mouth and forced them down his bone-dry throat.

Before the bitter, nasty taste of the pills left Cain's mouth, Cain froze. His senses shot into overdrive, his body tingled, and his entire being went on full alert. Belatedly, panic rushed through him in droves; he wondered if this was really his bedroom at all, or if he was still in the torture chamber hallucinating this picture of safety. Maybe his mind had played another trick on him, an attempt to lull him into thinking he was safe when he wasn't. *Doesn't matter.* Wherever Cain now was, a vibration had changed the air a moment ago. *I'm not alone.* As a clicking sound ricocheted around him, Cain's entire body went rigid. His mind raced. *What kind of weapon can make that kind of soft noise?* And how much could such a weapon hurt him when he found out?

Footsteps grew louder, and Cain could only think the demons had come for him again. He knew he needed to go limp and feign unconsciousness but his muscles had locked into place, paralyzing him, preventing him from even curling into a ball to protect himself. He could only wait for the next attack.

The shatter of glass penetrated Cain's mind first. And then, "Oh my God, Cain. Oh my God, you're awake." *Luke's voice.* Cain didn't relax. He didn't dare fool himself into believing it was real. "I had to go outside and talk with Caleb and Dr. Winters. I had to, or else he would have questioned why neither one of us was there. One of the horses hasn't been eating, and we didn't want to take a chance. Oh God, baby, I'm so sorry I wasn't here when you opened your eyes."

Luke then knelt on the floor, right in front of Cain, filling his vision. *Oh dear God.* Between the rapid-fire words coming from Luke's mouth, and the sight of his beautiful, yet haggard face, Cain started to believe this wasn't his Luke from the torture chamber. This Luke wore different clothes, and this one -- *oh, my, this one* -- his face was so much richer, detailed, and real.

*Is it really you?* Daring to hope, Cain reached out and touched the man before him. He smoothed his fingers over Luke's forehead, strong cheeks, and hard jaw. He traced his fingers over Luke's mouth, and in return, those lips pressed a kiss against the pads of his fingers. Lifting his gaze, Cain found gray eyes filmed with moisture, filled with real emotion, brimming with loving, protective feelings. This was a man who would never cause Cain pain.

*Oh Christ. No.* Right then, the memories -- full-on graphic images -- started rushing through Cain's brain, one after another, more and more and more. The pictures were of his fantasies while enduring torture -- entire scenarios where this man, this gentle, kind man, had done brutal things to him. Things that weren't real. Things Cain had made up in his head. Sick things that, in the end, Cain had welcomed with open arms.

Cain just managed to shove Luke out of the way and get his head over the side of the bed before he vomited.

# CHAPTER TWENTY-EIGHT

Cain didn't have anything in his system to throw up, but that didn't stop his body from heaving with razing, stripping coughs. Bile and aspirin came up and stung his esophagus, tasting like bitter poison as it pushed through the desert in his mouth. Cain coughed and choked every bit of awfulness from his body and then wiped his mouth with the back of his dirty hand. His bloody, bruised, *disgusting* hand.

"I need to take a shower." Cain's voice was full of sandpaper and he could not meet Luke's stare. He rolled onto his back once more and focused on the ceiling. Christ, he couldn't look at Luke. "I want to take a shower right now."

Out of the corner of his eye, Cain watched Luke grab a towel off the card table and begin to clean up Cain's mess.

"Do you think you can make it to the bathroom?" Luke asked.

Cain kept his stare straight up and blinked back ugly tears that wanted to fall. "I don't know," he admitted, hating himself for the weakness.

With the bundled-up towel in hand, Luke disappeared through the bedroom door. Thirty seconds later he came back empty-handed. He stood at the foot of the bed, his body tight and laced with frustration. Wide, pained eyes fell on Cain, studying him, and the scrutiny only made Cain feel dirtier. "I don't know, baby," Luke said as he rounded the bed and sat on the edge, facing Cain, "you haven't eaten or had anything to drink in three and a half days. I can't help you if you fall and hurt yourself."

"I have to shower." Cain's voice remained stripped raw. Thank God he could blame the sickness and not the hidden, panicked desperation roiling through him. "I have to get clean right now."

His lips tight, Luke finally nodded. As he stood, he pointed at a cane hooked on the headboard. "Grab the cane and get to it then." He stepped out of the way, but he made it clear with his widened stance and the way he crossed his arms that he had no intention of leaving Cain to do this without an audience. "You are your own man, Hawk. I am your partner, not your parent, and I'm not going to tell you what you can and cannot do. You can heal in your own way all you want, but you are going to have to put up with me watching every step while it happens, and you damn well can't do a thing about it. So get that belligerent, pissed-off look off your face right now."

"How can you even tell what kind of look it is," Cain mumbled as he rolled to his side, "when you can't even see it beneath the crap covering every inch of my face?"

"Because I don't need to see your whole face, Hawk," Luke snapped back. "You say everything with your eyes, and I read them better than anyone. Don't ever forget it."

*Shit.* Cain squeezed his eyes shut. Luke's knowledge of Cain was exactly why Cain couldn't face him yet. Not with these terrible memories flickering in his brain like a wraith, haunting him with a truth he didn't want to know. He needed to get to the shower and begin the first step in washing away this filth living inside him, for good.

While forcing himself into a sitting position, Cain winced as his middle squeezed like a vise and a stabbing pain knifed him in the side.

He didn't want to think about what kind of injuries could cause that kind of hurt. Not right now. He needed the cleansing effect of water more than he cared about any pain racking his body. *Move, damn it. Now.* Cain managed to get his bruised, stiff legs over the side of the bed and his feet touching the floor -- a very good first step. With a move that tore fiery pain through his ribs, Cain got the cane and set the rubber base on the floor. Pressing with both hands, he tested its sturdiness. When the wooden rod held, he pushed to his feet -- where he promptly crashed to the floor when oceans of dizziness swam in his head and his damaged legs collapsed beneath him. As the head of the cane jammed Cain under the chin and shoved his teeth together in a bone-jarring clatter, Cain cursed a litany of foul words.

In a shot, Luke dropped to the floor beside Cain. Worry etched new lines into his features, and his hands dug into his thighs, clearly as a means to keep from reaching out to help. "Jesus Christ, Hawk. Damn it. I knew it was too soon for you to do this. Are you okay?"

"A fall to the floor won't kill me, Luke." Cain's voice sounded hard to his ears. Too hard, but damn it, he couldn't have Luke so close right now. He hadn't prepared himself to have this perceptive man scrutinize him yet. "If being the bitch of twelve vindictive demons didn't do me in, then I am pretty damn sure I'm not going to be bested by my own floor. Now get out of the way so I can crawl to my goddamned fucking shower. Christ, man. Give me some room."

Luke's gaze turned stormy, as dark a gray as Cain had ever seen it, but he slid away from Cain and got back to his feet. He stayed out of the way, as requested, and he didn't say a word as Cain did exactly what he'd said he would. Cain crawled the entire way to the bathroom -- although it was more along the lines of what babies do before they actually get to crawling, something along the lines of a glorified drag. Christ, every single muscle in Cain's body -- places he had never even been aware existed -- shrieked and shouted at him to stop the insanity the entire way.

He couldn't, though. Cain couldn't because the voices in his head screamed louder, and those were the ones spurring him onward. Those terrible voices were the ones giving him the strength to crawl up the side of the tub and climb in. Those awful, ugly visions were the things that somehow allowed Cain to overcome the weakness in his legs. Those disgusting images of what he'd done were what pushed him to his feet and kept him from falling over when he stood up in the tub. Although slumped against the wall, barely upright, Cain knew the nastiness clutching at him inside was what allowed him to reach for the shower curtain that would temporarily shut the rest of the world away.

"Don't close that." From the open doorway, Luke gave that order, and interrupted the thoughts in Cain's pained mind. Luke came into the bathroom, put the toilet seat down, and took a seat. "I'll clean up any water that spills onto the floor." Such agonizing patience laced Luke's voice, and it only made Cain feel guiltier for his previous cruelty. "I need to be able to see you while you're in there. I need to know you haven't fallen and cracked you head open on the tile. Leave the curtain open."

Cain didn't have the strength to fight Luke. More than that, he was too close to the water, something he desperately needed, to delay any longer. He turned both spigots on full blast, uncaring of the water's temperature, just so long as he got lots of it. The spray rained down on him in cool droves, blasting his chest and stomach with the power of its full force, but Cain didn't care. He leaned his shoulder against the shower wall, putting his balance and weight there, and then tilted his head down to watch the rusty brown water run in rivulets down his body to then swirl into the drain before disappearing.

Each circle of dirty water was quickly replaced by another. As it was, Cain let the drum of the shower spray attack a different part of his body, one battered bit at a time. The pressure from the water slowly worked away the caked-in blood, sweat, excrement, puke, and antibacterial cleanser from his body. The water cleansed his flesh, revealing what was hidden beneath one piece at a time. As it did, the true state of Cain's body became clear. It wasn't pretty.

Cain closed his eyes, unable to look just then. He wasn't ready. Sliding forward, he tilted his face up into the force of the water. The stinging spits of water shot little stickpins into his cheeks, forehead, and nose, but he didn't care. He opened his mouth to let in the first droplets of liquid his parched tongue had tasted in three days. The water was lukewarm, but it was heavenly, and Cain drank it up as would Whisky at her red bowl on the hottest summer day.

With that need for liquid temporarily assuaged, Cain pushed his head fully under the shower spray, turned his face downward, and let the force of the water pull the buildup of grease, gunk, and grime from his hair. If only a shower could clean out the dirtiness inside his mind just as easily.

*Please.* Cain's chest constricted, and silent tears filled his eyes. He let them fall, knowing even with Luke sitting three feet away the water protected him from Luke's scrutiny. Heartsick, Cain reached for the soap on memory. A new bar of Ivory soap sat right where it should be, and a jolt of normalcy punched Cain in the gut. The placement of the soap was a small thing, but a real snippet of his old routine. Cain desperately needed predictability right now, enough that he would cling to it in the form of a bar of soap.

After grabbing a washcloth and lathering it with the soap, Cain began to wash himself in slow, steady increments, mindful of every small cut and laceration marring his flesh, of every tender bruise discoloring his body, and of the blistered, burned skin across his lower stomach under his belly button. The soap stung his flesh like a son of a bitch, but Cain welcomed the sharp bursts of pain. These pains were of the healing variety, and thus Cain would not only tolerate them, he would welcome them.

By the time Cain finished washing his chest, stomach, and arms, he'd depleted what little strength he had. The mere thought of crawling back to the bed right now exhausted him, so instead decided to take a good, long soak in the bath. It didn't even matter that it wouldn't be a hot bath; all that mattered was that he could rest. After using his foot to push the drain stopper down, Cain moved down like a mountain climber going in reverse; he used the spigots, soap tray, and lip of the tub as handholds, not stopping until he lowered himself into the tub. Gingerly pushing himself backward, he stretched until his spine hit the wall. With an exhausted sigh, he laid his head to rest on the cool tile.

Sitting back warmed Cain inside -- for about two minutes. Then his muscles stopped quivering, his heart stopped pounding at the physical strain he'd put himself through, and dark thoughts pushed front and center in his mind again. Along with those thoughts came terrible, terrible pictures of Cain's time in the torture chamber, and the horrific things he'd done during those twelve endless hours. Dirty images consumed Cain, so awful that no bathtub full of water would ever wash them away. Cain feared that nothing could, when with everything in his soul, he only wanted to forget. *Please.* Cain shuddered. *Make it all go away.*

"Feeling any better?" Luke's voice broke into the silence, startling Cain, and made him snap his eyes open.

Cain couldn't say for sure whether he'd simply forgotten about Luke's presence in the bathroom, or if he'd just wished so hard that Luke couldn't see him right now, in this state, that he'd convinced himself of its truth. No such luck. From the edge of his vision, Cain could see Luke. The man, so achingly beautiful, leaned back against the porcelain commode, arms crossed against his chest, waiting. Cain had never felt so ugly in his life. This kind of casual intimacy -- sharing a bathroom with a man, with Luke -- had been Cain's greatest fantasy, his dream. Now it was a nightmare.

"I'm fine." Cain barely pushed that falsehood past his lips. Fingering the edge of the tub, he stared at the soap floating on top of the water, then looked at his legs, searching for a patch of skin that wasn't cut up or covered with a dark purple bruise. "Getting cleaned up is half the battle. I feel one hundred percent better already."

"Liar." Luke spat out the word, and it echoed against the tiles in the bathroom, resonating in the air until it landed on Cain and sank into his core with a ripping, gutting pain.

"What?" Cain quickly looked at Luke, but just as fast tore his gaze away. "What are you talking about?"

"Let me ask you something, Hawk," Luke said, his voice full of challenge. "Are we going to do this dance every time something happens to you that tests your faith in me?"

Forcing himself, Cain lifted his focus. The stare waiting for him blazed with silver fire. "What?" A stabbing pain lanced Cain's insides -- a hurt that had nothing to do with his beating. "Of course I have faith in you, Luke. I have every faith in you."

"Then pull your head out of your ass and start talking to me, damn it." The coddling man who had cleaned up Cain's vomit less than an hour ago no longer existed in this Luke before him now. "Do you think I haven't noticed this is the first time you've looked me in the eyes since you woke up? Do you think I don't know that you're biting my head off and pushing me away for a reason? I know you. It wasn't that long ago that I was a dozen steps away from walking off this property for good before you finally broke down and let me in, before you finally told me the truth about what was making you so scared. Then it happened again when you thought I'd hate you because you'd intimidated MacLesten in your demon form. I had to drag that out of you too, before you would own up to it.

"So I'm asking you now, Cain, once again." Luke's entire being held nothing but laser focus. All trained on Cain. "Is this something I have to look forward to dealing with for the rest of our lives? Is it going to be a constant battle to get you to open up to me? Are you always going to hide from me when something hurts you? Is this what I have to prepare for, repeatedly, in our future?"

Terrible pressure built behind Cain's eyes again. He stared up at the white ceiling, blinking, blinking, blinking until it passed and he could find his voice. "Would you leave me if I said it was?"

"Goddamnit, you frustrate me." Luke pushed forward and dropped to his knees on the wet floor, only the separation of the low tub wall between them. Reaching over, Luke took Cain's chin in his hand, forced his gaze from the ceiling down to his, and wouldn't let him look away. "No, honey," Luke said gently. "I wouldn't leave you over it. Okay? I'm not going anywhere, no matter how many headaches you give me with this solitary, stoic thing you have going on. I'm not ever leaving you, and you can put money on that."

Luke's kindness, his unconditional love, obliterated what

little strength and resolve Cain still possessed. Everything that had happened in the torture chamber, and now hearing Luke, even while angry, still promising that he wouldn't leave Cain alone ever again, crushed the bottle holding his emotions in check. Beyond his will, Cain began to shake and shudder. Burying his face in his hands, he drew his knees up and folded himself into a ball as sobs wracked his entire being.

"Oh, honey." Luke's voice cracked. "Please don't do this to yourself. It doesn't have to be so damn hard." Reaching over the tub, Luke drew Cain into the circle of his strong arms.

Stroking Cain's back, Luke rocked Cain as best he could in their awkward position. He whispered soothing words, ones that slowly penetrated Cain's psyche. Luke then pulled away -- just the smallest amount -- and brushed his fingers through Cain's hair, smiling softly at him while pushing strands of hair away from Cain's forehead and tucking them behind his ears. The intimacy of such a small kindness from the man he loved was everything Cain had ever wanted; it was why he'd gone through the Changing Gauntlet in the first place, and the simple gesture became Cain's undoing.

Luke kissed the top of Cain's head. As he did, more tears leaked out of Cain and onto Luke's shirtfront. "You have got to start showing a little bit of faith in my staying power," Luke said as he rocked Cain in the band of his arms. "There is nothing you could ever tell me that is so bad it could change how much I admire and respect you. You have to start believing that nothing you say to me is going to make me stop loving you. Talk to me, baby, and tell me what has you so distraught."

Cain withdrew, and Luke let him go. Wiping his eyes, hell, his whole damn face in an effort to get the weary off of it, Cain exhaled. "You were there," Cain admitted, his voice thick and raspy. If he wanted to be a real man, he had to accept everything inside him, the good and the bad. "In my mind, at a certain point, you were suddenly there with me in the torture chamber. Once you were there, you stayed with me for the next five hours until it was over."

"Okay." Sitting back on his heels, Luke clasped his arms around his knees and put his full focus on Cain. "But can you elaborate a little bit and tell me why that is so disturbing to you now?"

"Ohhhkay…" Cain chuckled, the sound gritty with nerves and shame. "You don't ask for much from me, do you?"

"Only everything." Luke offered a lopsided smile. "Just like you demand from me."

"Right." Exhausted to the very marrow of his bones, Cain leaned back against the shower wall. Swallowing convulsively, he forced down the lump sitting in his throat, choking him with his fear, and began. "Through a lot of the torture, I did all right. I floated in and out of consciousness; I did cry and beg them to stop, but mentally, I was okay. I managed to get in some good hits on a few of them every once in a while, before they would overpower me and start pummeling me again, but basically I was all right. As long as I didn't use the words 'I give up' or 'I quit,' then they knew I wasn't truly surrendering."

"Which you knew going in, based on what Caleb told you."

"Right, and like I said, I was doing okay." Cain blinked rapidly as the memories stirred him up again and pushed out a weakness it shamed him to let Luke see. "But then something happened, something I should have prepared myself for, but I didn't…and… and when it did, I wasn't okay anymore. It…it had me sobbing and nearly broke me right from the start."

"Say it, Hawk," Luke pressed. "Say it out loud and claim it. Make it your event, and not theirs."

"Funny you should say that." Cain laughed, the sound rusty. He had to, or he would throw up again. Rolling his head on the tile, he faced Luke, meeting that open, guileless gaze he loved so much. "Because that was exactly what I did." Paralyzing fear tightened Cain's chest and turned his mouth to cotton, but he refused to look away now. "When one of them started violating me with a stone rod, it was the one thing I couldn't take. It was the one…one thing, Luke…" Needing to stop, mad at himself, Cain slashed a hand across his wet cheek. "It was the one thing that was just between us, and when… when he took it…when he took it and turned it violent and ugly, I begged him to stop. It was a sacrilege of what we do together, and I couldn't take it. When he asked me if I wanted to quit, I opened my mouth to say yes. I was going to say yes; I was going to forfeit. But before I could, you were suddenly there with me, and I didn't say it."

A deep furrow marred Luke's brow. "Okay. But, honey, why is that tearing you up inside so much right now? What has made you afraid to even look at me?"

"Don't you see?" Cain cried, agony scraping his voice to shreds. "I brought you there. In my own twisted head, I brought you there, and I put you behind me. More than that, I put you inside me, Luke. My sick head put you in the most violent, dehumanizing act that can happen to a person, and I made myself like it. I came, Luke. While that animal was raping me, I was so completely convinced it was you, I had an orgasm while it happened. How disgusting is that?"

"Hawk --"

"Oh, no, no." Cain cut a swath across the air with his arm. "That wasn't even the end of it. My time with you as the image of whatever Naverto happened to be taking his turn on me didn't end with that. No, from that point on, every hit that I took, every crack of the paddle, every slash of the leather... It was you delivering that pain and humiliation to me, not a demon. From the point you showed up in my head that first time, all the way through to the next thing I remember, which was waking up just a little while ago, I had no concept of the demons torturing me anymore. Do you understand what I'm telling you? I got through almost half of that Changing Gauntlet because I put the picture of man I love, you, in my head, and I had you beat me into submission. And all the while, I heard your voice at my ear -- which I know was all in my mind -- telling me that each hit was proof of your love. So guess what, Luke? I reveled in every blow you delivered, and even though I told you what you did to me hurt me unbearably, you assured me it would be okay because it was all done in love, and I believed you.

"How disturbing and wrong is that?" Cain growled and smashed his fist against the shower wall, but barely registered the impact. "How sick must I be, somewhere deep in my brain that I don't want to see, that I could create something like that so convincingly that I even tricked my body into getting excited by it? How could I do that and not believe I'm completely perverted?"

"Hey, hey, hey." Shooting forward, Luke put his hand over Cain's mouth. He got right in Cain's face, and his stare didn't waver. "There is nothing sick or wrong or perverse about you, Cain Hawkins. I don't want to hear you talking about yourself like that ever again. I won't stand for it. You did what you had to do to survive; that's all."

His eyes pleading, Cain pushed Luke's hand away from his mouth. "But why did it have to be that way?" he asked, searching, begging for answers, for absolution. "Why did I take what you mean to me and taint it like that? Why would I take your face and your voice, which are the gentlest, most loving things in my life, and put them on the ugliest, most disgusting act that has ever happened to me? I must be sick and twisted in some terrible way. Buried deep inside, I must want you to hurt me, and I just didn't know it until it was forced out of me in a desperate situation."

Luke shifted off his heels to sit on the edge of the tub. "No, honey, that's not true. You don't."

"Yes."

"No," Luke said again. He feathered his fingers over the bruises on Cain's face. Cain shivered but then reared back in fear. Luke seemed to understand Cain needed some space and he backed off. "All right. I won't touch you right now. Let me ask you something else instead. Can I do that?"

Like a child, Cain bit the edge of his lip and nodded.

"Okay." Luke held Cain's gaze, trapped him. The unwavering strength in Luke's eyes wouldn't let Cain break the hold. "Let me ask you this: have you ever, in your life -- and I'm talking well before you met me, and we started having sex -- have you ever associated violence with the sex you've always wished you could have? Have you ever, in any of your sexual fantasies, imagined me, or some other man, hitting you, or beating you, or humiliating you, and you getting off on it, in any way?"

"No."

"Okay." Luke nodded. "How about right now? Is any part of you excited by the thought of me hurting you physically?"

"No."

"And even if you were, do you think there is any part of me that would ever agree to it? Really hurt you? Not just a little bit of sexual play? Do you think I could hurt you in the way I did during the Changing Gauntlet?"

"No."

"Okay." Taking Cain's bruised hand, Luke brought the knuckles to his lips, pressing tiny kisses on the scraped-raw skin. "So think about all of that, Hawk. Think about what it means. Think about the fact that you were in the most dangerous situation you've ever faced in your entire life. Think about the fact that you knew, somewhere deep in your soul, you knew that you could not give up, that you had to get through it. Somehow, you had to get through it. Think about how scared you were. How scared were you, baby?"

"I was terrified."

"And you didn't know those demons. You knew the limits of what they were supposed to be allowed to do, but you couldn't be sure they would actually follow those rules. Were you ever afraid they were doing too much? Were you ever afraid you were going to die?"

As tears streamed slowly down Cain's cheeks, he nodded. "All the time."

"Yet beneath that terror, you also knew you couldn't give up, or else you would be right back where you started. Right?"

"Worse," Cain corrected. "The Traveler showed up while I was there. He'd figured out what I was. So if I didn't get through that gauntlet, I would have been executed anyway."

"Okay, even more pressure. In your desperation, in your absolute need to survive this thing, you conjure me. Right?"

"Yes."

"So why me? Don't think about it; just tell me from your gut. Why? Don't think, just speak. Why? Right now, Cain. Why?"

"Because…because…" Cain struggled to make words come out through the unbearable tightness locking him up inside. "Because the only thing I know for sure in this world is *you*. I know that *you* would never hurt me. I know that *you* would never lie to me. So I knew that if *you* said I could stand the pain, and if *you* promised that I wasn't going to die, and *you* swore that you weren't going to kill me, then I could trust it and believe my torment would come to an end eventually. It had to be *you* because I needed someone...someone..."

Fresh memories of the brutalizing pain Cain had suffered rushed to the surface and almost dragged him under. But as before, Luke held his hand and wouldn't let go. Cain locked in on the depth in Luke's stare and pulled the strength he needed from the endless well living inside this man. "I needed someone who could make love to me... because...because otherwise the rape from that stone rod would have broken me. It would have made me quit, and you were the only one whose voice and touch could get me through it. I needed you to be there with me. Even if it was just in my head. Even if it wasn't real, I needed you."

"There's nothing shameful in that," Luke told him, his smile so welcoming in sliced the sweetest pain through Cain's heart. "Nothing shameful, sick, or perverted; nothing you should ever hang your head over." Luke scooted closer, took Cain's face in his hands, and tilted his head back until they looked into each other's eyes. "Do you remember what I told you the night before you left to face the council?"

With tears streaming down his face, Cain nodded.

Apparently that wasn't good enough. Luke asked again, "What did I tell you? You give me the words. You say them out loud."

Cain reached up and covered Luke's hands with his. It was a small connection, but Christ, he needed it right now more than he needed to breathe. "You said that nothing is wrong when it comes to surviving. You said to do whatever it takes to come back to you. And...and I did."

"Yes, baby." Tears filled Luke's eyes too. "You did. You sure did." He leaned down and pressed his lips to Cain's. This time, Cain clung to the touch, needing the closeness desperately. Too much emotion constricted his chest, but once again, he welcomed this pain.

Luke broke their kiss, but bussed a loving kiss on Cain's bruised cheeks, forehead, and nose, before wiping the tears from Cain's face and pulling away. "You're going to be okay," Luke told him. "You're going to get through this, and on the other end we're both going to be all right. I promise."

Because Luke made the promise -- the real Luke this time -- Cain let himself start believing he would survive and have a future with the man he loved.

# CHAPTER TWENTY-NINE

Stirring in bed, Cain stretched his arms, working out the kinks in his sore muscles as he awoke from yet another of his many recent catnaps. He knew recovering from trauma took time, but he itched with impatience. This weakness had hung around far too long for his liking. Recovery was one boring-ass bitch.

Cain blinked the sleep from his eyes and then rolled his head on the pillow. The perfection his stare landed on made his breath catch in his chest. *My Luke.* "Did I ever tell you how sexy you look in your glasses?" Cain mumbled, his voice thick from sleep.

With a laptop resting on his thighs, Luke glanced up and met Cain's stare. The man sat in a recliner with his feet kicked up on the bed, and he looked as casual and beautiful as could be in his jeans and a blue western-yoked shirt. As Luke glanced from his computer to Cain and then to the computer again, Cain could swear his man's cheeks heated.

"Well?" Cain asked. "Have I ever told you how sexy those glasses make you look? Because they do. You look good enough to eat." With a rough groan, Cain remembered the necessary imposed celibacy in their lives right now. He just hadn't been strong enough for sex yet. Beyond that, though, they'd both figured they couldn't risk any sexual intimacy being construed as aiding in Cain's recovery. "Sweetheart, when you look all studious like that, you make me very, very hungry."

"Don't tease me, Hawk. I just wear them for reading." Luke slid the wire frames off his nose and tossed them on the nightstand. Leaning forward, he put the computer on the nightstand too. "Besides, if you keep thinking like that, you're only going to give yourself a hard-on you have to take care of with your own hand."

Frustration welled in Cain, forcing another grumble. When his first thought involved going back and beating the shit out of the council that had done this to him, rather than on any one particular pain in his body, he figured he'd very nearly healed completely from his beating.

Still, with a sigh, Cain said, "You're right." He traced little circles into the sheet with his fingers. "So tell me how the horses are doing today? Christ, I miss being with them." He suddenly jammed his fist into the mattress, dislodging the sheet loosely covering his body. "I hate that you feel like you have to be cooped up in here with me. You're not working with them as much as I know you'd like to."

"The horses are fine," Luke assured him, "and so am I. I've already been warned by Caleb and Cassie that if I try to thank them for helping one more time they're going to tape my mouth shut. Don't rile yourself up. Everything and everyone you love is doing just fine."

"Still…"

"Everyone but you, honey…" Luke cut off Cain's complaint. "You still have one hell of a bruised up body to work back to full health, and you don't need to do anything that will set you back." Moving to perch on the side of the bed, Luke stretched his arm across Cain's legs and braced his hand on the mattress. With the other, he tickled Cain's belly button, using the very tip of his finger, and worked down to the gauze patch covering Cain's burn. "Like this."

Luke tapped the woven strip of material taped between Cain's belly button and the waistband of his sweats. "Maybe you should think about changing the dressing and applying another coat of ointment."

"Yes, mother," Cain commented, and rolled his eyes.

Luke leaned down and pressed a kiss to Cain's lips, lingering with his warmth for just a moment, but pulled away before Cain could part his lips to deepen the contact. As Luke pulled back, his gray gaze twinkled with too much satisfaction for Cain's comfort. "Now you know how I felt when you brought me home from the hospital."

Without more than a look exchanged, Cain started to peel the medical tape away from his flesh.

"What I had, compared to this," Luke shared, "was nothing."

"Oh, yeah." Cain snorted. "Just a bullet wound that landed inches from your heart and took ten years off of my life. Yeah, that's nothing."

Luke made a sarcastic face, but quickly dropped his attention to the burn Cain had revealed. Reaching out, Luke fingered the ridges of the wound on Cain's belly. "Have you looked at this thing since you first covered it up?"

"Not really." Luke's tone drew Cain's attention down to his stomach. "Just long enough to slap some ointment on it and cover it up again. Why?"

Luke touched Cain's stomach again, and the contact made his belly quiver. "Maybe you can't see it because it's upside down to you, but that's not just a burn, Hawk. It's a word. Fe-all-tóir." After sounding the word out, Luke looked up, his eyes wide. "*Fealltóir.* What does that mean?"

Before Cain could say that he didn't know, Caleb, his voice deep, responded from the doorway. "Fealltóir," he said, his jaw clenching wildly. Cassie stood beside him. "Damn it. Sons of bitches." Caleb walked into the room to take a closer look, Cassie hot on his heels. "It's Gaelic. Translated, it means 'traitor.' It apparently wasn't enough to beat you senseless and almost kill you; those bastards have permanently branded you too."

"Oh." Cain reached over to his medicine table and grabbed the tube of ointment he wanted. "Well" -- he fingered the bumpy letters with the healing salve and then covered the scar back up -- "okay. I guess that's that, then."

"That's that, then?" Caleb mimicked, his voice rising. "They have permanently scarred your body with an insult. Aren't you pissed off?"

Cain immediately looked to Luke. "Does it bother you?" Cain asked for Caleb's sake; he already knew Luke's answer.

Luke shrugged and asked back, "Do my scars bother you?"

"Darlin'" -- Cain smiled intimately -- "you already know the answer to that."

Luke rubbed Cain's leg. "Now that I think about it, it's kind of sexy. I mean, you got it going through hell so we could be together. Whenever I look at it, it's just going to affirm how much you want us to be together. When it heals up, I'm gonna end up loving it."

"Geez Louise." Caleb rolled his eyes. "God save me from the disgusting sappiness of people in love."

The other three in the room laughed a secret chuckle Caleb did not understand.

From the other side of the bed, Cassie said, "Just you wait, Caleb Hawkins. I will find you the perfect mate and get you together with her, just like I did for Cain and Luke here."

Cain threw back his head and hooted. Cassie sure had matchmaking delusions of grandeur. "What the hell? You are crazy, Cassie." He met her mutinous glare. "If anyone is responsible, it's your husband and his ridiculously insane jealously. That is what drove him to beg me to take Luke out of your house."

"Oh yeah?" Cassie arched an eyebrow that suddenly made Cain sweat. "And who knows my husband's irrational jealousy, and how he reacts to it, better than I do? Who do you think was whispering in his ear about how tired you looked every time I saw you? Who do you think planted the seed that you might need help with the horses? Who do you think gave Luke no choice but to come home with me and let me nurse him back to health?"

Cain's mouth hung open, too stunned to speak. He looked at Luke and saw his eyes were equally wide.

"That's right, boys," Cassie said with a triumphant smile. "That would be me. I'd been trying to figure out a way to get the two of you together ever since I learned Cain was gay. I already knew that Luke was. I already knew you both had a love of horses. I also knew you had a similar work ethic, that you both fiercely love your respective families, and that you were each strong enough to handle what it would mean to be a gay couple in this town." Her eyes suddenly misting, Cassie added, "Why do you think I was so upset that night when I discovered you could be executed, Cain? I couldn't confess anything when Caleb uttered those words in Connor's office; I was too horrified by what I'd done. I thought for sure I'd put you right into an early grave by pushing you and Luke into such close proximity. Thank God for Caleb, or else I don't know if my marriage to Connor would have survived telling him what I'd done."

"There's the silver lining," Luke mused softly, his eyes alight with new understanding.

Cain reached out and rubbed the back of Luke's hand, just wanting to touch his man. "What do you mean, darlin'?"

Luke's gentle smile was confident and wise beyond his years. "I mean that my mother raised me and my sister to believe everything happens for a reason, even if we can't always see it. I have to admit that when I was having the shit beaten out of me by MacLesten, and then going through the painful recovery process, I didn't see how there could be any great purpose in what that beast did to me. Now I see that the trust I had in one person that day -- Cassie -- led me to you."

Cain brought Luke's hand to his lips and pressed a kiss to the center of his palm. In his deepest soul, Cain believed that his body, his very being, had been created for this man. *For Luke.* "Right," he agreed, love choking his voice.

Cassie pinched the air and raised her arm out to the side, as if making a small, country-girl curtsey. "And thank you, thank you, thank you very much. No need for applause. It was all in a day's work."

With a few big strides, Caleb rounded the bed and clamped a

hand over Cassie's mouth. "I'm going to get her out of here before she starts demanding a stud fee."

"Hmhey," Cassie mumbled from under Caleb's hand.

Caleb continued, "We just came inside to tell you that we gave Night Runner and Laura's Love a good, energizing workout today. All of the horses have been fed too. They're settled in for the evening, and now we have to go. Otherwise, Connor is going to wonder why he's sitting at a table with MacLesten's estate attorneys all by himself when he expects me and Cassie to be there."

"Do you think we're gonna get the land?" Cain asked.

Caleb nodded. "We've put the best offer in, and you know how people just seem to give Connor what he wants."

"But not if we turn Connor into a bear around those attorneys while he's waiting for us," Cassie pointed out. "So we really do have to get going or else --" A heavy thud hit the front door right then, hard enough to put a steel rod in everyone's spine.

With a smile, Cassie said, "Or else" -- she rolled her eyes -- "Connor is going to come beat your door down looking for me. I'll be right back."

"Ooh, ooh...Caleb, Caleb..." With little boy excitement humming through Cain, he caught Caleb's attention. "Get closer to the door and listen in. There are going to be wicked, under-her-breath, heated words from Cassie that are going to make Connor explode. Go hear what she says."

Wearing a wicked grin in return, Caleb nodded and even slipped out of the room to do Cain's bidding.

Luke just shook his head. "Good God, Hawk, you guys really are siblings in the truest sense of the word. You have that whole 'gang up on one brother and torment him' thing down pat. I swear to God you'd think the two of you were twelve years old and conspiring to hide in the closet and eavesdrop while Connor makes out on the other side."

"Nah." Cain waved Luke's comment away. "It's just that we both watched Connor fall in love with Cassie and torment himself with this dream of a perfect life that he never thought he could have.

So now it's fun to see him living it while he digests that it's not all making love under the moonlight the way he dreamed. She can render him speechless like no one else, and for me and Caleb, seeing our autocratic brother completely lose his thoughts because of what Cassie means to him... Well, let's just say it's a delicious bit of fun for us at his expense." Right then, Caleb and Cassie reappeared at the door. Narrowing his stare, Cain asked, "Where's Con?"

"It wasn't Connor," Cassie shared. She moved back into the room and handed Cain a slip of paper. "It was this. It was attached to the outside of the front door by the blade of a knife. That must have been the noise we heard."

Cain looked down at the thick sheet of paper. As he read the missive, his hands started trembling. He looked up at Cassie first and then Caleb. His heart thudded so hard he felt certain everyone in the room must be able to see it. "This isn't a prank? You really found this on my door?"

"We would never do that to you." Caleb spoke for the both of them. "It's real."

With nothing more than a nod, they both quietly left.

"What are they talking about?" Luke grabbed the paper out of Cain's hand, his gaze darkening as he began to read. "*You are an embarrassment we no longer claim. May you die a painful human death, for you are no longer one of us. You are Naverto no more. Good riddance.*" Luke looked up at Cain, his eyes as wide as Cain had ever seen them. "Is this what I think it is?"

"I think so," Cain said, his voice soft. He was so, so very afraid to hope, though.

Closing his eyes, Cain focused within and searched for the demon, thought about the being that had always lived inside him, and imagined himself pulling the beast out, in the way he'd trained himself to do. In silence, in darkness, he waited for the shift, for the beginnings of the pain that wasn't really a pain, and tried to force the change. Every muscle tensed, and pain did indeed course through him -- but it was the same residual discomfort from bruises and cuts he'd been living with during his slow recovery for a month now. It wasn't the deep internal hurt of the demon emerging.

*The demon is gone.*

Cain covered his mouth to hold in a sob. "Oh Christ, Luke." Cain looked to his man, searching that gray gaze he loved so much. There it was, so beautiful and sure; Cain reached out, snaked his hand around Luke's neck and dragged him forward, onto his lap, until their foreheads touched. Discomfort sliced through Cain as Luke landed on him, but he dismissed the pain entirely. Feeling Luke on top of him, knowing he never had to hide this passion ever again, obliterated any pain still living inside him. His eyes surely shining much too bright, Cain uttered, "I think the test is over. I think I'm free."

In response, Luke vaulted off the bed and out of Cain's arms in a shot.

# CHAPTER THIRTY

Luke turned his back on Cain, and the blood drained from Cain's limbs, leaving him numb. Old insecurities, new fears -- everything Cain now had to deal with that was a part of most people's teenage crushes, first loves, and practice relationships -- Cain now had to navigate as a novice in his relationship with Luke. Only, this wasn't just a first love or a first relationship for Cain; it was the only one he ever intended to have. The only one he wanted to have. Cain intended to spend the rest of his life with Luke; this was the man for whom he would do anything in the world.

*Hell, I already did.*

Damn it, Cain hadn't put his body and mind through hell only to have Luke pull away from him. Not when they'd finally gotten an answer to their prayers. Not when for the first time, truly, in every way, they could be together without fear of everything crashing down around them when some demon force ripped apart.

"What's the matter, Luke?" The silence from this man cut Cain up inside; he couldn't bear it. "Why are you doing this?"

Luke's entire body stiffened. "Just give me a minute," Luke answered, his voice low and strained. "I just…just give me a minute. I need a minute."

"Why?" Cain growled. He no longer cared about being polite, he just wanted answers, something to make this sinking feeling in his stomach go away. "I just told you we're finally free to be together, in the way we've been dreaming about, and your first reaction is to pull away. You didn't like it when I tried to do that to you. I get that now, Luke, because I goddamned don't understand this, and I sure as hell don't like it one bit. So spit it out, right damn now. Tell me what's wrong."

"It's nothing," Luke insisted, his back still to Cain. "It's just… just when you told me we were free… I had an unexpected reaction to it."

Well, that fucking didn't make Cain feel any better. "What kind of reaction?" His tone was clipped and hard.

Luke finally turned around, and the bulge jutting against the front of his jeans immediately became clear. A small dark wet spot had also formed there. *Shit.* Cain's neck broke out in a sweat, and his cock jumped in his sweats the longer he stared.

Forcing himself, he tore his stare from Luke's erection to the man's eyes. "Jesus Christ, Luke." Relief flooded Cain's entire being, making him dizzy. His legs were already weak enough; thank God he was lying down "You almost gave me a goddamned heart attack, all because you didn't want me to see your erection?" Just as fast as the tension had filled Cain, it drained away, and a slow, hungry smile appeared. "Come here, darlin'." He patted his chest. "We'll take care of that wood right now."

"See, I knew you would do that." Fiery passion filled Luke's tone. "You're not ready yet."

"Who the hell says I'm not ready?" Pushing his sweats down past his hips, Cain let Luke see the proof for himself. "I'm damn well ready to take you, darlin'." Just with speaking those words, Cain's dick jumped against his stomach. "I've been ready for at least a week."

"No," Luke corrected. "Your cock is ready, but the rest of your body isn't. Damn it, baby, don't tell me you don't hurt; you grunted in pain when you pulled me on top of you not five minutes ago."

*Damn it.* Cain should have known this man would pick up on any visible discomfort in Cain and take that pain right into his heart. His Luke was so very attuned to every subtle nuance in Cain's behavior.

"I am still sore," Cain finally admitted. He didn't see any sense in lying about it; it wasn't as if he didn't still look like he'd been used as a punching bag -- which he had. "But I need you, Luke. I need for us to be together, physically, in some way. I need to feel the beginnings of that connection again in order to start believing this is real."

"I don't know." Luke remained too far away, his hands stuffed in his back pockets. "I would never forgive myself if I set back your recovery; if you ended up hurting yourself in some very real way. Remember, you're human now. You're vulnerable to human injuries, just like the rest of us." He suddenly swore, and his stare widened. "God, baby, we don't even know the age of the human body they gave you. It might be older than we think."

Cain chuckled. "Worried you've tied yourself to an old man, are you?"

"No." Clearly horrified that he'd been misunderstood, Luke rushed to the side of the bed. "That's not what I meant. I love you. I don't care how old you are."

Before Luke thought better and stepped away, Cain grabbed his hand and effectively shut him up. "Relax, darlin'." Cain tugged Luke until the man's kneecaps dug into the side of the bed. "I'm only teasing. If I could translate where I was in my demon life to human years, then I'm around thirty-five years old. I did take pretty good care of myself; that hasn't changed." A thought suddenly filled Cain, one that forced out a chuckle. "Although I will cut down on the amount of red meat I consume. In fact, you may end up with a full-fledged vegetarian on your hands."

A smile emerging, Luke brushed back the hair on Cain's forehead. "I think I can handle a cowboy vegetarian with a soft heart." He leaned down to press a kiss to Cain's forehead and let his lips linger there for a moment. As he pulled back he added, "I think I'll like it a whole lot."

Cain fucking melted under the loving, gentle attention from Luke, but Christ, his entire being hungered for intimacy with this man, and he needed more. "At the very least, I can handle your cock." As Cain said that, his body hummed with anticipation. After scooting up to lean against the headboard, he adjusted the pillows at the small of his back. "I haven't had your taste in my mouth in a month, Luke. I miss it. I ache for it. Let me just sit here and take care of you. Just give me that. Please." He reached out and started working the buckle holding up Luke's jeans.

As if without conscious thought, Luke groaned and leaned in closer. "I would say you drive a hard bargain" -- Luke ripped open the snaps on his shirt and shrugged out of it, revealing his beautiful, perfect chest -- "but I'm clearly getting the better end of this deal."

"Not from my perspective you're not." Just thinking about getting Luke's big prick into his mouth and making the man come made Cain even stiffer.

With permission given, Cain got to work undoing Luke's button-fly jeans. When Cain pushed Luke's jeans and underwear down past his buttocks to his hips, and his fully erect cock slipped free, Luke gasped. He shoved his jeans down even farther on his own, not stopping until they got caught up in his cowboy boots.

Luke went to kneel. Cain knew he intended to remove his pants, so Cain shot out his hand and squeezed Luke's hip. "Leave them on like that," Cain said. He let his attention drop to the jeans and underwear bunched around Luke's boots, and the sight pushed a pearl of early seed from his cock. With a soft groan, he grinned and lifted his focus back to Luke. "When you look like this, it makes me think you were too excited and couldn't even spare a second to get your clothes all the way off. It's sexy. I like it."

"When you put it like that" -- Luke managed to get on the bed and straddle Cain, his boots resting in a point between Cain's thighs -- "it makes me damn excited too. Slide down just a little bit, baby." Luke held out his long, lovely cock. "I'll be right there, and you won't have to do very much work at all."

Getting a strong whiff of dark, musky sexuality combined with honey -- Luke's fragrance -- Cain moaned and opened his mouth. With a secret smile, Luke slid his cock past Cain's lips, all the way into his mouth. The smooth, velvet-hard pole pushed its way to the back of Cain's throat. *Christ, yes.* Cain sucked and pulled on Luke's rigid shaft, and then tickled his tongue back and forth around the underside of his man's wonderful, hot penis. Above him, Luke moaned, and Cain warmed in a place deep inside. Damn, he'd missed this. With just one month of abstinence between them, he hadn't realized how much this part of his relationship with Luke had meant to him, until just now. Cain had missed Luke's decadent, masculine aroma; he'd missed the slurping sound as he dragged his mouth up and down Luke's cock; getting the shaft all slippery and wet, and in some cases, getting it ready to take his ass. Cain had missed Luke pumping his hips back and forth against his face, helping Cain set a rhythm Luke needed in order to come. He'd missed reaching up and tweaking Luke's nipples into hard little points, of causing the man to gyrate and flex those sexy slim hips of his as he struggled to deal with the pleasure Cain wreaked upon his body. Cain had missed the sheer, unadulterated intimacy of the things he did with Luke, things he'd never done with anyone else, and that he somehow knew, deep in his soul, he never would.

Luke braced his hands on the headboard and fucked Cain's mouth with his long, slender prick. "Oh goddamn it, Hawk." As Luke stared down, watching Cain feast on his cock, pleasure pinched his face. He gasped, and his lips parted, as if he could not get enough air into his lungs. "You take care of my dick in a way no one else ever has. Damn it." He shoved his burning-hot length deep into Cain's mouth, and Cain's throat muscles were already well trained to take the deeper filling. "You're so fucking good. You'll make me come too fast, baby."

For just a moment, Cain let Luke's penis slide out of his mouth. "I want you to." Cain wrapped his hand around the base of Luke's erection and started to pump its length. "Come for me." He licked the head of Luke's penis and swirled the rim with the tip of his tongue. Luke's entire body seized tight, and Cain could see the muscles bulging in his arms as he put a death grip of the lip of the headboard. Once more, Cain flicked his tongue across Luke's slit, and then added, "I want you to come in my mouth." He slipped just the first couple inches of Luke's dick past his lips, and with everything in him, started to suck. *Come for me, darlin'.* Cain reveled in pleasing Luke and making him lose control. He added his other hand to the mix and played with Luke's cum-filled balls. *Right now.*

*Oh God.* Luke shuddered as insane need, desire, and joy coursed through his cock. He never had a chance. Cain gave him a thorough handjob, teased his nuts, and sucked him off at the same time. Watching everything happen from above, getting lost in the intent delight mapping Cain's face, Luke found he didn't have the willpower to hold back his release. His balls drew up, unbearably tight to his body. *Fuck.* His heart stopped beating as he hung, suspended between life and death, on the precipice of something magnificent.

A rush of ridiculously focused pleasure rocked through Luke and kick-started his heart. Ripples of sensation raced through his lower belly, swelling his prick to an acute sensitivity, something bordering on pain. Cain kept sucking Luke deeply, though, and unable to fight it, Luke cried out as semen started pumping out of his cock in endless gushes, right into Cain's warm, welcoming mouth. *Yes.*

On the other end, Cain's heart beat just as fast, and he loved Luke's loss of control as much as Luke did, if not more. Luke's cock pulsed inside Cain's mouth, coating his tongue with salty, thick cum. Cain continued to suck on the mushroom head of Luke's penis, through every jerk of the man's body as he achieved release, and drained him. From the first sharp cry Luke gave, all the way to the final deep sigh as the stamina left Luke, Cain swirled his tongue around Luke's cock and sucked him hard. In the aftermath, Luke slumped, and the movement slid his length free from the warm protection of Cain's mouth.

With one move, Cain wrapped his hand around Luke's neck and dragged him down for a hard, searing kiss. He took Luke's mouth like a man starved, slashing his lips across Luke's and parting the man's mouth for full penetration. Cain needed this too -- the connection of kissing Luke. Luke quickly took control, holding Cain's head in place as he sucked Cain's tongue deep inside the wet vacuum of his mouth, and Cain cried out with needful pleasure. He wrapped his arms around Luke and squeezed him close, needing him so much he forgot about the state of his body until Luke pressed against his ribs. Cain gasped as a sharp stab pierced his middle. In a heartbeat, Luke broke their kiss and pulled away.

Cain didn't care about pain. Not right now. "Please, Luke." Cain's eyes shone bright with love and need, he felt certain of it, but he didn't care. "I need to be inside you. I need to feel that connection between us in order to feel human -- in order to feel completely alive in a way I never have before. Please, I don't care about any discomfort; I just need to feel you wrapped around me; I need to experience that thing only we do together."

"Oh, baby" -- Luke smoothed his fingers over Cain's face -- "I can't even imagine what this must be like for you. To be the same person, but also to feel this piece of you gone that used to be part of who you were. You must not be sure who you are anymore."

Luke's observation delved way too close for comfort to Cain's deepest fears. Reaching up, he took one of Luke's hands and brought it to his mouth. He kissed the center of Luke's palm, smiling as Luke shifted his fingers and rubbed his thumb against Cain's lower lip.

Cain looked into Luke's eyes, and his heart swelled at the loving patience he found there. "As long as I know I can still love you," he shared, his voice choked, "then everything else will eventually start to feel normal too. I need to love you, Luke. It's the only thing I know right now that will make everything else all right."

Luke seemed to struggle with the request, but finally, he nodded. "Okay, but I set the pace. That's the only way. Understand?"

"Sweetheart" -- Luke's restrictions pulled a grin from Cain -- "I don't even need a pace. I just need to be inside you."

"That's good." Chuckling, Luke reached over to the nightstand. "Because that's about the pace I was going to set. Lie back down, baby, and I'll get on top."

Cain did as instructed and watched Luke through lust-filled eyes. Without having to be told, Luke shifted and gave Cain a view of his ass as he fingered his pucker and worked lube into his hole. The sight of that digit disappearing into Luke's body was still as maddeningly arousing as the first time Cain had witnessed it; his cock strained, hard and painful, against his stomach. "Do you remember that first night in your old room down at the barn?" As Cain asked, he reached out and covered Luke's probing fingers with his own, just to feel the way Luke's hand moved as he worked lubricant into his rectum. Christ, it was so fucking hot to see. "Do you remember when I ordered you to turn around so I could watch you do this very thing?"

"Hell, yes," Luke answered. He pulled his fingers out of his hole, then turned his attention to Cain's cock and slicked up the shaft with the clear liquid too. As he moved his focus up Cain's stomach and chest to his face, his gaze heated with gray fire. The sight of Luke with hungry eyes was as arousing as the hand he still had on Cain's erection. "I still use the memory of our first time together to jerk off in the shower in the mornings sometimes."

"Invite me in next time," Cain requested, his gaze falling to half-mast.

"When you're better," Luke promised.

Luke then crawled over Cain's abdomen and spread his thighs, settling himself as best he could with his feet still tangled up in his jeans. Luke settled his booted feet in between Cain's thighs again and spread his knees to rest alongside Cain's hips. Cain watched intently as Luke then reached behind himself and in between their bodies. He wrapped his hand around the base of Cain's cock, held the shaft straight up, and then slowly, oh-so-slowly, lowered himself down until his puckered hole kissed the sensitive tip of Cain's penis.

*Oh yes.* Then, for Cain, it wasn't about looking anymore; it was all about feeling. "Oh Christ…Luke…" As Luke wiggled on Cain a little bit, Cain keened, his voice hoarse. Then, Christ, then Luke took Cain inside his body, and the wicked beauty of Luke's burning hot ass enveloping Cain's straining cock pushed another low moan from his core. "Oh God… God, Luke…"

"You all right?" Luke asked. He didn't stop to wait for an answer though. He kept pressing, pressing, and didn't halt his descent until he had his cheeks resting on Cain's pubic hair, with Cain's dick tucked all the up his wonderful ass.

Barely getting out a, "Yeah," Cain moaned as Luke's scorching channel pulsed with fluttering life around his prick. Looking up, Cain locked his stare on the silver glittering in Luke's eyes. "I always forget how fucking tight you are until I get inside you again. Come here." He drew Luke down until they were chest-to-chest and the man he loved draped him completely.

"Your injuries." Worry filled Luke's tone, but Cain dragged his man down the rest of the way and shut him up with a kiss.

As Cain deepened the kiss, the tension slowly left Luke's body. Tasting, lingering on Luke's insanely lush mouth, Cain didn't let up until Luke completely relaxed into a puddle on top of him. Murmuring his pleasure, Cain then grazed and licked and kissed his way across Luke's hard, square jaw. Luke tilted his head to the side, giving Cain complete access in a way Cain loved. With every soft lick from Cain, Luke hummed in response. Cain kissed his way up Luke's cheek to have his way with the man's ear. *Mmm…*

Darting his tongue inside, Cain started mimicking the action he wanted to mirror with his cock. Luke yelped a little "Oh!" and made Cain rather arrogantly proud. His chest swelled with pride at his sexual prowess, but then Luke busted his bubble by adding, "Damn it, I left the computer running. It's been on all this time."

Cain turned to look at the nightstand, shivering as Luke's rough jaw rubbed against his flesh.

Stretching, Luke tried to reach the keyboard to turn off the computer, but Cain wrapped his arms around Luke and held him in place. He still had his cock happily buried in Luke's ass, and he did not intend to let the man move enough to dislodge the hot, delicious connection. "Don't worry about it." Cain turned Luke to face him and planted a soft, loving kiss on his lips. "If the battery dies before we're finished, we'll just recharge it."

A telltale stain of red covered Luke's cheeks just then -- the same one that had flushed Luke's skin earlier when Cain had awoken from his nap. His brow furrowing, Cain asked, "What were you working on?" He'd assumed the blush from earlier had risen as a result of teasing Luke about his glasses, but now he wasn't so sure. "What was so interesting? Now that I think about it, you didn't realize right away I was awake. And that's weird, Luke. You always seem to have a sixth sense for when I'm about to open my eyes."

Luke only reddened even further, and the proverbial cat had definitely put a LoJack on his tongue.

"What?" Cain prodded, wildly curious now. "You can tell me. I won't judge you if you were looking at porn or something like that."

Luke stretched his arm again; this time he managed to graze his finger across the mouse pad. When the screensaver's swimming sharks disappeared, a website appeared. One Cain did not recognize or comprehend. *Definitely not porn.* Puzzled, Cain looked to Luke for an explanation.

"I think I have an idea for your horses, Hawk," Luke began softly, his voice wavering a bit.

"Our horses, darlin'," Cain corrected. He smoothed his hand down Luke's scarred back. "Everything I own is yours too."

"It's the same for me." With a shrug, and another pinking of his cheeks, Luke added, "Not that I have very much."

Christ, Cain wanted to tuck this man under him and love him forever. Brushing his fingers through Luke's dark locks, he said back, just as gently, "You apparently have an idea, sweetheart, so why don't you tell me what it is. I want to hear it."

After biting his lip, Luke blurted, "I don't think you should sell the horses. You love them too much, and I think it would break your heart each time you had to let one go. I don't think you'd ever feel one hundred percent secure that wherever they go they won't somehow end up abused and mistreated again."

"You're right." Thickness lodged in Cain's throat and made it hard to speak. He'd never gotten around to telling Luke about his problem with figuring out what to do with the horses. Too much had happened too quickly, and he hadn't wanted to burden Luke with a problem that wouldn't matter if he'd ended up dead. But in the end, it hadn't been necessary for Cain to speak one word; Luke had figured him out all on his own. Cain should have known. Studying Luke's earnest stare, he asked, "What do you think we should do with them?"

"I think we should open a therapeutic horse farm, for people with special needs. That's what I've spent the last week on the Internet researching. These special farms are a place where people like my mom can come and learn to ride, and where they can feel safe knowing that we trained each and every animal before we put anyone on them. I think it might be good for the horses too -- being around people who will be so loving and profoundly grateful for the opportunity to ride." Luke bit his lip again, and his eyes rounded wide. "So, what do you think?"

A rage of ridiculously powerful emotions slashed through Cain, and he roughly whispered, "I think I love you so damn much." In a rush, he rolled his hips up into Luke, needing to feel their connection again. He hissed as his cock slid deliciously within Luke's tight ass, the hot slide rubbing every sensitive nerve ending on his prick. With a gasp, Luke shifted, and his channel clenched Cain in a powerful wave. It felt so fucking good to be inside Luke again, and Cain never wanted to leave. *I'm finally home.*

Cain leaned up and captured Luke's mouth with his, clinging there, nipping and biting and delving his tongue inside for a taste. He tore his mouth away, but his emotions still swirled within. "I love you more than is probably healthy, but I don't care because I don't think I can ever stop." Reaching up, he brushed his fingers over Luke's cheeks and forehead, then pushed his hands through the dark thickness of Luke's hair, and got positively lost in Luke's eyes. "I love your idea." Sliding his eyes closed, Cain pulled Luke to him again, and murmured against his lips, "I think it's the most freakin' genius goddamned idea I've ever heard."

"Thank you." Luke's blush returned in full force.

"I really do love it." Cain's brain started churning at a million miles a minute. "But I won't do it without you being on board as a full partner."

Luke paled, and his eyes grew darkly wild. "What do you mean?" He tried to pull away, but Cain held him tight. "I don't know anything about business, Hawk. I barely got through high school. I don't want to be an anchor around your neck."

"Honey, that's not even possible," Cain vowed, no hesitation in his response.

Luke's mouth still pulled with lines of tension. "But I don't have any money to be a partner with you."

"You bring so much more to me than money, Luke." Cain squeezed the man and held him close, adding, "You bring complete trust and faith, and that is more valuable in a partner than any endless supply of money. I promise you that. I don't want to be partners with your bank account, Luke Forrester; I want to be partners with you."

Moisture filmed Luke's pale gaze, and he trembled. "You really want me to have equal say in everything, top to bottom?"

"Yes. Do this with me, darlin'." Pure enthusiasm and joy rushed through Cain's system, made his blood race, and reheated his loins. With a happy, lust-filled growl, he pushed his cock up into Luke's ass again and began the slow burn of friction between their bodies. "Let's do this together, you and me, and create this life we've both been thinking about since the day you walked onto this land. Let's make it real. Build a life with me, one that fifty years from now we can still be proud of and still get excited about." Cain rocked his hips, keeping them on a slow burn, and locked his gaze to Luke's. "What do you say, Luke? Will you make a commitment to me, to us, to creating a life that will bond us to each other forever?"

As Luke circled his ass on Cain's full penetration, he offered an oh-so-gentle answering smile. With a sharp little breathless exhale, he said, "I don't need a business in order to be bonded to you forever,

Hawk." He wiped a streak of wetness from the edge of Cain's eye just then, one Cain hadn't even realized was there. "But if you want me as your partner, then I want to do it."

Cain's chest squeezed with unbearable tightness and a sob choked his throat. It was so much...so much more than he ever could have dreamed when he'd walked in on Connor and Cassie making love in the office almost two years ago. So much envy and jealousy had filled him that day -- so powerfully that he'd built this cabin in order to get away from the pain of constantly witnessing something he'd known for a certainty he was never meant to have. He'd felt so desperately alone back then, and all he'd wanted to do was hide. Like Luke had said before, though, in every hardship existed a silver lining. In the throes of that pain and in wanting to get away, Cain had created a sanctuary and put himself out of contact with most of the rest of the world. Luke had invaded his hideaway, though, had found a way in, and in so doing had given Cain such strength, and had broken through to him to the point where he'd made it impossible for Cain to ignore what his heart and body wanted. Which was a man to love. A special man. A man that could have only ever been Luke.

Cain blinked through the wetness of tears he couldn't keep at bay, and looked up at the understanding living right on the surface of Luke's beautiful gaze. "I love you," Cain whispered thickly. A tidal wave of emotion rolled through him, leaving him weak. "I love you so much."

"I know you do, baby," Luke replied, and brushed more wetness from Cain's cheeks. "But you don't have to cry. You don't have to be sad or afraid, not ever again." With that vow, Luke shifted, planted his hands on the bed, and started to move his hips. Cain's cock, still embedded deep inside Luke's warm, welcoming body, screamed back to life. "Because I'm here now, and I'm always going to make it better."

"Ride me, Luke," Cain begged. He struggled to lift his hips and join in; struggled just as hard not to come right on the spot. "Ride me in the way only you can. Make everything better."

Luke did. He torturously, slowly, rode Cain's cock, making love to him, until Cain cried with pleasure and exploded deep inside Luke's ass. With Cain's first jolt, Luke shouted and covered Cain's stomach with seed.

Luke was right again. Being with Luke, like this, did make everything better.

In fact, as Cain pulled Luke down and fused their mouths together in a searing, loving kiss, Cain understood that having Luke made everything damn near perfect.

# Epilogue

**Eighteen Months Later**

"Jesus, Hawk." Luke whistled as he adjusted the man's collar for him. "You look so damn handsome today."

Heat stained Cain's cheeks and warmth infused his entire being. He never got tired of listening to Luke's delusions about his physical attractiveness. Instead of correcting him, though, Cain said, "Damn it, darlin', I don't want to look *handsome*. I want to look *competent*."

"Well" -- Luke leaned in and gave Cain a quick peck on the lips -- "you *look* that too."

"Thanks. You look fucking gorgeous yourself." Cain smoothed his hand over the small of Luke's back, over the crisp, clean feel of the newly ironed, western-yoked shirt, just above where the fabric was tucked into Luke's softly faded jeans. "But you look damned capable too." As Cain leaned around Luke to grab his watch off the dresser, he bussed a kiss to his man's temple. "How are you feeling?"

After a year and a half of reworking the parcel of land Connor and Caleb had sold them, and after creating some nice, natural-feeling trails on said land, and after building a second barn to house

348

the horses still in training, and after interviewing nurses and phys.cal therapists in order to have someone medically trained on hand when clients were on the property… After doing a thousand other things just like those, today was the day Cain and Luke would meet their first few customers and take them riding.

They were starting out part-time, having people in on Fridays, Saturdays, and Sundays until they got the feel for it, until they worked out the kinks that always came with a new business. They'd done their research; they'd visited other therapeutic horse farms and had taken notes of the things that they'd liked, and those they didn't. Most important to both men, though, the horses were now comfortable and ready to deal with a different kind of rider.

Luke's mom had been a wonder, not only riding the animals herself and making them comfortable with her, but also networking online with other people with special needs who were interesting in riding. She'd found some people whom she trusted, and they'd been invited to come and ride the horses -- traveling and accommodations on Cain and Luke's dime. Test time was necessary for the horses; it was important to let them feel different people with different kinds of harness saddles on their backs. These tasks and rituals had to be done over and over again until the horses took to being ridden by strangers just as easily as by Cain or Luke.

The training and preparation were all over now. They'd had a small party last night with their families and a few friends, including Nate Palmer, who'd crafted all of the special saddles to each horse's specs himself. Sheriff Boone and his son, both of whom had become good friends to Cain and Luke after that whole nightmare with MacLesten, had attended as well.

The grunt work and physical labor of getting a business like this up and running had been damn hard; hearing encouraging words during the party last night from the people who loved them had been special, but now it was time to get to business. Now it was time to see if they'd done everything needed in order to make this work.

"So" -- Cain touched his forehead to Luke's, kept them close, and looked into the blurry closeness of his eyes -- "are you ready to do this?"


Luke slid his hands up Cain's chest to around his neck and caressed the short tufts of hair there. He never took this love he had with Cain for granted, and he never forgot to say a prayer of thanks that they were both alive to share it. The pure blue light of adoration in Cain's eyes always lit up brighter and shone in Luke's direction when he entered a room. *Good God; he's beautiful, inside and out.* Luke didn't know how to be anything other than his best when Cain looked his way.

"I get all the courage and confidence I need just from looking in your eyes, Hawk," Luke shared. A combination of tenderness for this man and excitement for the next course of their lives filled him up whole. He leaned in, closed the distance between them, and sank his way into a slow, sweet kiss, smiling against Cain's mouth as he felt the other man's tongue dart out and lick his. Luke grinned without embarrassment, feeling the contented happiness latch on, all the way down in his core. Luke pressed a fast, chaste kiss to Cain's lips, and then reluctantly pulled away.

"Now that we've said good morning properly" -- Luke twined his fingers with Cain's and tugged him through the bedroom to the front door -- "let's go feed our horses so that we can get this day started."


"You got it, darlin'." Cain chuckled and happily let himself be led by the man he loved. "Your wish is my command."

Luke's bark of laughter was loud and joyful, but the look he threw Cain over his shoulder was full of heated promise. "That's right," he teased. "And don't you ever forget it."

"No, Luke," Cain murmured, his heart somehow finding a way to get fuller, although he didn't know how such a feat was possible. "I promise; I won't."

And he never did.

THE END

# ABOUT THE AUTHOR

I am an air force brat and spent most of my growing up years living overseas in Italy and England, as well as Florida, Georgia, Ohio, and Virginia while we were stateside. I now live in Florida once again with my big, wonderfully pushy family and my three-legged cat, Harry. I have been reading romance novels since I was twelve years old, and twenty-five years later I still adore them. Currently, I have an unexplainable obsession with hockey goaltenders, zombies, and an unabashed affection for *The Daily Show* with Jon Stewart.

Find me on the web at
**www.camerondane.com**

Printed in Great Britain
by Amazon

45421601R10210